Praise fo[...]rst
Tes[...],
[...]spect

"Entertaining."
—*Publishers Weekly*

"Rowe writes a classic whodunit . . . a world-class writer."
—*Sydney Morning Herald*

"Rowe's language seems, with each book, to become more terse and straightforward, not a word wasted. The pace in this one is unflagging."
—*Australian Book Review*

"A classic mystery puzzler . . . A very entertaining read that is recommended for all aficionados of good crime novels."
—*Canberra Times*

"Pleasant and engaging . . . Rowe is very good with the little details of human business—inappropriate dress, misconstrued meanings, and the messy conflict between work and personal life."
—*Sunday Age* (Melbourne)

By Jennifer Rowe
Published by The Ballantine Publishing Group:

SUSPECT
SOMETHING WICKED

SOMETHING WICKED

Jennifer Rowe

BALLANTINE BOOKS • NEW YORK

A Ballantine Book
Published by The Ballantine Publishing Group
Copyright © 1998 by Jennifer Rowe

All rights reserved under International and Pan-American Copyright Conventions. Published in the United States by The Ballantine Publishing Group, a division of Random House, Inc., New York, and distributed in Canada by Random House of Canada Limited, Toronto. Originally published in Australia by Allen & Unwin in 1998.

Ballantine and colophon are registered trademarks of Random House, Inc.

www.randomhouse.com/BB/

Library of Congress Catalog Card Number: 99-90599

ISBN 0-345-42795-5

Manufactured in the United States of America

First American Edition: December 1999

10   9   8   7   6   5   4   3   2   1

By the pricking of my thumbs
Something wicked this way comes

Macbeth, William Shakespeare

One

He knew she'd come to him if he waited long enough. She'd drift, slim and white, from the bottom of the slope, from the aromatic shade of the pine forest, flitting up through the long grass towards him, as she had the first time. Or she'd come down through the orchard, the scent of thyme and lavender from the herb gardens still clinging to her hands, hair and clothes. She would come.

He twisted fence wire, working slowly, forcing patience, waiting. The wire was stiff. The green-handled pliers fitted his hand awkwardly, and already a chafe mark ran warm and red across the ball of his thumb. A year of weekend work had done little to toughen his skin. And maybe, he reflected vaguely, he hadn't done very much hard work over recent months. Somehow, things had started to slip.

He sweated lightly. The sun was warm on his back, and there was no breeze. The long, pale gold grass on the other side of the fence, like the grass of his own paddock, was heavy with seed. It bent and swayed, stirred by the chirruping, rasping insects that crawled through its stems and around its roots, eating and being eaten. In the pine trees the big black cockatoos screeched, greedily tearing at the cones, vandalizing the trees, snapping off branch tips thicker than his thumb, tossing them carelessly aside to fall to the dense brown carpet of needles below.

Nearly a year ago, when he'd first come here—the very first day he'd taken possession of the place—the black cockatoos had been screeching just like this. He'd walked, exhilarated, exultant, in his new elastic-sided boots, down from the

1

house, through the long grass of the paddock towards the pines and the creek below.

It was strange to think that all the time she had been watching him from the other side of the fence. He hadn't even looked that way. But she was there. She'd admitted it, one day. She was shy about it, but she admitted it. She said she'd stood where he was standing now, at the place where the rough, towering border of cherry laurels ended, where the sagging wire and drunken posts of the fence were bare, and watched him striding tall, hands in jacket pockets. She said she'd wondered about him, thought he was splendid. Astral used words like that. "Splendid."

When she described what she'd seen, in her low, unaccented voice, he could see himself through her eyes with the clarity of a film. Alone and slightly smiling, eyes narrowed against the sun, he walked down the sloping land towards the trees. His boots trod heavily, blazing a clear trail through the drying grass. You could still see where he had passed long after he disappeared into the pines.

He hadn't known she was watching him. Not consciously. But sometimes now he wondered if her presence, her concentration on him, had somehow communicated itself to his unconscious mind. That would explain the elation that had possessed him that day—that feeling that something transforming was happening, that feeling of being special, and twice as alive as usual.

He'd tried to describe the feeling to friends at the advertising agency where he worked, when on the following Monday they'd asked him how his first weekend in the mountain house had gone. Listening indulgently, they were patronizing or romantic in response, explaining away the unexplainable.

They could understand how he felt, they said. It was the natural excitement of all first times. It was pride in claiming a new possession. It was the beauty and the clean, fresh air. It was the satisfaction of a primeval drive, a rediscovery of man's need to be close to the land. But nothing they said could destroy the wonder. He'd never forget the sense of enchantment that came over him as he moved into the forest that first day.

It was another world there. Sound from outside was muffled, but he could clearly hear the creek (his creek!) running at the foot of the slope, and the birds' beaks cracking cones and wood above his head.

Shafts of golden light pierced the shadows. Scarlet toadstools covered in white spots, like the toadstools in an old-fashioned children's story book, studded the thick, brown carpet under the trees. They'd appeared since he last visited the place. It seemed miraculous.

Among the toadstools lay the bright green tips of pine branches, each one like a tiny Christmas tree, thickly needled, studded with perfect, miniature cones. Some of the pieces were as long as his forearm. Their dark, knobbly stems weren't broken or ragged. The parrots' beaks had cut them cleanly through, as though with secateurs. They were fresh, lush, exotic.

He started picking them up. It seemed such a waste to leave them. You could sell them, in the city. He was sure of it. He thought with smug compassion of the people who would buy his pine bouquets. City people, who had to spend their weekends in town. Who had no place in the mountains, no big, old rhododendron bushes, or grassy paddock, no pines or toadstools, no creek, or parrots either.

He kept gathering more and more of the pine tips till he had a huge, tangy, prickly armful. When he got back to the house he stood his booty in jugs, jars, buckets—anything he could find that would hold water. He put the containers in every room—even the bathroom. They filled the house with the smell of the forest. And that night, after he'd lit the fire in the fireplace, telling himself that it really was cold enough to warrant a fire, he'd sat on the sagging old couch that had come with the house, ate bread and cheese and drank small, cold bottles of beer, made plans and lists, and felt—complete.

Remembering, he found himself smiling with bittersweet nostalgia, as though contemplating himself as a much younger man—fresh, keen and naive, in a long-distant past. Yet it had only been a year—a little less than a year. So much had happened since then.

He wiped the light sweat from his forehead with the back

of his hand and became suddenly aware that the insects had stilled. He looked up quickly. His stomach turned over.

Astral was standing a meter or two from the fence, watching him gravely, waiting for him to notice her. She'd come so quietly, her bare, sun-browned feet pressing through the grass so softly that he hadn't heard her. The long, shapeless white shift she wore, its cheap cotton softened and thinned by countless washings, seemed translucent, and clung where it touched that slim girl's body, so cool, so strangely still, passive, accepting . . .

"Hi," he said, casually, his tongue thick and clumsy in his mouth. His palms were damp. Her smooth, narrow lips turned up at the corners. But she said nothing. She just looked, her eyes wary dark blue pools fringed with black, her shoulders a little bent and half-turned, as though at any moment she would run.

"What's the matter? Astral?" He kept his voice gentle. He didn't want to startle her.

"Could you come in, Jonathon?" she murmured, still hanging back, one hand holding a branch of the last cherry laurel as if to keep herself grounded.

"Come in?" he repeated stupidly. There was a thud, deep in his chest. He hadn't expected this. Not this. He wasn't, somehow, ready for it, despite all he'd thought, planned and imagined over the long days and nights of this last week.

She nodded, and waited. The parrots screeched in the pine trees.

Jonathon knew he couldn't refuse. It would be absurd to refuse.

He put the pliers on the fence post, bent and scrambled awkwardly through the fence, pushing his way between the two top strands of wire. He made a clumsy business of it, catching his foot and half-stumbling. Astral hadn't stumbled when she crossed the fence-line last weekend, he thought dimly—but then, of course, Astral was graceful in everything she did. And whereas here, where the fence had been repaired, the wire was tautly strung between its posts, in the forest many of the old posts were half-rotted, leaning drunkenly, and the wire was rusted and slack.

He straightened and glanced involuntarily behind him. It was very strange to be on the other side of the fence, on the Haven side, and to see his own property as Astral had been seeing it for so long. His little house looked cute. His paddock basked in the sun, sloping gently to where the forest began.

He turned back to Astral, who was quietly watching him.

"What is it, sweetheart?" he said softly. The endearment was automatic, but somehow, he didn't dare approach her. It was always like this. Every time was like the first time. He could never tell what she was thinking, or what he could expect.

Instead of answering she came closer, and took his hand. The pressure of her slim, work-roughened fingers sent a thrill through him. He reached for her, but she moved back, still holding his hand, and began leading him away from the fence and up towards the apple orchard. His heart thudding wildly, he let her take him.

The orchard closed green around them. Lank grass was soft underfoot. The apple trees were old, their trunks covered in lichen, but the tangled boughs overhead were magically laden with gleaming red fruit, ready for picking. It was like a sort of paradise. Stretch out your hand, and you could eat. But Jonathon knew that the paradise was poisoned. The red fruit looked evil to him. Fallen fruit rotted on the ground, teeming with ants, gleaming with the slime of the slugs and snails that feasted secretly on the flesh at night.

Astral led him on, out of the trees, up a few railwaysleeper steps. Now he could see the garden. It was just as he'd imagined it. The fastidiously cared-for vegetable beds, smelling of chicken manure, heaped with mulch; the fragrant herb gardens, the great banks of lavender and rosemary humming with bees, the rambling roses already covered in ripening scarlet hips. Beyond the gardens, white sheets hung from a clothesline strung between two posts and propped up with a wooden pole. And beyond that, tree-shrouded, vine-hung and dim, was the house.

Four months ago, in the summer, when Jonathon and Astral first started meeting by the dividing fence—or a few weeks on, anyway, when he realized that the meetings were becoming a regular thing—he'd suggested that he should pay her family a formal visit. After all, she hadn't even turned seventeen then. She was very (adorably!) young.

Previously he'd been quite content to come and go on his weekend visits without encouraging notice from the people next door. He enjoyed the solitude of his mountain retreat, and it was easy to avoid even thinking about the house that huddled on the land beside his own at the bottom of the winding track called Lily Lane. Haven was so secret, so enclosed by the dense, dark-leaved shrubs that followed the fence-line almost all the way down to the forest, that for all he could see of it from his own house it could have been wild forest or wasteland.

He had known, of course, that his neighbors were unusual. That had been clear from the first dry comments he received when he told some of the village shopkeepers where he lived. His property was well known to them, it seemed. An old man called Ivan had lived there for many years, so Jonathon's place, to the locals, was "Ivan's place." And it was also "the place next-door to Haven." The word "Haven" was always accompanied by a wry or disapproving grimace.

The shopkeepers, once they got to know him, were plainly keen to swap gossip. But in those early months Jonathon hadn't pursued the matter. He'd taken care, in fact, not to appear more than casually interested, even when (especially when) he heard about Haven's celebrity inhabitant. He preferred to be perceived as a man who took celebrities in his stride.

He wasn't concerned about his neighbors. They didn't worry him, he didn't worry them. That was how he put it to himself, and to city friends who asked. Until he met Astral, eight or so months after he took possession of his property, he hadn't seen a single one of the Haven denizens at home or—to his knowledge—in the village. And that suited him perfectly.

But once he had started seeing Astral, it ceased to suit him. Increasingly, he felt uncomfortable about the thought that the household next door was perhaps unaware of the relationship. (In a few short weeks he had started to think of it as a "relationship.") He didn't like the idea that there was something covert about it. He felt he ought to make himself known.

It wasn't a thing that would have occurred to him in the city. But here it seemed the proper, the responsible thing to do. And maybe, he realized now, he was lamely trying to put Astral in perspective, making an effort to fight the spell that was gradually, thread by thread, enmeshing him.

But she resisted his suggestion. She fobbed him off with vague murmuring, her silky, pale-brown hair swinging as she shook her head. A little amused, he thought she was titillated by their innocently clandestine meetings, and wanted, romantically, to hug the secret to herself.

But, as more weeks passed, as their relationship deepened, as they talked, as he started to gain a sense of her daily life from the small, vivid details she let slip while she spoke of other things, he realized it wasn't as simple as that. A meeting with the family next door would not be a matter of drinking tea, polite and constrained, in some dim, old-fashioned sitting room, or at an oilcloth-covered table in a kitchen where herbs hung in bunches from the ceiling. Haven didn't welcome strangers. He probed, but Astral was reticent, and froze up as soon as he asked direct questions about her family.

Curious, he at last started fishing for more information in the village.

As before, the shopkeepers were more than ready to talk. They were well used to him by now. Ever since he bought Ivan's place he'd been stopping at Oakdale on his way from town to buy his Saturday milk, bread, fruit and meat. For over eight months he'd been making the Sunday morning pilgrimage for a paper, a take-away cappuccino and the small, warm apple pies that early on had become an essential part of his weekend routine. He was known at the hardware shop and the wine shop, and often wandered around the nursery.

People responded to his cautious bait with a torrent of information about the family at Haven. He had no idea how much of what they told him was true. But, with his grandmother's pursed-lip phrase flying unbidden to his mind from the past, he told himself that there was no smoke without fire.

He was shocked. And shocked as much by his own reaction—fascinated distaste, prurient curiosity—as by anything else. There was no question, even then, of his disentangling himself. It was already too late. Though at that time they'd barely touched, seeing Astral had gradually become not just a highlight but the focus of Jonathon's weekends in the mountains. Already he'd begun inventing work that would take him into the paddock, or sitting on the veranda for hours, pretending to read, watching for the glimmer of white by the fence-line, afraid to go into the house in case he missed her.

Sometimes she'd stay for an hour. Sometimes just for minutes. Sometimes she'd come to the fence twice or three times in a day. Those were good days. Sometimes she wouldn't come at all. Those days were empty, bleak, wasted. She never apologized or explained her absence. He learned not to press her. If he did, she'd grow silent, and soon afterwards drift away.

He stopped suggesting he meet her mother, her mother's de facto, her sisters. He stopped suggesting she let him take her out, to dinner, or a film. All he had heard had made him realize that such talk had been ridiculous. Astral, had she been other than she was, might have laughed in his face. She knew that if he revealed himself as an interested party, she'd be overtly forbidden to see him, and she would have to obey. Secrecy was her safeguard. She didn't want to lose him.

He didn't want to lose her, either. He couldn't face the thought of losing her, even then. And later, of course. Later . . .

Jonathon blinked rapidly, forcing his thoughts back to the present. Astral was leading him through the lavender now. Waves of sweetness surrounded them. The buzzing of the bees seemed abnormally loud.

Ahead, beyond the clothesline, the house lay low under the trees. Long ago it had been painted white, but the paint had faded and flaked away so that now the old timber was ridged and gray, like the bark of the apple trees. The vines that clung to its veranda posts had spread and twined together to hang in great swags from the shadowed roof, concealing the windows.

Jonathon's skin crawled. There was a sense of brooding

menace about the place, and he had the strong feeling that they were being watched. Frantically he scrabbled around in his mind for something to say. Something natural, that would make her talk to him, tell him what to expect.

"I don't think this is a good idea, Astral," he said, just loudly enough for her to hear. "If he's home he won't like me coming in this way, from the back. Or is he out? Or gone? Astral . . . ?"

She turned her head. "Please," she said in a low voice. Her hand tightened. He stared helplessly. He couldn't make himself break free.

She veered slightly to the right, moving through some shrubs and past a rainwater tank to the side of the house, where there was a small, bare dirt yard partly closed in by several rotting wooden sheds, a stack of firewood and a wire hen house the gate of which sagged open. Sharp-eyed hens, brown, black and white, scratched, crooning, around the yard, and pecked in the grass beyond it.

"Where are we going?" Jonathon whispered, holding back a little. "Astral, are you sure . . . ?" His voice faded.

Standing by the closed door of the largest shed, turning silently to face them, were two more young women, both dressed like Astral, both with long, loose hair. Jonathon knew at once who they were. Astral's descriptions of her older sisters had been very accurate.

The tall, dark-haired one, the one with the closed, handsome, brooding face and her arms full of lavender branches, was Bliss, the eldest. The other, plainer, plumper and fairer, carrying a basket with a cloth folded over the contents, was the middle sister, Skye. Her eyebrows and eyelashes were so fair as to be almost invisible. Her eyes were pale blue, slightly protruding, and utterly expressionless.

Without haste, Astral led Jonathon over to them.

"He was by the fence," she said, as if a question had been asked. "We need him to tell us."

Bliss and Skye looked at one another, then at Jonathon. Neither of them spoke.

Jonathon wet his lips with his tongue and cleared his throat. There was a faint, unpleasant smell in the yard. Hens picked at dried mud around his feet. He wanted to turn and run. He was way out of his depth here. He glanced behind him at the shadowed house, but inside no one stirred.

"We were told to wait," Bliss said. Her voice was beautiful—low, controlled and even.

"It has been too long," replied Astral. "Jonathon will know."

Bliss and Skye glanced at one another again. Then Bliss gave a tiny nod. Skye lifted the heavy latch of the shed door. The door swung open. A vile, sickening smell billowed out into the yard on a wave of heat.

"No!" Jonathon heard his own voice screaming.

On a heap of straw on the shed floor lay a swollen, stinking horror that had once been a man. Candles flickered at the thing's head and feet. Lavender branches were ranged carefully by its sides.

A roaring began in Jonathon's ears. Crying incoherently, he staggered back, overwhelming nausea rising, burning in his throat. But Astral's face was floating in front of him. Her mouth was moving.

"It is Adam, Jonathon," her voice was saying. "We have done all we can for him. But it has been six days already and he has not returned to us. He has changed very much. I think he is truly dead. Don't you?"

TWO

Senior Detective Tessa Vance was in her sunlit bedroom, dressing for a wedding. She looked in the mirror, saw a fair vision in misty blue, and was very glad she'd splurged on a new dress for the occasion. Not just because it was a compliment to Pete and Lori, whom she liked. Not just because weddings were times for celebration, and fine clothes were part of that. But also because it was so good, for once, to see herself in soft pastels, to be rid of the severely tailored, drab-colored suits she wore to work, to enjoy the sensation of light, silky fabric against her skin. It made her feel more like a woman and less like a workhorse than she'd felt for quite a while. Made her remember, as well, that sunshine and flowers, laughter and life, were just as real as darkness and fear, grief and death. A thing that in her line of work it was easy to forget.

She glanced at the pager lying on the bed with her handbag. She was on call. But so far the pager had maintained a welcome silence. She hoped, very much, that it would continue to do so. She wanted to enjoy this golden day.

She brushed her lips with a final touch of lipstick. She was ready.

And the hat? . . .

Tessa glanced uneasily at the romantic little hat lying on the dressing table. She'd seen it in a shop window just after buying the dress, and bought it on an impulse she now couldn't explain. Fine blue straw, tiny flowers and a wisp of veiling, the hat was a confection, a folly, a dream.

I must have been mad. I never wear hats like that. Why on earth did I? . . .

11

You know why. Because you adored it as soon as you saw it. Because it's charming and feminine and you felt like being a girl for once. Because it matched the dress so perfectly that it seemed like fate. You have to wear it. It cost . . .

I don't have to wear it if I don't want to.

You're scared. Scared of looking different. Scared of looking like you're trying. Go on, wear it. Why not? Why not? Let him see you looking . . .

Tessa picked up the hat and put it on.

It was perfect. It framed her face, emphasizing her eyes and her cheekbones. Her light hair shone beneath its hazy blue, curling around it in soft, fair waves.

Why not? Let him see . . .

She turned to pick up her handbag and, at that exact moment, her pager began to beep.

Senior Detective Steve Hayden was on the phone in his own bedroom listening to his father's slow voice. He glanced at his watch. There was no need to rush the conversation. He was dressed and ready to leave, and the church wasn't far away.

"Better let you go, then, son," his father said. "Your mum's giving me the hurry-up. You've got this do on, she says. Wedding, or something."

"It's okay, Dad," said Steve easily. "It's not till eleven. Plenty of time."

"Beautiful day for it," his father said. "Is up here, anyhow. Had a bit of rain yest'dy, though."

"That's good. How much?" Steve grinned. He and his father always ended up talking about the weather.

The answer to his question was prolonged, for apparently there had been some argument as to the exact amount of rain that had fallen. Steve listened absently, staring at the leafy branches moving gently outside his window against a background of tower blocks and blue sky. His father was speaking from a place where the sky was bigger, and bluer. Where gum trees didn't have to struggle for light between tall buildings but spread themselves over the hills and through gullies, clustered along the banks of creeks and bunched together in rolling paddocks, making pictures, and shade for cattle. A world away from city hype and office politics, suits and ties, and Central Homicide. Once, Steve thought, it was his world. No more.

The familiar wave of homesickness rolled softly over him. He resisted it, turning his face away from it, as he always had. Even in the old days, when it was so much stronger, with so much more power to hurt, he had refused to give in to it. There was no point in regretting things that couldn't be changed. The boy who'd thought he'd live forever on the land had been wrong, that's all. The cards just hadn't fallen that way.

Inside the jacket hanging on the back of a chair, the pager sounded. Automatically, he reached for it, turning away from the window, and the view.

"Dad, I've got to go," he said into the phone. "Got to call in. Looks like I'm working."

"No rest for the wicked," his father responded laconically. "Ah, well. That's how it goes."

Steve suppressed a sigh. "Yep," he murmured. "That's how it goes."

Two hours later, Tessa slowed the car to a crawl as the road she'd been following narrowed and its gentle slope became an alarming plunge. She glanced at Steve lying back in the passenger seat with tie and collar loosened and his eyes closed. He looked peaceful, but she was sick of silence. The brief she'd been given when she called in had disturbed her, grimly shadowing the bright day. The closer they came to facing the reality of the death of Adam Quinn the more her feeling of foreboding grew.

"I think we're almost there," she said aloud. "We're in Lily Lane. The 'No Through Road' sign's just ahead."

"Good-oh," Steve answered, without opening his eyes.

Her eyes flickered to the car clock. "Pete and Lori will be married by now," she said.

He smiled amiably. "Long ago. Hope he knows what he's doing."

"Hope she knows what *she's* doing," Tessa retorted.

The smile widened, the eyes opened. Steve sat up straighter in his seat, fastened his top shirt button, pulled up the knot of his tie and smoothed the back of his hair. He peered with interest through the windscreen as the car bumped past the NO THROUGH ROAD sign and onto a rough, narrow strip of aged and potholed bitumen that wound down into the valley below. On the right of the track, the ground fell away in a tangle of brushy scrub that dropped unbroken to the valley floor. On the left rose a high bank covered with ferns, honeysuckle and wild berry bushes from which red and green parrots flapped, shrieking, as they passed.

"I don't know what you're supposed to do if you meet anyone coming the other way," Tessa said.

"You just back up."

"Sounds like a good way to die," she growled. She hunched over the wheel, glaring moodily at the road ahead.

"Shame we didn't get to the wedding." Steve knew how women felt about these things.

Tessa shrugged.

"At least we didn't have to change," he said, pulling his tie into place.

Tessa looked down ruefully at her sober brown trouser suit, and forbore to answer.

Not long afterwards the lane petered out completely, widening into a rough, rutted turning circle edged with pines, banksias, wattles, gum trees and more berry bushes. Two dirt tracks, closed off by farm gates, led down from the circle, one directly ahead of them, one straggling off to the right.

The track that ran straight ahead was marked with a charmingly ancient fence post bearing a wooden letterbox to which some brass numbers had been screwed. The posts that supported the wire fence on either side of the gate were relatively new, Tessa noted. Presumably the old post, valued for its authentically rustic appearance, had been carefully retained when the fence was repaired. Through gaps in the trees beyond the gate you could see glimpses of the valley below— a red tin roof, the tops of pine trees—and above and beyond, a breathtaking blue-green view of distant hills and sky.

"That's the neighbor's place," Steve said, glancing at his notebook. "Guy who rang the cops. Jonathon Stoller. He only comes up on weekends."

He got out of the car and strolled over to the right-hand gate. He opened it, and Tessa rolled the car gently through the opening, noticing the faded, hand-lettered sign swinging from the wire, but unable to read what it said. She felt instantly claustrophobic as the gate swung shut behind the car and a mass of dark green enclosed her.

"Secluded little spot," Steve joked as he slipped back into his seat.

Tessa eased the car forward, her foot on the brake. The drive was steep. Twigs and old cones snapped under the wheels, and leaves brushed the doors and windows as they moved down, down through a dark tunnel the walls of which became even more impenetrable as trees gave way to towering evergreen shrubs with stiff, glossy leaves.

"What did the sign say?" she asked, to break the silence.

"Haven."

The double line of shrubs broke at last. Ahead was a weatherboard house with a low, rust-spotted roof and a wraparound veranda, the side of which was partly closed off by a mishmash of fibro sheeting and recycled windows.

The track ended at a broad patch of lush grass that edged a flat, bare earth yard at the side of the house. A line of stepping stones meandered away towards the front of the house. Presumably it represented the official entrance path, but the stones were almost hidden by the weeds growing beside and between them. The front door of Haven, apparently, was rarely, if ever, used. The side door, giving off to the yard, was the common way in and out of the house.

Hens pecked around the wheels of a battered ute, the police four-wheel drive vehicle and various other cars that had been parked on the grass. Tessa pulled to a stop at the back of the group.

"Here we go again," said Steve, climbing out and stretching.

Crime-scene tape. Voices. Figures. Uniforms.

Haven. A strange place for Adam Quinn to die.

Jonathon sat in the Haven living room, waiting. Waiting for what, he didn't know. The police had asked him a few

questions, then they'd left him with the three girls and a female constable who had a face like a scone, even to the small,
brown sultana eyes. His watch told him that it had been hours
since, heaving and choking, he'd run next door to phone for
help, to gasp that oh, God, there'd been an—accident. That
Adam Quinn, of Haven, Lily Lane, was dead. But he'd hardly
been aware of time passing.

He could have gone home and waited there, he suspected,
and he wanted with all his strength to do that, but he couldn't
leave Astral to face this horror alone. She had no idea, none,
of what it meant. Of Rachel Brydie, her mother, there was
still no sign. When the police asked, Skye and Bliss had said
simply that Mother was out, and they didn't know where
she was.

Astral was sitting beside him, very still. He wanted to talk
to her, but Skye and Bliss were sitting opposite them, staring.
He couldn't speak in front of them. It made him shudder inside to think of what they'd done, how they'd spent the last six
days. He found himself compulsively glancing over and over
again at their hands. Those sun-browned hands—Skye's angular, long-fingered; Bliss's plump, pink-tipped, with nails
bitten down to the quick—smoothing, anointing and caress-
ing the darkening, bloating skin of that dead thing in the shed,
day after day, while the flesh rotted and the blowflies came.

Astral. Had she too . . . ? His stomach churned. Had they
made her help them? Had the hand that had led him up
through the orchard, through the herb garden, touched . . . ?

He cursed himself for a fool. He should have known. He
should have realized that something like this might happen.
With bitter hindsight he realized that indirectly Astral had
said enough over the past few months for an intelligent
person to have been able to predict this—all this. But he
hadn't really listened. Hadn't really thought. For months he'd
thought only of her. Of getting time with her alone; of
keeping their secret. Till last Sunday. And then, he hadn't
thought at all. What he'd felt couldn't be called thought. He
knew that, now.

Bliss and Skye were watching him. Somber dark eyes;
poppy pale eyes. What did they know? What had Astral told

them? What would she, and they, tell their mother, and the police?

He felt the sweat pricking on his back and chest. As if she sensed his tension, Astral turned to look at him, her face troubled.

"Are you afraid?" she whispered.

He shook his head. "There's nothing to be afraid of," he said gently.

"Because of Astral, we disobeyed. We will be punished." Skye's voice was high-pitched, and hysteria lurked behind its singsong cadences. Jonathon glanced at her, met those light eyes with distaste.

"You did nothing wrong," he said evenly.

"There are strangers at Haven," said Skye. "It is forbidden. And when Adam returns . . ."

"Be still, Skye!" ordered Bliss. "What is done is done."

Astral moaned softly. Jonathon felt her body quiver as she pressed against him. Hot blood rushed to his head. Desire mixed with irritation, shame and a sort of dread convulsed him. It was like a sickness.

"For God's sake!" he mumbled thickly. "This is crazy!" He put his arm around Astral's shoulders and held her. "Can't you get it through your heads, you people? It's over! He can't hurt you any more. He's dead. Dead!"

He became aware of slight movement from the scone-faced policewoman, sitting so silently in her corner. He glanced at her. She was writing something in the notebook balanced on her knee.

Every move we make, he thought. Every word we utter. She'll tell them.

With Steve beside her, Tessa stood at the door of the shed. A generator roared, powering the lights that flooded the dim space. Inside, the blue-uniformed figure of Dee Suzeraine moved around, nostrils pinched, video camera glued to one eye. In the background, members of Lance Fisk's forensic team, their faces reflecting their physical distress, dourly poked around the walls, through the dark, piled-up mess of grimy terracotta pots, bits of wood and pipe, rusty tools, bags of chicken feed and bales of lucerne hay.

Perhaps, once, the shed had housed a tractor, or even been used for milking, Tessa thought. But that was a long time ago. Now, in common with the other outbuildings lining the yard, it was just about derelict. Rough rafters, clean and bare, supported a rusty tin roof. The walls were gappy where here and there a rotted timber had fallen away. The packed earth floor was littered with dirty straw, dead leaves, feathers and chicken droppings—everywhere but in the center, where the body lay. There, the floor had been swept scrupulously clean. The smell—decay mixed with lavender oil—was appalling, but pathologist Tootsie Soames was bending over the grotesque, oozing, purple-clad shape on the floor, showing no sign of discomfort.

"She's incredible," muttered Dee, escaping from the shed with relief. She looked around for a suitable place to stand and made for the chicken pen.

Tessa felt queasy.

You've seen decomposed bodies before.

This is awful. Dressed in purple, like a king. Beard's starting to come away . . . They've been washing him . . . The maggots . . .

"We've seen enough, haven't we?" muttered Steve. He moved away to join Dee. Tessa followed.

"This is a good spot," Dee called cheerfully as they approached. "Chooks smell so bad you can't smell the other." She squatted to take a photograph of a brown hen which had stalked back into the pen on her approach and was now watching her through the wire, its red comb flopping over one black eye.

"Where's Fisk?"

"There's been a fire around the other side of the house. He's there, with Thorne. He's in a filthy mood. Fisk, I mean. With Thorne, how could you tell?"

She turned round to grin at them, then her face froze into a look of polite inquiry.

Inspector Thorne was approaching from the house. It was

impossible to tell if he'd heard the joke, or not. He nodded at Tessa and Steve.

"Nasty business," he said mildly. "According to the witnesses, it happened last Sunday night. The witnesses, such as they are, are in the house. Bliss, Astral and Skye Brydie." He turned up his eyes slightly as he pronounced the names. "Lived here with Quinn and their mother. Mad as meat-axes, the pack of them."

"They really thought he was going to come back to life?"

"So they claim," said Thorne. "But the youngest—Astral Brydie—apparently started thinking maybe after six days it was just a bit iffy—"

"Not to mention whiffy," Dee put in.

Thorne turned to her. "I think Sergeant Fisk could use your services in the burnt-out part of the house, Constable."

Dee ducked her head, and went.

"This morning Astral asked the man next door to come in and take a look—against the wishes of her sisters, I gather," Thorne continued. "You realize the body's been interfered with, of course."

Steve nodded. "They've been cleaning it with lavender oil."

"And the rest," said Thorne dryly. "Forensics won't have an easy time in that shed. The girls swept the floor around the body, and they've been tramping in and out since Monday morning, fiddling round with candles and flowers and so on."

Steve grinned. "Do Fisk good to have a bit of a challenge."

"It's no joke, Hayden. They've cleaned the gun, too," snapped Thorne. "They say they knew Adam'd want them to."

"Are they—simple, or something?" asked Tessa, trying to get a grip on the situation.

"Hard to say." Thorne frowned. "Brainwashed might be a better way to look at it. They make sense when they're talking about things other than Adam Quinn. A kind of sense." He grimaced. "It's a weird setup."

"He didn't leave a note, I gather," said Steve.

Thorne shook his head. "Nothing found so far."

Tessa glanced at the dim, low farmhouse, its rafters

festooned with spiderwebs, its vines, overlush, crawling unchecked.

What went on here?

She moistened her lips. "What a way for Adam Quinn to end up," she said. "He was huge when I was at school."

"I've never heard of him," said Steve.

"You must have. His records sold heaps."

He shrugged laconically. "I wasn't into that stuff."

"He was incredible on stage. Of course he didn't have the beard then."

"What happened to him, then? I mean, how come he dropped out?"

"I think he burned out. He made a fortune. Started drinking. Got into drugs. He was married and divorced again six months later. He got caught in a hotel room with a thirteen-year-old. All that sort of stuff. He had a couple of albums that flopped. Then I think he had some sort of breakdown, and just faded out."

"Up with the rocket, down with the stick," said Thorne, with some satisfaction.

Tootsie came out into the air, blinking and stripping off her gloves. She strode over to them.

"Gunshot wound to the forehead. Dead about a week, I'd say," she said briskly. "Could be less. Decomposition's very well advanced, but it's hot in there."

"So what do we reckon?" Steve asked. "Suicide?"

"That's what it looks like to me. At this stage."

"That's what it *would* look like, if someone planned it that way," said Thorne.

"You think they did?" Tessa asked. "You're talking about the Brydie sisters and their mother?"

He raised his eyebrows. "Why not? They could have killed him while he was asleep in bed, and dragged him out here."

"No." Tootsie shook her head. "If he wasn't shot where he lies I'll eat my hat. And if he didn't do it himself, I don't know who did. He's a big man. In good shape, too—muscles like iron. It's hard to imagine he was forced flat on his back by a few women. Even acting together."

"So he sets fire to the house then comes out here, lies down and tops himself, that it?" drawled Steve.

Tootsie shrugged. "It's the most likely explanation," she said primly. "A .22, like the girls said, by the look of it. The bullet'll be embedded in the dirt under the straw. They'll find it as soon as we can get the body out."

Steve rubbed his chin with his hand, looking around the yard. "Locals obviously weren't so happy to call it suicide," he said at last. "McCaffrey didn't waste any time calling us in, did he?"

Thorne hesitated. "You'll want to have a word with Sergeant McCaffrey and the constables—Ingres and Williams—yourself," he said slowly at last. "There seems to have been some local feeling about this place. About the Brydie women—particularly the mother, Rachel Brydie. She's lived here for a long time—twenty-five years or so. Adam Quinn moved in with her and the girls about four and a half years ago."

"Mrs. Brydie's not here, I gather," said Tessa. "Where is she?"

"You tell me and we'll both know," said Thorne. "Go in and see if you can get the girls to talk, Tessa. Get rid of Stoller while you're at it—tell him he can go home. Steve can get his story there, after he's seen the burnt-out room." He turned to Steve. "We'll go in by the front door. It's open. Best, I think, that the women don't see us poking around. I don't want any hysterics."

Steve looked around, frowning. "This place's got a bad feeling about it," he muttered. "And they call it Haven. Some haven."

Tessa shivered. She agreed with him.

Three

The village of Oakdale lay about two kilometers away from Haven, on the other side of the highway and the railway line that together crossed the mountains, climbing up, then winding down, connecting Sydney to the plains of the west. The village was beside the railway station and near enough to the best-known views to be a handy stopping-off point for tourists.

Oakdale was small and almost excessively pretty. In spring, clematis, camellias, wisteria, azaleas and cherry trees blossomed in the old gardens that surrounded it. In autumn, Japanese maples and liquidambars flamed, and tulip trees, ashes and oaks glowed gold. The quaint shops that sheltered under their awnings along the tree-lined main street had either been there since the village began, or had been built to look as if they had. Charm was Oakdale's stock-in-trade, and the charm was fiercely nurtured. The gift shops, cafés, galleries and antique shops lived and died by it.

During the working week the village was quiet as the locals went about their business. People greeted one another in the main street, stopped to chat as they bought their meat, their fruit and veg, their paper or their groceries. Women enfolded in lilac capes spent restful hours having their hair permed in the Oakdale Hair Salon. The men in utes with blue or brown dogs in the back parked easily near the cake shop when they stopped to buy their pies for lunch. The gift shop owners were bored. The cappuccino machines in the cafés worked seldom.

But at the weekend the village changed character as the tourists arrived, surging up from the city on Friday night and

Saturday morning, ready for two days of mountain air, sight-seeing and spending. The shopowners went on the alert. Their usual customers kept out of the way, or maintained a low profile. The main street streamed with cars. The footpaths streamed with people. The waitresses in the cafés ran backwards and forwards with baskets of scones, strawberry jam and cream in little glass dishes, pots of tea, cappuccinos and flat whites, long blacks and cafe lattés, hot chocolate for the romantics and milkshakes for the kids. Cash registers sang in the galleries. Dreamers stood in line across the real estate agents' windows, pointing out to each other this photograph or that—Cute Cottage, Mountain Hideaway, Golden Oldie, Cozy Log Cabin, Turn-of-the-Century Magnificence—exclaiming at the low, low prices, doing their math. The disabled-parking-only zone in front of the church was always, eventually, filled by someone quite able-bodied, but too brash or desperate to care what anyone thought of them.

This Saturday was no exception. But this Saturday, unknown to the visitors, a tide of rumor and fascinated speculation was moving, bubbling just beneath the pretty surface, behind the village smiles.

The news spread around corners, in back rooms, through car windows, between brasserie courtyard and kitchen, in murmured meetings on the street.

Adam Quinn was dead. Adam Quinn had been dead a week. Adam Quinn had killed himself last Sunday night—with a knife, with a gun, with an ax. There'd been a fire at Haven. It was half-burnt away. Inside it was weird, a health hazard, like a hovel, like a jail, like something out of the movies. There was a big, black cauldron on the stove. There was a special room full of herbs and drugs and bottles and weird mixtures. Haven was crawling with police. Police from the city. Homicide police. That meant murder. Adam Quinn had been drugged, poisoned, shot through the head. Rachel Brydie had run away. The Brydie girls were being questioned. The Brydie girls had poisoned Adam Quinn. Because he wanted to leave them. Because they wanted his money. Because their mother had told them to. Because their mother had left. Because they'd finally gone over the edge. It was shocking. It was a tragedy. Adam Quinn, the local celebrity, so famous, with pots of money, but always so natural, so friendly, just like anyone else, had been sucked dry, drugged and murdered by the Brydies. When you thought about it, it was bound to happen. Something like this was bound to happen. Everyone had thought so. Everyone had known it was only a matter of time.

Lyn Weisenhoff, whose husband Carl ran the wine shop in the main street, heard several versions of what had happened to Adam Quinn when she dropped her daughter off to ballet class at the church hall. Her informant was a woman called Freda Ridge, who owned the CountryWise boutique and whose husband, Charles, was one of the two local real estate agents.

Freda was short, square and red of face, with a gleaming, blond pageboy bob. She was full of bounding energy, and Lyn always found conversation with her exhausting.

Particularly so today. Not only was Lyn frightened and revolted by what Freda was saying, barking at her, really, in the rapid-fire monolog that was her specialty, but all the time cars were braking behind, and then angrily swerving around, Freda's white Mercedes which she had recklessly double-parked outside the hall. Freda had her back to the road, and was either sublimely unaware, or taking no notice, of the furious toots and often obscene shouts of the balked motorists, But Lyn felt as embarrassed as if the car were her own.

". . . an absolute tragedy," Freda Ridge was saying. "Remember when he first came, and we heard he was looking for a place? And we were all so thrilled? I mean, it was a real chance for the village, wasn't it? I said so at the time. Look what happened when Paul Hogan went to Byron Bay. It put the place on the map. The world map."

"He—Adam—didn't want any publicity though, Freda. He just wanted—"

Freda flapped a hand dismissively. "Oh, I understand all about that," she declared inaccurately. "But people would have *known*, Lyn. That's the important thing. Charles showed him some gorgeous places. I mean, you'd give your eyeteeth for some of them—" Crossly, she jingled her car keys in the pocket of her jacket. "And then, what does he do but throw it all away and take up with that terrible woman. Of all people! It was a travesty. I said so at the time. A travesty." Her brow knotted at the thought of the wasted opportunity.

"It was his choice, Freda," Lyn protested, against her better judgment.

"Rubbish! Heaven knows what lies she told him. Or what she did to get him to move in with her. Well . . ." Freda pursed her lips. "Well, no, you can imagine what she *did*. With her history. God knows, she's had enough practice. She probably knows every trick in the book. It makes you sick to think the things she probably does for them. But what he'd see in her in the first place I can't begin to understand."

"She's quite striking-looking, really," murmured Lyn. She winced slightly as she said it. How bizarre, for her of all people to be defending Rachel Brydie. But Freda was a fool if she couldn't see how attractive the woman's high-cheekboned, haggard looks might be to some men. And that air of fatalism, and otherworldliness. And that reputation. Impossible to combat, for anyone ordinary. For anyone, for example, with soft, limp brown hair that escaped unceasingly from its pins, a long, pale, pleasant face and a willowy, apologetic sort of body, and whose life was an open book consisting of endless, short chapters with titles like: "Defleaing the Dog," "Doing the Shopping," "Treating Angus's Plantar Wart," "Serving in the Shop," and "Cooking Spaghetti Bolognese."

The other woman snorted. "She might have been attractive once, but honestly, Lyn, she gets round like a hag—I mean, she doesn't do a thing to herself. It's one thing for young girls to get around in long dresses with their hair flowing everywhere and so on. But a woman her age? And grim! My God! Charles says just looking at her gives him the shivers. He says he'd rather go to bed with a snake."

Lyn silently considered Charles Ridge—a hearty man with a beer belly and a well-trimmed moustache, who wore shorts and long socks and a golf club tie. She thought that Charles would have had more chance of persuading a snake into bed than getting within spitting distance of Rachel Brydie. Maybe that was the problem.

"And imagine taking on a woman with three half-wit daughters who don't have a snowflake's chance in hell of ever making anything of their lives," Freda was going on. "It was madness. Madness! No decent and normal man—"

"Adam Quinn wasn't decent and normal, though, was he?" Lyn muttered. Her head felt as though it was going to burst.

Cut off in full flow, Freda stared, then started to bluster. "Well—he wasn't *average*, if that's what you mean, Lyn," she said hotly. "You wouldn't expect him to be, would you? But I don't know why you'd say he wasn't *decent*. You mean all those tales about his past and so on, do you? Well, I don't know about all that. That was all publicity hype and paper talk, if you ask me. Up to a point."

Finding that her companion remained silent, she tossed her head slightly and went on.

"Whatever the case, you realize there'll be publicity," she said, jingling her car keys in her pocket. "They'll be up here in droves for sure. Wanting interviews—who knew him and so on. Pictures of the village. I've been thinking—we'd better get a special street committee meeting organized. Discuss how we're going to play it. It'll have to be tonight. I've got Daniel's birthday party this afternoon, too. Sixteen ten-year-olds, can you imagine? Of all the times! *And* I've got Mum staying. Isn't it always the way? Still, can't be helped. I'll book our usual table—seven-thirty too late for you?"

Behind her, a green four-wheel drive balked at the Mercedes and found itself hemmed in as the cars behind it overtook it one after the other. The driver glowered, muttering, peering into his rear-vision mirror.

"Oh, well, Freda, I don't know if I can make it tonight," Lyn protested feebly, pushing back a few straggling wisps of hair, feeling for loose pins.

"No, no, you'll have to make it. We have to act fast on this, you know, Lyn," said Freda severely. "We don't want our image going down the tubes at this stage. Everything's been going so well. We've got to take charge. Clamp down on anything nasty before it starts." She pulled out her keys, turned around and strode to her car. The driver of the green four-wheel drive glared at her and she stared him down, expressionless. He looked back at his rear-vision mirror, saw a chance for escape, put his foot down, and stalled.

Trying not to look at him, Lyn followed Freda, bleating ineffectually. "Juliette won't want to give us a table tonight. It's Saturday. Saturdays are busy for them. Tuesdays—"

"I know what day it is, Lyn! But this is an emergency. And we *always* go to Martin's. Juliette won't mind, for once. It's not as if we don't pay at all, is it? You're not suggesting one of us cater, are you? Well, I certainly can't. Not in a million years. Not when I've just run a kid's birthday party."

"No, of course not, but anyway—" Lyn made an effort "—anyway, is there any point in having a special meeting, really? I don't see how we can control—"

"Of course we can! It's just a matter of sticking together. Well, I'd better love you and leave you." Freda hauled her car door open and clambered behind the wheel. "Sorry to rush off. I've got to get home and ice the blasted cake. Tonight. Seven-thirty. All right? If you really can't make it, send Carl."

The green four-wheel drive lurched around the Mercedes and jerked away with a screech of tires.

"Mad," said Freda, peering after it. She slammed the door, then wound down the window. "Just stop off at the bookshop on your way back and tell Floss it's all confirmed, will you? Michael's still sick—she'll have to come instead of him. You can let Maryanne Lamplough know as well, if you think of it."

There was a lump in Lyn's throat. She swallowed, feeling as though she could hardly breathe. "Michael's no better?" she heard herself say.

"Apparently not." Freda frowned. "I called into the bookshop this morning. Floss said he'd rung in earlier and he sounded terrible. I said to her, 'Why on earth doesn't he go to the doctor, Floss?' And she said he just refused—it's all that natural remedy, power of the mind business. Well, you know where all that stupidity comes from, and you'd think he'd have more sense, a so-called intelligent man like him." She rolled her eyes. "Anyway, must fly. You tell Floss and whatever. I'll ring the others. Bye."

The Mercedes roared to life. Behind it, a man in a station wagon braked suddenly and leaned on his horn. Freda glanced vaguely behind her, waved a casual hand and put her foot to the floor. In seconds she was gone.

Lyn hesitated on the gutter. Dull anger churned in her stomach. Why did she let the woman get away with it? Why couldn't she just have said, calmly and firmly, "No, Freda. I can't make it tonight, and neither can Carl. Have the meeting without us. Or don't have it at all. It's pointless anyway."

"Completely pointless," she said aloud, then glanced around to see if anyone had heard her. She pushed some loosening hairpins in again, and, seeing a break in the traffic, dashed across the road. She had to get back to the shop. Carl was on his own, and by now the place would be getting busy.

When she got back to the shop, she'd have to tell Carl about Adam Quinn. The thought of facing him, telling him, seeing his face change, keeping her own face still and bland, almost frightened her. She hesitated again, nibbling at her lip. She decided to go to the supermarket and buy bread and milk on the way. The supermaket would be crowded. Maybe, if she delayed a bit, someone else would have told him by the time she got there.

And that, at least, would be something.

Mrs. Verna Larkin, of the Bide-A-While bed-and-breakfast establishment conveniently situated a short taxi ride from the station, heard about the doings at Haven when her teenage daughter Melissa, the only one of her children still living at home, came back all agog from the village patisserie with the bread rolls. Mrs. Larkin offered "lunchtime picnic baskets" as part of her service, and tastefully filled bread rolls, she'd found, were not only quicker and easier to make than sandwiches, but looked more impressive.

"They say he's been dead for ages," Melissa whispered, eyes sparkling, pretty, triangular face alive with ghoulish delight. "Weeks, or something. He was all black and swollen up. Just lying on the ground, in a chook shed, with candles all around him. Isn't it awful?"

Mrs. Larkin automatically took the bag of rolls from her

daughter in her left hand, and just as automatically crossed herself with her right. It came into her mind, quite suddenly, that it had been a long, long time since she'd been to Mass. Of course she knew why. To go to Mass she'd have to go to confession first. And that was out of the question, what with one thing and another.

Ages ago she'd decided that she couldn't face telling nice old Father Pernane that she was committing mortal sin on a regular basis with Duncan Drewe, one of the taxi drivers who ferried guests between the station and Bide-A-While. Let alone that she was on the pill. Father Pernane had absolved her for so much in the past. She couldn't bear to disappoint him again. She hadn't been sure whether he would view the fornication or the contraception with the more gravity, and as she had no intention of giving up either of them, she'd let the matter drift.

But drifting away from the disciplines of the church had meant drifting away from her past. Like a piece of kelp dislodged from the seabed, she had gained her freedom, but lost her roots. These days she found it hard to identify with the adolescent Verna Malloy who had planned to be a nun. Who had wept for sinners, and prayed on her knees every morning and every night. Who had pleaded with her mother to let her cut her curling, waist-length hair short, because vanity was a sin.

The years had flown. That life seemed like a dream.

Now Mrs. Larkin sometimes looked in the mirror and wondered how it could be that, so quickly, it seemed, the idealistic, stainless Verna Malloy, size 8, God's child, had been transmogrified into practical, perimenopausal Verna Larkin, size 14, Paddy Larkin's widow, Paul, Matthew and Melissa's mother, Bide-A-While's proprietor, taxi driver's scarlet woman, so much else.

And no going back.

She'd thought occasionally of going to confession somewhere where she wasn't known. But obscurely it seemed to her that this would be creeping and dishonest, and wouldn't count. And Father Pernane would surely say something, if she turned up at Mass without having turned up at his confessional first. To avoid embarrassing explanations she'd have to confess in two parts: mortal sins to a stranger, venial sins to Father Pernane. And that was a kind of dishonesty in itself.

Mrs. Larkin, turning to put the still-warm rolls on her kitchen bench, felt uncomfortable thinking of it. So, as was her way, she let her thoughts slide into other, less dangerous channels. Despite momentary lapses, no doubt induced by hormonal changes, she was a natural optimist.

She had time yet to be shriven. She was in good health. Barring accident, she should live to a good old age, she thought. She had the genes for it. Her mother had died peacefully at home at eighty-six, with every tooth in her head, despite keeping boiled lollies under her pillow to suck if she woke at night.

Melissa was chattering on, her voice high and animated yet strangely distant, like background radio noise. "Louie at the cake shop, you know, her sister's boyfriend Russell's in the police. Mum? So Louie knew absolutely *everything* . . ."

In the fullness of time, Mrs. Larkin thought vaguely, the pill would be no longer an issue. Her fertility was already in question. So that was one thing. And at some point, sad to say, it was fairly certain that Duncan Drewe would also no longer be an issue.

Already their weekly lovemaking sessions, though still comforting, and something to look forward to, had become rather mechanical. On Thursday night, staring at her bare, pink toes, which were pointing towards the ceiling at the time, Mrs. Larkin had found herself thinking that for the weekend breakfasts, a few button mushrooms might be nice with the bacon and eggs instead of grilled tomato, for a change. And given the time he took, maybe Duncan had had his mind on other things, too. The state of his taxi's brakes, which they'd discussed at dinner, maybe.

Duncan worried a lot about the cab. Of course it was his livelihood, but his concern with the vehicle seemed excessive to Mrs. Larkin. It came from spending too much time in the thing. She often told him that he should walk about a bit while waiting for fares at the station, instead of sitting behind the wheel reading the paper . . .

"Mum!" Melissa was jiggling up and down, urgent for her

mother's full attention. "They'll probably put Mrs. Brydie away now, don't you reckon?"

"Why?" asked Verna Larkin dimly, feeling for a knife in the kitchen drawer. Shredded lettuce, cream cheese, smoked salmon, a few capers . . . honey-baked ham, tomato and relish . . .

"Well, she must've done it! Don't you reckon? She's run away."

Mrs. Larkin felt a jolt, deep in her stomach. "Run?"

"Louie says Russell says Astral and the others are on their own there. It was the guy next door who found the body. You know, the city guy who bought Ivan's place? Who always wears the red-checked shirt? Who always buys the apple pies on Sundays?"

"Stoller."

"Yes, him. Louie says Russell said he chucked up when he saw it. Well, you would, wouldn't you? I'd've had a heart attack. He was shot in the head." Melissa giggled, clapping a hand over her mouth. "I mean, Adam Quinn was. Louie says he had a hole in his forehead like this." She put the tips of her thumb and index finger together to make a circle. "They'll probably put the sisters away too, Louie says. I mean, they'll have to now, won't they? Loonies like that—"

"What have they—"

"Mum, I *told* you. They put candles round him. They've been sort of feeling him and rubbing stuff into him and decorating him and worshipping him and stuff—"

"Oh, God!"

"—for a whole week. They're really mad. I mean, we always knew they were mad, but I mean, this means they're *really* mad. They reckoned he was going to rise from the dead, like Jesus or something. That's what they told the cops. And Louie says Russell said his hair was falling out, and he stank like—"

"Melissa!"

"Well he did!"

"I don't want to hear. Get the capers out, will you?"

Mrs. Larkin's hands split bread rolls, spread cream cheese,

separated slices of smoked salmon, pink and damp and paper thin. Black pepper . . .

"It's so awful!" said her daughter, rooting around in the crowded refrigerator. Bottles and bowls scraped together, setting Mrs. Larkin's teeth on edge.

"In the door," she snapped. The lettuce was already shredded, ready in a bowl.

Pluck out handfuls, heap it up. Lettuce is cheap . . .

Melissa found the capers and brought the jar over to the bench. Her sojourn at the fridge had changed her mood. "Actually, it's really hard to take it in. It's a real shock. It's sort of incredible, isn't it?" she said in a soft and wondering voice. "I mean, we actually knew him. He was actually here, in our own house."

"That was years ago."

Years ago.

"He was really nice to me. He bought me a toffee apple at the market. Even after he went to Haven to live he always used to say hello if I saw him at the shops. He always said, 'Hello, Melissa, how's tricks?' You know, I told you. Oh, I feel awful now. I mean, I sort of forgot about—before. Everyone was talking about it, and they were all excited, and I forgot. How could I?"

Mrs. Larkin glanced up, and fought down a wave of impatience. Her daughter's hands were clasped, her lips were trembling, and the bright eyes were misting over as she willed the tears to come.

"We hardly knew him, Melissa," she heard herself saying. "Don't get all worked up."

"You don't understand!" The feeling of injustice did the trick and Melissa's eyes overflowed. She rushed, sobbing, from the kitchen.

She's just young, Mrs. Larkin reminded herself. She leaned on the kitchen bench. Suddenly she felt extremely tired. She would have liked to sit down. She would have liked a nice, hot cup of tea. But the picnic baskets had to be finished.

She reached for the caper jar.

Four

Crossing the gray boards of the veranda to the side door of the house, Tessa saw that the closed-off area to her right was screened by a faded curtain bearing a grapevine pattern. She pulled the curtain aside and looked in. The small room contained a cracked and peeling bath, some concrete tubs, an old-fashioned hand wringer and a wood-fired copper for boiling water.

No power. They do the washing by hand. They have to boil water to have a bath. But Adam Quinn must have been a multimillionaire by the time he dropped out. What happened to him?

The doorway was shielded by a wire screen door. It creaked as she opened it, and rattled as it banged lightly shut behind her. A familiar sound. A sound from her childhood.

Granny's place. Back door.

Dimness. Silence. The smell of spices and wood smoke. She was in the kitchen. There was a large, scrubbed central table, probably used only for food preparation since no chairs were gathered around it. There was the first meat safe she'd ever seen outside a folk museum. There was a big, black fuel stove, radiating heat. Ladles of all sizes were hanging from hooks screwed into the mantelpiece. A great black iron pot stood on the stove.

Witches' cauldron.

Pull yourself together!

Everything was scrupulously clean and tidy. The boards of the floor were gray and smooth with scrubbing. A brass tap was fastened to the unlined wall, its pipe leading, presumably, to the tank outside. A metal bucket stood beneath it. A

33

kerosene lamp and several candles in tin holders stood on the mantelpiece and on the meat safe.

No power. Even in here. They live like . . .

Bunches of dried herbs hung from the ceiling rafters—thyme, oregano, marjoram, rosemary, bay leaves and others Tessa couldn't name. Nailed to the wall was a poster-sized calendar. It was the only newish thing in the room, but even so it looked faded, printed in dull green on recycled paper. It was headed "Harmony with Nature" in flowing script. A simpler legend at the bottom stated: "Courtesy O'Malley's Bookshop." The thing was a promotional giveaway, Tessa guessed, from some bookshop which perhaps specialized in new-age publications. Every day bore a diagram of the appropriate phase of the moon, and sketched astrological signs danced around the margins. The calendar had been marked all over with pencilled reminders, all in the same hand.

Curious, Tessa went to look more closely. The notes were all about work to be done—mostly in the gardens. Composting, weeding, planting, mulching, harvesting, pruning . . . There seemed to be nothing personal at all. No birthdays, no visits, no outings, no holidays had been marked. Only one date was ringed: the 5th of January, a new moon day, but there was no note beside it, nothing to indicate why it was important.

There was something very depressing about this relentless catalog of tasks unrelieved by any hint of gaiety or celebration. Tessa felt instinctively that on New Year's Eve the calendar would be taken down and another, the same or very similar, would be put up, ready to be filled with the same tasks, expressed in the same words.

A round of labor, never-ending.

"Can I help you?"

Tessa turned to meet the sharply inquiring eyes of a stockily built, uniformed policewoman standing at the door that led into the rest of the house.

"Tessa Vance, Central Homicide," she said, showing her identification.

The constable's jaw dropped in an expression of surprise which quickly became a grin of pleasure. "Hey, what d'you know about that?" she exclaimed. "I didn't realize they had any women in Homicide. That's great. How is it?"

"Oh, fine," Tessa murmured idiotically.

The constable nodded, still beaming. Then she seemed to remember where she was. "Oh, look, sorry—Constable Rochette Williams," she said, arranging her features into a more official expression. "I've been sitting with—you know—them."

Furtively she moved further into the kitchen. "They're in there," she muttered, gesturing with her thumb into the room from which she'd just come. "Just sitting. Hardly saying a thing."

"The Brydie sisters," said Tessa, making sure.

Rochette Williams nodded vigorously. "Plus the guy from next door. He was the one who rang us. Looks like death warmed up. Not that I blame him."

"The body was pretty terrible," Tessa agreed.

"It's not just that," Constable Williams said, lowering her voice even more. "It's the company he's keeping. I ask you. W-ei-rd!" She rolled her eyes.

What is this?

"Right," said Tessa, in what she hoped was a brisk and efficient manner. "I'll go and have a chat with them."

"D'you want me?" Constable Williams was looking eager. "I mean, I've never seen a homicide investigation before. No one much ever gets killed round here—except for accidents and loonies jumping off cliffs. I'd really like to see—you know, how you operate and that."

Operate?

"Oh, sure," said Tessa, fighting back her misgivings. "I'd like you to sit in. But I'm going to send Jonathon Stoller home—talk to the sisters alone. Apparently they haven't been making much sense. So—"

"Sense?!" Constable Williams looked scornful. "They couldn't make sense if they tried all week. They're a bunch of fruitcakes."

She bent forward, frowning intently. "Look, believe me," she hissed. "I grew up round here. Bliss and Skye Brydie were at the school when I was. I was older, of course. But you couldn't miss them. They were *weird*, even when they were little. And as for their mother—well! I could tell you things—"

"We'll have to talk—later," Tessa interrupted quickly. "But I've got to get some kind of statement from them now."

Constable Williams nodded. "Course. You go for it. And you're right about getting rid of Stoller. You'll do better without him there." Her small eyes narrowed. "I reckon he's got something going with the youngest one, Astral."

"Something going? You mean a sexual relationship?"

Constable Williams guffawed. "Yeah. He's been getting into her knickers all right or I'm losing my touch. How about that? Talk about taking advantage. Not that it's carnal knowledge or anything. She'd be seventeen or so by now. But still—it's a bit rough. It's not as though she's normal. That's men for you."

Interesting.

"Anyhow, it hasn't been going on for long, I'd say," Constable Williams whispered on. "A few weeks or so at the most."

"Why do you say that?" Tessa was, against her better judgment, vastly intrigued by this example of mountain wisdom.

"Well, you can tell, can't you?" jeered Constable Williams. "He can hardly keep his hands off her. And don't tell me a bloke like that's going to stay that hot for all that long." She paused. "I mean," she added flatly, "they don't, do they? Once the novelty's worn off?"

"I guess not." Tessa looked at her companion appraisingly. Constable Rochette Williams was obviously sharper than she looked.

Steve and Thorne had entered the house by the front door. They had found it unlocked, though frosted with spiderweb and plainly seldom used. A narrow hallway ran towards the back of the house, doors leading off both sides.

"Door on your left leads straight into the living room," muttered Thorne. "Bedroom doors are on the right. This is where the fire was." He nudged open the first right-hand door. The room beyond still smelled of smoke. Part of one fibro-lined wall and a section of the floor had been severely burned and the ceiling was scorched and smoke-blackened. But attempts had been made to clean up. Holes had been carefully stuffed with clean rags, and the floor had been swept and scrubbed.

There were three narrow iron beds in the room, all neatly made. There was a low shelf on which stood three hairbrushes, a candlestick and some matches. There was a single oak cupboard with hanging space on one side and shelves on the other. The hanging space contained half a dozen long white dresses; the same number of shapeless, ankle-length gray woollen skirts; three pairs of brown leather sandals; and three pairs of heavy shoes. Stacked on the shelves were some thick stockings, a pile of plain white underclothes, three gray woollen shawls and three identical hand-knitted sweaters.

And that was all.

"Locals say the mother believed in the simple life," said Thorne dryly.

"Looks like it," Steve murmured.

He squatted to look at the burnt floorboards. He bent his head, and sniffed.

"Petrol. You can still smell it."

"Indeed."

Steve turned to see Lance Fisk standing in the doorway.

"Petrol-soaked rags and a piece of old carpet," said Fisk. "The remains, including what's left of the petrol can, are in the incinerator outside. Initially there would have been little noise, and more smoke than fire. Deadly. The women were lucky they woke before it killed them."

"Quinn wanted them to die in their sleep," Steve suggested.

"We don't know he lit the fire," growled Thorne. "The girls could have done it themselves as a blind. Or the mother could have done it."

"Or someone else, I guess. But who? These people don't seem to have exactly had a wide social circle."

"I hate to interrupt. But were you going to look at the other bedroom?" Fisk inquired politely.

"Thought we would," said Thorne easily. "Have you finished there?"

Fisk raised an eyebrow. "Hardly. But nor have we finished

here. So I would be grateful if you moved. And the master bedroom does shed some light. In a negative sort of way."

He stood back and held out an arm. "After you," he invited.

Steve reflected that Fisk could be extremely offensive when things weren't going his way.

In the kitchen, Tessa was briefing an excited Constable Williams. "Listen," she said, "I want you to go and find the other detective—Detective Steve Hayden—and tell him what you just told me about Stoller and Astral. Detective Hayden's going to take Stoller's statement. Tell him I sent you. He'll be interested in what you have to say. Okay?"

"Right!" Constable Williams was instantly poised for action. "What does he look like? Any idea where he is?"

"He should be looking at the burnt-out bedroom with Inspector Thorne. He's about my age—tall and dark—wearing a gray suit, a pale blue shirt and gray-striped tie."

She paused, very aware of the other woman's interested gaze. *She's on to you.*

Tessa resisted the thought and pressed on: "Don't go through the living room. We don't want to get the Brydies all stirred up. Go outside and in again by the front door."

"Okay," Constable Williams's eyes were shining. "Then I come back?"

"Sure. I'll see you inside." Tessa moved to the doorway that led to the living room.

"Watch yourself," she heard Constable Williams hiss as she crossed the threshold. She wondered if the people inside the room had heard it too.

The living room was quite large and starkly simple, its only decoration a painting hanging over the fireplace—a huge head and shoulders portrait of Adam Quinn. Slightly surreal, vividly—almost savagely—colored, it was the first thing you saw when you entered, and it dominated the room. Quinn had been painted against an abstract background of jagged red and black lines. He was wearing a purple robe, like the one he'd been wearing when he died. His hair and beard were long—black streaked with gray. His face was gaunt and arresting. Deep lines scored his forehead, and made furrows from nose to chin. His magnetic dark eyes, the eyes Tessa remembered from publicity photographs and posters in her teenage years, were deeply shadowed, wild and haunted-looking.

Horrible.

The fire had been neatly laid, ready for lighting, and an armchair covered with an embroidered shawl was drawn up in front of it. But no one was sitting in the chair. The four people in the room were instead grouped at the long, bare dining table which had wooden benches on either side and chairs at both ends.

They were sitting on the benches, two by two, facing one another across the table. On one side were two young women wearing very simple, white, long-sleeved shifts that reached their ankles. Bliss and Skye Brydie, Tessa guessed. Their hair was long and shining, their feet were bare. Their eyes seemed strangely vacant as they watched Tessa approach them, her steps loud and echoing on the bare boards.

On the other side of the table was another, younger, girl, dressed exactly like her sisters. This must be Astral. And perched uncomfortably beside her was a smooth-looking man in a checked shirt, new-looking, well-ironed jeans and shiny elastic-sided boots. Jonathon Stoller.

The bedroom at the back of the house was about the same size as the girls' bedroom. Fisk ushered Steve and Thorne in, directing them to stand on the plastic strip he'd placed on the floor.

Two windows—one at the back, one at the side, looked out to the shadowed veranda and the gardens beyond. A white and pale blue Chinese rug covered the floor. The double bed, heaped with pillows, starched white spread, white blankets and smooth white sheets now pulled back to expose the mattress beneath, had been placed under the back window. It was reflected in a full-length mirror set into the elaborate antique wardrobe on the opposite wall.

It was a simple but beautiful room. Yet Steve found it unpleasant. It was its air of controlled perfection, maybe. Or maybe it was the contrast between it and the room he'd just left that made his stomach churn.

Fisk went to the wardrobe and, with the air of a conjurer, opened all the doors to expose the contents.

The space was filled with clothes—expensive, conventional men's clothes, slightly out of date, several robes like the one in which Adam Quinn died—scarlet, black and deep blue—and a few long dark-red shifts. One of the shelves was full of unopened bottles of gin standing in rows. One opened bottle, a quarter full, stood in the front with a crystal glass beside it.

Without a word Fisk indicated the bed.

"No staining, no visible blood," he said tightly. "It would be an enormous surprise to me if there were any blood whatsoever."

"The girls said they've been changing the sheets and pillowcases," Thorne reminded him.

"My dementia is not so far advanced that I don't remember that, Malcolm!" snapped Fisk. "But if the subject was shot in bed the blood from that head wound would not just have stained the sheets. The pillows, the blankets and the mattress show no sign of having been stained, or washed. Neither does the floor rug, or any other piece of bedding in the house."

"It'll all be tested, though, presumably," Steve put in unwisely.

Fisk drew himself up. "Naturally," he said. "I am simply keeping you abreast of the situation at present. And giving you my opinion. For what it's worth."

He glowered at them and left the room.

"He's upset," said Thorne.

"Obviously."

"He's stuck with the shed as the crime scene." Thorne permitted himself a small smile.

"So are we," said Steve thoughtfully. "So it looks like suicide after all."

"As you say. It looks like it." But Thorne's expression made it very clear that he wasn't going to leave it at that.

There was a sound from the doorway. Fisk was back. "A highly excited female constable is at the front door, asking for Detective Hayden," he said. "I persuaded her to stay where she was. She declines to leave a message. Perhaps you could see to her. When it's convenient."

In the living room, Tessa had introduced herself and shown her identification. The Brydie sisters didn't react. They just stared. She wasn't even sure if they'd understood what she'd said. But the man flushed slowly red.

"H-Homicide?" he stuttered. "Why did they call Homicide? What is this? Quinn killed himself—didn't he?"

"We just want to make sure of that—Mr. Stoller, is it?"

You sound like someone in a movie. You sound as if you're trying to sound like someone in a movie.

But he was nodding dumbly.

"Mr. Stoller, you can go back next door now. We think it would be better to take your statement there." Tessa smiled officially at him, being brisk, brooking no argument.

He half-rose, licked his lips, looked down at the young girl by his side. "I'm not sure . . ." he muttered. "I mean—I don't like leaving Astral—all of them—on their own. They're not—used to this sort of thing, if you know what I mean. They've—ah—had a hard time." His eyes were fixed on Tessa's face, as though trying to communicate something to her.

They've had a hard time.

The fair sister laughed—a high, whinnying laugh. The dark girl next to her frowned.

"It is only necessary to tell the truth," she said, in a rich, beautiful voice. "The truth cannot harm us."

"That's right," said Tessa, fascinated, but feeling like a gross hypocrite.

The girl next to the man moved slightly. He spun round and looked at her, his face transparent with longing. Longing to go, longing to be begged to stay.

"Should I go? Astral?"

"If you are asked to go, you should go," she said softly. "It is better to obey."

Are these people for real?

"Detective Hayden will see you over at your place soon,"

said Tessa, as Stoller hesitated. He finally nodded his head and scrambled awkwardly over the bench.

"I'll see you later," he said to Astral in a low voice. The girl smiled at him, then looked down at her hands. She didn't raise her head as he walked to the kitchen door and out of the room. But Bliss and Skye looked after him, expressionless, only relaxing as they heard the screen door open and slam behind him.

Tessa sat down at the head of the table. She felt rather than saw the involuntary movements all the girls made, and glanced up. Three faces—like, and yet unlike—seemed calm. But the eyes had widened, and the plump, fair girl had pressed her fingers against her lips.

You're sitting in his chair. Quinn always sat here.

The screen door squeaked and banged again. Heavy steps tramped through the kitchen, and then Constable Williams came into the room. She nodded conspiratorially at Tessa and plumped herself down on an upright chair that had been placed against the wall, near the door. Her previous post, presumably. She took out her notebook and waited, pencil poised.

Okay, Vance. Let's see you operate.

I don't know where to start. I should separate them.

What's the point? They've had nearly a week to get their story straight.

Still . . .

Tessa leaned on the table, and looked around at the closed faces. Bliss. Skye. Astral. Their eyes were full of secrets.

They're hiding something.

Shake them up.

"Tell me," she said pleasantly. "Who did the painting over the mantelpiece?"

Five

Jonathon Stoller toiled up the Haven driveway. He'd decided to go back next door through the front gate rather than taking a shortcut across the fence-line. He didn't want to climb over the fence. It seemed wrong. Too familiar. Too casual, under the circumstances. There were police everywhere. And the thing in the shed . . .

He turned his mind away from that and walked faster. He rehearsed what he would say when it came time to make his statement. He wondered what Astral was telling the quiet female detective with the beautiful eyes.

He was nearly at the top of the drive. At last! He reached the gate and leaned on it, panting. Why had he walked so fast? His heart was pounding painfully in his chest. His legs were aching and trembling. His head felt thick, as though it were stuffed with wool. His throat was suddenly dry. He remembered that he had a bottle of wine in the refrigerator at the house. He comforted himself with the thought that he would open it. His tongue tingled at the thought. Then he remembered the detective. Detective Hayden. If Hayden found Jonathon drinking wine in the morning he'd make up his mind that he was a drunk. As bad as Adam Quinn.

Jonathon let himself through the gate and stumbled out of the shadows, through the scrub to the turning circle. There he paused again, and automatically glanced at his watch. He was astounded to see that it read 2:13. He squinted at the numbers, half-thinking that he was reading them wrongly, that moving so suddenly from dimness into bright sunlight had affected his eyes. But the seconds clicked by, and 2:13 changed to 2:14 as he looked.

43

He rubbed the back of his hand over his damp forehead as his head slowly cleared. He snorted with exhausted laughter. Of course, he realized, he'd been at Haven for hours. Time seemed to him to have stood still there, but time didn't stand still in real life. The morning had gone. No wonder he was tired, thirsty and hungry. And of course it would be quite okay to be seen having a glass of wine at this time of day.

His thoughts ran on. And why would he imagine the police would think anything of him having a drink, anyway? He'd had a terrible shock, hadn't he? He deserved a drink to settle his nerves, surely. Whatever time it was.

He walked to his own gate and opened it. His little house waited for him down below. A refuge. Soon to be invaded, though. He felt queasy, thinking of the detective who would soon be questioning him. He'd never been in trouble with the police before.

Then he realized that his thinking was getting confused again, and shook his head impatiently. He wasn't in trouble. He was a witness. Just a witness. There was nothing to worry about. Nothing at all.

The sound of a car coming down the lane penetrated his thoughts. He turned to look, and swore. More police. How many more?

But the car that rounded the last bend and bumped slowly down towards the turning circle was a burgundy four-wheel drive of the same make as his own. At the wheel was a handsome, proud-looking—almost arrogant-looking—woman with a short, expertly fashioned cap of thick, silver-white hair.

Jonathon recognized her as someone he'd seen a few times before, in his first half-year in Oakdale. He'd noticed her at the wine shop, the delicatessen, the patisserie—places like that. But he hadn't seen her for months, now. Six months, at least. She was wearing sunglasses today, but the hair was very distinctive and the high-cheekboned face unmistakable.

He'd wondered about her when he'd seen her in the village. She was a bit of a mystery. On the one hand her confident, relaxed air and the cane basket she carried over her arm made her look very much at home, yet on the other hand she seemed out of place. He couldn't quite see how she fitted in.

She was too young for retirement to mountain bliss and golf—despite that white hair, she couldn't be more than fifty. She'd probably had black hair when she was young, and had gone gray very early. She wore no wedding ring, and anyway looked too independent to have followed a retiring partner into obscurity. That very good haircut bespoke a city hairdresser, surely. And when he'd seen her, she'd always been alone.

She could have been an artist, or a writer. There were plenty of those up here, plying their lonely trade surrounded by beauty, in houses they could never afford in town, occasionally journeying to the big smoke to go to films, sit in inner-city coffee shops and see the agents, publishers or gallery owners who hawked their wares. But somehow Jonathon didn't think so. His experience of writers and artists outside the advertising world was limited, but silver-hair (as he called her to himself) didn't have that sensitive, diffident look he imagined they'd have. And her clothes were too neat.

Was she a boutique owner, perhaps? The manager of one of the tourist hotels? A gallery administrator?

The mystery had amused and slightly piqued him for a while, but he'd never thought of asking any of his local acquaintances who the white-haired woman was. He wouldn't want to seem too interested in a perfect stranger. And by the time he met Astral he hadn't seen the woman for some time. He'd assumed, really, that she'd moved away.

But, it seemed, she hadn't. And now she was here. For what purpose he couldn't imagine.

The woman turned her car towards the Haven gate. Then she saw Jonathon watching her and lifted an arm. Jonathon lingered obediently while she pulled the car up. She jumped out, leaving the engine running, and strode towards him. Her figure was boyish, athletic. She was wearing blue jeans and a blue-and-white striped open-necked shirt with the sleeves rolled up to the elbows.

"Hi. Fiona Klein," she said, holding out her hand across the gate.

Jonathon took the hand and shook it. Her grip was firm. Like the handshakes of the women he met in business, in the city. For some reason this reassured him. "Jonathon Stoller," he responded.

She smiled briefly. Her teeth were white and even, but the smile had no real warmth in it. He felt that behind the sunglasses her eyes were appraising. "I thought you must be," she said. "We've seen each other at the shops a few times, haven't we?"

Without waiting for an answer she jerked her head down towards the Haven gate. "What's going on down there?" she demanded.

"Ah—there's been a bit of trouble—" Jonathon began cautiously, but she cut him off with an impatient wave of her hand.

"Oh, I know about Adam Quinn," she said. "I know you found him. He'd been dead a week, or something. In a shed. Revolting! It's all over the village that he shot himself. Well—that was only a matter of time. No—I mean, what's going on now? Are the girls all right?"

He didn't know how to answer, so he avoided the question. "They're talking to one of the detectives," he said.

"Detectives? What detectives?"

"Homicide detectives, from Sydney."

She went very still. "Homicide," she repeated, as though testing out the word for herself.

"Just in case," Jonathon added. He'd meant to sound balanced, reassuring, levelheaded, but when the words left his lips they sounded inane.

A curious expression appeared on Fiona Klein's face. " 'Just in case.' So. And what does Rachel Brydie think about that?" she asked softly.

"She's not there. No one seems to know where she is."

The woman's eyebrows shot up, then she nodded, and her strong mouth tightened. "She's gone off and left them to it," she muttered. Then suddenly, astonishingly, she bared her teeth in a snarl of rage. "Irresponsible, selfish bitch!"

"Are you a friend of the family?" asked Jonathon. He almost winced as the words left his lips. Why, he wondered, did everything he said to this woman come out sounding idiotic?

"I taught Astral in high school," Fiona Klein murmured. "English."

A high school teacher! That was a surprise. Jonathon mentally adjusted himself.

"You're still teaching?" he asked cautiously.

Again that brief flash of white teeth. "No I'm not, actually. I've been away. In Italy. Why do you ask?"

"Oh—I don't know. You don't look like a schoolteacher, that's all."

The smile disappeared. The woman lifted her chin and adjusted her sunglasses. He realized that he might have sounded as though he was flirting with her. The idea filled him with embarrassment and a kind of disgust.

"I can't imagine Astral at school," he blurted out. He just wanted to say Astral's name. Link himself with her in some way.

Fiona Klein pulled off her sunglasses and turned to look at the Haven gate.

"She was good," she said. "There were problems, as you can imagine, but she was dealing with that, and she would have done very well, if she'd been allowed to stay on. But, oh, no. The bare minimum, that was all the formal education Astral was going to get. Kept her more malleable, didn't it?" Her mouth twisted.

Jonathon couldn't answer for a moment. There was a sour swelling at the back of his throat. He'd thought he was Astral's only contact with the outside world. But Astral had confided in Fiona Klein, too. Before she ever met Jonathon. Before . . .

"How long have you been away?" he asked finally. He'd tried to make the question sound like a pleasantry, but his voice was a croak.

"Five months," she said briefly. She wasn't thinking about him.

There was a pause, then she straightened, as if she'd made a decision. "I'm going down there," she said. "Those girls shouldn't be left alone with the police. And they'll need somewhere to stay tonight."

"I don't think they'll let you in," he mumbled. "The detectives want to see the girls on their own. They made me leave."

"Did they?" She didn't turn around. "And they really think it's murder, do they?"

He wished he could see her face.

"I don't know what they really think," he said. "I wish I did."

In the Haven living room, the light was dim. The veranda with its heavy fringe of vine enfolded the house, blocking out the sun. The portrait of Adam Quinn brooded over the gathering at the table. Mother's painting, Bliss, Astral and Skye had told Tessa. Mother likes to paint sometimes.

Tessa sat at the head of the table, pushing forward with her questions. She couldn't see Constable Williams, behind her, but could almost feel those sharp eyes boring into the back of her neck.

The girls were being cooperative. You couldn't say they weren't. But talking to them was like grasping at wisps of mist. They volunteered nothing, and seemed utterly passive. Whether it was genuine passivity or a result of intense emotional control, Tessa couldn't tell. Their strangely formal manner of speech, their long pauses for thought, made everything they said sound unreal at first. Their habit of finishing each other's sentences using exactly the same tone made talking to them seem like talking to one person with three voices. But once you got used to it, it started to seem natural. And of course it was natural, Tessa told herself—a natural consequence of spending all their time together, with no other company.

No other source of outside influence either. There was no phone. No television set. No radio. No newspapers or magazines. No books that Tessa could see, except for a few books on herbs and a copy of Henley's formulas.

They're totally isolated. Their world begins and ends here.

Astral was seventeen. Skye was nineteen. Bliss was twenty-one. None of them knew anything about their father. When Tessa asked them, they looked at one another, bemused, as if, perhaps, they'd never thought about it before.

They were born at Haven, they said, and had always lived here. When they were young, they went to school. But now they were able to stay at home. They work in the Haven gardens. Weeding, tending, planting according to the phases of the moon, helping their mother to make the Haven herbal products they used to sell at the local Sunday market. Flower waters, soaps, ointments, creams, lavender bags, potpourri—things like that.

"You don't sell them now?" asked Tessa.

Astral shook her head. "Not now. Not for a long time."

"Why not?"

They stared. "Adam says there is no need," said Bliss finally.

"Adam looks after us now," said Skye. "He will always look after us."

"How long has he been with you?" Tessa realized too late that she had caught their habit of speaking about Adam Quinn in the present tense. She didn't correct herself. It seemed better not to disturb Bliss and Skye by insisting on the fact that he was dead.

Four and a half years ago, Adam was visiting the town, they told her, obviously repeating something they'd been told many times. He was looking for a good place to live, to put down roots, far away from the city and the life he used to know. He met their mother at the markets. He knew at once that fate had intended him to know her. He came to Haven. He stayed.

Bliss took over the Sunday market stall after that. Their mother preferred to stay at home, once Adam came, she said. Astral and Skye were still at school, then. They heard some girls at the school talking about Adam. Saying that he had been a singer in the city. But they knew nothing about that. He never talked about it.

"Did you like Adam?"

Again they stared, and looked at one another. Then they all glanced at the portrait above the fireplace.

"Do you like him?" Tessa persisted.

"Adam is good to us," said Astral softly.

"We were poor until he came," said Skye.

Your turn, Bliss.

"He has given us everything we have," Bliss chimed in on cue. "He loves us. We are his family."

They sound as if they're repeating a lesson.

I'd say they are.

"When did you last—?"

Don't say when did you last see Adam alive. That won't get you anywhere.

"When did you last—speak to Adam? Or see him—walking around."

"He said goodnight to us on Sunday night," said Bliss.

"Last Sunday night?"

"Yes."

This is like wading through treacle.

"What time was that?"

"At nine o'clock. That is our time—unless there is planting to be done."

"Where were you when he spoke to you?"

"In our room." The girls exchanged glances once more. Where else would they be, the glances seemed to say.

"And where was your mother?"

"She was out."

"Had your mother ever gone out at night before? Leaving you with Adam?"

"Yes. Many times. We are safe with Adam." This time it was Skye who had spoken. But the other two nodded in agreement.

"So Adam said goodnight to you—what happened then?"

"He gave us each a cup of his drink," said Astral. "A cup filled to the top. He made us drink it all."

"What drink?"

"Adam's drink. He keeps it in his room. It is alcohol." She pronounced the word carefully, and paused before going on. "It looks like water—but it tastes—burning. I did not like it. None of us liked it."

"I said nothing," said Skye.

"But you did not like it," Astral answered calmly. "And Bliss did not like it, either. Your faces told me." She turned to Tessa. For the first time she seemed actually to want to explain something. "I told Adam we did not like the drink, and asked if we could be excused, but Adam said we could not. He said the drink was good for us. That it would help us to sleep. He said that if we did not drink, we would dream bad things. Things might come for us, out of the mist. Our candle was nearly burnt away. There was no moon, and mist had come up to the windows."

Bliss frowned. Whether at the memory or in disapproval at Astral's loquacity it was impossible to say.

"So you drank. What happened then, Astral?" urged Tessa.

"I felt dizzy and sick and lay down. I saw Adam looking down at me. He said, 'Now, sleep.' My eyes were so heavy . . .'"

Bliss took up the story. "Skye and I lay down also. We felt ill. The drink had not agreed with us. Astral was asleep. Adam put out the candle and left us. Skye began snoring. Then I slept, too."

"But you woke . . ." Tessa prompted.

"I dreamt of thunder, and woke, and the room was filled with smoke," said Bliss softly. "There was smoke, and fire. Mist still hung at the window. I woke Skye. Astral would not wake."

"We pulled Astral out," said Skye. "We called Mother and Adam, but they did not answer. We took Astral outside, and then we went back—"

"But Mother and Adam were not in their bed," said Bliss. "They were nowhere in the house. So we put out the fire with water from the kitchen and smothered the ashes with earth. Then we went back to Astral."

"I woke up with them calling me," whispered Astral. "The mist was all around me like a cloud. I was coughing. My throat was sore . . ."

"You were soon recovered," Bliss cut in. She seemed almost angry, as if she thought Astral was trying to gain sympathy, or draw attention to herself. Astral, the youngest, had already proved herself to be a weak reed, deficient in the stoicism that life in this family seemed to require.

"And then?" Tessa persisted.

"We dressed, and sat here until morning," said Bliss simply.

"Here, at this table?"

"Yes. We thought Adam would soon come back and tell us what we should do. But he did not come."

Skye's lip trembled. It was the first overt sign of emotion she had shown. "We waited until sunrise, and still he did not return," she said, in that light, high voice that was such a contrast to Bliss's rich, mellow one. "Then we went outside. The door of the big shed was open. We went to close it . . ." She stopped short.

"Adam was lying there, on his back," said Astral. "He had a hole in his forehead. The rifle was on his chest. We felt him, but his heart was not beating. He was dead."

Skye suddenly clenched her plump fists and beat them on the table. "Astral, do not say that," she moaned. "Adam will be disappointed. We have told you and told you—" She broke off as Bliss put her hand over the fists and gently held them still.

"He will not be disappointed. He is dead," Astral insisted. But her voice wavered.

"Adam is not dead, Astral," Bliss said patiently. "He can never die. He will never leave us."

There was a very slight sound from the kitchen doorway as Constable Williams shifted in her chair.

Mad as meat-axes.

Keep control.

"Why do you think that Adam can never die, Bliss?" asked Tessa.

Bliss turned to look at her. "He told us," she said, as if that answered the question fully and completely. "He has died before, many times, and risen again."

Don't argue.

Tessa took a deep breath. "So you found him in the shed. And then—"

"We talked about what we should do," said Bliss. "Astral thought as we did—then. We agreed that we should care for Adam, while he was making himself new. Everything should be fitting when he woke. So we did what we thought best."

"The gun—"

"The gun must always be cleaned and put away after use," chanted Skye. She had calmed down now that they were no longer disputing Adam's immortality.

"And then?"

Blank looks. No answer.

Tessa tried again. "I mean, that was nearly a week ago," she said. "What have you been doing since?"

"We have been doing our work, we have been caring for Adam, and waiting," said Bliss.

Waiting for the corpse to sit up and say hi.

"And your mother didn't come back?" asked Tessa.

They all shook their heads.

"Mother would say to do as Adam wished," said Skye, as though this ended the matter.

Give up on Mum. Go back to the story. Get it straight.

"So what happened this morning?"

"When we opened the shed, Astral would not do her work," murmured Bliss. "She said she had stopped believing that Adam would return. She said she thought that he was truly dead, dead forever. Like a shot fox, or a dead bird."

"We told her she must keep faith," put in Skye, her voice rising. "But she would not be still."

Bliss looked at her, and she fell silent. "Astral said the man next door came to his house on Saturdays," Bliss said evenly. "She said she was going to ask him."

Tessa turned to Astral, sitting very still and staring straight ahead. Her eyes looked almost black. She looked partly defiant, partly frightened.

What's going on in her mind?

"Astral? You know Mr. Stoller?" she asked gently.

Astral looked down at her lap.

Hiding her eyes.

"Astral?"

"I have seen him," the girl said in a low voice. "Mending the fence."

Tessa restrained herself from glancing at Constable Williams, alert against the wall.

Leave it. For now.

"You saw him by the fence and asked him to come in to see Adam? So he'd tell you what to do?"

The bent head moved in a slight nod.

"She brought him to where Adam was." Skye's eyes were glassy and bulging, her voice just above a whisper. It was almost as if, even now, she couldn't believe it.

"It really was the best thing to do, you know," Tessa said gently.

"It was wrong," said Bliss, in the tone of one who is not arguing, but simply explaining. "A stranger to Haven could not understand, and would not know." Her lips tightened. "Astral has no patience, no faith. Adam has corrected her for that, many times. But she does not learn."

"Now the house is full of strangers," Skye broke in. "Adam will be disappointed. He will correct all of us."

Her eyes flickered with dread.

"What do you mean?" asked Tessa, her heart sinking. "What do you mean, 'correct' you?"

Skye raised her eyes to a shelf near the kitchen doorway, just above Constable Williams's head. A bamboo cane rested there, propped against the wall.

Six

Jonathon sat on his back veranda, staring out at the pine forest and drinking wine, waiting for Detective Hayden to come. He felt unreal, and haunted by a sense of foreboding. The feeling had been with him all morning, and the meeting with Fiona Klein had made it worse. For her to turn up so unexpectedly, after so many months and at just this time, was bizarre. Like something that would happen in a play. It was as though it was a sort of sign. An omen. The hero sees the silver-haired woman at the beginning; he sees the silver-haired woman at the end.

The end. Was this the end?

Jonathon poured another glass. If Hayden found him half-pissed, so much the better. He'd already decided that it was perfectly natural for a man to have a few drinks at a time like this. It would be, in a way, more suspicious if he didn't.

The black cockatoos screeched in the pines. One was perched at the very top of a tree, swaying dangerously, eating from a scrap of pine cone clutched in one claw. At this distance, silhouetted against the sky, it looked uncannily like a crouching animal—a possum, or even a monkey. But he'd been fooled by this illusion before. Then, for minutes, he'd stared, his spine prickling, until he'd understood. Now he could see the claw, the bending head, for what it was, straightaway.

He was waiting for the police to come. He, Jonathon Stoller. And, he was sure, he would have to explain about Astral. About everything.

He gulped wine. It came to his mind how easily he might have avoided all this. He might have bought that other house—the one on the other side of the highway, the fashionable side. If he'd bought that cute, well-kept two-bedroom timber cottage, painted dark cream and heritage green, with a red, high-pitched roof, half an acre of established garden—wonderful old camellias—walking distance from the village, he would never have settled here, at the end of Lily Lane. He'd never have met Astral. He might have heard about the weirdo family at Haven through village gossip, even seen Adam Quinn or one of the girls at the shops. But it wouldn't have mattered to him. It would have been nothing to do with him.

If he hadn't haggled about the price of the camellia house he would have got it. Charles Ridge, the agent at Ridge Real Estate, had told him that he was the first one to see it. But he had haggled. He'd made an offer of twelve thousand under the asking price. He'd only been looking for a couple of weeks, driving up from Sydney on the weekends, and people said vendors always asked ten to fifteen thousand more than they were willing to accept up here.

Perhaps that was true. But the second person to see the camellia house had agreed to the asking price straight away. The house was sold by the time Jonathon rang Charles Ridge back to find out why he hadn't heard from him.

Jonathon was most upset. He had started thinking of the house as his. He blamed Ridge for not letting him know that he had a rival. He would have been willing to pay more. But as Ridge pointed out, rather huffily, it wasn't a sole agency. There were two real estate agents in Oakdale, and the property was listed at both of them. He hadn't shown the successful buyer the house. And if Jonathon had offered the asking price straightaway, the property would have been his.

A few weeks later, Ridge showed him this place. And then Jonathon thought it was fate. Fate had withheld the camellia house from him so that this miracle could happen. So that he could have Ivan's place, with its five acres, its dreamy view, its creek and its forest.

Fate.

But even having bought the property, he might never have found himself in his present bind if he hadn't bothered with the boundary fence. The cherry-laurel hedge, after all, was dense and high enough to serve as a barrier between the properties, except for that part right down near the forest. But the rotten posts and sagging wire had irritated Jonathon every time he sat on his veranda or walked in the paddock. He knew the owners next door wouldn't be interested in sharing costs. Why should they? The hedge was on their side. So he'd started to fix the fence himself, and one Sunday saw Astral, wandering up from the forest on her side of the fence, barefoot in the long grass.

She'd looked ethereal, unearthly, that first time. For an instant he'd thought that she was some sort of vision. She'd been crying. Her cheeks were wet with tears. He spoke to her, asked what was wrong. She didn't answer that. Just asked his name. She seemed shy, and frightened, and she soon ran back to the house. But the following weekend she was there again, walking from the forest, glancing over to the fence-line. And so it had begun.

If he'd kept her at arm's length in the first place, or if he'd listened to his own misgivings, and cut the relationship off before it went too far . . .

But he hadn't done that.

He'd told himself it was only friendship. That it would always be only friendship. She needed him, and he was responding to that. He wouldn't take advantage of her innocence. But after they'd been meeting for about five weeks, one late afternoon in the last days of summer, she fell silent and looked up into his eyes. They were very close. He took her face in his hands and gently kissed her narrow lips. And in that moment, everything changed.

He felt her trembling under his hands. He smelled the warm, soft sweetness of her. His own body seemed to be melting. He could hardly stand.

She drew away from him at last, breathing fast and lightly, crossing her arms across her breasts as if to hide the nipples jutting under the thin white cloth. Then she said, "I have to go" and backed slowly away, disappearing at last into the green tangles and long shadows of the orchard. Jonathon stood where he was for a long time, leaning on the fence post, panting like an oversexed teenager.

He drove back to the city an hour later in a state of

euphoria. The mood persisted through Monday and Tuesday. He couldn't eat, and a sickening thrill fluttered in his chest and stomach every time he relived the kiss over the fence. He had to keep resisting the urge to drop everything and rush back to the mountains.

On Wednesday, after a night of disturbing dreams, he woke tense, anxious and even embarrassed. Realities started crowding in on him as he showered, ate mechanically and went to work. The situation seemed intolerable.

By Thursday, he was feeling like a fool. A little kiss over the fence and he was acting as though he was seventeen himself. It was absurd. He knew he had to take control. He knew what he had to do.

He asked some friends from work to a casual Saturday lunch in the courtyard of his townhouse; two couples to whom he owed hospitality—Gavin and Louise, Drew and Seana—and a woman called Liz who'd been with the firm for a couple of months. Liz was tall, vivacious and bright, with a ready laugh and a clever, waspish tongue. She had very short auburn hair, a sensual mouth, and long, well-shaped legs. She was extremely attractive. He couldn't think why he hadn't tried to get to know her better before this. Except, perhaps, that she showed her gums when she smiled, and her nose was so sharply pointed that its tip was white and that, by the time he met her, he was absorbed by Astral.

He spent Friday lunchtime buying wine, flowers and paper napkins, Friday evening cleaning and tidying the flat. He told himself it would be fun, for once, to spend the weekend in town. It would be good for him, too. You couldn't hide away in the sticks all the time. You had to keep up your social contacts.

He'd decided to keep lunch simple—prawns with ginger and garlic (he could cook those quickly on the barbecue, and they looked impressive), salad, bread. Then he could make his special individual lemon soufflés for dessert. His sister had shown him how to make these years ago, and he'd discovered that they were always much appreciated. People often couldn't believe he actually made them himself, and would stand in the kitchen watching, amazed, as he folded stiffly

beaten egg whites into lemony custard with practiced ease
and spooned the light mixture into small, white dishes. And
when the soufflés came out of the oven all puffy and faintly
crusty and golden on the top, smelling delicious, they would
gasp and cheer, and call others to see. It was very satisfying.

He went to the fish markets on Saturday morning so that he
could be sure that the prawns would be perfectly fresh. It had
seemed like a good idea on Friday, but the traffic was terrible
and the crowds at the markets were dense and pushy. He managed to secure his prawns, then fought the crowds again for
salad vegetables. By the time he got home, the prawn pack-
age had leaked on his trousers and it was quite late. Then he
realized that he'd forgotten the bread, and had to go back out
for it. While he was at the patisserie he also bought a French
glazed apple flan and some King Island cream. He no longer
felt like making lemon soufflés.

He managed to get himself changed, the prawns mari-
nating, the table set, the barbecue heating and the salad partly
prepared, before his guests arrived. It was a rush, but he did it.
Luckily they were all a discreet twenty minutes late, arriving
at his door almost at the same moment. All the women kissed
him on both cheeks, and so did Gavin, who'd spent years in
L.A. Drew shook hands, and everyone teased him about it.

They sat in the courtyard drinking chilled white wine, and
said how marvelous the weather was, how lucky Jonathon
was to have the courtyard, how nice that Jonathon was in
town for the weekend for once, and how pleasant it was to be
there relaxing, and how it was the simple things that counted.
Then, while Jonathon brought out the bread, the salad and the
green prawns ready for cooking, they all started gossiping
about work.

Jonathon stood at the barbecue, isolated in the smoke. It
was hot in the courtyard. A tiny headache nagged behind his
eyes. He stared at the carefully marinated prawns on their big
white plate, fiddling at them with his barbecue tongs, wondering if he should have bought more, or less, wondering if
the barbecue was hot enough. He gulped at his wine, looked
over at his guests—and suddenly it was as though they were
from another planet.

The women were insect-like—leaning on their angular elbows, nodding their small, smooth heads. Their big, painted eyes stared. Their mouths worked as they chewed celery sticks, chattering and laughing, their long legs rubbing together in designer denim. The men seemed bizarrely smooth-skinned and strangely pale. Their hands, clutching wine glasses, gesturing, were small and pudgy with carefully cut, white-rimmed nails.

Jonathon broke out into a sweat. He couldn't think of a single thing he would want to say to these people. These are my friends, he told himself. But it seemed incredible.

The prawns sizzled and grew pink on the barbecue plate. He turned them over mechanically. He registered that they smelled good. He reminded himself that he mustn't overcook them. His headache grew worse.

When the prawns were done he put them on their platter and took them, hot and fragrant, to the table, forgetting the garnish of lemon slices and cress he'd planned. With as much courtesy as he could muster he told his guests to help themselves, to enjoy. Then he went inside. While he was swallowing headache pills with a handful of water from the bathroom tap, he looked at himself in the mirror and barely recognized his own face. His head was pounding. He looked at his watch. It was just after one o'clock.

Into his vacant mind rushed a picture of Astral, far away, a world away, drifting through the long grass down by the forest, looking across the fence, to see if he was there. How many times this morning had she walked that way and been disappointed?

She would have expected to see his car parked outside his house at nine this morning. He had almost always arrived by then. But not today. Today he hadn't arrived at nine, or ten, or eleven, or twelve. He hadn't arrived at all.

What must she be feeling? What must she be thinking?

Something seemed to grip him in the pit of the stomach. He hadn't considered this before. Not to have considered it seemed like madness, but it was true. He'd been totally absorbed in solving what he perceived as a problem that was his alone. He'd been concentrating on keeping his resolve firm, and his thoughts on the straight and narrow. Not till this moment had it occurred to him to wonder what his absence might mean to her.

But last weekend he had kissed her . . .

The memory, firmly held back for days, broke through with a surge of power that took away his breath. His fingers curled at the memory of her body quivering under his hands. He moaned quietly to himself, pressing his burning forehead against the coolness of the mirror.

What was he doing here? What had possessed him, to think he wanted to be away from her? Now through his own folly he was trapped in his townhouse with a bunch of chattering strangers while she . . .

He closed his eyes.

After a few moments he managed to pull himself together and go back out to the courtyard. He felt as though he'd been away for hours, but it had only been a few minutes. The guests seemed hardly to have noticed his absence. They were feeding happily, lips moist and gleaming. The prawns were still warm. The courtyard was thick with the smell of seafood, olive oil, garlic, perfume and barbecue smoke, and echoing with the sounds of eating, talk, and meaningless laughter. You wouldn't have thought five people could make so much noise.

He wanted nothing more than for them to finish their food and leave, but he knew that relief was hours away. His guests had all come in cabs so that they could have a long, boozy lunch without fear. Having indulged in that expense, they weren't about to waste it by being abstemious and leaving early. They, furthermore, knew that Jonathon's lunch would be considered a failure if it didn't last at least until four or even five, and as they made it a practice never to attend failed entertainments, they stayed and stayed.

The afternoon seemed endless. Jonathon, in misery, feeling as though he was operating behind glass, created errands to release himself from the bondage of conversation. Refusing all offers of help, he cleared dishes, served dessert, coffee, and (when requested) more wine, changed CDs and even stacked the dishwasher while the group in the courtyard politely ignored what they must by now (he told himself) see as his odd behavior—unless they were too hazy with wine to notice.

By four he'd run out of excuses to leave the table, and was sitting in an agony of bored impatience, willing them to go, barely able to be civil, totally unable to respond. At four-thirty Gavin and Louise glanced at one another, and started murmuring about calling a cab. Seana looked at her watch with a little cry, and laid her hand on Drew's sleeve, saying she'd had no idea how late it was! It had all been such fun! They must go, too. Liz smiled and murmured, and crossed her long legs, sipping wine. Her glass was still half-full.

Jonathon knew that they were all expecting him to ask Liz to stay. They were waiting for him to protest that they couldn't all leave him flat, that Liz must stay to keep him company, help him drink the last of the wine, help him watch the sun go down.

But of course he didn't say it, and as the moment passed, Liz touched the side of her smooth cap of hair and suggested she share a cab with Drew and Seana, whose terrace house was in the same suburb as her own.

Fifteen minutes later, Jonathon was standing at the door waving them off. Ten minutes after that he was in his car, driving to the mountains.

It was growing dark by the time he reached Oakdale. The rhododendron bushes in front of his empty house were hulking black shapes. The cherry laurel hedge brooded on the boundary, its leafy tips silhouetted against the sky.

He went into the house and turned on all the lights. Perhaps they would shine through chinks in the hedge, telling Astral that at last he had arrived.

He went out onto the back veranda, into the paddock and over to the fence. But she wasn't there. Why should she be there? It was late, too late. She'd probably been waiting for him all day. He had failed her.

He went back to the house and sat in the living room, lights blazing, far into the night. He had some mad idea she might contrive to come to him—slip out of her bedroom while her family slept, creep through the garden and over the fence, and come to him. Every creak, every rustle outside made his heart leap. But of course she didn't appear. He went to bed long after midnight, hazy with wine, dulled by disappointment, leaving all the lights on. Just in case.

In the morning he didn't make his accustomed visit to the village for supplies and the paper. He couldn't bear the thought that he might miss her. He went out into the paddock and started mending the fence. He was just fiddling, he knew it. And she didn't come.

As if to make up for his idiocy he changed his job. He tried to work properly, hacking angrily at a patch of blackberry that had been on his list for removal from the edge of the pine forest since his arrival. He'd resolved never to use poisons on his property. But the blackberry thicket proved too much for him, defeating his inadequate cutting tools, tearing at his clothes, crosshatching with smarting scarlet tears the skin of his hands, arms and legs.

After two hours Astral had still not come to the fence. Finally, sweating, exhausted and humiliated, cursing himself, he retreated to his back veranda where he drank beer till his head was spinning, watching for the glimmer of white by the fence-line that would tell him she was there. It never came.

At two o'clock he staggered into the house, threw himself down on the couch, and slept. He woke hours later, skin tight and prickling, mouth sour and dry, every muscle aching. The light had dimmed. He'd slept the afternoon away. In numb misery he had a shower, painted his scratches with antiseptic, and changed, ready to go back to town.

He was about to leave when he realized that the back veranda table was still littered with beer bottles. He almost left them, but couldn't bring himself to do it, and went outside. As he packed the bottles into a box, he glanced one last time across the boundary. And Astral was there. She wasn't at the fence. She wasn't looking his way. But she was there, walking, head bowed, down to the forest. In seconds the shadows of the trees had swallowed her up. But by that time he was down the steps, and running.

And after that day, for Jonathon, there was no turning back.

There were still misgivings, of course. Driving back to town, his mind filled with Astral, his hands, face and clothes fragrant with the scent of her, he would start thinking how this would look to others. He was ten years older than this girl, and her life was so bizarre, she was so damaged, she was so completely unused to the ways of the world, that she was, effectively, a child. The closer he got to the city lights, the more uncomfortable he would become. He'd promise himself that the next time—next weekend—he'd tell her that something would have to be done. That he would have to confront Adam Quinn.

But by the time the working week had passed, and it was again Saturday morning, his resolution would have melted into longing. He would meet Astral by the fence. He would delay talking to her about Quinn, procrastinating, unwilling to break the spell. Later, in the forest, he would finally raise the matter, softly, gently, so as not to startle her. She would grow silent, trembling in his arms. She would turn her face up to his, her eyes beseeching. Then he would forget, and another weekend would pass in a dream with their secret intact, Jonathon's misgivings, sense and even anger displaced by shamed complicity.

Seven

While Jonathon was dwelling feverishly on the past, Fiona Klein was, as always, concentrating on the present and the future. She was, also as usual, exerting her considerable force of personality to try to get her way. But the uniformed constable who had stopped her crossing the scene-of-crime tape strung across the Haven yard was proving recalcitrant.

He'd told her his name: Constable Russell Ingres. He'd written down her name, address, and phone number in a small ring-bound notebook. He'd promised to let Astral, Skye and Bliss Brydie know that Miss Fiona Klein was available for any help they might require. He'd carefully noted that Miss Klein was not a relative, but wished to see them. He'd noted that she wanted to see them as a matter of urgency. He'd stolidly repeated that at the moment the young women were in good health, but were not available, because they were giving statements to a detective from Sydney. He'd also repeated his request that Fiona stay, for the moment, exactly where she was. Another detective would be with her shortly.

"I don't want to see a detective, Constable Ingres. I want to see those young women. Now, please," said Fiona, having decided that her velvet glove, such as it was, was in this case hampering her iron fist and should be abandoned. "It's quite inappropriate for them to be questioned on their own. Someone should be with them. I gather their mother isn't here."

Constable Ingres, who was not normally an aggressive man, found his spine prickling with irritation. He was already out of sorts. It was in his opinion bloody insulting to be relegated to guard duty while the city detectives ponced around

interviewing the suspects. It wasn't as if he and Sergeant Mc-
Caffrey couldn't have handled this. Russell had assumed they
would.

But because Quinn was famous—or had been—McCaffrey
had suddenly lost his nerve and called in Central Homicide.
He was regretting it now, but now it was too late. Left alone
they'd have wrapped the case up overnight. Instead they were
lumbered with a bunch of bleeding-heart city types in fancy
suits who were going to mess everything up.

And now here was this woman Klein on her high horse,
treating him like some servant. Russell had occasionally met
women like her before, and they always had this effect on
him. He thought Fiona's confident, cultivated voice was affected, that her clothes were inappropriate to her age, and that
her manner was offensively superior. He didn't like the way
she'd just left her car in the middle of the track, blocking it.
He even objected to her hair, which seemed to sum her up: the
silver-white color, which any less confident woman of her
age would have had tinted, and the haircut that was too short,
too smooth and too smart—a show-off sort of haircut, in his
opinion.

He therefore looked severely at Fiona Klein and said: "And
how do you gather that, ma'am?"

"I beg your pardon?"

"How do you know that Mrs. Brydie's away from home?"

Fiona's brows drew together above her sunglasses. "I met
the next-door neighbor on my way down here," she said
haughtily. "He told me."

Constable Ingres nodded slowly, tapping his notebook.

"Why? Is it a secret?" demanded Fiona Klein.

She was a little bit rattled, or she wouldn't have asked. So
in that sense, Constable Ingres's ploy had been successful. He
was quietly pleased.

"Not to say a secret," he said. "I was just interested in how
you knew. Just routine."

It always worried them when you said, "Just routine."

Briefly, he wondered why it was he'd never seen this
woman before. He'd been working in this area for six months.
You'd think he'd have bumped into her, one way or another.

She wasn't the type to keep a low profile. She was the type who'd come into the station or ring up at the drop of a hat, if she had a complaint or something to report. And you'd notice her at the shops and round the traps.

He was just about to put this to her when he saw her look with interest over his shoulder. He turned to see the tall figure of Steve Hayden coming towards them from the front of the house. The female pathologist who'd been mucking round with the body in the shed came up to Hayden and said a few words. Hayden nodded, and glanced towards Constable Ingres and Fiona Klein.

They were going to move the body. And Klein's car was blocking the exit. Now she was going to get a flea in her ear. Constable Ingres felt warm satisfaction at the thought.

The pathologist went back to the shed, and Hayden strode towards them.

"Miss Fiona Klein," said Russell Ingres, as soon as Hayden got within earshot, and before Miss Klein could pre-empt him. "She's keen to see the Brydies. She's not keen to leave till she does."

"Right." Hayden nodded, his face giving nothing away. "They're being interviewed at this moment, Miss Klein."

"So I understand," the woman said crisply. "I heard about what happened. I know the girls—well. I came to see if there was anything I could do. Anything at all."

"Would you be able to put them up for a while?"

"Yes, of course I would."

"Well that'd be a big help. They'll have to move out of here for a couple of days."

The woman's brow wrinkled. "I'd have hoped they'd move out for good!" she said.

Steve shrugged. "That's up to them, I guess," he said easily. "And their mother."

She lifted her chin, tight-lipped. "I would like to see them," she said.

"That your car, Miss Klein?" asked Steve, indicating the maroon four-wheel drive.

"Yes."

"You'll have to move it, I'm afraid. We've got to keep the

access clear. I've got to go next door now. How about you give me a lift up to the top of the track? You can park up there. Someone'll come and get you when the statements are finished. Shouldn't be too long."

Klein hesitated, then nodded shortly. She would have liked to argue, Russell could see that, but she couldn't, really. After all, she had to move the car. Funny, really, how people always agreed to move their cars, even when they were happy to argue black-and-blue about moving themselves. He'd noticed it before.

Steve ducked under the scene-of-crime tape. "You'll brief Inspector Thorne?" he said to Russell. Without waiting for an answer he nodded pleasantly and walked off with Fiona Klein.

"Lived up here long?" Russell heard him ask in a friendly way. "Four and a half years," the woman answered. "I transferred from . . ." They moved out of earshot after that, but Russell, looking after them, could see that the conversation was continuing. By the time they reached the car they were chatting quite comfortably, and Klein was actually smiling.

Looks as if he fancies her, thought Russell disgustedly, watching Steve open the car door for Klein, and close it after her. Funny taste, some blokes have got.

Then another thought occurred to him. Hayden could be pumping the woman for information about the Brydies. Doing it casually, so she wouldn't get the wind up.

And if that was the case, he must have decided, like Sergeant McCaffrey, that the suicide story was fishy—whatever that pathologist woman had said about Quinn dying in the shed. Otherwise he wouldn't bother.

The maroon car backed, turned and drove back up the track, soon screened from view by the overhanging shrubs.

Hayden must think the weird sisters did it, Russell thought. Them, or their loopy mother.

He hitched at his belt and turned to face the yard again. He was smiling slightly. The thought didn't displease him at all.

"Any idea where Mrs. Brydie could be?" Steve was asking Fiona Klein.

Fiona shook her head, concentrating on the track ahead. He couldn't see her eyes, but her mouth had tightened again. Obviously, Rachel Brydie wasn't one of her favorite people.

"She could be anywhere," she said. "She's a complete neurotic. Imagine her going off and leaving those girls to cope with a dead body on their own."

"We don't know she did," said Steve, watching her. "The girls say she was gone before Quinn died."

"They'd say anything she told them to say," Fiona snapped. She was gripping the wheel so hard that her knuckles were white. Steve said nothing. She glanced at him, realized that he was watching her, and smiled wryly.

"She makes me mad," she murmured. She relaxed her hands, flexing them one at a time. Her fingers were short and strong, with blunt-cut but well-manicured nails. She wore two rings on one hand and one on the other. The rings were all broad bands of gold inlaid with what looked like black enamel in different, intricate patterns. Unusual. Steve liked them.

"Would you know if she's ever gone off for as long as a week before?" Steve asked.

A shrug. "I wouldn't have thought so. She's obsessed with this place—keeping the system going. She's got this thing about planting according to the moon. I can't tell you how often Astral came to school looking like death because she'd been up half the night working in the garden."

The gate was ahead. Fiona slowed the car to a crawl. "She'd spend recess and lunchtime sitting under a tree half-asleep," she went on, staring straight ahead. "Not that it really mattered to her. She didn't have friends to talk to, poor little thing. The other kids wouldn't go near her. Half of them thought she was crazy, and the other half thought she was subnormal—the way she spoke, the things she said—all that. In fact, she was brighter than all the rest of them put together."

The remainder of the smile twisted into a grimace. "Her mother should have been reported to Child Welfare, or whatever it's called now."

"Did you ever do that?"

"Oh, no."

"Can I ask why?"

Another shrug. "I talked to a few of the other staff about it. They knew all about the Brydies. They'd taught Skye and Bliss. They said there were no real grounds for a complaint that would stick. Not without the girls' cooperation, and that was out of the question. And—I don't know—it's tricky, in a small place like this."

"Yeah—it would be." Steve waited. He knew there was more to come. This woman wanted to talk. Or needed to.

She sighed heavily. "I tried to have a word with Rachel Brydie but she wouldn't come to the school, and by that time she'd stopped running her Sunday market stall, so I couldn't get to her that way. I wrote her a few notes, but she never answered. Finally Astral came to see me and asked me not to go on trying to get in touch. She said she knew that she and her family didn't live like other people did, but she was happy with what she had. She was really extraordinary. Very self-possessed and calm. Amazing for her age."

The fingers tapped restlessly on the wheel. "In the end I thought it would just make things harder for her at home if I kept on stirring the possum. And of course she always turned up to school. She did her homework. She was a very good student, in fact. Very perceptive. Wonderful imagination. Marvelous flair for drama."

"A good actor, you mean?" The question was asked lazily, but Fiona wasn't deceived. She cocked her head at him and again that mobile mouth twisted into a wry smile.

"Being a good actor on the stage does not necessarily mean being a good liar in a real-life situation, Detective Hayden," she said firmly. "I wouldn't want you to think—"

"I don't think anything yet, Miss Klein," said Steve.

"Please don't keep calling me that!" she snapped, suddenly showing her nerves. "It reminds me of teaching. Can't you call me by my first name?"

"Sure. Didn't you like being a teacher?"

Fiona shifted uncomfortably in her seat. "I used to. But you know how it is—you move on." She cleared her throat. "I've been away for a few months. In Italy. Got spoiled."

They reached the gate, and she stopped the car.

"It must have been hard to come back," Steve prompted.

"In a way." Fiona looked down at the rings on her fingers. Maybe she'd bought them in Florence, or Rome, Steve thought. Brought them back here, on her fingers, to a little town in the mountains west of Sydney. To the idea of a small school, smartass teenagers whispering in back rows, a staff room full of people who didn't want to see your photographs . . .

But she was talking again.

"So really, I'm not the ideal person for you to speak to about the Brydies," she was saying, almost reluctantly. "I only got back here yesterday. I've been unpacking. I don't really know what's been going on while I've been away."

She paused for a moment. "And even before that—it's not as though I ever came here—to Haven," she added. Her tone was odd. It was as if she was speaking more to herself than him—rationalizing something in her mind. "No one comes here."

"But you came here today."

"I heard what had happened—heard that Adam Quinn was dead and Rachel Brydie was missing. Word spreads fast—" she smiled ruefully "—in a small place like this."

Steve got out to open the gate. He glanced back at the car, at the woman sitting rigidly at the wheel. He found Fiona Klein very interesting. He wondered what Tessa would make of her.

Klein seemed very confident, very assured. But underneath that cool exterior there was a lot going on. He was certain, furthermore, that there was a great deal more she could tell him about her relationship with the Brydies, if she chose. He'd get over to see her in the morning, and see if he could break down a bit of that reserve.

She'd sounded almost guilty when she'd spoken about her trip—as if it had been wrong for her to go away for so long. But why should she feel like that? She said she'd never been to Haven before. She said she didn't really know Skye and Bliss. She plainly had no time for Rachel Brydie. And she didn't seem to be grieving for Adam Quinn.

But she wasn't the sort of woman to rush to the scene of a tragedy out of ghoulish curiosity. She wasn't the charitable sort who would trouble herself over people she barely knew, either.

But she was here. She'd rushed over here as soon as she'd heard that Quinn was dead. She'd demanded to see the Brydie sisters, and refused to leave till she did.

Why?

Standing in the yard, watching the body of Adam Quinn, securely encased in a blue body bag, being carried from the shed, Tessa, too, was asking why. She faced Thorne, briefing him, forcing herself to speak clearly and calmly, while an internal dialog raged.

"He beat them. He's been beating them for years."

Why did they put up with it? Why didn't they just leave?

Where would they go?

Somewhere. Anywhere.

Don't blame the victims.

"Their mother too, I'd say," she heard her own level voice continuing. "They're terrified of him." Her stomach was churning.

He deserved—

You're a homicide detective.

He deserved to die.

Thorne appeared not to notice her distress. "Pretty good motive there. Have they said where the mother went?"

"They still say they don't know. They say she just told them to go on with their work, and to do what Adam told them to do, and left. Sometime last Sunday afternoon."

"They're giving us the runaround."

The body was being loaded into the mortuary van now. Under the lights in the shed Lance Fisk crouched, intent, forceps probing through stained and stinking straw.

Tessa looked around. "Has Steve gone to see Stoller?"

"Yes. I gather Constable Williams thinks there's something going on between him and the youngest girl."

"Astral." Somehow it seemed important that he be forced to put names to them.

"Astral." But Thorne wasn't really paying attention. "Whether Williams is on the ball or not, I'm not sure Stoller's going to be able to help us much," he said, after a moment. "The mother's the key to this. She can't be far away. Wherever she went, she went on foot. The ute's the only vehicle at Haven, and it's still here."

She knew what he was thinking. It was what she was thinking, too. Rachel Brydie might have killed Quinn, and run. She wouldn't be the first woman to have killed a man because she couldn't imagine herself escaping from him any other way.

"The girls could have lit the fire themselves," she said unwillingly. "Their mother could have told them what to do—what to say—"

"Yes." Thorne was still thoughtful. "You think they're lying? Covering for her?"

"I don't—think so. Or at least—"

You don't know. That's what you mean.

"Well, come on, Tessa, spit it out!" snapped Thorne impatiently.

"I think they're holding back on something. But I don't know what it is. I don't know what's missing. They all say the same thing. It's like talking to one person, not three. Except that Astral puts in the most detail. And I think Skye's the one who's most scared."

"Skye's the fair one with the poppy eyes, right?"

Tessa nodded.

He talks as if she's not human.

"She's the weak link, then."

"You know, it's not out of the question that they're telling the truth, as far as they know it," Tessa burst out. "What if Rachel Brydie came home, found that Quinn had set fire to the house, and killed him?"

"Then ran off without putting the fire out? Letting her daughters burn to death?" Thorne shook his head and turned away to stare at the house. "It's just as likely she murdered Quinn and set fire to the place herself. She sounds mad enough."

"If you listen to the local people, yes. But do you want to?" Tessa glanced at the bulky constable standing by the scene-of-crime tape. Russell Ingres had had plenty to say when she first arrived. She knew exactly where he stood.

Thorne turned back to face her. "Don't get a bee in your bonnet about this, Tessa," he said mildly. "Keep on track. We're here to find out what happened. We use whatever information we can get. We don't blind ourselves with emotion."

"Or prejudice, I hope!" The words were scarcely out of Tessa's mouth before she regretted them.

What a prig you sound.

Thorne smiled briefly, blandly. "Quite," he said. "The constable you've got in there. Constable Williams. Is she satisfactory?"

"Yes."

"Thought she might be. She has the look. Okay, you get her to stay with the other girls, and you have a go at the fair one. Skye. Alone. All right?"

"Fine."

He deserved to die.

Thorne looked at her quizzically. "You do realize that the odds against those girls or their mother being guilty of anything are bloody high, don't you?"

He'd changed sides, caught her on the back foot. She gaped at him.

"How do terrorized women typically kill their men?" he inquired.

"While they're asleep in bed."

"Right. Especially if they're as big and powerful as Quinn. But it doesn't look as though Quinn was killed in bed, does it? Unless he made a habit of sleeping with the chooks."

"Fisk still has to confirm . . ."

He waved a hand dismissively. "Of course. A lot of things have to be confirmed. Which is my point. That's what we're here for. To investigate. And part of that investigation is to trace Rachel Brydie and get her side of things. Correct?"

His voice was bland, but his eyes were hard.

He's snowing you. All that about odds, that's . . .

"Correct."

"Off you go, then. Get them to give you a picture of their mother, while you're at it. And—" Thorne pushed a note into her hand "—tell them they'll have to move out of the house for a while. This woman—Fiona Klein—called by while you were inside. She's offered to take them. She's a friend of the family, she says. If they don't want to stay with her, we can put them up somewhere."

"They won't want to leave."

"No. Very likely not. But they'll have to, won't they?"

The doors of the mortuary van slammed shut. The engine started, and Tessa watched as the van began bumping over the grass towards the drive. Up it would go, out the gate, into Lily Lane, past the bank of berry bushes and honeysuckle, frightening the parrots. It would weave around the twists and bends, turn left into Lilac Street, right at Furze Avenue and at last find the highway. Then it would travel down, down to the plains and onto the motorway. And speed on to the city.

Four and a half years ago Adam Quinn had come to Haven. Now he was leaving it. It was free of him.

But the air seemed no sweeter now that the body had gone. The atmosphere of decay still hung heavy in the yard. It wasn't just the odor of death. It was the old, rotting wood of the buildings where in every crack and corner fat spiders crouched in webs knobbly with the shrouded husks of their victims. It was the vines that were slowly overwhelming the house and the sheds that lined the courtyard, crawling on and upward, layer upon layer, though many of their leaves were blotched and holed by disease. It was—fear, that wouldn't go away.

The hens pecked, crooning, in the dried mud, the limp grass. Every now and then one of them would look up, its black eye blankly manic. Tessa felt a chill. She'd be glad to leave this place.

"Got it!" It was Lance Fisk's voice, uncharacteristically jubilant. He was still crouching, but now he was holding the forceps at eye level, staring at the dark object he'd just unearthed from the shed floor.

"He found the slug," muttered Thorne. He seemed almost disappointed.

By contrast, Tootsie Soames looked pleased with herself.

She crossed the yard to join them. "I told you it'd be there, Malcolm," she said. "Even Lance told you it'd be there."

Thorne grunted.

Tootsie smiled sweetly at him. "Well, I'm off," she said, "and as my old dad would have said, I'm leaving as well. Not a minute too soon either. I don't like this place."

She turned to go, and then looked back. "God willing, I'll be doing the autopsy on Mr. Quinn tonight, Tessa. The state he's in, the sooner the better. I'll schedule it, and let you know. When do you think you and Steve will be back?"

Thorne looked up. "I'll be attending," he said. "I'm keeping Vance and Hayden up here for a couple of days."

What?

Tootsie glanced at Tessa as if she'd spoken aloud, and made a sympathetic face.

"You've brought your overnight bag, presumably?" Thorne asked, turning to Tessa with a smile.

"Yes. But I didn't think—"

"No point running up and down. Waste of time." Thorne was watching Fisk bagging the bullet and directing some of his people to collect the sodden straw. "Something about this smells to high heaven," he went on, apparently intending no pun. "We're going to find out what it is." He jerked his head around and looked fixedly at Tessa. "Right?"

"Yes, sir."

What's he on about? Why not just leave it? Suicide. It was obviously . . .

There's no suicide note. And where's Rachel Brydie? That's what's bugging Thorne. Rachel Brydie. Find her, and that'll be the end of it.

Find her . . .

Eight

When Tessa returned to the living room, the Brydies were sitting in exactly the same positions as before. None showed the slightest sign of restlessness. Constable Williams, still on her chair by the door, glanced up as Tessa came in and shook her head very slightly. Apparently there had been no conversation to report.

Tessa sat down at the head of the table, and was again aware of a frisson. She was aware of three pairs of eyes regarding her with fascinated dread. A feeling of pity mixed with rage swept through her. How cowed did you have to be to look like that, just because someone sat in a chair? She glanced at the armchair drawn up by the fireplace. Adam Quinn had sat there, in state. Rachel Brydie had not shared the fire, as she had shared Quinn's starched, white bed. She had sat with Bliss, Skye and Astral at the table or nowhere, it seemed. Why had she allowed it? This was her house.

Tessa was aware that the silence had gone on too long. She cleared her throat, and spoke:

"I know this is very hard for you all. I'm sorry. But when—something like this—happens, the police have to investigate. It's our job. Do you understand?"

Three nods. Slightly bewildered, she thought. Bliss, Skye and Astral were plainly not used to apologies—or explanations.

"I'm afraid we're going to have to ask you to leave the house for a few days. A friend of yours, a Miss Klein, has offered to have you stay with her."

Inevitably, the girls glanced at one another. Tessa waited.

"Miss Klein left the school," said Astral finally. "She went away. She said she was not coming back. She went to Italy." She made it sound like outer space.

"She must have changed her mind," said Tessa. "Anyway, she's here now, and she's offering to have you. You can stay with her if you like. Or if you'd rather, we can book you into a hotel."

Again she waited. There was no response.

"Do you understand?" she asked gently. "Bliss?" She looked at the oldest girl.

"We cannot leave Haven," said Bliss, just as gently.

Oh, God.

Just tell them. It's what they're used to.

Tessa forced some firmness into her voice. "It can't be helped, I'm afraid. But you'll be able to come back quite soon, if you want to."

"We must see to Adam," Bliss said, as if she hadn't spoken.

"And we must do our work," Skye added.

"The work can wait for a couple of days. And—Adam's body has been taken away now. We're going to look after it for you."

Bliss and Skye froze. But Astral gasped and leaned forward, gripping the edge of the table. Her eyes were wide. Something like hope seemed to be flickering there, fighting with the fear. "You have taken him?" she breathed.

Tessa nodded.

Skye made a strangled sound, covered her mouth, and looked up with horror at the brooding portrait above the fireplace.

"Don't be frightened," said Tessa quickly. "There's nothing to be frightened of." She leaned forward. "Really. He can't hurt you. Not any more. He's gone. Finished."

They didn't believe her—or at least, Bliss and Skye didn't. She could see that. But there was no point in arguing with them, or trying to make them see reason. She stood up.

"Come on. You'll need to pack a few things," she said, trying to sound brisk, to offer no choice. "Constable Williams will help." She turned and beckoned to Rochette Williams, who sprang from her chair like a released jack-in-the-box, and almost bounded across the room to stand behind her.

"I thought perhaps that Bliss and Astral could do the

packing," Tessa went on. "I'd like Skye to show me around a bit, before we go."

That's transparent. It's obvious you want to get Skye alone. Can't be helped.

The young women still hadn't moved. Tessa pushed her chair firmly under the table as a signal that the conversation was at an end, and action was required. "Ready, then?" she prompted.

Astral slipped from the bench and got up. The other two remained seated.

"We cannot leave here," said Bliss slowly. "It is forbidden. We cannot go with strangers. It is forbidden."

"Forbidden," Skye repeated. Her plump fingers, the nails shredded to the quick, were plucking at the thin stuff of her sleeve.

"Hey!" barked Constable Williams, her voice shockingly loud in the quiet room. "Don't give us that stuff. You do what the detective says. Now!"

Furious, Tessa spun around, but as she did she caught movement from the corner of her eye. She turned back to see Bliss and Skye swinging their legs over the bench. In a moment they were standing, watching her, passively awaiting further orders.

"Thank you," Tessa said. With difficulty she reined in her anger. She was angry with Williams for being a bully. She was angry with the Brydies for responding to bullying when they wouldn't respond to reason or kindness. And she was very angry with herself for losing the initiative.

"Will you accept Miss Klein's invitation, Bliss?" she asked tightly. "Or do you want to be booked into a hotel?"

Bliss hesitated. She seemed, for once, not to know what to say. She frowned, and glanced at Astral.

"It would be best to stay with Miss Klein," Astral said softly.

"Mother said—" Skye began in a high voice. But Bliss cut across her.

"We cannot stay with Miss Klein, Astral. Adam was angry when she tried to interfere before. When she tried to say you should stay at school. Adam does not like the school. He told you to stay away from her."

Skye whimpered, and went back to plucking at her sleeve.

"Adam did not like her interfering, that is true," Astral murmured, moving around the table to join her sisters. "But he would not want us to stay with strangers. Miss Klein knows us. And it is different now. She is no longer a teacher at the school. There is nothing to stop her from helping us now."

She's managing them.

"Or there is Jonathon," Astral added slyly. "He would help us, too. If we asked him. Miss Klein could visit us there."

The mention of Jonathon was apparently enough to decide Bliss. She looked darkly at Tessa. "We will go to Miss Klein," she said. It was as though she had just chosen between two forms of torture.

Tessa nodded. "All right, then. Now, you go along with Constable Williams and pack. Enough clothes and things for a couple of days. Are any of you on any medication?"

"We do not pollute our bodies with drugs at Haven," said Bliss.

Only straight gin, that's all.

"All right, then." Tessa held out her arm to Skye. "You come with me, Skye."

Skye hung back.

"I will show you what you want to see," said Bliss.

"No. You go with Constable Williams, please. Skye?"

Tessa heard the hardness in her own voice, and almost wondered at it. Now *she* was being a bully. It seemed required. Was it the girls' strange mixture of stubbornness and passivity that created it? Or the atmosphere of this place?

She glanced at the portrait on the wall. Adam Quinn's saturnine features glowered down at her. His expression seemed not so much menacing now, as taunting. If Tessa was fanciful, she could think that he was still haunting Haven. Still pulling the strings. Corrupting and debasing everyone who came here.

She could think that. If she was fanciful. But she wasn't.

She jerked her head slightly at Rochette Williams, who strode forward, separated Bliss and Astral from Skye like a tough little dog cutting out sheep, and herded her charges expertly from the room.

The door closed behind them, and Skye faced Tessa alone. Her mouth hung slightly open. Her pale blue eyes were wide in the plump, soft face.

Lamb to the slaughter.

"I won't bite, you know," Tessa exclaimed impulsively.

The girl's eyes opened even wider. A hand crept to her mouth.

She didn't understand what you meant. She thinks you're crazy.

I will be crazy if I have to deal with this lot much longer.

Tessa pulled herself together. "I need a picture of your mother, Skye," she said, slowly and firmly. "Are there any photographs of her here, anywhere?"

The girl shook her head. "No photographs," she said.

Tessa sighed, turned away, and then on impulse turned quickly back. She caught Skye's eyes unguarded. And in that pale blue vacancy a strange expression was flickering. It was instantly suppressed, but Tessa had seen it. Was it—triumph?

No photographs . . .

"Perhaps there's a painting, or a drawing, then?" she asked quickly.

She watched Skye try to think, to find a way out, and fail. The rounded shoulders slumped.

"Yes," the girl said in a flat voice.

"Where is it?"

"With Mother's other paintings. In her workroom."

"Right. We'll go and look for it now, then. Come on."

Jonathon Stoller's little cottage was in strong contrast to the house next door. Steve liked it a lot. It was the sort of place he himself would have liked to have owned. It had a homey feel. It nestled on its land as though it had grown out of it a long time ago, reached maturity and stayed, spreading its roots deep into the soil. It was a shame, Steve thought, that its owner was not so impressive.

He had knocked several times at the door, when he first arrived. Getting no answer, he had even opened the door a little and called, with no result. Finally, he had strolled around the back, to find Stoller sitting on his back veranda, with his feet on the railings, drinking wine. There were two bottles standing by the leg of his chair—one empty, one three-quarters full. He'd obviously been drinking ever since he got home—and drinking fast.

The man wasn't unfriendly. He offered a chair, a glass of wine. But he was slurring and plainly very far from sober.

Steve accepted the chair and refused a drink, cursing his own sloppiness in having delayed the interview so long. He hadn't considered the possibility that Jonathon would effectively render himself useless as a witness in the interim. He watched Jonathon pour himself another glass, wondering if he should stay or go. Nothing the man said while he was in this state could really be relied on. On the other hand, the alcohol might have loosened his tongue enough for some useful impressions to be gained.

Jonathon had launched into a rambling monolog. He seemed to be laboring under the impression that he'd been somehow hardly done by. He kept talking about other houses he might have bought, other courses his life might have taken. Tears came into his eyes as he said Astral's name, and he referred several times to "old silver-hair"—Fiona Klein, Steve realized, after the first few references. What Fiona had to do with Jonathon Stoller's state of well-being Steve found difficult to understand.

"You know Miss Klein?" he asked.

"No," said the other man sulkily. "I never met her till today. I met her on the drive, on the way back here. She said she was going to see Astral. Said she was her teacher, or something." His voice and manner were tinged with jealousy, as if he resented anyone but himself having a relationship with Astral Brydie. "Is Astral going to stay with her?" he asked abruptly.

"I wouldn't know, sir. Miss Klein has made the offer. She seems to know the family reasonably well."

"She can't know them all that well. Astral never mentioned her to me," Jonathon said sullenly. He was looking over to the Haven side of the fence. There were uniformed men searching the grounds. You could see them at the bottom of the paddock, where the hedge of shrubs that stretched along the fence-line finished. They were there by Thorne's orders, searching for Rachel Brydie in every possible hiding place. Searching for recently disturbed earth, too—just in case. Soon they would move across the fence, to Jonathon's land. Maybe already they were there, in his forest, hidden by the trees.

"I don't know why they're bothering to look down there," mumbled Jonathon. "She's been gone a week. She'd hardly hide in the forest for a week, would she?"

His voice was full of disdain for the incompetence and stupidity of the police. Steve didn't bother to correct his opinion, or to point out that they only had the Brydie girls' word for it that their mother had been gone a week. For all Stoller knew she could have slipped down to the forest five minutes before Astral led him to the shed. She could be quietly waiting down by the creek for all the fuss to die down. From what Fiona Klein had said, this would be just her form.

Steve stretched out his legs. It was pleasant, on the veranda. The view was breathtaking. The forest at the bottom of the gentle slope was deep green and shady. Full of promise, and secrets.

"Do you know Mrs. Brydie well?" Steve asked.

Jonathon shook his head somberly, staring into his wineglass. "Never even met her," he said, and, inexplicably, laughed. "Never met any of them, except Astral."

"You know Astral pretty well, though," said Steve quietly.

"What d'you mean by that?" The other man was suddenly pugnacious.

"Well, she asked you to help her this morning," Steve said peaceably. "She obviously felt she could trust you."

Jonathon nodded. His chin sank to his chest. "She trusts me," he mumbled. "God, I had no idea. No idea . . . " The wine glass tilted slightly in his hand.

"You didn't suspect what she was going to show you?"

"God, no." The man looked up, his face a mask of disgusted horror. "God, never in my wildest dreams." He bent his mouth to his glass and drank thirstily. "I knew they had some funny ideas," he mumbled. "I knew Quinn had them under his thumb. They believed every word he said. But . . ." His voice trailed off again.

"They say they thought Quinn was going to come back to life."

"How could they think that? How could anyone?"

There was no answer to that. Steve glanced at his notebook.

"You told Constable Ingres that you spoke to Astral last Sunday afternoon, Mr. Stoller. What time was that?"

"I've said all this! I said goodbye to her at about four-thirty. Then I left to go back to town. He's got all the details."

"How long had you been talking before four-thirty, sir?"

"Oh—you know, a while," Jonathon said vaguely. "Half an hour, or an hour or something."

Steve made a note, aware of the other man's eyes on him. He glanced up. "Half an hour or an hour," he repeated slowly. "And you were standing by the fence all that time, were you?"

"Oh, well, we might have moved around a bit—you know, walked up and down or whatever . . . What does it matter?" Suddenly Jonathon was pugnacious again. "I told the other guy all this. Why do I have to say it all again?"

"Just checking I've got it straight, sir. Was the meeting last Sunday different in any way from other meetings you and Astral have had?"

Jonathon's eyes flickered. "No. What do you mean different? Why do you ask that?" He reached for the bottle and filled his glass again, keeping his head down.

Steve's feeling that the man was hiding something strengthened. "Did Astral seem to have anything on her mind?" he asked. "Did she tell you anything that might have happened that day? Say anything about her mother, or stepfather?"

"No," Jonathon said tightly. Now he was tense and watchful, blinking rapidly as if trying to fight off the effects of the alcohol, as if he knew that he should, at this moment in the interview, have his wits about him.

"Are you sure, Mr. Stoller?" Steve persisted. "Astral was exactly as normal?"

The other man paused. "At the beginning, she was a bit upset, I suppose," he muttered, after a moment.

"Go on."

"It's nothing," Jonathon mumbled. He was obviously already regretting his statement. "I mean, nothing important. I don't want you making more of it than it's worth." He drank, taking his time.

Steve waited. Finally Jonathon heaved an exaggerated sigh and went on.

"She was just a bit upset, that's all. She'd been walking down in the forest, before she came up to meet me. She often goes down there. The creek's a sort of refuge for her. No one else in the family seems to go there. She came up to where I was—I was mending the fence down there." He pointed towards the place where the hedge of shrubs ended, leaving the wire fence bare. "She'd been crying."

"Did she tell you what the matter was?"

"No."

"Didn't you ask her, Mr. Stoller?"

Jonathon made an irritated gesture. Some wine slopped out of his glass onto his hand, but he didn't appear to notice. "You don't understand," he said pettishly. "She was often upset. The first time I saw her—the very first time, months ago—she'd been crying. I mean, the life she led in that place—it was bloody terrible."

His face had darkened. His eyes narrowed as he stared at the distant hills. "It was appalling. Unbearable," he slurred. "Would you expect her to be laughing and singing with all that going on?"

"All what going on, sir?" Steve asked the question calmly, but his interest had quickened. Just how much did Jonathon Stoller know of life at Haven?

The other man glanced at him and seemed to return to some sort of awareness of his own position. He leaned down to get the wine bottle, noticed that his hand was dripping, and shook it. Drops of wine spattered over the dusty veranda boards.

"At Haven they're supposed to just work, meditate and sleep. Be in harmony with nature, or something. Their mother's some sort of middle-aged hippie. A real nutbag. She thinks the world's evil and corrupted. She didn't like the girls to go out, or mix with other people or anything like that, in case they got polluted."

He grimaced. "Might have been all right. But then their mother took up with Quinn. She met him while she was running a stall at the markets. She seems to have decided he was some sort of guru. Brought him home. He just took over. Started all these rules, and rituals."

Unguarded, his face was twisted into an expression of disgusted fascination. "He was mad. Astral was terrified of him. They all were."

"Were they physically afraid?" Steve asked quietly. "Was Quinn violent?"

He'd thought he had to ask the question. But as soon as he had, he regretted it. He should have let the man talk without interruption.

Stoller's face had closed up. "He could've been," he said rapidly. "How would I know? But it was more than that. It was a mental thing. Like mind control. He told them something, they believed it. He made them believe it. It was incredible. They thought he could read their minds, for God's sake! I told Astral it was crazy, but—"

He broke off, bent, fumbled again for the partly filled bottle, and finally secured it. The empty bottle was knocked over in the process, and he froze, watching as it rolled over the boards, finally coming to a stop at the veranda railing. Apparently satisfied, he filled his glass to the brim, and sipped.

He seemed to be determined to wipe himself out, thought Steve. Soon he'd be incapable of making any sense at all. But he was still relatively rational now. He'd fallen silent, as if he'd lost his train of thought. More likely he'd thought better of what he'd been going to say.

"Astral didn't believe you when you said Quinn couldn't read her mind," Steve prompted.

"Yes," the other man mumbled. "I mean, no, she didn't believe me. Or I don't think she did. Hard to say. She said she guarded her thoughts when he was around. She tried to. That's what she said."

He glanced up. "Look," he said roughly, "you probably think I should have done something about it. Told someone.

But who was I supposed to tell? The cops wouldn't have done anything about it. Astral and her mother and sisters would just have said there wasn't a problem. Plus Quinn's a big shot around this town. People think he's the ant's pants. I'd've been left with egg on my face, and made things worse."

"You didn't think of confronting Quinn privately?"

"Think of it? Of course I bloody thought of it!" Stoller's face creased into a frown. "But Astral begged me not to. She begged me." His eyes were glazed with memory, his mouth hard. There's something there, thought Steve. He's remembering something specific.

"You've known Astral for—four months or so?"

"Yes." Stoller looked down at his glass. "It seems longer," he murmured.

"Did her mother or Adam Quinn know you were meeting her regularly?"

"Of course they didn't. Quinn would have stopped it. She didn't want that."

"What exactly is your relationship with Astral Brydie, Mr. Stoller?"

The bent head jerked slightly. He's been waiting for that, Steve thought.

"She liked having someone to talk to," Stoller mumbled. "Someone outside her bloody family. God, you can understand that, can't you?" He looked up defiantly. His eyes were dull and slightly bloodshot. "I helped her," he said. "Because of me she started to understand what's what. I mean, about the real world. Okay, she might have waited till I got back before she did anything about Quinn's body. But at least she did something then. Even though the other two were against it. So being with me has done her good. Right?"

Steve wondered whether he should press the point, act directly on the hint that Tessa, via Constable Rochette Williams, had given him, and decided against it. Badgering a drunk was a bad way to get to the truth, if you didn't want to buy trouble. Tomorrow he'd question Jonathon Stoller again. Take an official statement. Tomorrow Stoller would, presumably, be sober, and more inclined to be reasonable about the risks of lying.

"Right?" Stoller repeated.

Steve nodded, and got to his feet. "I'll leave it there, I think, Mr. Stoller. I'll come back and see you tomorrow morning. You'll still be here, will you?"

Stoller looked up at him blearily. "Why do you want to talk to me again? I've told you everything I know. And all I know is, that bastard tried to kill those girls, then killed himself. All I did was find the body and call the cops. I'm just a witness, right?"

"Do you know of any reason why Adam Quinn should try to murder the Brydie sisters, then commit suicide, last Sunday night, sir?" Steve asked formally.

Jonathon shook his head. "I've got no idea," he said. He drank deeply, looked out into the distance. "But it doesn't matter what I think anyway. Doesn't matter what any of us think. Quinn was insane. A bloody megalomaniac, if you ask me. Megalomaniacs make up their own reasons for things. Maybe something upset him. Maybe Mum Brydie got the irrits and pissed off on him. Maybe she found another man and gave him the arse. Have you thought of that?"

He reached for the wine bottle. "Whatever," he said. "I'm just a witness. It's got nothing to do with me."

Nine

Skye hung back in the doorway of the workroom and watched as the tall man with gray-streaked hair—Sergeant Fisk—and the detective called Tessa Vance searched through the paintings stacked in rows against the walls. They were both wearing transparent gloves. The gloves smoothed out all the wrinkles in their fingers, and made their hands look pale, as though they didn't belong to human beings. Four strange hands, pale and smooth, touching Mother's paintings.

There were so many paintings. Some had frames, but a lot were just boards. They were piled up against one another all around the walls of the workroom as though they didn't matter at all.

It had always been like that. It was as though, once she'd finished a painting, Mother stopped caring about it, no matter how long she had spent on making it. Once it had dried she would just prop it against the wall with the others, and go on to something else.

Sometimes, before Adam came, she would have to paint new pictures over ones she had already done, because there was no money. But Adam's money paid for new boards and canvases, and paints and brushes, too, so after he came the number of paintings in the workroom grew quite fast. But Mother still stacked them up, out of sight. Only one was ever put up on the wall, over the fireplace, to watch them. Those eyes, following you, knowing you . . .

Skye's fingers stole to her lips. The puffy, pink tips weren't bitter any more as they slipped into her mouth. There was nothing to remind her not to explore them with her tongue and her teeth, searching for a ragged edge, a tiny hook of nail she could worry and nip off.

The detectives were moving to another stack of paintings now. It was frightening to see strange people in this room. It was frightening to think they were here because she had brought them here. But what else could she have done? Tessa Vance had tricked her into telling about the painting. Bliss or Astral might have been able to avoid the trick, but she couldn't. They knew that she couldn't.

That was why they had looked at her as they did when they left the room with Rochette Williams. They were warning her to be careful. And that was why, Skye dimly realized, Tessa Vance had wanted to talk to her alone. Tessa Vance was a detective. Detectives were clever. Tessa Vance thought that Skye would tell her things that Astral and Bliss wouldn't.

And Skye had told about the painting. So Tessa Vance must think she was stupid. Skye felt a tightness in her chest and at the bottom of her stomach. It was anger. With her free hands she plucked at the sleeve of her dress, watching Tessa Vance bending over the paintings with the man. I'm not stupid, she thought at them.

At school, she'd always been able to pass her tests. She could remember things. She could remember whole pages of books, if she tried. But when people tried to tease her or trick her she got upset, and frightened, and couldn't think quickly enough. People had always been able to play tricks on her, and make her do things, and they always had—when all she wanted was to be quiet, and to be left alone.

At school other children had done it all the time—hiding her ruler, and her hat, stealing her lunch and then taking it to pieces in the playground and showing each other. She remembered how they'd always laugh and hold their noses because her sandwich was dark, hard homemade bread with hard-boiled egg and things from the gardens inside, instead of proper white sliced, buttered bread with ham or cheese or peanut butter.

They thought it was funny that Skye brought a jar of flour-and-water paste to school, instead of shop-bought paste, too. Mother said the flour-and-water paste was quite good enough for school, but in summer it sometimes went bad, and smelled, before the jar was finished. The children said Skye smelled, too. She told them she didn't. But they still said she did. They said she wiped her bottom with her fingers, because the stuff Mother painted on her nails to stop her biting them stained her fingertips with brown.

While Bliss was still at the school it wasn't so bad. Bliss stayed with Skye at recess and lunchtime, and walked home with her. But Bliss was two years older, and when she left to go to high school Skye had two years of misery. Astral had started school as well by then, of course, but Astral was younger, and she didn't help. In some ways she made it worse, because at first Astral used to shout at the other children, and even fight them, if they took her things. That got them both into trouble.

Skye wanted to stay home, after Bliss went to high school, but Mother said she couldn't. The law said children had to go to school, and Mother didn't want any trouble. Once a teacher told Bliss that they could all be taught at home, if their mother would teach them. The teacher wrote a letter to Mother about it. Mother put the letter in the fire. She said that she had too much work to do in the gardens to be a teacher. But often, when they came home, Mother wouldn't be in the gardens at all. She would be out, or in the workroom, painting her pictures.

Skye felt a sting in her fingertip. She took it from her mouth and glanced down at it. It was bleeding.

Tessa glanced at the girl standing by the door. Skye's pale blue eyes were blank with what looked like despair.

I've done this to her.

That's ridiculous.

Her finger's bleeding . . .

Is it your fault she bites her nails? You have to do your job.

"Tessa?" Fisk was indicating one of the paintings he'd uncovered near the back of one of the stacks. Tessa looked. It was a group portrait done on a big piece of board: the Brydie sisters as young children. They were naked, sitting on the grass, with bunches of herbs in their hands. The painting had been rendered with only middling skill, but unlike many of the others they'd seen, it had been finished with enormous care and attention to detail. The sisters were easily recognizable: Bliss, a dark, serious little girl; Skye, fair and wide-eyed; Astral, very pretty at four or five, her narrow lips curved into a fixed half-smile.

It could have been one of those cute, sentimental pictures of early childhood, but it was far from that. Beetles and worms crawled in the grass around the girls' feet. There were fat snails hanging from the leaves of the herbs they held. Behind and around them, mottled vines writhed like snakes. It was a crude and rather horrible rendition of innocence threatened by corruption.

"Unusual," Fisk murmured, raising one eyebrow. He was being discreet because of the watching Skye.

He scanned the painting for another few moments, then fastidiously eased it forward to uncover the one behind it. Another abstract. A huge mass of purple and black. What it was supposed to represent or suggest, Tessa couldn't begin to imagine. As Fisk studied it before moving to the next, she controlled her impatience. He wasn't capable of just flipping through the paintings to find the one they were looking for. It wasn't in his nature to skim. But at this rate the job would take an hour.

There were hundreds of paintings in the room. Some were signed RB, others were unsigned. But plainly they had all been painted by Rachel Brydie. All bore the same trademarks of vivid color, jagged shapes and background movement. Most were abstracts. Some were still lifes, the same subjects painted over and over again—bowls and jugs, fruit and flowers, knotty pieces of wood, snail shells and stones, a straw hat. No landscapes, unless you could call the few paintings of the house landscapes. Strange, Tessa thought. Living with beauty all around you, and locking yourself in a dusty room to paint empty snail shells and abstracts like bad dreams.

Fisk tipped the black-and-purple painting forward, and suddenly, there it was—a large, framed half-length portrait of a gaunt, ravaged beauty with long, gray-streaked black hair. The woman was wearing a long-sleeved scarlet dress. Clasped around her neck was a beaten silver necklace with the crescent moon as its centerpiece.

Tessa turned to the girl hovering by the door. "Can you see? Is this your mother, Skye?" she asked.

The girl nodded, shrinking. Her protuberant eyes, lashes and brows invisible, seemed to swim in her pale face. It seemed incredible that she had sprung from the womb of the woman in the portrait. You could see a shadow of Bliss in that dark seriousness. You could see Astral in the remains of the beauty. But there was nothing of Skye.

The artist had been merciless. She'd looked straight into a mirror and painted what she saw there. She hadn't attempted to soften or smooth the harsh lines that scored the skin of the forehead and the corners of the mouth. She hadn't, by the look of it, even combed her hair.

"I think I've seen that face before," murmured Fisk. He frowned, and rubbed his chin, staring at the strong nose, the huge, staring dark eyes, the straight, black brows.

"On your way here, you mean? Where?" Tessa whispered urgently.

"Oh, no. A long time ago. When she was younger. Just can't think where. Leave it with me."

There was no point in pestering him. Frustrated, Tessa tugged at the portrait's frame. It didn't move. Its base was firmly wedged in place.

"Patience," murmured Fisk. Methodically, he began moving the paintings stacked in front of the portrait. Finally it was exposed completely. He turned to Tessa. "Perhaps you could fetch Constable Suzeraine on your way out," he hinted politely.

Tessa had no wish to stay. She nodded and ushered Skye from the room.

As they left the living room and went through the kitchen towards the back door, Skye took a deep breath. "What is he going to do with it?" she whispered. "Is he going to take it away?"

A question. At last. She's showing an interest.

She's scared.

Thorne said she was the weak link.

"I don't think so," Tessa said. "It's so big, you see. I think he's planning to have it photographed." She pushed open the screen door, and they walked out into the yard.

Skye was silent, her face uncomprehending. She stared around the yard. The police invasion was complete, here. The generator pulsed, filling the air with its sound. Cords lay tangled on the ground. Light streamed from the open shed door. Inside you could see men and women in overalls moving around. And where Adam Quinn had lain, there was only a white outline. Nothing else. Not a candle, not a lavender sprig, not a piece of straw. Just a small patch of bare, packed earth in a sea of rubbish.

Constable Williams, Bliss and Astral were waiting at the yard edge, beside one of the police cars. Each was carrying a pathetically small bundle of clothes. Dee Suzeraine was standing with them. Thorne's car was gone, Tessa noted. He hadn't wasted any time. Fleetingly, she wondered whether he'd organized any accommodation for her and Steve before he left. It was unlikely.

"Dee?" called Tessa. "You're wanted inside."

Dee grabbed her camera case and left the group by the car. The few hens that remained outside their pen scattered as she crossed the yard. "Through there," Tessa said, gesturing towards the back door as she reached them. "First door to your right, off the living room. Fisk needs a good, clear pic of a painting."

Dee nodded, smiled briefly at Skye, and disappeared.

"Is she a photographer?" asked Skye.

Another question. How about that?

"That's right."

"But she's a policewoman."

"Yes. Dee's a police photographer. She'll take a picture of the painting, then we'll have copies made of the prints."

Skye's bewildered expression didn't change. You could swear that she had no idea what was going on. Yet she'd prevaricated about the painting's existence. Maybe that had simply been instinctive—the result of a lifetime's training: Tell them nothing, then they can't criticize; tell them nothing, then they can't hurt us.

"We need to be able to show people what your mother looks like, you see," she told the girl. She found herself speaking slowly and clearly, as though to a young child, or to a person for whom English was a second language. "It'll help us to find her. Do you understand?"

"Yes." The voice was barely a sigh.

"You want her to be found, don't you?"

"Yes." But the soft face seemed to quiver. The eyes were fixed on the watching figures of Astral and Bliss on the other side of the yard.

Tessa moved a little, to block as far as possible the girl's view of her sisters, and theirs of her. "Maybe you already know where she's gone, Skye," she said gently. "If you do, it would be just as well to tell us, don't you think? For her sake. And for yours, and your sisters'."

Skye hung her head.

"I think you do know where she is," Tessa said. "Or approximately."

The bent, fair head moved slowly from side to side.

She does know. Definitely.

Tessa strengthened her voice. "Skye, this matter can't be closed until we hear what your mother has to say about it—until we find out where she's been all this time. I'm sure you wish we'd all go away and leave you alone, but we can't do that until we find her."

Not completely true.

Near enough.

Skye's lips opened. Tessa held her breath.

She's going to crack. She's going to tell.

The girl raised her head. "Mother went out," she said, her voice high and trembling. "She just went out."

"Tell me, Skye," Tessa whispered. "Tell me. Don't be frightened."

"No—" The blue eyes widened, then suddenly squeezed shut. Skye pressed her hands to her ears. Then she was screaming, rocking from side to side. "No! Don't make me!" she shrieked, her voice rising shrilly over the burr of the generator. "I won't! No more! No more!"

"What's happening here?" shouted an angry female voice from the driveway.

Tessa glanced behind her. She'd thought Bliss or Astral had called out, but they were standing utterly still, making no move to come to their sister's aid, just watching gravely. Rochette Williams, on the other hand, had already turned to confront the silver-haired woman in sunglasses who was now striding over the grass towards them, having surprised, and thus easily outpaced, her escort, the red-faced Constable Ingres.

Here's trouble.

"You can't make me!" wailed Skye. "I won't—"

Tessa turned back to her. "Skye! Stop that!" she ordered harshly.

The girl broke off in mid-scream and stood silent, mouth half-open, hands still loosely over her ears.

She was panting. Her face was pink. Her eyes, wild but tearless, stared over Tessa's shoulder at the group by the cars.

"Is that Miss Klein?" Tessa asked evenly.

Skye nodded.

Did she see Klein coming down the drive? Did she put on that act for Klein's benefit?

I don't think it was an act. She lost control. It was like a violin string snapping.

She knows where her mother is. Make her tell.

She won't. She's terrified.

Tessa gave up. "Come on," she sighed.

With Skye trailing behind her she walked over to the group waiting by the police cars. Constable Ingres, still red-faced, and Rochette Williams were now standing shoulder to shoulder between the yard and the woman with silver hair, who had Bliss and Astral on either side of her and who regarded Tessa with strong disapproval.

"Miss Klein?" Tessa said. "Detective Tessa Vance, Homicide. Sorry to have kept you waiting. Bliss, Skye and Astral can go now."

"Thank you. If you're quite finished." Fiona Klein's voice was very cold. She adjusted her sunglasses and looked at Skye. "Are you all right?" she asked.

Skye nodded dumbly, glanced at her sisters and then hastily looked away again.

"The hens must be locked in for the night," said Bliss. "It is already past their time."

"We'll do that," snapped Rochette Williams.

Fiona ignored her and spoke directly to Tessa. She was plainly very angry, but keeping herself under control. Her handsome face was taut. "I can't understand how you can justify bullying these girls," she said. "Surely you can see they're not up to it."

"Miss Klein, there's been no bullying . . ."

Not true.

". . . but we have to locate their mother."

"We do not know where she is," said Bliss in a low voice.

"Well, there you are," snapped Miss Klein. "They can't help you."

"I think they can," Tessa said. "And I'd suggest you talk it over with them tonight. If Mrs. Brydie isn't located by tomorrow morning I'll have to talk to them all again." She couldn't resist looking quickly at Skye to see how she took this. But the soft, pink face was blankly stubborn now, and the fingertips had crept between the moist lips. Skye had for the moment retreated to some safe, familiar place in her mind where no one could touch her.

Tessa turned to Astral and threw her final card. "Look, you're the one who did the sensible thing this morning, Astral. You got a friend to help you. Okay. Do the sensible thing again. Tonight you tell Miss Klein everything you know. Everything you've told me, and anything else at all that you haven't told me. She'll know what to do about it."

There was no response. Tessa nodded briskly to Klein. "We'll have a word with you in the morning," she said, and turned away. She felt irritated, and a failure. "Constable Williams?" she called over her shoulder. "Could you come with me, please?"

She strode off towards the house, letting Rochette Williams follow. She didn't really know what she was going to do with her, but she felt the need to get her away from Russell

Ingres. Their shoulder to shoulder stance was unpleasantly reminiscent of her memories of classes in riot control.

"Didn't do any good with Skye, huh?" said Williams's voice from behind her. Tessa shook her head and kept going. A hen flapped, panic-stricken and squawking, out of her way and straight through the door of the fowl house. "Good shot," said Constable Williams approvingly.

Tessa stopped. "Constable," she said wearily, "would you know if Inspector Thorne made any arrangements for Detective Hayden and me before he left?"

"He asked me to fix it. He said, not too far away, and not too expensive. I've booked you in at this bed and breakfast just round the corner from the shops. It's called Bide-A-While. Supposed to be all right. You get a decent breakfast there, they say, and it's not too noisy. Not like some of the others."

Bide-A-While?

"Sounds fine," said Tessa.

"Two single rooms," Constable Williams added casually. "If that's okay."

Tessa turned to face her, working with all her strength to maintain a dignified and aloof expression. Constable Williams returned her gaze blandly. "It doesn't do dinners, of course," she added. "But there are quite a few places for that in the village. Nice quiet places. I'll write you a list."

Nice quiet places.

She means romantic. She means . . .

"You'd better join us," said Tessa recklessly. "You said you had information about the Brydies."

"Well, yeah. Of course I do. But I could—"

"No. Steve should hear it direct. We'll do it over dinner. If you're free."

"Free?" Constable Williams grinned. "Sure, I'm free."

"Good. All right, then. What about that pub on the highway? Does it have a restaurant?"

"Swans? Oh, sure. But they have entertainment Saturday nights, and it's Bouncy Bernadette's night tonight. They'll be all booked out."

Bouncy Bernadette?

Don't ask.

"Will you book us in somewhere else, then? Anywhere at all."

"No problem."

No problem.

Ten

It was nearly dark and growing chilly by the time Tessa and Steve finished a check of properties in Lily Lane and the surrounding streets, and with very little to show for their efforts, drove on to the village of Oakdale. Rochette Williams's precise directions led them easily thereafter to the bed-and-breakfast establishment so unpromisingly called Bide-A-While. Neither of them had been expecting much. Both of them had a surprise.

In the dusk, its curtained windows and the leadlights in its front door glowing with light, the house was extraordinarily beautiful. Graceful and perfectly proportioned, with a high-pitched green iron roof and old timbers painted warm cream, it nestled in the middle of a huge garden that in spring would be a mass of blossom and was now almost as beautiful—rich with fruit, berries and flaming leaves.

"How would you like to own a place like this?" Steve murmured enviously as they walked up the gravelled front path to the steps.

"You'd have to live way up here to afford it," responded Tessa.

"Would that be so bad?" He looked at her quizzically.

Tessa hesitated.

Say no.

I'm not going to lie to him to please him.

"It's beautiful here," she said. "I mean, in the mountains. But—there's something sort of, mournful, about the atmosphere, isn't there?"

He grinned. "City folks," he teased. "You get depressed if

100

you can't see traffic lights or a Coke sign from where you're standing at any given moment."

But he was disappointed.

"It's that place—Haven," she said. "Tucked away in its lovely hidden valley, but everything human decaying. And such—awful things happened there. Things no one else knew about. It gave me a bad feeling. I can't get rid of it."

He nodded somberly.

He rang the doorbell. The leadlights in the doors, Tessa saw, were decorated with waratahs and kookaburras. Original or reproduction? she wondered. And why would they seem so much prettier if they were original? That didn't make sense. And yet it was true.

The door was answered by a smiling, middle-aged woman with dangling earrings and thick, wavy auburn hair twisted into a knot high on the back of her head. Her eyes were liberally decorated with blue eyeshadow and mascara. Her generous mouth gleamed with freshly applied lipstick. She had the kind of fully fleshed face that seems ordinary at first, but becomes more and more attractive as it grows familiar. She introduced herself as Verna Larkin, their hostess.

Fluttering a little, she led them along the broad, tiled hallway—the original tiles, Tessa decided. The bedroom doors on their left bore nameplates featuring flowers—Wattle and Waratah—with appropriate illustrations. Through a doorway on the right they caught a glimpse of a bright, chintzy sitting room where a fire already burned and several youngish people sat on the edges of their chairs chatting politely. They were killing time, presumably, till it was time to go out for dinner.

Mrs. Larkin led them on, past a bathroom, two more bedrooms (Rose and Bluebell) and a small room marked TV, presumably for those who couldn't do without the box even for a weekend.

The house was formally set out at the front, but rambling at the back. Steve and Tessa's bedrooms were in an added-on section there, down a corridor from the breakfast room and on either side of a small bathroom.

"These are all I've got left, being the weekend," Mrs.

Larkin explained, adding mysteriously: "but anyway, I suppose you'd rather be at the back." Possibly, Tessa thought, she imagined that, being detectives, these guests would be doing a lot of creeping around during the night, and would need to be able to slip out of the house unobserved.

Mrs. Larkin opened the bathroom door, presumably to show that it contained all the required facilities. "I hope you don't mind sharing," she said. "Rochette Williams said it would be all right, but—"

"It's fine," said Tessa, glancing in at her room. The flower-bordered ceramic plate on the door bore the legend "Lilac" in flowing script and the room had been relentlessly decorated to carry through its theme, right down to the box of mauve tissues on the bedside table and the potpourri jar on the dressing table.

"I'm planning to put in ensuites everywhere eventually. I mean, the tourists expect it these days, don't they? But you know how it is. Plumbing's so expensive!" Mrs. Larkin chattered on. "And some of the rooms really aren't big enough. Anyway . . ."

"We'll manage," said Steve. He grinned at her. "Very nice," he added, looking in at his own room. It was labeled "Fern," and was a symphony in green.

Mrs. Larkin smiled and patted her hair in response to the grin.

"There's another bathroom at the front," she said. "Just off the hall, next to 'Wattle,' and across from the living room. There's a washroom off the breakfast room, as well."

Lavatory arrangements having been explained, she hesitated. "Rochette Williams didn't say how long . . . ?" she inquired delicately.

"We're not sure," said Steve. "It could be just for tonight, or we might need a couple more days. Would it be okay to—?"

"Oh, yes, of *course*. I was just asking because you could change rooms, for tomorrow night, if you were staying on. 'Wattle,' 'Rose' and 'Waratah' all have ensuites. Though they're at the front of course. Anyway, I mean, I'm booked up now, but after tomorrow lunchtime, about, you'll have the place to yourselves. Everyone else goes home on Sunday. So you could swap. If you like. And I was wondering for the catering—the breakfasts, and so on. But we can take it day by day, can't we? If you come in late anytime, just help yourselves to tea and coffee, and a sandwich, from the kitchen. Melissa and I have our own quarters out the back. Don't hesitate to call me if you need me, will you?"

"We won't. Thanks." Steve flashed her another grin and she beamed at him.

"I've never had police in the house before," she giggled, laying a confidential hand on his arm. "Makes me quite nervous, actually."

There was a small sound from the end of the corridor. Tessa saw a teenage girl standing there watching them. She was dressed in black from head to foot, and her mass of curly blond hair had been pulled severely back from a small face that was a mask of tragedy.

Mrs. Larkin glanced over her shoulder. "Melissa, unpack the dishwasher, and start laying out the breakfast things, will you?" she called, rather sharply.

The girl in black silently retreated.

"My daughter," sighed Mrs. Larkin, turning back to Tessa and Steve.

"Anything the matter?" Steve asked.

The woman shrugged. "Teenagers," she murmured. "They're up, or they're down. There's always something, at her age. And if there isn't something, you have to make something up. You know." She wiped her hands distractedly against the sides of her floral skirt.

Melissa hadn't looked more than about sixteen or seventeen, Tessa thought. She followed up the idea.

"Would Melissa know Astral Brydie, by any chance?" she asked.

Mrs. Larkin's eyes widened. "Oh, well, she knows *of* her," she said carelessly. "Astral Brydie was in her year at school. But they weren't friends, or anything. And Astral left, of course." She frowned. "Did you want somewhere for the girls to stay, or something? I'm afraid I haven't got any more—"

"Oh, no," Tessa assured her. "They're okay. A friend's looking after them."

"Friend?" Mrs. Larkin looked surprised, then intensely interested. "*Not* the man next door? The one who found—"

"No. A Miss Klein. Fiona Klein. She was Astral's teacher, apparently."

"Oh . . . Right. Oh, yes. Of course." A strange expression flashed across Mrs. Larkin's face, and just as quickly disappeared. She looked down, brushing furiously at an imaginary thread on her skirt.

"I was just wondering," she gabbled. "Well, I mean, because the Brydies don't mix. The girls didn't even mix at school. Not that they had the chance, poor things. The other kids thought they were freaks. Their mother should be shot."

Realizing instantly that her phrasing was unfortunate, she went crimson. "Oh, what a terrible thing to say," she gasped. "I didn't mean—"

"Do you know Mrs. Brydie?" asked Tessa.

"Well, I know her as well as anyone." Mrs. Larkin was still flustered. "I mean, I've seen her around. She's been here a long time, you know, and it's not as if Oakdale's a big place. You'd see her at the shops sometimes, years ago, before the kids got old enough to run her messages for her. And she used to have a stall at the weekend market—I've bought potpourri from her in the past. That sort of thing. But I don't *know* her."

And I don't want to, her look seemed to say.

"Have you seen her at all this week?"

"This week? Oh, heavens, no. She hardly ever goes out. You hear things—I mean, people bump into her at odd times—but I haven't seen her myself for—well, it'd be over a year, probably." Mrs. Larkin patted her hair again, but tensely this time, glanced at her watch, and started to show signs of restlessness. "I'd better get on," she said. "Weekends . . ."

"Just one more thing, Mrs. Larkin."

The woman went very still. "Yes?"

"Mrs. Brydie seems to have left her home last Sunday afternoon, and her daughters can't tell us where she is. From your knowledge of her, can you suggest anywhere, anywhere at all, she might have gone?"

Verna Larkin shook her head. But Tessa had the fleeting

impression that her body had relaxed slightly. As though she'd breathed out, after holding her breath.

She's relieved. That wasn't the question she expected.

"Can't help you there," she said. Then she leaned forward. "I can tell you one thing, though," she added, her eyes narrowing. "Whatever Rachel Brydie's doing, and wherever she is, she's with a man."

Tessa's face must have shown her surprise, because the woman nodded vehemently. "Take it from me," she said.

"Heard something, have you?" asked Steve, wise in the ways of small communities.

Verna Larkin smoothed her skirt. "Nothing concrete," she said. "But leopards don't change their spots. I'm just going on past history."

"Mu-um!" Melissa's voice called plaintively from the breakfast room.

"Coming!" bellowed Verna. She started to move away. "Sorry. Have to run," she said.

But Tessa was determined to get at least one thing straight. "When you say past history, you mean Adam Quinn?"

"Oh, no. I mean, not specifically. Long before that. One man after another. I mean, look at those girls. Every one of them illegitimate."

"Their father—"

Verna snorted with laughter. "Fathers, you mean. They all had different fathers. Didn't you know that? Oh, yes. Rachel Brydie's always been one for the men. Just latched on to any drifter who turned up around the place. Didn't seem to matter to her how scruffy they were. They'd stay till they got sick of her, or she got sick of them—I don't know which—bit of both, I suppose—then they'd move on."

Her face took on a spiteful expression that sat oddly on her generous features. "Poor Adam was just the last in a long line," she went on. "Not that he knew it. *She* wouldn't have told him, and of course no one else did. He was completely taken in. You wouldn't think a man with his experience'd fall for it. But there you are."

Tessa was having to struggle to keep her own face expressionless. To stop herself from remembering that house, its claustrophobic, dread-ridden atmosphere, crimson and purple robes in a cupboard and a bamboo cane on the shelf by the kitchen door. To suppress her knowledge of the life Rachel Brydie and her daughters had led. To remember that Verna Larkin didn't know all that. Verna Larkin didn't know what the famous Adam Quinn had been, or become. She was going on small-town gossip and the typical small-town distrust of difference that would have prejudiced her against someone like Rachel Brydie from the start.

"We heard that Quinn was at Haven for four and a half years," Steve murmured.

"Oh, yes." Verna smiled unpleasantly. "Adam lasted longer than any of the others, but I'd say that's because he had a bit of class, and a lot of money. Rachel would have liked that. She doesn't have two pennies to rub together, you know. And it's not as if she's getting any younger. She probably worked harder than usual to keep him sweet." Her mouth twisted with fastidious disgust.

She scanned their faces, correctly read what she saw there, and put her hands on her hips. "Look," she said sharply. "None of us is perfect, and I'm no prude, believe me. Life's not easy for a woman, and you've got to take your happiness where you find it. But your kids have to come first. That's why Rachel Brydie's beyond the pale, as far as I'm concerned."

"Mu-um!" wailed the voice from the dining room.

Verna's brow puckered. Suddenly the hard look had disappeared from her face, leaving it soft, slack, and rather sad. "I don't know," she sighed. Then she lifted her chin. "I'll have to leave you. Make yourselves comfortable. And as for what I said—well, I'm sure you think I'm awful. I run off at the mouth. Always have. But you ask anyone." She spun around and walked rapidly down the corridor and into the breakfast room beyond.

"Melissa!" Tessa heard her say reprovingly. "Didn't I tell you—" The door swung shut behind her, muffling further sound.

They stood looking after her.

"Interesting," said Steve.

"Horrible. The whole town probably thinks the way she

does about the Brydies," muttered Tessa. "Just because they're different—"

He dismissed that with a wave of his hand. "I didn't mean that. I mean about the men."

Tessa shrugged. "We don't even know it's true."

"You shouldn't underestimate these people, Tessa. They're not fools, you know. The gossip machine mightn't always be dead accurate, but—"

"I know, I know," she interrupted impatiently. "Well, Rachel Brydie probably did have lovers. Why shouldn't she?"

"We hadn't thought of another man, had we?"

"No."

"It'd answer a few questions, wouldn't it?"

"Which questions?"

Steve stuck his hands in his pocket and leaned against the wall, watching her.

You sound sulky.

I hate this place. I hate these people.

"Which questions?" Tessa repeated, moderating her voice a little.

"Well, for a start, if Rachel went off with a guy, that'd explain her not telling her daughters where she was going," said Steve patiently. "Or telling them, and swearing them to secrecy. Right?"

"Yes. I guess."

"And it'd give Quinn a reason to kill himself—and try to take the girls with him, wouldn't it?"

He's right. Why didn't I see that?

Not thinking. Too busy being angry.

"You're right," Tessa said aloud.

"You don't look too happy about it."

She sighed and looked up at him. "I was just thinking I wasn't a detective's bootlace."

"Right." Steve levered himself off the wall, took his hands out of his pockets and picked up his overnight bag. "We've got over an hour till Rochette turns up," he said. "I'm going to grab twenty minutes shuteye."

"I don't understand how you can do that," Tessa complained.

"I'm tired."

What was he doing last night?

What does it matter to you?

"No—I mean, I don't understand how you can catnap," she said. "Fall asleep so quickly."

"Clear conscience."

"No conscience, if you ask me."

Steve grinned, slung his bag over his shoulder and pushed open the door of "Fern." "It's very green in here," he commented, then glanced back at her. "You okay?"

Tessa nodded, and picked up her own bag. "I'll have a shower," she said. "Get the cobwebs out of my head. I'm not thinking straight."

He went into his room and closed the door. She went into her lilac bower, kicked off her shoes and fossicked in her bag. It was her usual practice, when she was on call, to keep a packed overnight bag at the ready, to be slung in the boot of the car at a moment's notice. But now she wished she'd been less severely practical in her choices of spare clothes. Sadly, it would be the brown suit again for dinner.

She pulled the curtains aside and looked through the window. She found herself looking directly out onto a pleasant, bricked courtyard covered by a pergola over which scrambled a grapevine in bright color. Mist drifted over damp tables and benches, and a dripping barbecue. The other side of the courtyard was bounded by another wing of the house. Light shone from windows and a pair of glazed doors. The kitchen, Tessa guessed, though it was impossible to see clearly.

Turning away from the window she noticed that there was a terry-towelling bathrobe hanging on a hook on the back of the door. She hadn't expected that, in a bed-and-breakfast place. She stripped off her clothes, absurdly pleased, and blessed Mrs. Larkin's attention to detail.

In three minutes she was standing under the shower, turning her face up to the stream of warm water, reveling in it. She'd read in a magazine, once, that it damaged your skin to let the shower run on your face. Ever since, she'd felt slightly guilty when she did it.

Steve's just on the other side of the wall. Listening to the shower running.

He'll be asleep by now. What's wrong with you?

Abruptly she turned off the water, stepped out of the shower cubicle and started roughly rubbing herself dry with Mrs. Larkin's fluffy mauve towel. Rubbing like that was bad for your skin, too. You were supposed to pat yourself dry. Pat, pat, pat, blotting away the moisture. Like a ritual drying of a sacred object. Then you anointed yourself with body lotion.

The Brydie sisters wouldn't know what body lotion was.

The Brydie sisters anointed a decaying corpse with lavender oil for a week. Sacred object . . .

The shower seemed to have stimulated her, without actually clearing her thoughts. She wrapped herself in the bathrobe, which was so big (one size fits all!) that it would have wound around her twice. She pulled the sash tight.

Rachel Brydie's beyond the pale.

Adam will be disappointed . . . He will correct all of us.

Wherever she is, whatever she's doing, she's with a man.

Tessa left the bathroom, glancing instinctively to the end of the corridor, half-expecting to see the drooping, black-clad figure of Melissa watching tragically from the doorway. But there was no one there.

Anything wrong?

There's always something, at her age . . .

Just one more thing, Mrs. Larkin . . .

Verna Larkin had been tense, waiting for a question that never came. What question?

Tessa went into her room, hung up her towel and lay down on the bed. She was warm. Her skin was tingling. Her muscles were aching, but pleasantly—the aching of tension relaxed and relieved.

If Rachel Brydie was away with some man, they'd hear from her soon. Adam Quinn's death would be reported all over the country. Rachel would hear the news, somewhere, somehow, and get in touch. Tonight, or tomorrow. Surely. She'd know her daughters needed her.

They've needed her all along.

Rachel Brydie's beyond the pale . . .

What question?

Eleven

An hour later Steve and Tessa were standing outside Bide-A-While, waiting for Rochette Williams to pick them up. It was cold—amazingly cold, given the heat of the day. Mist was billowing around their feet and veiling the single street-light in their vicinity. Tessa shivered and wrapped her old coat around her, grateful that she'd got into the habit of leaving it in the back of the car with her gum boots. She could easily have neglected to bring a coat this weekend. It had been hard to believe, in the humid city, that she'd need one.

Rochette arrived right on time, her car headlights appearing quite suddenly out of the mist.

"I booked us into this place called Martin's," she said, as they got into the car, Tessa in the front, Steve in the back. "I've never been to it, but everyone says it's good. It's in the village. We could walk to it from here, but I may as well drive." There was a slight restraint in her manner that Tessa hadn't noticed before. Perhaps she felt self-conscious because she'd changed out of her uniform into a red, long-sleeved shirt, blue slacks and red-and-blue striped jerkin. She looked under her eyebrows at Tessa, noting the brown trouser suit. Tessa resisted the urge to tell her that she had nothing else to wear.

"Is it all right?" Rochette asked, jerking her head at Bide-A-While, its garden mysterious in the mist.

"It's fine," said Steve. "Beautiful old place, isn't it?"

"Oh, yeah," Rochette responded indifferently. She did an elaborately careful U-turn and began to drive very slowly back the way she'd come—not much faster than walking pace, in fact. She was, no doubt, being well-behaved on their account. Ahead, Tessa could see only mist. Thick and white, it closed in behind them, enveloping them, hiding them.

There was no moon, and mist had come up to the windows.

Which one of the Brydie girls had said that, this afternoon? Probably Astral. Her words painted pictures that stuck in your mind.

He said things might come for us, out of the mist . . .

Tessa wrapped her coat more firmly around her. The car tires swished on the dampening road.

"Has Bide-A-While been used as a bed-and-breakfast place for long?" she asked, to break the slightly uneasy silence.

"Seven, eight years or so. Verna Larkin's mother left it to her," said Rochette. "Verna could never have afforded it, otherwise. She turned it into a B & B after Paddy Larkin died. Paddy drank. Got violent, too, by all accounts. Didn't like Verna dying her hair. Always on at her about something or other. She would have divorced him but she couldn't, being a Catholic. And there were three kids. Anyhow, Paddy got run over by a train, luckily, and he had life insurance."

It was hard to know how to respond to that. "I didn't realize you knew Mrs. Larkin," said Tessa lamely.

Rochette glanced at her in surprise. "I don't," she said. "But you hear things."

Small towns . . .

"She's a character, isn't she?" said Steve easily. "We had a bit of a chat. Hasn't got much time for Rachel Brydie, has she?"

"Not a lot. From what I hear."

"She reckons Rachel could have gone off with a new boyfriend."

Rochette looked interested. "I hadn't thought of that," she admitted. "But she could be right, you know. If Rachel found someone to take her on she'd probably have jumped at it. It's not as if she was having a great time at home, eh? As it turns out."

To put it mildly.

"Would she have left her daughters behind, though?" said Tessa, worrying away at the thought.

"Fiona Klein seemed to think she would," Steve put in.

"Which reminds me, Tessa, didn't you think Larkin was put out when we said the girls were staying with Klein?"

Tessa turned in her seat to look at him. "Yes. Or—no—not exactly upset. But very interested. Why, do you think?"

"Have to ask her, won't we?"

"There's something else, too. Didn't you get the feeling she was waiting for us to ask her something? Then was relieved when we didn't?"

Steve shrugged. "We'll get to it," he said comfortably, and put his hands behind his head.

As Tessa turned back to face the front again she glanced at Rochette Williams. Their driver was hunched over the wheel, staring through the mist, and, very slightly, smiling. There was something rather smug about that smile.

She thinks we're up ourselves.

Or she knows more than she's telling.

"I presume no one's called in about seeing Rachel Brydie last weekend, or since, Rochette?" Tessa asked, a bit abruptly.

"Not that I've heard. But it's been on local radio and so on, as per request. Taxi drivers all say no. The railway station's unattended on the weekends, so that's useless. The neighbors were no good, I guess?"

Back to you, Detective Vance.

"No. There aren't many of them to start with. No one saw her on the road, or noticed a strange car . . ."

"But as they pointed out," said Steve from the back, "they weren't looking."

"Plus there was heavy mist last Sunday," Rochette said brightly. "Worse than this, and started earlier. Mid-afternoon."

"Right. So they told us," muttered Tessa. "Mine all said they wouldn't have seen anyone cutting through their properties either, if it was low down, away from the house. Rachel could have kept right off Lily Lane. She could have gone down to the creek, and followed it for a while then gone up to the turnoff and on to the station, or even crossed the creek and climbed up through the bush to that road that runs along the ridge . . . what is it?"

"Furze Avenue," Rochette said helpfully.

"That's right. But of course she'd only do that if she was

hiding. If she didn't want to take the slightest risk of being seen."

"Seen by the neighbors, or Quinn?" Rochette murmured.

Tessa shrugged.

"No one noticed the smoke from the fire, because of the mist," Steve said. "But there was one thing, a woman just up from the narrow bit of Lily Lane—a Dr. Iris Greenlander—"

"Old Iris, eh?" said Rochette with interest. "Geeze, she must be a hundred by now. How's her knee?"

She braked at the corner and cautiously turned left into the Oakdale main street, where the mist hung light and damp and fairy lights outlined the gables of the buildings and glowed in the branches of the trees like fallen stars.

"She didn't say a word about her knee," said Steve patiently. "What she did say was that she thought she heard a single shot at about nine-thirty on Sunday night. She didn't think anything of it. People shoot foxes around there all the time, she says. That right?"

"Yeah. They all keep chooks on that side of the line," said Rochette, stopping the car and preparing to park.

Tessa stirred impatiently. "Nine-thirty would be about right. Bliss said she dreamed of thunder just before she woke. We can presume that it was the shot that roused her . . ."

"Can we?" Steve sounded amused.

"I think so. Real sounds often work their way into dreams."

Backing into her parking spot, Rochette launched into a sprightly supporting anecdote about fighting tomcats, and her Auntie Nell's nightmare about an ax-murderer. By the time the story ended, with Auntie Nell half-strangling her bedmate, Uncle Bill, while believing she was fighting for her life, they were all out of the car.

Not surprisingly, there were few people to be seen. The shops were all closed, their footpath signs and bargain tables taken in for the night, but the wine shop a few doors up from where they were standing was still open, and the four tactfully spaced restaurants hummed with music and conversation behind their drawn curtains.

"Martin's is up there on the corner. Might be an idea to call in at the wine shop on the way," said Rochette. She was just

the driver, and a humble constable, her tone implied. It was
up to them. Nothing to do with her. But it was plain from the
parking spot she'd chosen that she considered a stop at the
wine shop appropriate.

"Good plan." Steve glanced at her with thoughtful ap-
proval. "Martin's isn't licensed, I take it?"

"No. But they'll open a bottle for you."

We shouldn't drink on duty.

Wowser. We're not on duty. Exactly.

"Should be champagne," Steve was saying. "We missed a
wedding for this, didn't we, Tess?"

Tessa nodded. She realized that she'd forgotten completely about the wedding. This morning seemed a year ago,
a world away.

A big, fair man with a red face and a loose, sulky mouth
stood behind the counter of the wine shop. He nodded, un-
smiling, and hitched at his belt as they came in.

"G'day, Rochette," he said.

"Carl," Rochette Williams acknowledged. She gestured at
Tessa and Steve. "This is Tessa Vance and Steve Hayden.
Homicide detectives from Sydney."

"Entertaining the nobs, are you?" The man still didn't
smile, but Rochette seemed unruffled. Carl Weisenhoff, presumably, affected a tough manner as a matter of course when
confronting strangers.

"Just popped in for some wine. We're eating at Martin's,"
said Rochette, leaning on the counter.

"Heard you were," the man said. "Leo came in for a bottle
of Calvados, earlier. Bunch of old ducks he had in at
lunchtime all ordered the apple pancakes and ran him out."

Rochette sniggered.

Small town . . .

"Want to come and help me choose the wine?" Steve said
to Tessa. She shrugged and shook her head. "Whatever," she
said. She knew little about wine and felt prickly, anyway,
about giving anyone the impression that she and Steve were a
couple.

He wandered off to the wine racks. Tessa and Rochette remained at the front of the shop, facing the big man over the counter.

"You're on your own tonight, Carl," Rochette commented, looking around.

"Yeah. Dave's got the flu." The man's small eyes slid in Tessa's direction. Rochette, too, glanced at her. Feeling unwelcome, she turned and moved a little away to look at the bottles ranged on shelves behind her. Sherry. She didn't like sherry, much. She wasn't interested in looking at Carl Weisenhoff's range. But she could pretend, and so the time would pass.

"You heard about Adam Quinn?" she heard Rochette say in a low voice. She edged further away. If Rochette was going to be indiscreet, she didn't want to know about it.

At the back of the shop, Steve was carefully examining wine labels.

Hurry up, Steve. How long can it take? Just get anything.

Weisenhoff was muttering. Grumbling phrases reached Tessa's unwilling ears.

". . . shock of my life . . . like hens with their heads cut off . . . some bloody meeting . . . I said to Lyn, if you think I'm going to waste my time with that crew of bloody wankers . . ."

Rochette was murmuring sympathetically.

Tessa moved on to the spirits. Brandy, whisky, gin . . .

Come on, Steve.

Weisenhoff's voice went up a notch.

". . . any of them come in here asking bloody questions they'll wish they . . ."

Is he talking about the police?

Can't be. Rochette is *the police.*

". . . I said, they'll print anything they bloody like anyhow . . ."

Journalists. He means journalists. Asking about Adam Quinn. Why would they come here, especially?

Quinn was a drinker.

Quinn was a drinker. Gin. Ten bottles of gin, lined up in the bedroom cupboard. Shelf crowded. Did he buy them here? When . . . ?

Rochette was speaking again. Asking a question. Then

Weisenhoff was answering. He'd lowered his voice again, now. Tessa had to strain to catch the odd phrase.

". . . carton, last Saturday afternoon . . . shocking . . . eyes like piss-holes in snow. I said . . . kill yourself if you go on like this, mate . . ."

Quinn picked up a carton of gin last Saturday.

". . . hear the Brydie woman pissed off and left the girls to . . . Russell Ingres was in earlier . . . reckons they . . . Fiona Klein . . . didn't even know she . . ."

Steve came up, holding out two bottles. One red, one white. "Thought we'd get both," he murmured. "We don't know what we're eating, do we? These okay by you? Or will I change them?"

"They're fine." Tessa barely glanced at the bottles. She was still trying to overhear the conversation at the counter. Steve bent towards her.

"Come on. You're cramping her style," he murmured in her ear. "We'll hear all about it at dinner."

Shocked, Tessa raised her eyebrows at him. He grinned, tucked a hand under her elbow and led her to the back of the shop. "There are ways and ways, you know, Detective," he said. He was delighted at her discomfiture.

What is this?

He's saying all this was a plan. Rochette's working. That's why we're here. She thinks Weisenhoff's going to be useful. She's showing us to him, casually, so he'll get used to the idea of us. Now she's doing a bit of preliminary softening up, finding out a few things, on the pretext of chatting indiscreetly while we're busy. So that tomorrow . . .

Why didn't she say?

She assumed we'd get it.

Why should we?

Steve did.

Tessa grimaced at the rows of wine bottles waiting for her inspection.

"Let's have champagne," she said loudly. "Let's toast Pete and Lori. I'll pay."

Her phone trilled in her handbag. Surprised, she fished it out and answered, while Rochette and Carl Weisenhoff watched with interest from the front counter.

"Fisk here."

"Fisk? Where are you?" She could hear the sound of traffic.

"In that oasis halfway down the freeway. Groceries, fast food, rest rooms, petrol and a car wash. Appalling. If they set up camp stretchers you could live here. I think some of the people here do. They certainly look like it. I stopped off to call."

"What is it?"

"That portrait. You'll recall I thought I recognized the face?"

"Yes." Tessa knew better than to hurry him.

"It came to me. It was in a magazine I read at the dentist. Many years ago. Twenty-six years ago, to be exact."

"Fisk!" Tessa exclaimed. How could the man possibly remember . . .

"I remember particularly," said Fisk loftily, ignoring the interruption, "because I was unfortunately having two wisdom teeth extracted, and had to wait forty-five minutes for the privilege. The dentist had overbooked. It was disgraceful."

He paused. Tessa jiggled with impatience, bit her tongue, and glanced at Steve. He looked amused.

"I read the article because of the accompanying photograph." Fisk's voice was thin and distant-sounding. The traffic sounds almost overwhelmed it. "She had a very distinctive face, even then. The photograph was very memorable. Unlike the prose, which was execrable. It wasn't an interview, you understand. It was what you might call an unauthorized profile. And why they bothered it's hard to fathom. It's not as though she was particularly well-known. It must have been a filler."

Oh, Fisk, get on with it!

" 'Tragic Rachel' was the headline," Fisk went on reminiscently. He was obviously enjoying this supreme example of his talent for total recall. "And I must say, there was plenty of tragedy. She was orphaned at fifteen—car crash, I think. Marriage, at twenty, while she was still a drama student, to Lloyd Perez—a theatrical producer-director. He 'discovered' her, as they say, then left his wife for her. They made it all sound very romantic in the article, called him a Svengali and so on, but he must have been a good twenty-five years older than Rachel Brydie was, and—"

"Fisk, how can you *remember* all this?"

"Oh, well." Fisk hesitated, then decided to come clean. "I daresay the mention of Perez made the article stick in my mind," he admitted reluctantly. "He did a bit of Shakespeare. He liked Chekhov, too. I'd seen several of his productions. Liked his work. I'd read he'd died—"

"Died?" Tessa gasped the word. Too loudly, because she noted Rochette and Carl glance at one another. Steve was prospecting in the refrigerator cabinet for champagne, apparently taking no notice at all. He was too old a hand to hang around waiting for tidbits of information that he'd soon enough get in full.

"Very sad," said Fisk calmly. "He and Rachel did very well for a few years. But it went sour, as these things tend to do. He was already effectively an alcoholic when she met him and it started showing. The work suffered. He had a few rocky productions, then two complete duds in a row. Then he suicided."

"Suicide . . ." This time Tessa remembered to keep her voice down. She just breathed the word.

"Don't jump to any conclusions," snapped Fisk. "Remember your psychology."

"I am remembering it. What happened to Rachel after that?"

"According to the article she had some sort of catastrophic breakdown and retired from public life. Tragic loss to the world of theatre, it said. Well, it would. Whether it's true or not I can't say. I never saw her on the stage. Presumably she eventually recovered, sold what little was left of Perez's assets and—"

"Moved up here. She's been here for twenty-five years, apparently."

No wonder she called the place Haven.

It probably was a haven, too. Until . . .

"Well, there you are," said Fisk. "Thought I'd let you know.

Not that it helps particularly with the present problem. But it fills the story out."

"Yes. Thanks. Thanks very much."

"I'll let you go and be on my way. I want to be on time for the postmortem. No doubt we'll be in touch tomorrow morning. Have a good evening," Fisk said politely, and cut the connection.

Twelve

"So she's a natural victim. Perfect prey for Quinn." Steve sipped champagne "This is good," he added absentmindedly.

The champagne *was* good, thought Tessa. It didn't suit the weather, the occasion, the place, her pocket or her mood, but it had been a pleasure to defy all those. It had been a pleasure, too, to see the barely concealed surprise on Rochette Williams's face when she carried the bottle to the counter. It was nice to do something, however small, that Constable Williams didn't expect, for once.

Martin's restaurant was good, too, if you could go by atmosphere and appearances. It was warmly lit, and artfully arranged to seem relaxed, but intimate. Flowered curtains were drawn across the windows, shutting out the darkness, the cold and the mist. The old polished floorboards gleamed warm red-brown. There were flowers and antique silver on a sideboard, a fire burning in the fireplace. The restful restaurant sounds of background music, low voices and the soft chinking of knives and forks on china filled the room.

Every table was occupied. In one corner five women and a man sat hunched over their food, engaged in earnest conversation. At least, four of the women and the man were talking. The other woman was very definitely out of it. Her pale face was bored and irritated.

"That's Carl's wife, Lyn," Rochette whispered. "The main street committee's called an emergency meeting. Because of Quinn popping off. They don't want any bad publicity for Oakdale, see?"

"Did you know the street committee was meeting here?"

asked Tessa suspiciously. She saw Lyn Weisenhoff glance their way and bite her lip.

They know who we are.

"Well, they always meet here," Rochette said, the picture of innocence.

Their table was in a corner. A young woman who had introduced herself as Juliette had dealt with the champagne, brought bread rolls and taken their orders from the simple but impressive menu with a perfect mix of friendliness and practiced efficiency. Then she'd left them to themselves.

Rochette leaned forward, her glass clutched in her hand. "Why do you say Rachel Brydie's a victim?" she demanded. "I really don't understand why you say that, just because her first husband knocked himself off. She never looked like a victim to me. When I was a kid I was scared to death of her. We all were. We thought she was a witch. Long hair streaming down, weird clothes—you should see her!"

"I have seen her," said Tessa softly, remembering the portrait.

"Think about it, Rochette," said Steve. "Every man she's ever been involved with has let her down. They've all been drunks, drifters, pigs—they've all preyed on her."

"It was her choice. She chose them."

"That's the awful part," urged Tessa. "She chose them. That's what often happens. People choose the same type, all the time. As though they can't help themselves."

Rochette pursed her lips. "I don't go for all that psycho stuff," she sniffed. "If you ask me, Rachel Brydie knew exactly what she was doing, every step of the way. She might've bitten off more than she could chew with Adam Quinn, but she fixed that, in the end, didn't she?"

"You think she killed him?" Now it was Tessa's turn to lean forward, glass in hand. "Then why didn't she wait till he was asleep and kill him in bed?"

"He was a drunk. He could've passed out—"

"In that filthy shed?"

"She could've drugged him. Or poisoned him. She's practically a witch, you know. She knows all sorts of stuff about herbs and seeds and stuff."

"You mean she gave Quinn something that acted so fast he couldn't even make it to the bedroom?"

"It's possible."

Tessa snorted. Steve decided it was time to intervene.

"The postmortem's being done," he said peacefully. "There'll be tissue analysis, chemical tests and so on. If Quinn was drugged or poisoned or tied up or hit on the head before being shot we'll find out about it. All right? Let's just take it easy. The food'll be coming soon."

There was a moment's silence. But it wasn't restful.

"Your boss thinks it's murder," muttered Rochette.

She's right there. She's smart. She picks up on things.

She's prejudiced. She picks up on things that fit her narrow views.

Be fair.

"Look," Tessa exclaimed, "Rochette, I'm not dismissing anything, right? I'm simply saying that it's most likely that Quinn tried to murder Bliss, Skye and Astral and then committed suicide because Rachel ran out on him."

She noticed that a couple of people at the street committee table were glancing her way, and took a deep breath.

Take it easy.

"Remember, Haven was Rachel's house," she went on more quietly. "Quinn thought he was secure there—but what if he suddenly realized that Rachel had found a new man? Someone she could ask for help—who might stand up to Quinn—throw him out?"

"You're saying she goes away with this guy—" Steve began.

"She goes away with this guy, leaving the girls to cover for her, tell Quinn some story about how she just went out, and they don't know where," Tessa interrupted.

"They're still telling the same story now," Rochette pointed out.

Tessa shrugged. "Maybe they really don't know about the boyfriend. Maybe they really don't know where Rachel is, or who she's with. Anyway, Quinn finds out or guesses what's doing. His mad little kingdom is threatened, isn't it? He's angry. Wild. He's probably very drunk anyway. He wants revenge. So he drugs the girls, and sets the fire. He leaves them to smother in the smoke, and burn with the house. But he doesn't like the idea of burning to death himself, so he goes to the shed and lays himself out and uses the gun."

"Why?" Rochette asked bluntly. "I mean, why lie down?"

"Maybe it was a sort of ceremony. Maybe he'd started to believe his own propaganda, and thought he'd rise from the dead stronger than ever. Who knows?"

"Megalomaniacs make up their own reasons for things," murmured Steve.

"What?"

"Just something Jonathon Stoller said."

Rochette maintained a stubborn silence.

Steve cleared his throat. "The problem with the murder-suicide theory—Thorne's problem with the murder-suicide theory—is that he's seen a lot of them. So have I—so have you, Tess—but not as many as he has. And it's not that common for the killer to kill himself without making sure that the victims are actually dead. Is it?"

"It happens."

"Sometimes. But Adam Quinn doesn't sound like the sort of man who'd take the chance the girls were going to survive, does he? Why didn't he wait and make sure? Better still, why didn't he shoot them, as well as himself?"

"He might have thought they'd run away before he could get them all," said Tessa.

"Nah. They were stonkered on gin. They weren't going anywhere," said Rochette flatly.

Tessa tried again. "He might have thought the shots would attract too much attention. Someone might have come and stopped him before he had the chance of killing himself."

"Nah," Rochette said again. "Not round Haven. Old Dr. Iris told you—if they even noticed they'd just think it was someone banging away at a fox they sprung having a go at the chooks."

She leaned back in her chair. "No. I reckon our boss is right, and yours is too. Whatever your mate Tootsie finds when she cuts Quinn up, it was murder. Somehow, it was murder. And I'll tell you why I think so. I don't know much about murderers, but I know a lot about drunks. According to Carl Weisenhoff, Quinn bought a full case of gin last Saturday. Quinn told Carl he was all out. Finished his last bottle on Friday. A case is twelve bottles, right? But there were ten bottles lined up in that bedroom cupboard. He'd hardly started on the stuff when he got the chop. And I don't care how angry he was. That's just not on."

She looked across the room and her face brightened. The kitchen door had swung open and Juliette was bearing down on them with steaming plates and dishes. Their food was on its way.

At home in his little red-roofed house, Jonathon Stoller was eating sardines on toast. He knew he had to eat something so he could keep the headache pills down. Whiteness swirled at his windows. The forest, the paddock and even his driveway had been blotted out. It was as if they didn't exist— as if his house was an island in the mist.

He had the radio on—for company, and so he could hear the news bulletins every half hour. He'd heard the story of Adam Quinn's death repeated several times by now, always in the same words. The report was brief, but accurate—based on a police media unit press release, he assumed. It contained a request for information as to the whereabouts of Rachel Brydie, so he knew that they still hadn't found her.

For the first time Jonathon wished he'd bought a TV set for the house. He'd decided not to—often told his friends at work how great it was to be rid of the tyranny of the box on weekends. He was always so gloriously tired after a long day in the fresh air, he often said, that Saturday nights for him were a simple meal, a good book, and bed early. He was often up at dawn the next day. Up with the kookaburras. Some of his friends said they envied him. Others, more honest, perhaps, said it sounded like hell, and they thought he was mad.

But if he had a TV set now he could watch something, take his mind off things. There might be a movie. If it was bad, so much the better. It might put him to sleep.

For he didn't see how he could sleep.

He'd turned his mobile phone off. He was afraid someone

would ring him. Not the police—after this afternoon they wouldn't try to talk to him again till morning. But one of his friends, who'd heard the news. They all knew that Adam Quinn lived next door to him. He'd mentioned it to them, carefully casual, as soon as he found out himself. A celebrity, even a faded one, gave the locale cachet, and Quinn's checkered past merely added to the glamor.

One or more of them were bound to be trying him, right now. He couldn't face the thought of speaking to them, answering their avid questions.

If he lied to them—about Astral, about how well he knew her, they might find out, later, that he'd lied. Whether they found out depended entirely on what he and Astral told the police, what she told Bliss and Skye, what she told Fiona Klein, what the press picked up. But it was a risk. If he told his friends the truth about Astral, he'd have to explain why he knew how she was living, and did nothing.

They wouldn't understand. He barely understood himself. He'd always thought of himself as streetwise, but he hadn't been able to focus on most of the things Astral had confided in him or let slip over the past months, let alone what she had admitted to him, finally, last Sunday.

A wave of heat swept over him, even now, thinking of it. It had been like turning over a stone and finding some nameless, disgusting thing underneath. It was like a headline in the kinds of magazines he'd be embarrassed to be seen buying or even reading at the dentist's. Consumed by a dark, possessive, primitive rage he hadn't known he was capable of, he'd told her he wasn't going to stay out of it any more. She could see he meant it. Literally, she'd nearly fainted. She'd begged him, kneeling in front of him and embracing his ankles in an agony of fear.

And he had wavered, bent to her, given in. Even then.

How could he explain it?

He couldn't explain it. So he couldn't talk to his friends. There was only one person he wanted to talk to. Astral.

But Astral wouldn't call. She'd seen his mobile phone, and marvelled at it, when he brought it down to the fence one day because he was waiting to hear from a guy who was going to quote on new guttering for the house. But she didn't know his number.

And he didn't know where she was. It was the first time, he realized, that he hadn't known—known exactly.

When he'd finally screwed up his courage and gone next door to try to see her, the police officer on duty had told him that the sisters had gone to stay with a friend. Jonathan knew what that meant. Astral was with Fiona Klein—who had a house somewhere in Oakdale, presumably. But where in Oakdale?

His head was heavy and there was a feeling of aching emptiness in his chest. He hadn't, somehow, expected the girls to leave Haven. He'd just assumed that they'd stay on there, for the time being. It had been a shock to find that Fiona Klein had taken charge of them.

He didn't like the idea. He hadn't liked Klein. She'd seemed—what?—proprietorial, that was the word—about Astral. And after all, Jonathon was the one who had the right to be proprietorial, if anyone did.

But of course Klein wasn't to know that. And he hadn't offered to have Astral, Bliss and Skye at his place. He'd been with them all morning, and he'd never thought to suggest it. It hadn't occurred to him that it was an option, and Astral would never have presumed she had the right to ask. She never presumed anything.

Jonathon moved restlessly, pushing away his plate. He'd blown it. He'd made too many assumptions. He had only himself to blame. Though maybe Bliss and Skye wouldn't have agreed to come to him, anyway. They hadn't been happy about Astral calling him in in the first place.

This thought made him feel a bit better. He reached out to his plate again, and nibbled at a crust of toast. He stared at the phone. Turned off. Silent. If only he'd given Astral the number. Why hadn't he? Because there was no phone at Haven, he told himself. And Astral rarely went out. She didn't have access to a phone.

But Fiona Klein would have a phone.

The thought drifted into his mind and he blinked at it stupidly, then actually boxed his own ears in frustration. Of course! What was wrong with him? How stupid could he be? He was acting as if his brains had been scrambled.

He leaped up and got the local phone directory from the shelf. The local directory had always amused him. It was so thin—white pages at the front, yellow pages at the back. Now he was just grateful for its reassuring brevity. He flicked through the pages. He found the Kleins. There weren't many—and there was only one in Oakdale. Klein, F.W. 12 Greys Lookout Drive.

Jonathon grabbed his phone, turned it on. The tiny time it took to react was agony. He punched in the number.

Engaged signal. He was absurdly disappointed. He waited three minutes, redialed. Still busy. Who could the woman be talking to? The police?

He waited five minutes before calling again, and when the engaged signal sounded once more, flew into a temper. He paced around the room, and rang again. Engaged. He sat doggedly pressing the recall button over and over again, cursing and gritting his teeth.

Thirteen

Lyn Weisenhoff sat with her back to the wall in her usual spot at the street committee's usual table in the most discreet corner of Martin's restaurant. Her plate had been taken away, the delicate scraps of veal glazed with translucent golden-brown sauce, the fragrant rice, even the coriander garnish, almost untouched. A full glass of wine stood in front of her. They'd refilled it without asking her. She knew she wouldn't drink it.

As always, Martin's was a pleasant place to be. It had been truly inspired of Michael O'Malley to suggest a couple of years ago, on his first joining the committee, that the bi-monthly meeting could be held here, over dinner, instead of at the members' houses in rotation as had been the practice. He for one, he said, didn't want to cater. He had enough trouble feeding himself. And Martin's was always very slow on Tuesdays. Juliette and Leo would give the committee mate's rates, he was sure, for a fixed-price meal.

Freda Ridge had resisted the suggestion at first. She quite enjoyed being able to display her home, her cooking and her household management skills when it was her or Charles's turn to play host. Freda was incredibly efficient in everything she did. When the committee arrived at Freda's place, an imaginative but easily served meal was always ready, the table was set, the children were bathed, fed and tucked away downstairs doing homework or playing quietly, the house was pleasantly tidy and the answering machine was on.

The same could not be said for the evenings at anyone else's house. Notably the Weisenhoffs'.

It wasn't as though she was a bad manager, Lyn thought resentfully. Things bumped along in average fashion normally. But committee meetings were always held on weeknights when, after her stint in the wine shop, it was always a rush for her to get the children organized, the house tidy and any kind of meal cooked. Weeknights were not the time for entertaining.

Her cooking was chancy under pressure, for a start. And Carl, of course, resenting and despising the whole committee thing, was unhelpful in the extreme. Unlike Charles Ridge, who on meeting nights ran obediently along the tracks Freda had set down for him, doing in order the tasks she regarded as within his competence, Carl usually hung around grumbling, stirred up the children, then went out, leaving the bathroom steamy, the vanity basin strewn with hairs, and his towel on the floor.

And the children were less biddable than Freda's. Certainly, Freda had a teenage daughter called Heidi who appeared to be a model of competence where her younger brother and sister were concerned. But even when Heidi was out—at math's coaching, or a flute lesson, or engaging in some other worthy and enriching evening pursuit—the younger children behaved. Lyn's children did not. Whatever Lyn said to them, threatened them with or promised them, however carefully she had prepared, they didn't stay out of the way like the small Ridges. Unsupervised, they became overexcited, argumentative and destructive. They'd come wandering in together or in succession, clutching broken or injured toys, complaining about each other, wanting Lyn to referee arguments, saying they were hungry or thirsty, hot or cold. When the time came to put them to bed, they were clinging and wouldn't settle. Freda's children, on the other hand, kissed their parents sweetly, said polite goodnights to everyone else and put themselves to bed.

So enticing was the prospect of relief from what had become both an onerous duty and a regular opportunity for odious comparisons that for once Lyn found it easy to stand up to Freda. She enthusiastically embraced Michael O'Malley's suggestion to hold all future street committee meetings at Martin's. The other members of the committee agreed too—

so readily that Lyn did wonder afterwards if they found Freda's efficiency as daunting as she did.

On Tuesday nights they usually had the restaurant almost to themselves. But tonight, it was full. Every table was occupied, and several groups had been turned away. This made Lyn feel guilty and uncomfortable. Freda had said that Juliette Martin had been pleased to accept their booking, but Lyn doubted it. Juliette had probably cursed when she hung up the phone. What restaurateur in her right mind would be pleased to have a table for six taken up on the busiest night of the week by a group paying mate's rates?

In the corner of the room diagonally opposite from the street committee table sat Rochette Williams with the two Homicide detectives from Sydney. Carl had told Lyn they'd be here. She found it difficult not to keep looking at them. They were talking animatedly, but except on the odd occasion kept their voices down. She wondered what they were discussing.

Long ago—sometime during the main course—she'd tuned out of the conversation at her own table. She knew that no one would notice or care that she was being inattentive. And she was missing nothing. Floss Reitenberg talked. Charles Ridge talked. Freda talked. Maryanne Lamplough talked. Phillida Browning talked. Freda talked again.

If Michael O'Malley was here, he'd be talking too, and then the meeting might have got somewhere, because Michael, a cynical eyebrow raised, was always able to stop the others in their tracks when they strayed off into fanciful and time-wasting paths. But of course Michael wasn't here. Michael was at home, as he'd been all week, leaving the bookshop to Floss and a bewildered, hurriedly employed casual who Floss said didn't know Austen from Auden, and recommended stationery items to the undecided because "you were always safe with a calendar."

Lyn's eyes strayed to the fire. She didn't feel guilty on account of her inattention. She knew she was only at the meeting to add to the numbers. She knew she'd only been elected to it in the first place because she was enough of a bunny to accept nomination, and she offended no one. She had nothing to contribute. Her presence was totally unnecessary.

For an hour she had been bored, as she had known she would be. She had been irritated, as she had known she would be. She had said nothing, as she had known would be the case. From the start, the emergency meeting had been pointless, as such meetings always were in her experience.

Not that the main street committee had had a problem like this to discuss previously. The closest thing to it was that poor Japanese woman who'd been sideswiped and badly injured by a delivery truck while posing for a photograph beside her tourist bus. The death of Adam Quinn at Haven was more exciting altogether. It gave everyone the chance of airing his or her opinions and trotting out old anecdotes and grievances. Charles Ridge, expanding, enjoying being the only male present, had even managed to drag in his personal favorite, the Council's land and environment development policies, for blame and censure. As though five-acre lots unable to be subdivided, like Haven, somehow encouraged eccentricity, suicide, murder.

In a way, though, Lyn was grateful for the chance to be away from home tonight. She realized that she preferred sitting at the corner table at Martin's, bored witless, to sitting in front of the TV set alone with her thoughts while the kids slept and Carl talked Adam Quinn with Russell Ingres and the rest at Swans.

Carl usually had little time for Russell Ingres. A jumped-up little turd in uniform, he'd called him once to Lyn, when Russell got him for driving eighty in a seventy zone on the highway. But Russell had come into the shop just before Lyn left for home, and Carl was all over him.

It was only because Russell had inside information, of course. And Russell knew it, too. He wasn't giving anything away for nothing. Not to Carl. He made Carl work for every little tidbit. They circled each other like two dogs for ten minutes, their smiles like snarls, while Lyn watched from the sidelines, despising them both.

Carl wouldn't be very happy when she got home. He'd be sulky because he'd had to stay home to baby-sit. The whole macho Oakdale push would be at Swans tonight—scoffing down beer in the bar while Bouncy Bernadette wowed diners in the restaurant. Carl would be furious to be missing the boozy, leering discussion of the latest Brydie sensation. And they said women gossiped! Women had nothing on those men, as Lyn had often observed, seeing them in action in the shop.

It was very lucky, really, that Freda had organized the meeting. Lyn wouldn't have been able to stop Carl going out, if she'd been home to take care of the children. He wouldn't have listened to her. He never did. These days he was rarely home in the evenings, which suited Lyn just fine. But it was just as well to keep him away from Russell Ingres tonight. With a few drinks inside him, he could say anything.

Lyn shivered slightly, and drew her cardigan more tightly around her. She couldn't get warm. It was as though the fire was artificial—full of bright flames, but giving out no heat at all. Yet other people in the room were in shirtsleeves. Perhaps it was just Lyn's corner that was cold—a freakishly chill, drafty little air pocket that the heat somehow couldn't penetrate. Or maybe the chill was inside her, deep inside, like a hard, white lump of ice.

She became aware that Freda had now raised the question of who among them should be responsible for what she insisted on calling "media liaison." Everyone at the table was perfectly aware that Freda wanted this job for herself (and CountryWise), or failing that, for Charles (and Ridge Real Estate)—but was waiting for someone else to make the suggestion.

"What about Michael O'Malley?" Maryanne Lamplough said, looking brightly around. "He's *very* presentable, and *awfully* articulate, and the bookshop would make a *marvellous* background for TV interviews. Not too *commercial*-looking, you know?"

"Michael? Oh, no, I don't think so, Maryanne," said Freda, swelling almost visibly with irritation.

"I know he's had the flu," Maryanne continued, not to be squashed, "but he must be feeling *much* better by now, *surely*, and I just know he'd—"

"It's not a matter of his fitness, dear," snapped Freda. "His *physical* fitness. It's just that given poor Michael's past history, it could be a little bit awkward . . ."

She paused, significantly. Charles Ridge mumbled and guffawed. Floss and Phillida exchanged meaningful glances.

So it's begun, thought Lyn. Well, it was only a matter of time. Michael must know that. He knows this place. Who better?

"Why awkward, Freda?" asked Maryanne breathlessly, eyes wide. "Oh, have I said the wrong thing?"

Maryanne was a relative newcomer to Oakdale, having only taken over Oakdale Gifts and Fancies six months ago. She affected a tentative manner, and was fluttering and deferential, but she'd eased herself smoothly onto the street committee at the recent elections, and had been slowly building her power base ever since. In a year or two, Lyn thought, Maryanne would be giving Freda a run for her money as chief pushy person around the place.

And Freda knew it. "Oh, we wouldn't expect you to understand all the ins and outs, Maryanne," she said kindly. "It's always awkward, when you're new to a place. It's so easy to put your foot in it, isn't it?"

She let that sink in, then continued, lowering her voice and glancing at the detectives' table across the room. "It's just that Michael and Rachel Brydie were—close—at one time. Before Adam Quinn came along and stole Michael's thunder. And even after that—well, Michael's always been a great admirer of Mrs. Brydie's in his own quiet way, bless his heart. And of course Mrs. Brydie has—well—decamped. It might seem a bit—odd—in the village, if he were our spokesperson, under the circumstances. And if the press were to find out . . . Embarrassing. You see my point?" She paused triumphantly. "Now—any other suggestions? Lyn?"

Lyn jumped slightly. "Why don't you do it, Freda?" she murmured, following what she knew to be her cue.

Freda hesitated, and pursed her lips, as if considering the matter for the first time. "Yes, well, I'm rushed off my feet at the moment, but I could do it, I suppose," she said at last. "If you're all sure I'd be *presentable* and *articulate* enough." She laughed harshly.

Everyone but Maryanne Lamplough, who was smiling and pretending fluttering confusion, murmured and shifted in their seats. Even Charles, chuckling artificially along with his wife, had reddened with embarrassment, and his blunt fingers, tufted with black hair, drummed the tablecloth.

Lyn risked closing her eyes for a moment. Who was going to notice?

Michael O'Malley had long, smooth fingers. He didn't laugh often, but when he did he threw back his head so you saw the smooth skin of his throat above his open-necked shirt. His white teeth gleamed through his light-brown beard, and his intelligent gray eyes crinkled with mirth behind his gold-rimmed glasses.

Michael and Rachel Brydie were "close" at one time. That was what Freda had said. Her aim in saying it had been to put Maryanne Lamplough in her place, but she'd spoken the truth. Everyone knew it: Lyn most of all. What else had she thought about, standing in the bookshop sipping coffee from one of Michael O'Malley's cups, talking books with him, feeling the distance between them? How often had she wished that she was more capable of fooling herself? That she could pretend to see in Michael's disillusioned gray eyes, when he talked to her, that gleam of intrigued sensuality that lit them when he looked at Rachel Brydie?

Rachel Brydie was still missing, according to the news. The girls were staying with Fiona Klein, according to Russell Ingres. And Adam Quinn's body had been taken back to Sydney to be autopsied.

Lyn had seen a TV documentary about an autopsy. She'd read descriptions of autopsies in novels, too. She knew exactly what would happen.

They'd cut the body across from each armpit to the breastbone. Then they'd cut down the center right to the groin. They called that the Y incision. They'd take out all the internal organs, weigh them and measure them, and slice off pieces of them to test. With a little electric saw they'd cut through the skull, exposing the brain. And after they'd looked at the brain in place they'd cut it free and remove it, too.

And then Adam Quinn would be really dead. An empty carcass. Later, when they knew every single thing about him and the way he died—or thought they did—they'd put all the bits and pieces back inside the body, and sew it up again. Sometimes, Lyn had read, the organs were put back jumbled all together in a plastic bag. Vaguely she wondered if a body as decayed as Adam Quinn's had been could still be sewn back together. Or would the skin be—

"Lyn?" Freda's voice was bright, but tinged with reproach. Lyn opened her eyes to meet the amused gazes of the rest of the street committee. She felt her face warming, and knew that her chin, forehead and cheeks were staining unbecoming scarlet.

"I—was listening," she lied. "It's just—I've got a bit of a headache."

But even as Freda exclaimed, commiserated, fussed, signalled to the waitress, asked for aspirin, Lyn saw Floss and Phillida exchange a second meaningful glance.

They knew.

Tessa took a last, sublime mouthful of salmon and regretfully put down her knife and fork. It was possible, she thought, that she'd never eaten anything so delicious.

"The street committee party's breaking up," Steve commented, jerking his head slightly at the table across the room.

Tessa glanced up. The pale young woman—Lyn Weisenhoff—was edging awkwardly between the wall and the table, murmuring apologetically, clutching her handbag high against her chest with one hand, patting at her rather untidy hair with the other. Three of the other women had money out on the table, and were swapping notes and coins, presumably so they could pay their exact share of the bill.

Lyn rounded the table and headed for the door, determinedly staring straight ahead. A dangling hairpin fell onto her shoulder and then to the floor. She balked, then walked quickly on.

"She shouldn't wear her hair long, should she?" said

Rochette critically. "It hasn't got enough body." She shook her own cropped head. "I know some men've got a thing about long hair, but if you haven't got the wherewithal, there's no good crying for the moon." She wiped her plate clean with the last of her bread roll, and ate the resultant dripping morsel with appreciation.

"Looks pretty sick, doesn't she?" she added, watching poor Lyn say goodnight to Juliette and slip away into the night. "Maybe she's got something on her mind."

Why draw attention to Lyn Weisenhoff? Unless . . .

Rochette swallowed, licked her lips, and sighed. "Whatever was in that, it wasn't bad at all," she pronounced, pushing her knife and fork together, and her plate slightly away from her. "Anyone else having pud?"

"What could Lyn Weisenhoff have on her mind, Rochette?" asked Tessa.

Rochette made a face. "If you were married to a scumbag like Carl Weisenhoff you'd have a few things to think about, wouldn't you?" she said airily. "Like how much longer you could put up with him, for instance."

She's fudging. Don't let her get away with it. Not again.

Juliette approached and cleared their plates, accepting their compliments with a smile, and promising to pass them on to "Leo."

"She's Leo Martin's wife," Rochette told them, after she'd gone. "She really runs this place. Does all the accounts, and everything. Leo's just the cook."

"Just the cook?" grinned Steve. "He's a genius."

"He is. What's he doing up here?" said Tessa, without thinking.

They both stared at her.

Mistake.

"I think he likes it here," said Rochette stiffly. "Some people do."

Juliette came back with dessert menus and waited.

Rochette studied her menu with absorbed attention, finally ordering sticky toffee pudding and cream. Steve, predictably, went for the apple pie. Juliette looked in a friendly way at Tessa and raised her eyebrows.

You don't need dessert.

Chocolate. Chocolate mousse. Profiteroles with—

Tessa ordered lemon sorbet, was sorry as soon as the words left her mouth, and asked for chocolate mousse instead. Juliette left, smiling slightly to herself. She was slim as a whip, and looked as if even as a child her idea of indulgence had been two carrot sticks instead of one.

"Anorexic, if you ask me," said Rochette, eyeing the narrow retreating back.

"Never mind that. What else would you be thinking, if you were Lyn Weisenhoff?" Tessa demanded. She might have put her foot in it about country living, but she wasn't going to be trifled with by Constable Williams.

Rochette blinked innocently. "Oh, I dunno. Whether you'd rather have been doing the wild thing with someone else for the last few years, I guess."

"You're not saying she was in love with Adam Quinn, are you?" said Steve.

Rochette's little eyes gleamed. "Nah," she grinned. "He wasn't her type."

"Who *is* her type then?" snapped Tessa.

Rochette realized she was cornered, and gave in with good grace.

"The guy who runs the bookshop, I'd say," she said. "Lyn Weisenhoff's always in O'Malley's with her tongue hanging out."

It was an ugly phrase that didn't seem to fit the pale, inoffensive woman who'd slipped so apologetically from the restaurant. Perhaps Rochette realized this, because she immediately corrected herself. "I shouldn't really say, 'with her tongue hanging out,' " she said. "She doesn't make a big thing of it. But it's pretty obvious."

Three more people had left the street committee table now, and the two remaining, a short, hefty woman with a severely controlled blond pageboy bob and a plump man with a moustache—Freda and Charles Ridge, according to Rochette—were carefully counting notes and coins onto the tray that had held the bill. They were taking their time. Juliette hovered discreetly nearby. The moment they seemed satisfied she moved forward, smiling, took the money and firmly said goodbye.

The couple moved towards the door, and then the woman murmured something to the man and wheeled around, fumbling in her handbag.

"Freda wants a word," murmured Rochette. "I didn't think she'd be able to resist it." Her plain face was impassive, but her little eyes burned with triumph.

She planned this.

Tessa glanced at Steve. He was grinning, leaning back in his chair, preparing to enjoy himself.

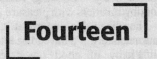
The next moment the Ridges were standing beside them, introducing themselves, and Rochette, rather grandly, was introducing Tessa and Steve in their turn.

"I do apologize for disturbing your dinner," said Freda Ridge, peering at them inquisitively and far from apologetically, taking in everything, from their clothes to the empty champagne bottle in the ice bucket by the table, "but I said to Charles, I really mustn't miss this opportunity to say hello, and to tell you if there's anything I can do, anything at all, you shouldn't hesitate to ask."

In her hand she had a pen and a small buff card, printed with the legend "CountryWise." Quickly she turned the card over and wrote down a phone number and the words "Main Street Committee Media Liaison Officer." She handed the card to Steve.

"I'm in the shop ten till three, before and after that at home at this number," she instructed, tapping the handwritten number with a well-manicured pink nail. "The answering machine is always on if I've popped out."

Steve thanked her gravely, and pocketed the card.

"Charles—give them your card, too," Freda Ridge ordered. "You never know."

The genial Charles obediently pulled out a small leather case of cards, slid one out with practiced ease, and passed it over.

Steve glanced at it. "How's the property market?" he asked pleasantly.

"Excellent, at the moment," said Charles. He eyed Steve

speculatively. "Looking round for something, are you? Mixing business with pleasure. Ha, ha!"

"I've been thinking about it," said Steve. "Not to live in, unfortunately. It'd have to be let—some of the time, anyway."

"Plenty of good investment properties round here." Charles rubbed his hands. "Rental market's very strong. Long lets, holiday lets—you name it." He got down to business. "Look, you come and see me and I'll fix you up with something, no worries. Got a list of good tenants crying out for places."

"Is that right?"

"Trust me! Lovely young couples looking for long lets. Waiting to buy their own place, or build, you know?"

He paused. Freda Ridge, smiling beside him, moved slightly. Tessa could have sworn she'd given her husband a tiny nudge. Prompting him to wind up the conversation? Or to say something else?

Presumably the latter, because Charles gave a small start, and became reanimated. "You want to help them, but it's not easy," he said, presumably still referring to lovely young couples. He caught his nose between thumb and forefinger and rubbed it vigorously.

"Had to turf one young pair out just recently," he went on, his eyes fixed on the wall behind Steve's head. "Owner was overseas, came back to the area earlier than she'd thought, wanted her place back—and do you think I could find them anything else? No way. Nothing available. Not a sausage. Finally did it, right on the knocker, the day before the lease expired, but it was a near thing."

"That was Fiona Klein's place, wasn't it, Charles?" said Freda, with a lumbering attempt at casualness.

Tessa almost smiled. So that was it. Freda Ridge was on a fishing expedition.

"Wasn't that awful? Putting you under that pressure. How could she just ring up, out of the blue, and expect you to let her break the lease?" Freda rattled on. She shook her head at the table in general. "Really, some owners are so—"

"Oh, well . . ." Charles interrupted smoothly, aware that whatever his wife's agenda might be, he was at that very moment in the presence of a prospective investor. "You can understand. It was awkward for her, wasn't it?" He beamed around. "But a lease is a lease. She only had to put up in a hotel for two weeks—not too bad—she had to buy a car, anyway . . ."

Two weeks. Klein's been back over two weeks. But Steve said . . .

Tessa looked quickly at Steve. His posture hadn't changed, but he was alert. She could see it.

". . . and she's right now back in her own place," Charles Ridge was continuing, anxious to make sure they understood everything was now hunky-dory. "I haven't seen her yet, but the house was left beautifully clean. I'm sure she's happy. And the Brinburns are all right, tucked up in Cranwell Road, happy as pigs in mud. So all's well that ends well."

"Well, yes. And really, it's lucky she did come back when she did, isn't it? I heard the Brydie girls were actually *staying* with her." Freda's wide-eyed innocence as she pursued the information she sought was obviously, excruciatingly fake. Whatever else the woman was, she was no actor.

Rachel Brydie was an actor.

The thought popped into Tessa's mind out of nowhere. She glanced at it, then forced it aside. That was something to think about later. It could mean everything, or nothing. And it wasn't germane to the issue at present. The issue of whether Fiona Klein had intentionally misled Steve about how long she'd been back in the country.

"I just couldn't *believe* they went to stay with her!" Freda Ridge was gushing. "I said to Charles, 'I just can't *believe* that!' Didn't I, Charles?"

Charles nodded unhappily.

"Is it true?" demanded Freda, suddenly growing weary of subtlety.

"Oh, yes," said Tessa. "Temporarily. We needed Haven empty for a little while, you see."

"Oh, I *see*," Freda breathed. "You *made* them leave. Right. I thought it was funny. I didn't think for a *minute* they'd actually go to stay with Fiona Klein by choice, whatever people said. Well, I mean—you know—it wouldn't be *my* cup of tea."

"Why's that, Mrs. Ridge?" asked Steve.

Freda Ridge looked at him archly, told him to call her Freda, and said Fiona Klein just wasn't her type of person.

Charles Ridge cleared his throat. "Takes all kinds. Ha, ha," he mumbled.

"They could have gone to a hotel. But they preferred Miss Klein's place," said Tessa shortly.

Freda pursed her lips. Her eyes glittered. "Wouldn't be my cup of tea," she repeated. "But there you are. And of course with their mother away—she *is* still away, isn't she?"

"As far as we know, yes."

"I heard an announcement on the news. On the radio. It said the police wanted to hear from her, or anyone who knew where she was."

"That's right."

Freda put her head on one side. "So it's *strange*, isn't it, that she hasn't turned up?" she said. "Unless she's staying away *deliberately*? I mean, I can't imagine Rachel Brydie being *unnoticed*, wherever she was. Can you, Charles?"

Charles shook his head, chuckling nervously.

"I mean," Freda continued, "the way she looks. It's—*extremely* distinctive. To put it mildly." She laughed.

Juliette approached the table with a tray. Nodding pleasantly to Freda and Charles, she began setting out the desserts in front of Tessa, Steve and Rochette.

Freda stared and tittered, entirely unabashed. "Well, don't they look yummy!" she exclaimed. "Don't our police do well for themselves?"

"No better than you did, I bet," said Rochette perkily. "And we only get ordinary meal allowances if we're away from home, you know. Any extra, we pay."

Freda wagged a finger at her. "Oh, I know all about that, Rochette," she said playfully. Then she smiled. "No, no. Just joking," she said. "It's good to see young people eat, isn't it, Charles? Charles and I have to watch our waistlines so we never have dessert—except for fresh fruit, frozen yogurt sometimes. Isn't that right, Charles?"

Charles mumbled, and gazed with longing at Steve's hot apple pie and cream.

Freda tugged at his arm. "We really must go and let these people finish their dinner in peace," she said, as though he was the one who had insisted on intruding. She twinkled at Tessa and Steve. "Now, don't you forget—call any time. And if you have any media inquiries about Oakdale generally, don't hesitate to put them on to me. Don't hesitate."

They both nodded and murmured appropriate reassurances, and, satisfied, Freda fluttered a hand at them and departed, with Charles in tow.

"All right, Rochette," said Steve firmly, as soon as they were alone. "What're you playing at?"

Constable Williams hesitated, her spoon hovering over her fragrant, steaming bowl. She raised her eyebrow. "Just giving you a tour of the zoo," she said, and grinned.

Tessa leaned forward. "Didn't you say Fiona Klein told you she'd only been back here for a couple of days?" she asked Steve.

He dug his spoon into his apple pie. "Yeah," he said slowly. "But I didn't ask her when she got back into the country. I didn't think about it." He frowned. "Think there's anything in it?"

"Could be."

Rochette was watching them, her mouth full of sticky toffee pudding and cream, her face a study in fascination.

. . . *see how you operate.*

Oh, God.

Rachel Brydie was an actor.

Why do you keep thinking about that? Why?

Fiona Klein's house lay low on its clifftop, shrouded in mist. On a clear day, the view from the deck that stretched across the entire back section of the house was a panorama of swooping chasm, soaring pink sandstone escarpment, and sky. On a clear night there was pure echoing blackness, spanned by a vast arc of stars. But tonight there was no sense of space, or even of darkness. The world outside the house was white. All sound was deadened. Mist filled the valley, overflowed onto the deck, and billowed against the windows, rising to the roof.

Inside the house, there was warmth and light, and music played softly in the living room. The cedar blinds were closed against the mist. The fuel stove glowed.

Fiona Klein sat watching the flames flicker in the heart of the stove. Her booted feet were propped on the hearth. Her hands hung loosely in her lap.

It was strange to be back. Yesterday, last night, she hadn't really thought about it. She'd been too busy unpacking, re-establishing herself in her territory, expunging all trace of her tenants, the scent or memory of whom had at first seemed to linger, despite the scrupulously clean state in which they'd left her house. They hadn't wanted to go. Maybe it was their resentment she could smell.

Now the tenants had disappeared, but the house was still alien. Bliss, Skye and Astral, silent and soft-footed, had filled it with their presence, and the presence remained, though they'd already gone to bed. Now they lay in Nicki's room—the room that had been officially Nicki's, when strangers called. Bliss and Skye were sleeping in the double bed. Astral was on a mattress on the floor beside them.

There was a spare bedroom kept for visitors—pleasant enough for one or two people, though without a view. Astral could have slept there. Fiona had suggested she did, in fact. But the sisters had preferred to huddle together in one room, like a litter of puppies. Fiona hadn't argued with them. They were frightened, subdued, and withdrawn. She'd let them drag the spare room mattress, pillow and the quilt into Nicki's room, and watched them make the beds, carefully spreading and tucking the linen only unpacked yesterday. Skye had run her fingers over the fabric, eyes widening at its smooth softness, but she'd made no comment.

Now they were sleeping, three parts of a whole, in a shelter they'd made for themselves. She was, effectively, alone.

The phone was off the hook. She hadn't wanted to talk to anyone. But now she glanced at it, got up and dialed Michael O'Malley's number.

He answered straightaway, as though he'd been waiting by the phone.

"It's Fiona," she said, without preamble.

"I've been trying to call you."

"I've had the phone off the hook. I've got Astral—and her sisters—here."

"I thought that might happen. What are they saying?" he asked quickly.

"Nothing much. They were very tired. They're asleep. Have you heard anything? About Rachel?"

"No. They're still putting out announcements. Every news bulletin. Asking for info."

"Have the police talked to you?"

"A couple called round." Michael's voice, as ever, revealed nothing. "They were doing the whole street. They said they thought she might have come through to my place, over the creek."

"What did you say?"

"I told them I wouldn't know. I told them to look. They poked around the house a bit. Then they left. They said they'd be back to look around again tomorrow, because my boundary adjoins part of Haven's."

"You all right?"

He laughed humorlessly. "As right as I'll ever be. Bet you're glad you came back when you did."

Her heart was pounding, but she lied fluently. "I am, actually."

"Right."

She knew that there was nothing to be gained from prolonging the conversation. There was no comfort to be gained from Michael O'Malley. Not tonight. He wasn't in the mood.

"Okay. Just rang to say hello. I'll let you get back to it, Michael," she said.

He laughed again. "Get back to what?"

"You know what I mean. Take care."

"You too."

She hung up, dissatisfied, took the phone off the hook again, and walked back to the fire. The problem with having friendships with complicated people was that it was either almost embarrassing intimacy, or arm's length, with them. And the shared memory of the embarrassing intimacies made the arm's length times even more awkward and hard to take.

She'd rung Michael last night as well. And last night, too, he'd been strained and withdrawn. Grimacing, she faced the fact that he probably disapproved of her return. Michael, for all his casual manner, tended to be censorious, and he valued strength of mind above all things. If he interpreted her rush for home as weak or self-indulgent, he wouldn't say anything, but he'd lose respect for her.

"Bugger him, then," she murmured aloud, and stared at the glowing coals. It was time to heave another log into the stove, but she didn't move. The effort of getting up seemed too great.

This homecoming hadn't been what she'd imagined. And yet, what had she imagined, really? What had she thought, as she booked her ticket and packed, avoiding Nicki's eyes, stripping the big, airy terrazzo-floored room they'd shared of everything that was hers—every postcard, every pen and scrap of paper, because she knew that was what Nicki wanted? What had she thought, as they'd hugged and kissed, briefly, on the pavement when the taxi came, as if they were friends who'd meet again, as if seven years could just be kissed goodbye? What had she thought, as she waited in the airport, sat in the plane through half a day and one whole night, disembarked at Sydney airport? As she collected baggage, emerged into the bright, bleaching light then shuffled forward in the taxi queue, smelling the familiar smells, hearing the familiar accents, feeling hot, sticky, gritty and displaced?

She'd thought of nothing, she realized. There had been no clear pictures in her mind. Just trailing threads of disjointed thought and memory drifting in the mist that had engulfed her mind weeks ago, and half a world away. She had efficiently gone through the motions necessary to get her home, but she'd gone through them blindly, on automatic. Her conscious mind had been in spasm, aware of nothing but the agonizing, paralyzing knot of primitive emotions at its core: shock, fear, hope, and deep, simmering excitement.

The knot had gone, now. Reality had dug in its fingers and after a moment of pain the knot had loosened, unraveled, and disappeared. But in its place was emptiness.

Fiona glanced at her watch. About now, on the other side of the world, Nicki would be stirring from sleep. Her red hair would be a tousled mass of color on the pillow, the shorter, finer curls at the front clinging damply to her forehead and the sides of her neck, under her ears. Soon she'd get up, swinging her legs over the side of the high, white bed, planting her bare feet on the smooth, cold terrazzo floor, padding to the bathroom, leaving the smudgy prints of toes and heels where she trod.

There was a crucifix hanging on the wall over the bed. They'd joked about it, when they first moved in, but somehow they'd never taken it down. Maybe they were both superstitious—hoping for a blessing, against all the odds.

The blessing hadn't eventuated. It had been an odd, dislocated five months. Perhaps, if Fiona had been working, had been less cut adrift from everything that had given her life focus at home, they could have kept the truth from themselves a little longer. As it was, their estrangement had become more and more obvious.

Nicki went to class, came home at night and talked about music, and strangers. Fiona learned Italian, went to galleries, sat in the terrazzo-floored room with its long windows that swung open over the street, pecking at the play she'd always wished she had time to finish at home, but which here, now, seemed irredeemably pedestrian. The aching sense of loss that was like a sickness, growing rather than fading as it was supposed to do, drove her out into the streets again. She wandered the shops aimlessly, buying things for herself, for Nicki, for the room.

One afternoon, she'd bought the three gold and black enamel rings. Uncharacteristically dithering, she couldn't decide between them, and in the end she'd bought them all, though they were expensive. Nicki smiled when she saw them: smiled, tightly, when Fiona said she hadn't been able to choose. Only then did Fiona realize that her half-formed plan of giving Nicki one of the set was ludicrous. The existence of a third ring made such a gift impossible.

Eating, buying fruit at the markets, walking together on the streets that had seemed vibrating with life on first acquaintance but, to Fiona at least, now appeared merely overfamiliar and crowded, they were lighthearted and polite. They deferred to one another like courteous acquaintances. They never argued.

They each pretended, for a long time, that everything was all right—that the past, and affection, could carry them through, that Fiona's decision to come to Italy had been a real decision, not just an apology, a promise and an act of faith, or desperation, or both. They pretended that when, at last, Nicki began crawling into bed, saying goodnight and immediately turning her back to sleep, it was because she was tired, not because she feared that if they touched, the image burning behind Fiona's closed eyelids, fueling her passion, would be of someone else.

It had ended, finally. Of course, it had to. Looking back on it now, Fiona knew that the ending had become inevitable, and a new chapter of her life had begun, the moment she first met Astral Brydie.

Fifteen

"Feel like walking home, Tess?" Steve said, as they left the restaurant and strolled down the footpath, past the darkened shops, towards Rochette's car. The mist had thickened. The other side of the road was invisible.

No. I'm tired. It's cold. You can't see a thing.

He wants to talk.

We can talk at Bide-A-While.

His room, or yours?

"Sure," said Tessa. "Let's walk."

Rochette grinned. "Better you than me," she said. They passed the shuttered wine shop, her car came into view, and she pulled out her keys.

"Are there any more organized tours planned for tomorrow?" Tessa asked politely. "Or is it up to us, now?"

Constable Williams's black eyes sparkled. She put her head on one side and her face took on an expression of infinite cunning. "It's always been up to you," she answered. "I'm just watching, aren't I? Observing?"

"Are you?"

"Oh, yeah. It's really interesting, too." Rochette stopped at her car, and jingled her keys. "You're sure you don't want a lift?"

"We'll be right," said Steve.

"Yeah, well, it'll give you a chance to have a private natter, I guess," said Rochette blandly. "Sort a few things out, before you get home? See ya, then. Mind how you go."

"You too. It's not good driving weather."

"I'm used to it. Plus I know this place pretty well, don't forget."

149

"That's the understatement of the century," murmured Tessa, as they walked on. She stumbled slightly on the uneven pavement and felt Steve's hand slide under her arm, to steady her. "You realize she's playing us like trout, don't you?" she said, looking up at him.

Steve laughed. "Yeah. She's having a great time."

"Sleep well," they heard Constable Williams call raucously after them.

They turned. She was still standing by her car. Her stocky figure was half-hidden in the mist, but she was slightly crouched, and her teeth were flashing white. She was silently laughing.

Insubordinate, disrespectful . . .

Are you turning into Thorne, or something?

"Come on," Tessa said through gritted teeth. She spun round, pulling away from Steve's hand, and started to walk rapidly, watching her feet.

"Hey, take it easy," she heard him say behind her. She slowed, but only slightly, to let him catch up. "She's getting to you, is she?" he said, when he was again by her side.

Tessa said nothing.

"So," he murmured. "D'you reckon Fiona Klein lied deliberately?"

He's diverting your attention.

"I don't know. Surely she'd realize we'd find out when she arrived back from Italy, if we checked." Tessa walked on, her shoulders hunched. It was cold out here, after the warmth of the restaurant, and the mist seemed to make it hard to breathe.

"If we checked. But maybe we wouldn't." Steve was taking one easy pace to her two. "You can't check out everything. And we had no reason to think Fiona Klein had anything to do with this."

"Do we have a reason now?"

"I'm not sure." Steve rubbed his chin thoughtfully. "We're going to have a word with her in the morning, anyhow, aren't we? We'll check it out then."

They had reached the corner. Tessa stopped. "Those girls are there alone with her," she said.

"For that matter, she's alone with them," Steve responded.

"Most people round here'd think that was more of a problem. But it didn't seem to worry her. Do you want to check on them?"

Tessa nodded, and pulled out her phone. A dark-colored car passed them—a six-seater four-wheel drive, like so many of the vehicles up here, it bulked out of the mist and raced through the crossing without a pause. The driver must be a local, used to the roads, used to the weather conditions. But he—or she—was taking a risk. Visibility was very poor. Tessa checked Fiona Klein's number in her notebook, and rang. Engaged signal.

"She's still up, anyway. She's talking to someone," she said, cutting the connection. "I'll try again later."

They crossed the road and turned to the right. The road sloped down. The mist was impenetrable. There was no footpath here—only a wide grass verge lined with cherry trees.

"We shouldn't have said we'd walk. We'll probably get lost, now," Tessa snapped.

"How can we get lost? All we have to do is stay on this road. Bide-A-While's down the hill, just past that streetlight. Remember?"

"I don't remember anything."

He laughed. "Rochette *is* getting to you."

"Steve, she's setting us up."

"She's not, you know. Not the way you mean. Look— if you were a local, how would you feel about some suits coming up from Sydney to muscle in on this thing? Especially if they didn't straightaway accept your ideas, and started reinventing the wheel?"

"I'd be grateful for all the help I could—"

"Come on, Tessa. That's bullshit. You might put up with it, but you wouldn't like it. That sergeant—what's his name?— McCaffrey, and the constable—Ingres—are pretty pissed off, for a start. I'd say they've got their heads together and decided to give us just as much help as they have to to avoid being called obstructive. No more, no less."

"And Rochette?"

"Rochette's not playing their game. She's playing her own.

She's giving us a go. Setting out the pieces for us, seeing what we do with them."

Tour of the zoo.

"If she's got a theory she should—"

"I don't think she's got a theory. But she's got local knowledge. She knows the people who've had something to do with Haven, something to do with Quinn. She knows who's up who and who's paying the rent. She knows who we should be talking to, to get the full picture."

"Then why not just tell us? Give us a list. Or bring them in?"

Steve hesitated. She glanced at him quickly, saw him shaking his head in a resigned sort of way.

You're exposing your inexperience. You're making this harder for him.

He's being too tolerant. Why should we accept unprofessional behavior? From any of them?

"She's going to have to stay on here after we're gone, Tessa," Steve said gently, after a moment. "And this is a small place. If she openly breaks ranks with McCaffrey and Ingres she'll have a pretty thin time of it after this. Take it from me."

That's how it works, city girl.

Tessa felt her face warming with anger. "But that's—"

"That's life." He was quite unruffled. "Rochette knows what's what. But she doesn't like sitting on her hands. So she's getting round the problem. She's making sure we bump into the right people, and leaving it to us to ask the right questions and make the connections."

Tessa frowned into the mist. She realized that her hands, plunged deep in her coat pockets, had balled into fists. She consciously relaxed them.

"If it's murder, we haven't got time for this," she muttered.

"But you don't think it *is* murder, Tess," Steve reminded her lightly.

Now he's playing games.

He's only telling the truth. You don't think it's murder. Do you?

They walked on in silence for a moment.

"How far is it now?" Tessa asked abruptly.

"To Bide-A-While?"

"Yes."

"About—oh—a meter and a half."

She stopped dead, peering at the fence beside which they were walking. Sure enough, the Bide-A-While gate was just ahead.

"I didn't think we'd come that far," she said, confused.

"You were practically running."

"Sorry."

Steve pushed open the gate and they went in. The path was well lit. The lights made the garden magic. The mist drifted like smoke. Everywhere bouquets of wet, shining leaves shone through it, red, orange, yellow and green.

Slowly they paced the graveled path together. At the steps Tessa stopped, and turned her face up to meet his eyes. "Sorry," she repeated.

"What for?"

For being angry. For being prickly. For having no sense of humor. For shaking off your hand. For hating this place . . .

"For being—a problem."

"You're always a problem," he said lightly. "Will we go in, or would you rather stay out here and tear a few more strips off yourself?"

She forced a laugh. "We'd better go in. Get back to work."

"What work?"

"You're the one who says Rochette Williams is on our side. Why do you think she booked us in here, then? There must have been other places going. If Bide-A-While was an arbitrary choice, it was the only one she made today."

He nodded. "Larkin?"

"I suppose so."

They climbed the steps. The front door, its blood-red waratahs and perching kookaburras glowing, was on the latch. They went inside.

The hallway was warm, and smelled faintly of freshly brewed coffee, but the sitting room was empty except for a solitary bespectacled young man reading a book by the fire. He glanced up as they passed, but quickly looked down to his reading again. He was thin, with a neat, slightly balding head and an earnest look. Tessa idly wondered what he was doing here, in the mountains, all alone. A weekend's bushwalking, maybe. But didn't you usually do that with a group? Perhaps he was a birdwatcher.

They found Verna Larkin, and the source of the coffee aroma, in a big, light-filled kitchen beyond the breakfast room. The kitchen was roughly divided in half—benches, cupboards, equipment and stove at the end nearest the breakfast room, big table, chairs and dresser further on. Double doors in the center of this part of the room led out to the courtyard Tessa had seen from her bedroom window. Verna was standing at a bench at the business end of the room, arranging cup, coffee pot, milk and a small plate of chocolate-dipped shortbread on a tray. She greeted them like old friends.

"I've just made coffee for Bernie," she said. "Would you like a pot yourself? The fire's lovely, in there, Bernie says."

Bernie the birdwatcher.

"Tell you what, Verna," said Steve. "I'd love to make myself some tea. And the kitchen'll do me, if it's all the same to you."

The woman beamed. "You're one of my mob," she said. "I was just going to make tea for myself. I'll just take this in to Bernie. The tea things are by the kettle. One flat scoop'll do it."

She bustled out of the room with the tray.

"Mr. Charm," jeered Tessa. "Don't you hate yourself?"

"No point in making it harder, is it?" Steve filled the kettle. "Real tea," he said with satisfaction, opening a tin decorated with galahs and looking round for the teapot.

You'd think he didn't have another thing on his mind.

Tessa wandered down to the big table, stripped off her coat and sat down. Suddenly, she felt very tired. She looked around the room. Shelves of grinning china frogs, blue and white china, a pottery hedgehog sprouting alfalfa, jugs and pots, bowls and cookbooks ... long, clear benches ... gleaming pans and a great big stove ... gingham pot holders and linen tea towels ... high stools pushed against the short, high bench which divided the kitchen proper from the sitting area ... on that bench the phone, a potted plant, a scattered pile of lists and notes . . . on the wall nearby a Harmony with Nature calendar.

Courtesy O'Malley's bookshop.

Verna Larkin knows Michael O'Malley, who's fancied by Lyn Weisenhoff, who's married to Carl, who sold gin to Adam Quinn, who's dead . . .

Tessa hauled herself to her feet and went to have a look at the calendar. Like the one on the kitchen wall at Haven, Verna Larkin's calendar was covered with marks and notes. But Verna's marks were scrawled in pen of all colors, pencil, and even thick black felt-tip. Reminders of birthdays, visits, dentist's appointments and parties . . .

Tessa heard a sound behind her and turned to see Melissa coming in from the courtyard through the double doors. The girl was wearing a bright, waterproof jacket that contrasted oddly with her long, black clothes. Silently she pulled the jacket off, staring at them as though they were intruders in her space.

"G'day, Melissa," Steve said.

"Where's Mum?" Melissa asked abruptly.

"Taking some coffee to a guest inside," Steve said. "She won't be a minute." He poured boiling water into the round, brown teapot, taking his time, as though he himself wasn't a guest, but someone who was perfectly at home.

The ploy seemed to work, for Melissa sighed and sat down at the end of the table, dropping her jacket on the floor beside her. Her shoulders slumped. The silence grew heavy.

"You've been out with your friends, have you, Melissa?" asked Tessa, sitting back down at the table, feeling like a maiden aunt.

Steve brought the teapot to the table and put it down. The pot was now covered, Tessa saw, with a pale green hand-knitted tea cozy topped with a floppy bunch of pink and yellow woollen flowers. She hadn't seen a tea cozy like that since . . .

Granny's house. The teapot on the table, covered in its cozy. Mum and Dad, Granny and Pop, drinking tea out of fine, flowered cups, every cup different. Lace tablecloth. Saos, with tomato and sliced gherkin on top. Half a fruitcake, on the special plate with the dark blue and real gold rim. Fairy cakes, with jam and icing sugar sprinkled on the wings, piled on the glass plate with the little stand. Fairy cakes especially for Tessa. Tessa loves Granny's fairy cakes . . .

The slumped shoulders shrugged. "I didn't really feel like it," the girl said. "But I had to." She raised mournful eyes, and her bottom lip quivered. "Have—have they found out anything yet?" she asked tremulously. "About Adam? He didn't really kill himself, did he?"

Tessa's heart gave a tiny lurch. "We don't really know yet," she said, keeping her voice even.

"You knew him well, did you, Melissa?" asked Steve. He sounded sympathetic, and respectful.

The girl nodded. Tears started oozing from her reddened eyes. They came so easily that Tessa suspected she'd been weeping on and off all evening. "He was really nice to me," she whispered. "He really understood me. You know?" She reached down, fumbled in her jacket pocket and brought out a small, grubby and dog-eared pack of children's cards, secured by a rubber band. She held them out reverently. "He used to play cards with me, sometimes. Old Maid, and Cheat, and Fish. When he was here."

When he was here . . .

Steve glanced at Tessa, and moved to the refrigerator, for milk. "That must have been before he went to Haven, was it?" he asked casually.

"Yes. He was looking for a house to buy. But he never did. He really liked it here. He said. But then he did go. That awful Mrs. Brydie—she's so weird! I don't know how he could have done it!" Melissa blinked, but made no effort to wipe the tears away. A drop fell onto the tabletop, and she looked at it with miserable satisfaction.

"I've just been crying all day," she quavered. "I can't help it."

"Melissa!" Verna Larkin stood in the doorway, her face a mixture of exasperation and consternation.

Melissa looked sulky. "I'm not doing anything," she whined. "I'm just sitting here. They don't mind."

"Of course we don't," said Tessa soothingly.

"Would you like some tea, Melissa?" Steve offered. "It might make you feel better."

"There's nothing whatever the matter with her," snapped Verna. "She's worked herself into a state over nothing, that's all." She turned to her daughter, her hands on her ample hips. "Where have you been, Melissa?"

"You didn't say I couldn't go out!" her daughter countered. "You went out."

Verna glanced at Tessa and Steve apologetically, then faced her daughter once more. "I didn't say I minded, Melissa," she said, with the dangerous patience Tessa remembered her own mother displaying when Tessa showed defiance in front of strangers. "I just wanted to know where you were."

"At Amy's place. With Heidi and Leanne."

"I thought Heidi had been grounded."

"That was up yesterday." Melissa frowned. "That was so unfair. But d'you know what? Even though Heidi's been grounded for two weeks, and the time's up, and it's Saturday night, her mother goes, 'Your father and I have to go out to a meeting. You can thank your lucky stars Granny's here, Heidi, because otherwise you'd have to stay home and baby-sit.' Can you believe that?" She shook her head. "If I was Heidi, I'd really hate my parents."

"That's a terrible thing to say. I'm sure the Ridges are very nice people."

Charles and Freda Ridge!

Means nothing. Small town. But the other . . . Adam Quinn stayed here . . . why didn't Larkin tell us?

"They're horrible!" Melissa exclaimed passionately. "They're ruining her life! They make her go to that stuck-up try-hard school where none of her friends are, and they have to wear that stupid uniform. They're completely prejudiced about every boy she's ever liked. They don't even let her ring her own friends in the week. I mean, all she's got is weekends, and then they—"

"Melissa, it's late." Wearily, but effectively, Mrs. Larkin stemmed the flow. "Get off to bed."

Melissa pressed her lips together, picked up her jacket and

stood up, the cards clutched to her breast. "I'll just lie awake all night," she warned. "Heidi said *she* would."

"You'll be asleep in five minutes," said her mother. "Off you go!"

Melissa flounced to the door, trailing her jacket behind her. "She saw Mrs. Brydie, you know," she said recklessly.

If she'd sought to create an effect, she wasn't disappointed. In fact, she probably got more of a reaction than she'd bargained for. Tessa, Steve and her mother all reacted as if she'd thrown a hand grenade into the room. Verna exclaimed, and clapped her hand over her mouth. Tessa half-stood, and in a few strides Steve had crossed the room and was standing beside the girl, tall, dark and serious.

"You mean Heidi Ridge, Melissa?" he asked.

She nodded.

"When did she see Mrs. Brydie?"

"Last Sunday night," said Melissa warily. Plainly she already regretted her impulsive disclosure.

"Where?"

Melissa's eyes shifted. "I'm not exactly sure," she temporized.

"Melissa!" screeched her mother. "Are you making this up, or something?"

"Of course I'm not," said Melissa indignantly. "Heidi saw her. She told us. Leanne and Amy, and me."

Verna Larkin was scarlet. "Don't you girls know that the police have been asking over and over for information about—"

"Course we know," pouted Melissa. "But it's not as if— you know—it was *important*." She looked around, felt their unspoken disapproval, and flared up. "It's not as if it'd help anything, would it?" she argued. "I mean, everyone knows she's with a guy. And this was practically a whole week ago. They're probably in another state by now."

"Has Heidi told her parents about this, Melissa?" asked Tessa quietly.

Melissa hung her head and muttered something.

"Sorry, I didn't catch that," said Steve.

The girl raised her head. "She hasn't said anything. She wasn't s'posed to be there," she mumbled.

"Be where?"

"At the lake. She was s'posed to be home, looking after Cecilia and Daniel."

Scandalized, Verna took a step forward. "You mean that girl went out—running after some boy, I suppose—and left a seven-year-old and a ten-year-old alone in the—" she broke off as Tessa touched her arm.

Melissa tossed her head. "You see!" she accused. "That's exactly what everyone would say. That's what her horrible parents would say. She'd have got into real trouble, if she'd told. And it's not her fault. Cecilia and Daniel were completely okay. They were asleep, and they never wake up. Heidi locked the door and everything. And it wasn't as if she was going far. The lake's down from their place. And anyway, everyone else round here leaves their kids on their own, all the time—"

"They certainly do not!" exploded Verna, unable to hold her tongue.

"Well, they're stupid, then!" flashed Melissa, who had now gone too far for anything much else she said to matter.

"So your friend saw Rachel Brydie at the lake on Sunday night. That's the lake in the park on the other side of the highway from here. The Haven side. Right?" Steve's voice was calm and reassuring.

The girl nodded sullenly. "Just down from Heidi's place," she repeated, with a glance at her mother.

"What time did she see Mrs. Brydie?" Steve asked.

"About ten. She was waiting—" Again Melissa's eyes shifted to her mother, then returned quickly to Steve. "Just in case this—friend—of hers turned up. But he didn't. So she only stayed awhile, then she went." She pursed her lips. "I mean, you can't hang round for them forever, can you?" she added, with a belated attempt at worldly wisdom. "Like, they have their chance, and if they don't take it, that's their problem, isn't it?"

She wasn't looking for an answer. She and her friends had obviously discussed this point during the evening, and

reached their own conclusions. Steve brought her gently back
to the point. "And she's sure it was Rachel Brydie she saw?"

Melissa's eyes flickered. "I guess," she murmured.

"You mean she isn't sure?"

A shrug. "Heidi said it looked like her. She thought it was
her. But Mrs. Brydie was inside the car. So—"

"What sort of car?"

"Some four-wheel drive, Heidi said."

"Did she notice the color? Or the numberplate?"

"She didn't notice any of that. It was all misty. And, I mean,
she didn't know it mattered then, did she? She didn't even see
the guy properly. She didn't go close up, or anything. She
wasn't going to perv on them, was she? I mean, they were
parked. You know. And she didn't want—you know—them to
see her—looking."

"You mean they were kissing or something?" asked Steve.

Or something.

Melissa's eyes shifted again. "Sort of. I guess." Her mouth
curled in distaste. "It's really disgusting," she muttered.
"She's so *old.*"

Steve stuck his hands in his pockets. "We'd better have a
talk with Heidi," he suggested.

"Oh, *no!*" Melissa's eyes widened in panic. "Oh no, don't!
Her parents'll freak!" She ducked her head and clutched at
her hair with her hands, swaying. "Oh, I knew I shouldn't
have said anything," she moaned. "Oh, why did I?"

"You probably knew in your heart that it was terribly important," said Tessa mendaciously. "After all, you were close
to Adam Quinn. You probably had an instinct."

The girl looked up, still anxious, but obviously impressed
by this glamorous interpretation of her behavior. Her shoulders straightened a little. She lifted her chin. Her soft features
began rearranging themselves into what she no doubt intended to be a farseeing, tragic expression. "I am very instinctive," she admitted.

"What you are is a very silly girl," her mother snapped.
"Now go to bed."

But Melissa by now was impervious to insult. "Do you
want Heidi's phone number?" she asked Tessa heroically.

"It's okay," Tessa told her. "We've already got it."

Melissa's eyes widened with superstitious awe. "How?" she breathed, backing away a little. Her hand crept to her mouth. "Oh—you knew, didn't you? You knew all the time!"

And with that she darted through the double doors, and away across the courtyard. She flew like a bullet to a room at the end of the new wing and disappeared inside, slamming the door behind her.

Sixteen

"Kids!" groaned Verna Larkin. She let herself fall heavily into a chair. "I'm too old for this," she said, more to herself than to her guests. She sighed and reached automatically for the milk jug. "Do you both take milk?" she inquired.

"Yes, please," said Tessa. She watched as the woman began adding milk to each cup. "Verna, Melissa said that Adam Quinn was a guest here, before he went to Haven. Is that right?"

The plump, freckled, beringed hand jerked convulsively, and milk slopped onto the tabletop. "Oh, silly me!" Verna exclaimed. She put down the jug and went for a paper towel to wipe up the mess. Not until the milk was blotted up did she answer the question, and by that time she had recovered her equilibrium.

"Now, what were we saying? Oh, about Adam Quinn," she said. "Yes, he did stay here for a while."

"You didn't mention it."

Verna concentrated on pouring milk, and then tea. "Sugar?" she asked brightly.

"Please." Steve sat down at the table beside her. She gave him a brimming cup, and pushed the sugar bowl towards him with a cheery smile.

"I never thought to mention it," she said. "Heavens, it was *years* ago."

Ancient history, her tone implied. But there was strain behind her eyes, and she must have known they'd see it.

"How long was he with you exactly?" asked Tessa.

"About ten weeks, I think. Ten or twelve weeks."

"That's a long time."

"Oh, yes. But I've had other people stay as long. Nearly as long." Verna blinked at them over the rim of her cup. "Are you going to ring the Ridges?" she asked. Her bright blue eye-shadow made her look a bit like a parrot from this angle, Tessa thought. A secretive sort of parrot.

Steve glanced at his watch. "It's a bit late. I think it'll keep till morning, Tess?"

Tessa nodded. Having had a taste of Charles and Freda Ridge, she felt strongly that any revelations about their daughter's illicit activities last Sunday night would be best made in the cold light of day, when everyone was well rested. And anyway she was pretty sure that Heidi was going to be able to tell them no more than she'd told Melissa.

Steve seemed to be able to drink his tea scalding hot. He emptied his cup and stood up. "Might give the station a ring," he said. "Give them the word, anyhow. Tell them we'll confirm in the morning."

"There's that other call too, Steve," Tessa reminded him. For some reason she didn't want to mention Fiona Klein's name. She didn't want to mention the Brydie sisters either, though of course, she reminded herself, Verna Larkin already knew where the girls were. There was no secret about it. The whole town probably knew. Gossip was plainly a thriving industry in Oakdale.

"The phone's over there," said Verna, pointing. "Or there's one in the hall, if you like." She was very uneasy. What was she hiding? Tessa wondered, looking down at her own tea. And if she had something to hide, why had she agreed to have the police here at all? She could have easily told Rochette she was booked up—didn't have a spare room in the place. Verna didn't look like someone who would balk at the odd white lie.

"Thanks, but I'll use the mobile. Stretch my legs outside for a minute." Steve was already up, and heading for the door. "Save me some tea."

He thinks girl talk's required.

She'd talk to him more easily than she will to me.

The mist drifted outside the window over the kitchen sink. To Tessa, it was a bleak outlook. Perhaps Verna felt that way, too, because she followed Tessa's gaze, got up and pulled down the blind.

"Cozier," she said, unnecessarily.

Tessa decided to play it straight. "You know, Verna," she said. "I've been thinking that you know more about Adam Quinn than you're telling."

Verna blinked. She was plainly flustered. She'd been ready for subtle tactics, but not for this. She folded her arms protectively against her chest. "I—I don't know why you'd say that," she stammered.

Tessa looked her straight in the eye. "Did something happen, while he was here?" she asked.

"What sort of thing?" Verna tried to smile. Her top lip caught as it slid over her top teeth.

"You tell me."

Silence. Verna stood very still, her arms still folded.

Tessa moved in slowly. "Was he drinking?"

"He did drink, that's for sure. But he could hold it. At least he could in those days. It was never an embarrassment, if that's what you mean."

"Was there any trouble? With Melissa, for example?" Tessa asked, stabbing in the dark.

Verna's brow puckered. "Melissa? Adam got on well with Melissa. She's exaggerating the whole thing a bit, of course. They didn't see that much of each other, really. But as she says, he was always very nice to her."

"Not—overnice? Overaffectionate?" Tessa asked the question carefully. Some people reacted to this sort of suggestion with sudden, shocked anger. As though you were impugning the virtue of their child, rather than the adult in question.

But Verna Larkin laughed. It was a rather hysterical laugh, but there was no anger in it. "If you're asking did he interfere with Melissa while he was here, no he didn't," she said. "No way."

Tessa leaned forward. "You're absolutely certain, Verna?" she asked quietly.

"I couldn't be more positive." Verna flapped her hands in a gesture of derision and sat down at the table. "Look, give me some credit for knowing something about men, at least. I've had enough experience." Again she laughed. Her self-consciousness had vanished. "The whole idea's ridiculous. I can't tell you *how* ridiculous! Why on earth would you even *ask* such a thing?" Then her expression changed. "Oh, I know," she exclaimed. "They've been telling you stories in the village. They told you that when Adam took up with Rachel Brydie he was buying himself a harem, did they?"

Tessa shrugged, and waited.

Verna snorted. "If you haven't heard that one, you soon will. You'll hear some of the men say it, anyway. Nasty-minded so-and-sos. They love the idea themselves, if you ask me. Carl Weisenhoff in the wine shop's one of the worst. I feel sorry for his poor wife, I really do."

"Still, Adam Quinn had quite a reputation before he came here, didn't he?" Tessa said quietly. "There was a story about him and a thirteen-year-old in a hotel—"

"Well, I can tell you right now, that was just paper talk," Verna interrupted, her voice rising. "The girl was fifteen, she looked eighteen, she'd got into his room by pretending to be a cleaner, and there was no way in the world anything happened."

"Did Adam tell you that?"

Verna nodded. "Yes, he did, because I asked him. But he wasn't lying to me, if that's what you think. The police didn't charge him with anything—and they would have, wouldn't they, if there'd been anything in it? Even if something *had* happened with that girl, I'd never have had a moment's worry about Adam and Melissa. She was only eleven when he was here. A young eleven at that. Skinny little thing with scabby knees. She didn't even get her periods till she was thirteen. And whatever else Adam was into, he wasn't into little girls. You can take it from me."

She's very sure.

Whatever else Adam was into . . .

So that's how it was.

"You knew him very well, obviously," Tessa said.

Verna pulled herself up at once, realizing she'd betrayed

herself. "Well enough," she said cautiously. She pulled Tessa's empty cup towards her, and poured them both more tea.

Giving herself some time.

"You had an affair."

The other woman didn't respond. But her silence was eloquent.

Push her.

"Verna?"

Verna's mouth twitched. She fiddled with the flowers on top of the tea cozy. "I didn't realize he would have told people," she said bitterly. "I didn't think he was that sort. Rochette Williams worded you up, did she?"

"Rochette didn't say a word," Tessa said truthfully.

But Rochette knew. That's why she sent us here.

"So you had an affair . . ." she prompted.

"You'd hardly call it an affair on his side," Verna said flatly.

"What would you call it?"

The blue-ringed eyes were hard now. "My late husband would have called it getting your end in."

"What about on your side?"

"On my side?" Verna seemed to think about that. Finally, she sighed. "Probably much the same thing," she said. "If I was honest. I was lonely, you know? You get lonely. And I suppose I was flattered he wanted it, too." She drew herself up a little. "Not that I hold myself cheap. But, let's face it, Adam Quinn could have had anyone, really. Anyone he went after. That's how I felt about it, when it started."

The corners of her mouth drooped. She was thinking about something. Something she wasn't telling.

"Was he ever violent, Verna?" asked Tessa. "Did he ever hurt you?"

Verna's eyes widened, and color rushed into her cheeks. "Of course not!" she said loudly. "Why would you ask that? As if I'd put up with anything like that!"

You put up with it from Paddy. For years and years.

Leave it. For now.

Tessa sipped at her tea. "How did you feel when Quinn went off to live at Haven?"

The woman looked down, running one finger around the

rim of her cup. "I was quite glad, really," she said. "And that's the honest truth. Things had got a bit awkward."

"Why's that? Melissa?"

Verna looked startled. "Oh, no. She never knew about—Adam and me. Never had the faintest idea. It used to happen long after she'd gone to bed. After everyone had gone to bed—and never on weekends, when the house was full. We used his room. He'd ask me, and later I'd go to his room." She pressed her lips together, as though remembering something distasteful. Something she was ashamed of. "It was just that—you know how these things are—after a while it started wearing a bit thin. I could see it was never going to end up as anything permanent. And then . . ." Her voice trailed off. She didn't seem to know how to continue.

"Then Adam met Rachel Brydie," Tessa suggested gently.

Verna looked up. There was an odd expression on her face. As Tessa watched, trying to interpret it, it changed. Her mouth tweaked into a half-smile.

"That's right," she murmured. "Rachel Brydie was just what Adam wanted, apparently. He said she was. Once he'd met her, he lost interest in me. So we rattled around here being polite to each other and so on—then after a while he moved out and went to Haven."

"I can see why you'd be relieved."

Verna nodded soberly. "Oh, I won't say that I wasn't sorry, in a way, that it hadn't worked out. I mean, I'd liked him. And he was a good catch, wasn't he? A celebrity—people stopped him in the street—bags of money, and so on. But it's not much fun when you know you're no real good to a person, is it? When you've got to try too hard? It's a strain, then. And, actually—" she blushed slightly again "—it's not what I'm used to."

She lifted her chin. "My present fellow seems quite content, anyhow," she said defiantly. "He's just an ordinary sort of chap, but we get on fine."

Tessa smiled at her, and the smile came from her heart. Verna Larkin might be fallible, foolish and battered around by life, but she was a real human being. And there was something gallant about her. Something indomitable. Adam Quinn would have realized that, after a while. Verna had learned from her experience with Paddy Larkin. She wasn't going to knuckle under to another man—a lover of just a month or two. She'd become too strong to be a victim. In that sense, she'd won, and Rachel Brydie had lost.

If she's telling the truth.

There was a moment's silence, and then Verna stood up, brushing at her skirt as if to remove a scattering of imaginary crumbs. "Well, if you're happy here I'll go in and see if Bernie needs anything else," she said briskly. "He's tired out, poor boy."

She had apparently decided to return the atmosphere to normal by the simple expedient of pretending the recent conversation hadn't occurred. Tessa was, for the present, happy to cooperate.

"Bernie's a regular guest?"

"Oh, yes. He comes up every month. They'd like to have him more often, of course, and I think he'd like to do it, too. He loves it up here. But once a month is all he can manage, he says. He's booked up solid in town all the rest of the time. And as he says, that's where the money is. He can't really afford to refuse."

Booked up for bird watching?

Tessa's confusion must have shown on her face, because Verna laughed.

"Oh, sorry," she said. "I thought you must have been talking to him before. Bernie's a singer—well, a performer, I suppose you'd say. He's terrific. Funny as a circus. He comes up to do a show at Swans—just one show on a Saturday night. But I don't know where he gets the energy."

"Swans?" Tessa hesitated. "You mean the pub?" An amazing idea occurred to her. "Verna—Bernie's not—he's not—Bouncy Bernadette?"

Verna laughed again, uproariously this time. "Oh, you've seen the signs have you? Yeah, that's him. You wouldn't believe it, would you? To look at him? But you can't judge by appearances. Honestly, you wouldn't recognize him when he's all dolled up."

She went out, still laughing.

Steve came in through the back door a few minutes later, and found Tessa still sitting at the kitchen table stirring the sugar in the bowl with a spoon. She looked up.

"What took you so long?" she said.

"I wanted to give you plenty of time, so after I'd made the calls I walked around the block. Then Tootsie rang about the postmortem. Quinn had cirrhosis of the liver and an enlarged heart, but the gunshot wound to the head was definitely the cause of death."

"And he was shot where we found him, wasn't he? That's definite too?"

"Yep. That's the word according to Fisk. And Tootsie says there were no signs of drugs, except for alcohol. The tissue analysis will have to confirm that, of course, but she and Fisk are both pretty sure. There's no sign that Quinn was tied up or restrained either. It's still all pointing to suicide, in other words, but Thorne isn't convinced. He's still on about why Quinn left the girls alive, and why he didn't leave a note. And why Rachel Brydie hasn't rung in yet, for that matter. Any tea left?"

"There might be some. Have a look. How did you go with Fiona Klein?"

"No luck. I think the phone's off the hook. Think we should go round there?"

"Maybe. I don't know."

Steve pulled off his coat, sat down and picked up the teapot. He weighed it in his hand, decided there wasn't enough tea left in it to make another cup, and put it down with regret.

"How did you go with Verna?" he asked.

Tessa had gone back to stirring the sugar. "She and Adam Quinn had an affair, while he was here. She's obviously not particularly proud of it. She says there was no future in it, and she was relieved when he went off with Rachel Brydie."

"Is that the truth?"

"I don't know. I asked her about violence. She was cagey. Very defensive. I think it's quite likely he tried a few things on her she didn't like, but put up with, and she's ashamed of it."

"Anything there for us?"

"Maybe. I don't know."

"Tessa!"

"What?"

"Why do you keep saying 'I don't know'?"

She looked up from the sugar bowl. "Do I?"

"Yes."

She sighed, and threw down the spoon. "Well, maybe it's because I *don't* know. I don't know what to think, I don't know what to do, and I don't know why I don't know."

"You're tired."

"I'm not all that tired. I'm just confused." She rubbed her eyes. "Steve, that man we saw sitting by the fire when we came in—the guy who looked like a birdwatcher . . ."

"Yeah? What about him?"

"He's a drag queen called Bouncy Bernadette."

Steve shouted with laughter. "You're kidding!"

"No. Verna told me. And it really made me think, you know. There's something about this place. It's all so quiet and peaceful that it lulls you. It affects your instincts. It makes you underestimate people—take them at face value—in a way you never would in the city."

Steve put his elbow on the tabletop, leaned on his hand and looked at her quizzically. "I don't think I've been doing that," he said.

"No. You probably haven't. But I have."

"And this crisis of confidence is all down to Bouncy Bernadette, is it?"

She laughed, but distractedly.

He stood up. "I think we should both get some sleep," he said. He began clearing away the tea things. She got up to help him. She took the cups and saucers to the sink, and rinsed them absentmindedly. When she'd finished she lifted a corner of the blind and looked out. The mist was no longer billowing and swirling against the window. Now it hung heavily, like a thick white blanket against the glass. There was no earth, no sky, no living thing to be seen.

She turned round to Steve. "What about the Brydie girls, and Klein? Should we go round there?"

"It's nearly midnight," he said.

"You suggested it before. What if there's something wrong? Why is the phone off the hook?"

"They probably had some nuisance calls. Or the whole town was suddenly Klein's best friend and she got sick of it. Who knows?"

Tessa paced, worrying at it. "The house isn't far away, is it?"

"Wouldn't be more than five minutes. It's in Greys Lookout Drive. Number 12. Mind you, in this mist—"

"Steve, I think we should just go and have a look," she said. "I'm happy to go on my own, if you—"

"Come on," he said resignedly, and grabbed his coat from the back of a chair.

The car crawled along, blind in the mist. The headlights didn't help. On high beam they simply lit up the whiteness, making it even more impenetrable. Street signs and house numbers were scarce, and when they were present, they were almost invisible. Tessa had to keep getting out of the car to check them.

They drew up, finally, outside 12 Greys Lookout Drive. All they could see of it was a mass of trees, an open gate, and a narrow, curving driveway climbing steeply into nothingness.

"Looks like she's right on the escarpment," said Steve. "Not bad for a schoolteacher."

"Ex-schoolteacher. Maybe she came into money. We'd better walk up, don't you think? In case they're asleep and the sound of the car gives them a fright."

"We'll be more bloody likely to give them a fright creeping around the house on foot," Steve said. "But we'll walk anyway. I don't like the idea of driving up there in this. Let alone backing out again."

They locked the car and began the climb, using their flashlight to guide their steps. The drive was extremely, ridiculously steep. Plainly, whoever built the house hadn't imagined anyone tackling it on foot. Tessa stopped halfway up, gasping and panting. The absurdity of the situation suddenly struck her, and she started to laugh.

"This is madness," she snorted. "It's torture!"

"D'you want to go back?" Steve inquired patiently.

"Of course I don't!" she gasped, desperately trying to control both her laughter and her breathing. "We've come this far."

"Come on, then."

The drive twisted again, and again, and finally they saw the house above them, looming out of the mist. It was small and very modern, built into the cliff, no doubt architect-planned to blend into its surroundings, but far too self-conscious a design ever to do so. There was a double garage built into the under-story, but Fiona Klein's maroon four-wheel drive had been left outside, pulled up onto a paved area from which a steep flight of stone steps climbed to the front door. The left side of the house was in darkness, but light glowed behind the blinds that covered the windows on the right.

"Someone's awake, anyhow," murmured Steve. Tessa was irritated to note that he didn't seem out of breath at all.

They edged past the car and climbed the steps, finally reaching the narrow timber deck that led to the front entrance and also appeared to encircle the house, providing walkways to the back. Steve knocked quietly at the door.

No one came. The house was utterly still.

Yet there was so much light. It glowed behind the cedar blinds on the right of the door. It streamed through the narrow vertical gaps between the edges of the blinds and the window frames.

Tessa shaded her eyes and peeped through the nearest gap.

"Living room," she whispered. "Every light on. But there's no one there."

"We'll try the back," Steve whispered in return.

They followed the walkway around the house and discovered that at the back the building was at ground level. The walkway ended in a single step that led them on to a flat, rocky area dotted here and there with scrubby bushes and clumps of spiky grass. The entire back of the house was made up of sliding glass doors giving out onto the rock.

The silence was as thick as the mist. Nothing moved.

Tessa jumped as Steve took her arm. "Stay close to the house," his voice murmured in her ear. "We don't know how far away the cliff edge is."

Her heart thumped sickeningly at the thought of the hidden, yawning gulf so near. "Wouldn't there be a railing?" she asked wildly.

"I don't think so. You don't have to fence off natural hazards."

The remark was so typical of him, so practical and commonsensical, so calmly delivered, that it made her want to laugh, and settled her at the same time. His hand, as he shepherded her along, was warm and strong.

Here, as it had at the front of the house, light shone brightly through the gaps in the blinds. Then Tessa saw that one of the sliding doors was partly open. It had been pushed aside, and hadn't been closed properly. Someone had gone in this way—or come out.

Again, they knocked. Again, there was no answer. Tessa peered inside. She saw the living room from another perspective, and in far greater detail. It was split-level, painted off-white, with polished floorboards and a few rugs. There were two black leather couches and a coffee table grouped around a slow-combustion stove; a dining table and chairs closer to where Tessa was standing at the back. The room was warm and very tidy, but nothing stirred. A small kitchen led off to Tessa's right, but it was separated from the dining area only by a square archway, and she could see that it, too, was deserted.

"There's no one there," she whispered. "The phone's off the hook, all right. And, Steve, the CD player's still on."

"I don't like this much," Steve said casually. He raised his hand and this time he knocked with his flashlight sharply, loudly, against the metal lock of the door, and called.

Tessa was just turning away from the window when she caught a movement from the corner of her eye. It wasn't in the living room. It was in a doorway beyond. Just a flicker of white, a glimpse of long, light brown hair.

"There's someone there," she hissed. "In the dark part of the house. It's Astral, I think."

"Call her."

Tessa knocked at the sliding door. "Astral," she shouted through the opening. "It's Tessa Vance. We came to see if you were all right. Sorry if we've frightened you. Could you come to the door, please?"

The seconds ticked by. No one came.

Tessa glanced at Steve. His face was grim. She knocked again. "Astral, we're coming in now. Could you get Miss Klein, please?"

They pushed at the door and stepped into the living room. Still calling, they moved across the room, down a few stairs, over to the door where Tessa had seen Astral Brydie standing, and through to a narrow hallway.

Across the hallway was another door. It was gaping wide, but all was darkness inside.

"Astral?" Tessa called. "Bliss? Skye? Are you all right? Are you in there?"

With Steve close behind her she moved to the door, cautiously felt for the light switch, and flicked it on. Bliss, Skye and Astral, all wearing white cotton nightdresses, stood clustered together in the very furthest corner of the room. Their eyes were wide and dark. They looked terrified.

"It's only me," Tessa said. "I'm sorry if we frightened you. Where's Miss Klein?"

There was a moment's silence. Then Astral spoke.

"We do not know," she said. "We went to find her, when you came. But she is not in her room. She is not by the fire. I think that she has gone out."

"Gone out?" said Steve quietly. "Where could she have gone, at this time of night?"

But the girls said nothing more. And many hours had passed before Tessa, Steve and the others they had called to help them finally found all that remained of Fiona Klein.

Seventeen

"It was a terrible fall. She broke her neck." Tootsie, business-like in slacks, sweater and sturdy shoes, her hair still tangled and leaf-strewn from her climb back up to the house, looked down at the body bag being hauled up the cliff face, strapped to a stretcher. "And there's severe concussion. Either one could have killer her. I'll know more when I can get a good look at her."

"When did she die, Tootsie?" murmured Steve. His face was set. They'd been up all night, but Tessa knew fatigue wasn't his only problem.

"I'd say—oh—between about 9 P.M. and midnight," said Tootsie.

Steve grimaced.

While we were having dinner, fencing with Rochette and the Ridges. Or while we were walking home, arguing. Or while we were listening to Melissa. Or while I was talking to Verna. Or fiddling around talking about Bernie. Wasting time . . .

We couldn't have known.

We should have known. That's what he's thinking. But I never dreamt she'd be in danger. Never dreamt . . . If anything, I thought—

"The question is, did she jump, or was she pushed?" murmured Fisk, who had been standing silently by, gazing out at the incredible view. The sun had risen now. The sky was an arc of blue over a panorama of cliff face and bush that stretched as far as the eye could see. The last of the mist clung to the valley floor, rising from the green depths like smoke. Tessa glanced at him and he returned her look blandly.

"I can't tell you how she fell," Tootsie snapped. "I'm not psychic. But if I find any hand-shaped bruises between her shoulder blades, Lance, you'll be the first to know."

Fisk turned away, smiling slightly. He enjoyed ruffling Tootsie's feathers.

"Fiona didn't jump," Steve said soberly.

"Are you saying she wasn't the suicidal type, Detective?" drawled Fisk, raising an eyebrow.

"No, I'm not." Steve refused to be riled. "She was the type who might kill herself if she found out she had something terminal. Or if she was in a real bind and couldn't see a way out." He stuck his hands in his pockets and turned to look at the house. "But she would have left a note explaining exactly why she did it," he went on. "And she would have chosen a time and a place that wouldn't inconvenience anyone else. She saw herself as protecting the Brydies. She'd never have left them with another suicide on their hands."

"Another suicide?" It was Thorne, approaching from the walkway. "Bit too much of a good thing, wouldn't you say?"

"She could simply have tripped and fallen, you know." Tootsie waved her hand at the unguarded boulders of the cliff edge, the sheer drop to the valley below. "Look at this—it's a death trap. Especially if visibility was poor."

"Poor? It was nonexistent," said Steve. "And that's the point, isn't it?" He looked around. "I can't see this being an accident any more than I can see it being suicide. Why would Klein have been wandering around out here late at night in conditions like that?"

"Maybe she needed to think," Tessa murmured.

They all looked at her.

Explain.

"The girls were in the house. The living areas are all open plan. Maybe she wanted to be alone. She's been away for quite a while. She might have forgotten just how close the cliff edge was."

But even as she said the words, she knew how lame they sounded. She'd only seen Fiona Klein for a few brief minutes—but that had been quite long enough for her to know that the woman was no fool.

"Then what if she heard something?" she hazarded. "Came out to look. Fell—"

"What if she heard *someone*?" Steve said slowly. "Went outside to check . . ."

"You're saying it's a homicide, Steve?" asked Thorne bluntly.

"Yes, I am."

He's so serious. This isn't like him.

He feels responsible.

Thorne looked out over the cliff, to the escarpment on the other side of the valley. It was glowing pink in the sun.

"Have you considered that the only people known to be in the house at the time of this woman's death were the Brydie sisters?" he asked, his face showing not a flicker of expression.

And Tessa knew that already, all over Oakdale, people were waking, hearing the news, and saying the same thing.

Bliss, Skye, and Astral were still in the bedroom, where Tessa had first seen them. In all the hours that had passed they had dumbly refused to leave it, refused to dress, or eat, or drink, refused to speak. Even when told of Fiona Klein's death, they had said nothing. They had simply stood, bunched closely together, and stared, their eyes wide and dark. Rochette Williams had been called from her bed to supervise them. Puffy-eyed but dogged, she stood as Tessa came to the door.

"They sat down, in the end, but they still haven't said a thing," she muttered.

Tessa went into the room, skirting the mattress that still lay on the floor. The air was stale, dead and overwarm. The window was closed, and the blind drawn.

The sisters were sitting rigidly together on the end of the double bed, facing a low chest of drawers with a mirror above it. Their hands were clasped in their laps, but their shoulders were touching. None of them turned their heads to look at her. They didn't need to, she realized. They could see her reflection, as she could see theirs. They were very pale. There were deep shadows under their eyes. Their faces were tight with tension.

Tessa took the chair on which Rochette had been sitting and placed it carefully so that it faced the bed, with its back to the chest. She sat down with an air of deliberation and looked at the three faces before her, one by one. Bliss, Skye, Astral.

They've put Skye between them.

Skye's the weak link.

"We need to know exactly what happened last night," she said quietly. "Bliss?"

Bliss didn't even blink. Tessa felt a tremor of impatience. Suddenly the gloom and stuffiness of the room became unbearable. She got up and went to the window, pulling up the blind, letting in the morning sun. She unlocked the window and pulled it open. Cool air streamed in. Then she went back to her chair.

"I understand you've had a terrible shock," she said, leaning forward and keeping her voice even and sympathetic. "But Fiona Klein is dead. We don't know at the moment whether her death was an accident, or not. But we have to try to find out. Do you understand?"

They nodded. It was a response, at least, if a silent one. Somewhat encouraged, Tessa went on.

"You will have to answer my questions," she said firmly. "I need to know, for example, if anyone came to visit you or Miss Klein last night. Astral?"

Astral stirred. "We saw no one," she said in a low voice.

Progress.

"When did you see Miss Klein for the last time?"

"At nine o'clock, when we went to bed."

That is our time—unless there is planting to be done.

They're still following the rules.

"And when you went to bed, where was Miss Klein?"

"She was sitting by the stove. Listening to music."

"Had you talked to her before that?"

Astral blinked. "Yes," she said cautiously.

"And what did you talk about?"

"She showed us our room, and the bathroom. She said for

us to have a bath, if we liked, and gave us sheets to make our beds. She asked us what we would like to eat."

"But what did you actually talk about? Did she ask you about Adam Quinn, for example? About the night he died?"

"Adam is not dead," whispered Skye.

"Did she ask you?" Tessa persisted, as though the girl hadn't spoken.

All three silently shook their heads, left to right, right to left. It was uncanny, the way they so often behaved in concert. But tension radiated from their bodies like heat. Tension, and fear.

"Then did you talk to Miss Klein about your mother, as I suggested?" asked Tessa. "Did she ask you about your mother? About where she is?"

Astral bit her lip. "She asked us."

"But we told her nothing, Astral," exclaimed Skye. "We did not—"

"There was nothing to tell," Bliss broke in. "We do not know." Her voice was very low, but very firm.

Aware of Rochette's interested eyes on her, Tessa tried another line of questioning. "Did Miss Klein seem worried or upset about anything?" she asked. She didn't really expect a sensible answer to this. But she was surprised, as so often she'd been surprised when dealing with the Brydies, for Astral nodded thoughtfully.

"She seemed sad," she said. "Her eyes were sad, when we said goodnight."

Tessa felt a small thrill of triumph. Here was something, at least. She leaned forward even further in her chair, concentrating all her attention on Astral. "Do you know why Miss Klein would have been sad?" she asked.

The girl looked around the room. "I thought perhaps she was sad because she was here, and Nicki was far away, and we had filled her space."

"Nicki?"

"Miss Klein's friend. She has long red hair, and plays the flute."

"This is her room?"

"It was her room, when she lived here. Nicki is in Italy,

now. Where Miss Klein was. Miss Klein said they were going to be away for many years. But she came back alone."

It was impossible to read anything into Astral's expression. Impossible to tell if she had any thoughts or theories as to what the relationship between Fiona Klein and Nicki, the flute player with long red hair, might have been.

Tessa couldn't help looking once again at Rochette. Rochette hadn't changed position, but as she met Tessa's eyes her eyebrows lifted very slightly, giving her face a smugly knowing expression.

Irritated, Tessa turned back to the sisters. Her eyes were hot and prickling and her muscles ached from her exercise of the night. Sometime today she'd have to get a few hours' sleep. But not for quite a while yet.

More questions had to be asked. And asked now. That Fiona Klein had committed suicide was, perhaps, not quite so unlikely a proposition as it had first appeared, given what Astral had just said. There was possibly a broken relationship that would have to be taken into account. But Tessa's instincts were all against it—as they were, despite what she might have argued outside on the clifftop, against the idea of the woman's death being an accident.

That left only one option. Murder. Murder by whom?

By these girls in front of her? Or one of them acting alone? Out of madness, it would have to be, since in the absence of their mother Fiona Klein was apparently their only protector in this place, if you didn't count Jonathon Stoller.

By someone else? Someone who, perhaps, feared what the girls might have told Klein, or might tell her in the future, about the death of Adam Quinn? Or who was angry, because she had taken them in? Someone who came visiting in the night, lured Fiona Klein outside, and pushed her to her death?

The sisters were waiting. Tessa took a breath and began:

"There are just a couple more things. When you came in here to bed, did you shut the door?"

Astral shook her head.

"Miss Klein said to leave it open, for air," said Bliss, breaking her long silence. "Because she saw me close and lock the window."

"Do you always sleep with the window closed?"

"No. Never before." Bliss pressed her hands together. It was the only sign of stress she had so far actively displayed.

Skye whimpered.

"Were you afraid someone might get in, Skye?" Tessa asked, looking at her quickly. But Skye just ran her tongue over her lips, and didn't answer. Tessa turned her attention back to Astral and Bliss.

"After you'd gone to bed, did you hear anything—anything unusual?" she asked. "The phone ringing? Anyone walking outside, on the deck? Anything at all?"

"We heard the music, faintly." Astral paused. Her brow wrinkled slightly.

She's remembered something.

"What is it?" Tessa prompted gently.

"I was lying listening to the music. I was tired, but I could not sleep. Then I heard her speak."

"Miss Klein?"

"Yes. Her voice was low. It stopped and started again. I thought she was reading a poem aloud. She liked to say her poems aloud. I liked to listen."

"*Her* poems? You mean, poems she wrote herself?"

"Yes." Astral caught her bottom lip between her teeth. Her eyes had darkened, as though tears were threatening.

They were close. Closer than either of them admitted.

Adam did not like Fiona, it is true . . .

If Fiona Klein was a lesbian . . . how close were they?

Astral's seventeen. Klein must have been fifty. And she was her teacher.

It happens. Is that why Klein went away?

Adam did not like Miss Klein . . . He said she should not interfere . . .

Astral was still speaking. "Miss Klein wrote poems about many things. Ordinary things—like school, and the house, and things she thought about. She said her poems were like her diary. She said they helped her to solve her problems."

"Could you hear anything she said, Astral?"

Astral shook her head. "Except that, at the beginning, she said my name," she whispered.

Beside her, Skye twitched convulsively. But Bliss stared straight ahead, her body seeming even more rigidly in control than before.

Tessa thought rapidly. There had been no pen or paper in the living room. There hadn't been a book either. Just a chair drawn up by the stove, a coffee mug on the hearth.

But the phone was there.

"You said that her voice stopped and started, Astral. Do you think perhaps Miss Klein could have rung someone up on the phone?" she suggested.

The girl looked up. The idea had obviously not occurred to her. "I could hear no one else," she said doubtfully. "Just Miss Klein."

"You wouldn't hear the other person's voice, Astral," said Tessa. "Not on the phone. Not from here."

"Oh." Astral stared.

It was incredible. Even a toddler would have known that. But Astral hadn't. Yet she wasn't a child. She was a young woman of seventeen, living on the fringes of a thriving community. She'd been to school—mixed with other young people . . .

The Brydies don't mix.

It seemed that the sisters had passed through the school system like droplets of oil floating through a stream of water. Untouched, unaffected . . .

Brainwashed. Stultified. Kept in ignorance. For an idea. For a theory. Left prey to superstition and nameless dread. Left prey to the likes of Adam Quinn . . .

Rachel Brydie should be shot . . . Oh, sorry, what a terrible thing to say.

Tessa felt sick. "Did anything else happen after Miss Klein stopped speaking?" she asked. "Did you hear anything else?"

Astral shook her head. "Then there was only music. Then I slept. Bliss and Skye were already asleep."

"Is that true, Bliss?"

Bliss nodded.

"Skye?"

Skye opened her lips, apparently with difficulty, and spoke. "She said we were safe. She said the doors were locked. She covered the windows to hide the darkness and the mist. She said we would be safe, if we slept." Horribly, she laughed—a high, hysterical laugh—then glanced at her sisters and pressed her hand over her mouth.

Tessa fought off a feeling of repulsion.

She can't help it. She's half out of her mind.

Half out of her mind with fear. With the tension of keeping a secret.

"So you slept—and then?"

"We woke up. We heard a banging, and a calling, from the back of the house," whispered Astral. "I got up and opened the door, and the sound was louder. I looked into the big room and saw that Miss Klein was not by the stove any more. But all the lights were burning. I heard you call my name. I went to Miss Klein's room, but she was not there. I was afraid. I ran back to this room, to Bliss and Skye. And then you came."

So where do we go from here?

Tessa looked over to where Rochette Williams leaned against the doorjamb with her arms folded, like a jailer.

"I think you'd better get dressed now," she said, turning back to the sisters. "We'll need to talk some more, but we can't stay here. The police will have to search the house."

Bliss, Astral and Skye glanced at one another. As if on a signal, Bliss stood up.

"We would like to return to Haven," she said, with tense dignity. "It is not right for us to be away. Please take us back."

"I don't think—" Tessa hesitated. She wasn't quite sure of her ground.

"We must go back." Skye's voice was high and trembling. The tips of her fingers, swollen and red, plucked at her nightdress.

"You change into your day clothes now, and I'll ask about it for you," Tessa temporized. "All right?"

They hesitated, glanced at one another. Silently communicating, perhaps. Or just undecided.

"Yes," Bliss said at last. "We will."

Tessa waited, but they didn't move. The moment lengthened.

"Come on, then," barked Rochette from the door.

Skye made a small, distressed sound.

"We cannot dress in front of strangers," said Bliss. "It is forbidden."

"Now, look—" Rochette began, but Tessa quelled her with a glance.

"All right," she said quietly. "Come out when you're ready."

She got up, ushered Rochette outside, and closed the door behind them. Rochette's whole body was rigid with disapproval as they moved a little up the corridor and settled themselves to wait.

"You aren't really going to ask him to let them go home, are you?" she demanded.

"I'd like to. I think it would be better for them."

Rochette shook her head. "Dunno why we'd be doing them any favors. What if they nick off, like their loopy mother?"

"I don't think they'll do that. They're scared to be away from Haven."

"I'd be scared to stay there, if I was them. They're not normal, you know."

That's the understatement of the year.

" 'Specially that Skye," Rochette went on, making a sudden gesture of distaste. "She gives me the creeps. She's always given me the creeps."

Intolerant, prejudiced . . .

Skye gives you the creeps, too. Go on, admit it.

It's not her fault!

"It's not their fault," Tessa said aloud. "They've been brought up differently from other people. And Quinn— they're still terrified of him. Just as if he was still alive. They're victims, Rochette."

Rochette screwed up her mouth. "I don't know about victims," she said, looking at the ceiling. "It's not the Brydies who're dead, is it? It's Quinn and Klein. Wouldn't you call them the victims? Or have I got it wrong?"

She frowned at the closed door. "God knows what they're doing in there," she commented. "Dunno why you let them get changed on their own."

Tessa couldn't explain. She couldn't explain that to insist on watching Skye, Bliss and Astral taking off their clothes would seem like brutalizing them, and she thought they'd been brutalized enough already. Rochette would see that as weakness. The Brydies were suspects, as far as she was concerned, and as such, shouldn't be left alone.

Rochette sniffed. "Not much point in changing, anyhow, if you ask me," she said. "They'll only put on those white things. May as well stay in their nighties."

"When you knew Bliss and Skye at school—did they wear school uniforms like everyone else?" asked Tessa curiously.

"You joking? Do you reckon Rachel Brydie would've come at that? No way."

"Were they the only ones?"

"Just about." Rochette poked out her bottom lip. "There were a few others—but they wore, you know, ordinary clothes—T-shirts and shorts and that. The Brydies always wore those long white things their mother made—looked like the angels in the Christmas play. Stuck out like sore thumbs."

She considered the matter, head on one side. "Would've probably been okay if they'd gone to that progressive school up Gilly way. Those kids wear all sorts of stuff. But it costs a bomb, they say, so that was out."

"It must have been terribly hard for them."

Rochette shrugged. "They never acted like it was hard. Like, if anyone ever tried to be nice to them, you know, felt sorry for them or whatever, tried to get them to join in some game or whatever, they never would. They weren't ever grateful, or anything." Her eyes slewed sideways, taking in Tessa's reaction. " 'Course, it's not much fun, being pitied," she added, with one of those shrewd, surprising flashes of insight that every now and again punctured her habitual insensitivity.

"No." Tessa wondered if Rochette herself had had her share of unwanted pity. She imagined her, a plain and stocky teenager, standing all dressed up against the wall of the school hall year after year while others danced, her smart mouth and rough manner camouflaging her pain, till gradually the protective hide grew thick and impenetrable.

There were sounds inside the room. Movement, low voices—too low for separate words to be audible.

What are they saying to each other?

You shouldn't have left them alone.

They know where their mother is. Why didn't they tell Klein?

They say they didn't. But maybe they did. And now Klein's dead. You asked for it. You—

A scream of pain tore through the air. Shrill, piercing—

Tessa whirled around. In two strides she'd reached the bedroom door. She threw it open. It crashed against the wall and bounced back. Bliss, Skye and Astral stood by the bed, frozen in a bizarre tableau. There was a pungent smell in the air. Skye had wrapped her arms around her head. Astral was naked, cowering and sobbing, her nightgown clutched to the front of her body. Bliss's raised hand was horribly smeared with something thick and yellow.

"What are you doing?" shouted Tessa, clinging to the doorjamb, her heart hammering with shock.

Then she saw, and her stomach churned. Behind her she heard Rochette swearing softly, and the sound of feet approaching from the living room.

"Rochette, tell Inspector Thorne everything's all right," she said quickly. "I'll be out in a minute."

She went into the room and closed the door behind her.

Eighteen

Skye had taken her arms from her face and was wailing softly now, her cries mingling with Astral's sobbing. But Bliss was silent, her eyes filled with dread. Tessa crossed the room and touched her shoulder.

"It's all right, Bliss," she said gently. "I'm sorry I shouted. I didn't realize what you were doing. I know you didn't mean to hurt her."

Bliss opened dry lips, and when she spoke her voice was trembling. "I am at fault," she said. "But the salve is thick, and I touched too roughly. I was trying to hurry—"

Tessa winced, looking at the terrible cuts and weals that crisscrossed the back of Astral's body from the shoulder blades to the knees. The wounds looked about a week old. They were healing, but still stood out angrily red, scabbed and swollen, scored, horribly, over dozens of other, older scars, pink and white, broad and thin, that marked the skin.

Adam has corrected her . . . many times . . .

Tessa took a breath. It seemed a long time since she'd done so. "Astral," she said, as calmly as she could. "Did Adam Quinn do this to you?"

Astral screwed her eyes shut, clutching her nightgown to her chest.

Make her say it!

"Astral!" said Tessa sharply. "Please answer me! Did Adam do this?"

"Yes!" The girl almost gasped the word.

"When?"

"Last—Sunday afternoon."

Go on!

187

"Was your mother there?"

"No. She had gone out."

"Why did he beat you?"

"He—corrected me. I—had disobeyed."

"You *always* disobey!" shrieked Skye, her eyes bulging, her ruined fingers pressed to her lips. "You disappoint Adam again and again. And now—" With a choking gasp, she was mercifully silent.

Bliss was rigid. Her hand, the fingers still gleaming with the pungent yellow stuff, was curled like a claw.

"Sit down, Bliss," said Tessa.

She sat down on the bed like an automaton. Tessa went and stood in front of Astral. The girl was bent over, her chin almost on her chest. Tessa spoke to her slowly and clearly. "Astral, before Bliss finishes putting on the ointment, I'm going to ask Constable Suzeraine to come in and photograph these marks," she said.

Astral shook her head. "No one must see," she whispered. "It is forbidden. Strangers would not understand."

No, they bloody wouldn't.

Tessa forced sternness into her voice. "It's too late to worry about that now," she said. "I've seen. The wounds must be photographed. It's necessary."

In case you killed Quinn. Or your mother did. So your lawyer will have proof of self-defense, provocation . . . whatever. So they can see what he did to you.

There was no response.

"Then a doctor is going to look at you," Tessa continued.

"We do not see doctors," said Bliss, with an effort. "The tea-tree salve will heal the wounds. They are healing now. The salve always heals, if the wounds are clean. I have put it on every day, as is necessary. We know what must be done."

They know because it's happened so many times before. To all of them.

You knew that. They showed you the cane. You knew it.

I didn't know it was like this!

There was a knock on the door. "Tessa, you okay?" called Rochette's voice. Flat, matter-of-fact . . . normal.

"Fine," Tessa called back. "But Rochette—find Dee

Suzeraine—you know, the photographer? Ask her to come in here, will you? With the camera? As quick as she can. It's important."

"Right."

Astral had begun trembling all over. Tessa bent and pulled a sheet and quilt from the mattress on the floor. "Wrap these around you," she said. The girl made no move, so Tessa herself draped the covers around her. "The sheet first, then the quilt," she chattered. "There. Now you'll be warmer, won't you? Why don't you sit down with Bliss?"

Still Astral didn't answer, didn't move.

Hurry up, Dee.

"You remember Constable Suzeraine, don't you? The police photographer who was at Haven?" Tessa chattered on, filling the silence. "She'll take these photographs quite quickly, Astral, and then she'll go. You don't have to be embarrassed. No one will see the photographs except people who really have to. All right?"

If she refuses to let Dee do it, what then?

You're a witness. You can—

Another knock on the door, and then Dee was in the room, bringing with her the smell of the bush. Leaves and seed pods clung here and there to her uniform. She was chewing gum. She closed the door behind her and raised her eyebrows at Tessa, questioningly.

"Astral has some injuries I'd like you to photograph, Dee," said Tessa, with forced casualness. She met Dee's eyes.

Don't scare her, Dee.

Dee nodded, chewing. "Sure," she said. "No problem."

"Do you need her to move?"

"Oh, no. Just there'll be fine." Dee looked through her camera, focusing on Astral's shrouded back.

Rochette's told her.

"Whenever you're ready," Dee said laconically. "I'll be quick."

Gently, Tessa pulled the quilt and the sheet away from the girl's body. Dee's camera flashed. Once, twice, three times. Dee stepped closer, and the camera flashed again. Over and over. She was getting the whole picture. Working fast.

Making sure she got the old scars, as well as the new. She was the complete professional, as always. But her mouth was a hard, straight line, and when at last she dropped the camera, the eyes that met Tessa's were full of loathing.

"What a bastard," she muttered.

Tessa nodded, wrapping the sheet and quilt around Astral again. The girl hadn't moved, and neither had either of her sisters.

"We'll leave you to finish getting dressed now," Tessa said. "All right?"

Bliss stood up. She looked haggard.

"Please don't worry." Tessa knew even as she said the words that they were useless. These women needed more than counseling. They needed therapy. They were in the grip of a nightmare that never ended.

Fisk and Thorne were in the living room, thoughtfully regarding the slow-combustion stove, the door of which hung open. Thorne looked up, and raised an inquiring eyebrow as Tessa and Dee entered.

Briefly Tessa told him what had happened, what she'd seen. She kept her voice flat and matter-of-fact. She was a professional. She was, theoretically, unshockable. But inside, she was raging.

When she'd finished, Thorne was silent for a moment. "It's no more than we knew already, in effect," he said, finally. "Except for the timing. They didn't tell you before that Quinn beat Astral on the day he ended up dead, did they?"

"No. But they've been taught to keep it quiet."

"They might also have realized it wouldn't do them any good." Thorne thrust his hands into his pockets and jingled some change there. "It strengthens their motive."

He turned to Dee. "Get plenty of pics?" he inquired brusquely.

Dee nodded, stony-faced.

I didn't get the photographs done for you. It was for them.

Thorne was still jingling the money in his pockets. The sound grated on Tessa's nerves almost unbearably.

"I don't see where Klein fits in," he said. He seemed to be

talking to himself, but suddenly looked straight at Tessa. "Any ideas?"

She shook her head. "It wouldn't make sense for the girls to kill Fiona Klein, if that's what you mean," she said. "She could have protected them. Could have made sure they weren't unfairly treated. And they seem to know that. Certainly Astral does."

He regarded her calmly.

You sound aggressive.

I feel aggressive.

"What did they tell you about her?" he asked.

"They say they didn't hear or see anyone in the house other than Klein last night. But their own window was closed. If someone came around the side after they were asleep, they mightn't have heard."

"Every door was locked, except that one sliding door at the back," Fisk commented, from his place by the stove. "The window in Klein's room was open, but there's a fixed screen and it hasn't been tampered with."

Thorne nodded. "No way there was a break-in," he agreed. "And if she didn't have a visitor . . ."

"She might have," Tessa cut in. "I think she made a phone call—sometime after nine. Astral heard her talking, but couldn't make out any individual words except her own name."

He nodded, tight-lipped.

Are you going to tell him the rest? The possibility that Klein was gay . . . broken relationship . . . Astral . . .

Check it out first.

"Astral should see a doctor, but she won't," Tessa said.

"Is her back infected?"

Crusted, raw strips on tender, white . . .

"No, I don't think so."

"We can't force her," said Thorne. "But I've got a psych coming up from Sydney tomorrow. We've got to be careful . . ."

Careful we don't give the defense a handle on us. Careful we protect ourselves.

What about them? Who's going to protect them?

"They want to go back to Haven," said Tessa. "Can I take them back?"

"As far as I'm concerned, you can," said Fisk. "We're finished there." He tweaked at his trouser legs, crouched, and peered into the stove. "What others might think about it, I don't know," he added, without turning around.

"If we take them to the station they'll attract a lot of attention," Tessa said, speaking directly to Thorne. "They're very frightened. Especially now we've seen Astral's back. They've broken one of the golden rules. I think they'll talk more freely at home."

He considered the question briefly, then nodded. "They can go back for the moment," he said. "But don't go yourself. Send Williams along with them. Tell her to stick to them like glue, and not to be too friendly."

"That won't be too hard for her," muttered Tessa.

He smiled coldly. "Fine. It might be a good idea to let them stew for a while before you tackle them again. Steve's doing a check of the neighbors. When he gets back you can follow up that phone call. Plus the Brydie sighting at the lake last Sunday night. What did her daughters say about that, by the way?"

Tessa's stomach gave a sickening jolt and she felt the hot color rush to her face. Literally, in the search for Fiona Klein, in the discovery of the body and the shocked guilt and conjecture that followed, she had forgotten Melissa's tale. Forgotten that there was a possible lead to Rachel Brydie's whereabouts. Forgotten to tax the sisters with it.

How could I? Oh, God, what will he think?
Tough it out.

She fought for composure. "I haven't asked them about that, yet," she said.

"You will be asking them, though, won't you, Tessa?" Thorne murmured. "Before you send them home, maybe?"

He can see straight through you. He knows you forgot.

"Yes, sir. I'll do it now."

He nodded, smiling faintly, and turned back to Fisk.

Tessa hesitated. "Do we have anything on Fiona Klein's

next of kin yet?" she asked. "Astral mentioned someone called Nicki, who used to share this house. We should—"

"Of course. And I'm sure you will. As soon as you have a moment." He didn't even glance in her direction.

"Right." Tessa turned on her heel and rejoined Rochette in the hallway.

"They're taking their time," Rochette observed dourly, jerking her head towards the bedroom.

Tessa realized that the room had become very quiet. She tapped on the door. "Ready?" she called.

No answer. No sound.

Oh, God. Out the window . . . ?

Quickly, she turned the handle and pushed the door open.

But the sisters were there, sitting once again on the end of the bed. They wore their long white shifts, and had put sandals on their feet. They had brushed their hair. Their bundles were at their feet. Their hands were clasped in their laps. She met their eyes in the mirror. Shadowed, fearful.

Tessa stared at them helplessly. They all looked down at their hands.

She crossed the room and sat down in the chair, facing them. They didn't look up.

"I want to help you," she said softly. "But I can't, if you won't tell me the truth."

Silence.

They're natural victims.

Stop treating them with kid gloves. Wake them up. Shake them up!

"We've had a report that your mother was seen at the lake last Sunday night," she said loudly.

The reaction was instant. Obviously startled, the sisters jerked up their heads. They looked at one another, and then at Tessa. Skye's mouth was hanging slightly open. Her prominent eyes showed white around the blue.

Bliss recovered first. "Who saw her?" she asked. Her rich, low voice was perfectly in control. But the fact that she'd actually asked a question showed just how off balance she was.

"I can't tell you that just now," said Tessa. "But if it was your mother who was seen, she was in a four-wheel drive vehicle, and she was with someone else. Can you tell me who?"

Again they glanced at one another.

"No," said Astral, after a moment. "We cannot tell you."

Despite herself, Tessa felt a stab of irritated anger. "Can't, or won't?" she snapped.

She could feel them withdraw. Then, almost imperceptibly they drew closer together, gaining strength from one another. She heard a disgusted sniff from the door, and turned to look at Rochette. Constable Williams's disapproval was written all over her square, plain face. If this is how you operate, her expression seemed to say, I'm wasting my time.

She's right. You blew it. You should have separated them.

"Who do you know who has a car like that?" she demanded. "Do you know the sort of car I mean? There are quite a few around here. Miss Klein's car is one, for example."

"Jonathon's car is like Miss Klein's," murmured Astral.

"Any others, that you can think of?"

She shook her head.

"Has a car like that ever come to Haven?"

Astral seemed to be about to answer, but hesitated.

"Strangers do not come to Haven," droned Skye.

"Skye, please be quiet! Astral, answer me, please! What were you going to say?"

"There have been no such cars at Haven until yesterday. Yesterday, there were two," Astral said quietly. "Miss Klein's, at the gateway, and another one on the grass."

"Police vehicle," said Rochette flatly, all but turning up her eyes to the ceiling.

This is a farce.

Tessa stood up.

"All right, then," she said. "Constable Williams will take you back to Haven now."

In unison, Bliss, Skye and Astral bent to pick up their bundles, and stood up. Though they had asked to be allowed to go home, they seemed neither grateful, nor aware that they had been granted a concession, now that their wish had been granted. If anything, their expressionless faces and slightly drooping shoulders indicated resignation.

Again Tessa felt that flare of anger. Again she allowed it to show. She knew that its light was hardening her eyes as she looked them up and down. She heard it sharpen her voice as she spoke to them.

"Later today I'll be speaking to you again. I hope by then you'll have decided to be frank with me. Two people are dead, and you were present on both occasions. You're in a very dangerous positions."

She paused. The sisters stood silently, staring into space.

I'm not getting through to them. They aren't even listening to me.

Nothing you can say to them is worse than what they fear already.

Her anger died. She lowered her voice slightly. "Look, I know you're scared. I know you think that by keeping quiet you're protecting yourselves, and possibly your mother. But it's no good. You won't be able to keep it up forever."

Still there was no response.

"If you tell us all you know, we can help you!" Tessa exclaimed in frustration.

Astral spoke. "No one can help us," she said, her lips barely moving.

"Astral, you don't believe that!"

"Miss Klein tried to help us, and she is dead." The words were like a sigh.

"We don't even know yet how Miss Klein came to fall," said Tessa. "It could have been an accident. Or even suicide."

You don't believe that.

But the sisters were slowly shaking their heads. Left to right, right to left.

"It does not matter how it was," said Bliss. Her voice was patient, as if she was explaining something to a very young child. "She is dead. Because we disobeyed."

"Bliss, that's—"

"You are a stranger, and could not understand," said Bliss. It wasn't an accusation, just a statement.

"I said we should not go with her," Skye suddenly burst out, her voice quavering and high. She pulled and tore at the breast of her shift.

"Skye—" warned Bliss.

Skye half-sobbed, but went on. "We have done great wrong!" she moaned. "We have betrayed Adam. We have allowed his body to be touched by strangers. We left our work undone. We let ourselves be taken from Haven. And now he has shown us . . ."

Her voice trailed off into a dull whimpering.

"Adam Quinn is *dead*!" Tessa exclaimed, her skin crawling. "He's not responsible for Fiona Klein's death. He's dead, and gone, and he won't come back."

But Bliss, Skye and Astral stared at her, and their eyes were full of animal fear. Dumb. Trapped.

They don't believe you.

Astral . . .

Not even Astral. Not any more.

Nineteen

Sheena Rafael, the owner of 14 Greys Lookout Drive, was a small, plump old lady with a bunched-up face, bulging eyes, a tiny mouth and chin, a mop of frizzed hair in an unlikely shade of chestnut and vividly painted nails that were so long that they curved slightly downward at the tips. When she opened the door to Steve she was wearing what looked like a lime-green boilersuit teamed with a matching hand-knitted sleeveless jacket and vast sheepskin boots that came almost to her knees. Unlike her two Pekinese, to whom in other ways she bore an extraordinary likeness, she'd been delighted to see Steve, and invited him in, refusing to take no for an answer. The dogs, yapping furiously, made kamikaze darts for his trouser legs as he followed her to the back of the house.

Mrs. Rafael showed him into a lively, cluttered sitting room which adjoined the kitchen, had a spectacular view, and smelled about equally of incense, dog hair, coffee and raisin toast. A large electric heater warmed the space. A TV evangelist was mouthing soundlessly on the screen of a television set which sat on a mobile stand that had been pulled into the center of the room. A coffeepot, a single cup, and a plate of raisin toast stood on a low, glass-topped cane table near the windows. Mrs. Rafael obviously spent a lot of time sitting at this table. An armchair piled with cushions was drawn up to it. There were books and magazines on a shelf beside it, the phone was there, and you could see both the TV set and the view from her chair.

Mrs. Rafael made Steve sit down at the table, facing the view, toddled to the kitchen for another cup, and poured him some coffee. On the railing of a narrow veranda outside the

197

windows, rosellas and king parrots flapped and squawked around seed trays that had obviously been freshly filled. The dogs growled and blinked at the parrots, but presumably had learned from experience that the glass was impenetrable, and soon turned their backs on the windows to concentrate on glaring balefully at Steve, daring him to make the wrong move.

"Just ignore them," Mrs. Rafael laughed happily. "They're just jealous." Her voice slipped without warning into an alarming falsetto. "Dust dealous, aren't we, sweetie pies?" she crooned to the dogs. "Naughty, dealous wittle tings!" Both dogs showed their teeth. "Bweakfast-time!" she wheedled. She took two pieces of raisin toast from the plate in front of her, and offered them temptingly. The dogs each accepted one sulkily and, with an air of outraged dignity, allowed themselves to be lifted onto a nearby purple couch to eat.

Her babies taken care of, Mrs. Rafael sat down in her chair and turned her attention to Steven. She knew, of course, why he had come. A pair of binoculars lying on the table attested to her attempts to keep track of progress next door. She had been woken during the search, and ever since had sat right in her present spot, alternately dozing and trying her best to see what was happening. But as she explained, the bush between the two houses was thick, and the mist last night made it hard to see any further than her own veranda rail. It was only when the stretcher bearing Fiona Klein's shrouded body was being hauled up the cliff face that the old lady had been able to catch a glimpse of the action.

But before that, of course, the phone had been ringing. Thanks to the village news network, Mrs. Rafael had known that Fiona Klein was dead since very early this morning. She told Steve that it was a shocking, terrible thing. A tragedy. A woman like that, with her whole life in front of her. Mrs. Rafael shook her chestnut curls wistfully, but with no real sadness. She realized that this must be obvious, and apologized. She and Fiona's mother had been good friends and neighbors for many years, she told Steve. But she hadn't known Fiona at all well. And at her age, you got used to people passing on. She herself had lost her mother and father, her husband, both her brothers and most of her old friends.

Questioned further, she said that Fiona had inherited the house from her mother, Mavis, who had built it with Fiona's father years ago on the site of an old fibro dwelling—in the good old days when councils didn't want to interfere in everything you did with your own land. Fiona's father was an architect, and had designed the house himself. It was thought most unusual and innovative then, but of course it was nothing to the weird and wonderful things that were built nowadays.

As far as Mrs. Rafael knew, Fiona had no living relations. There had been a sister who was severely retarded, and who was in some sort of home for years. But she had died in her early twenties, poor thing. There was no one else. Mavis, just before she herself died, had told Mrs. Rafael that when she was gone, Fiona would have no one. She asked Mrs. Rafael to keep a friendly eye on her daughter if she came to live in the clifftop house. But Fiona was a very private sort of person, and didn't need an old neighbor interfering. That was obvious, from the first day she moved in. And it wasn't as if she didn't have company. She had a friend living with her for most of the time—a very nice young woman called Nicole— beautiful red hair, she had—who always waved, if she saw you in the street. Nicole would be the one they should contact, Mrs. Rafael said. She'd be very upset to hear the news. She was in Italy. Mr. Ridge at the estate agent's should be able to give the police her address.

She poured more coffee, and Steve asked her about the night before. Had she heard or seen anything that might help them?

He was a very nice young man, Mrs. Rafael thought. A little bit serious, perhaps. Very likely he worked too hard, like all the young did these days. They drove themselves, that was the trouble. But he was tall, dark and good-looking for all that. He had a beautiful smile when he did smile, and he had what in her young days they'd called bedroom eyes. Old as she was, Mrs. Rafael said to herself with some complacency, she still had an eye for a good-looking young man.

Last night, she told Steve, she had taken herself off to

Swans, as was her regular monthly habit, to have dinner and see Bouncy Bernadette's show.

"I go to see her every month, when she comes up to Swans. It's my little treat. She sings, you know, and in between she tells the funniest jokes. I don't know how she remembers them all. They're sometimes a little bit naughty, but nothing obscene, if you know what I mean. Just a bit of fun. Laugh! I nearly die. It really does me good." She leaned forward confidentially. "I have to be careful with the money these days, being a widow on a fixed income, you know," she said. "And of course I have to book a taxi to take me to and from, so that makes it an expensive night for me. But I'd rather do without dinners for a week than miss out." She twinkled, looking up at Steve roguishly. "Not that it ever comes to that, dear. That was just my little joke."

She chattered on about her night out, obviously enjoying the company and the chance to talk. Steve didn't try to stop the flow. In his experience witnesses like Mrs. Rafael did better if you let them settle themselves down.

"They always give me the same table right in front, these days, you know," Mrs. Rafael said. "And there's always a red rosebud in a vase waiting for me. Compliments of Bernadette. Isn't that lovely? I always bring it away with me. It lasts nearly a week in my bedroom, if I put aspirin in the water."

She paused at last. Steve took his chance, and asked about her homecoming last night. Relaxed and happy, Mrs. Rafael proceeded to tell him what he wanted to know.

She had arrived home as usual last night, just after 9:30. She looked quite carefully at Fiona's house as the taxi passed it, slowing down to turn into the driveway of number 14. Of course she knew that the Brydie sisters were staying with Fiona. Everyone at Swans knew about it, and she'd been quite the center of attention, because she lived next door.

"Not that I was able to tell people anything much," she added regretfully, "except that it was very quiet in there. But then, it always was. Fiona and Nicole weren't the ones for noisy parties or anything."

"And when you came home?" Steve persisted. "Did you

hear or see anything unusual then? When you arrived, or later?"

At last, his patience was rewarded. Mrs. Rafael's bunched-up face took on a thoughtful, puzzled expression. She sipped at her coffee, then put down her cup and leaned forward again.

"Well, I *did* happen to notice that while I'd been at Swan's, Fiona had for some reason brought her car down from the house and parked it in the road," she said. "It wasn't there at 6:30, when I left. I thought, that's funny. I wonder why she's done that? It's a terrible climb up to these houses. Then I thought that perhaps some workmen were coming to repave Fiona's garage area in the morning. That would account for her moving the car before she went to bed. Workmen always start so early. It was awkward for her, I thought, with guests in the house—"

"You're sure it was Fiona's car you saw, Mrs. Rafael?" Steve broke in.

The old lady seemed startled. "Well, I just assumed it was," she said breathlessly. "It looked exactly like it. Fiona has one of those cars like jeeps, you know. They must be very heavy to drive, I've always thought. Not that I've driven my-self for many years, dear. I never really enjoyed it, and anyway I'm sure taxis work out cheaper in the end, don't you think? Cars are so expensive to run. Anyway, I saw the car there, and I didn't see the numberplate or anything, or even the color, really, because of the mist. But I saw the shape, quite clearly. And who else's would it be?"

She nodded her head vigorously, convincing herself. "No one would have been visiting the house, would they? Every-one knew the Brydie girls were staying there—and that they'd be wanting their privacy. They've never liked talking to other people at any time."

She lowered her voice. "The mother is *most* peculiar, but I think the girls are probably just very shy, poor things, what-ever anyone else says. People can be very cruel, can't they, in the things they say?" She sighed. "I was really quite pleased when I heard that Adam Quinn had moved in with the mother. The girls were still quite young then, and I thought it would be wonderful for them. A man does make a big difference to a house."

Steve made no comment on that, but began leading her carefully through the rest of her story. There wasn't much to it.

Tired from her night out, Mrs. Rafael had made her babies their supper, let them out, then let them in again. She was in bed by 10:30, and was asleep, more or less, as soon as her head hit the pillow. She had heard nothing during the night. Nothing that she was aware of, anyway. Living with nature, as she did, there were always night noises—animals calling out, and so on—she said. But you got used to it. As she supposed people in Sydney got used to planes roaring overhead, and sirens and such. And of course, these days she was just a tiny bit deaf. Flirtatiously, she lifted a chestnut curl to show Steve her hearing aid. She didn't really need it, she said, but her daughter had thought it might make the television easier to hear. Of course she took the aid out at night. There was no point in hearing things you didn't want to hear, was there?

"And the doggies tend to snore a bit, too," she added, lowering her voice, presumably to avoid hurting their feelings.

Steve's visit didn't last much longer, after that. Mrs. Rafael was sorry to see him go, but understood, as she said, how busy he must be. At the door, she wished him luck in his investigations. She said she was sure he'd soon work out how poor Fiona had come to grief. She watched every mystery she could find on television, and read all the books, too, when they came into the library. She knew that they could do wonderful things nowadays, with computers and so on.

Steve walked down the winding steps leading to the street with the sound of the dogs yapping after him. Bidding him good riddance, he imagined. He turned once, and saw the plump little lime-green figure still standing behind the screen door. It lifted a hand and waved to him. He waved back and went on, reaching the bottom, trudging over the muddy strip that edged the road till he arrived at Fiona Klein's driveway and beginning the hard climb up again.

Back to the real world, he said to himself. Then he met the

Brydie sisters walking down the drive with Rochette, and wondered if it was.

"Going back to Haven," Rochette said briefly, and shut her mouth like a trap. Steve could have sworn he actually heard her lips snap together.

He nodded and watched Bliss, Skye and Astral glide by, their heads lowered, their flat sandals slapping softly on the concrete. As Rochette passed him in her turn, he gave her an inquiring look. Did Tessa get anything out of them? the look said.

"If it had been up to them, not a blinking sausage," she muttered. "But there's a bit of news. What about you?"

"Woman next door wasn't bad," he said.

She looked interested, but he couldn't elaborate in case the sisters heard, and she knew it. Wrinkling her nose, she lifted her hand in farewell, and stumped on down the drive.

So Thorne was letting the Brydies go for the moment, Steve thought, as he resumed his climb. It would have to be just for the moment. Thorne didn't give up that easily. He wondered what Rochette had meant by news. Something that the Brydies hadn't told, apparently. Or hadn't wanted to tell.

He reached the flat, paved area, and the parked four-wheel drive. He went over to the car and inspected it, without touching. It was well-kept, but not new. A couple of years old, he'd guess. Charles Ridge had mentioned that Fiona had had to buy a car. She must have got this secondhand. They'd have to check it out: one of the hundreds of routine jobs that even the strangest and most bizarre case must involve.

Routine didn't daunt Steve. It sometimes bored him, but he had long ago disciplined himself to accept that a certain level of tedium was necessary in his work, if he was to get what he wanted. There was something satisfying, he found, about the patient, persevering assembly of facts. Reward would come when, slowly but surely, the facts began to roll forward, one tipping on to another like a line of dominoes, clearing a straight track through irrelevancies, leading him forward to an irrevocable conclusion.

The roll usually started with something small. Often a tiny piece of information from a member of the public. And Steve was wondering whether the tidbit he'd just received from Sheena Rafael was going to prove important.

Mrs. Rafael was sharp enough, he thought, pacing around Fiona Klein's car. If she thought the car she'd seen outside the house at 9:30 was this one, then either it was, or it had looked very like it. Certainly a similar make, anyway. But it had been dark and misty, and she'd just seen the shape. It could have been any color.

Melissa had said that Heidi Ridge hadn't noticed the exact color of the four-wheel drive she saw at the lake last Sunday night. Could it have been the car Mrs. Rafael saw?

"Steve?"

He looked up, crinkling his eyes against the glare of the sun. Tessa was standing at the top of the steps.

"I think we ought to get this car checked out," he said.

She nodded, but absentmindedly, and didn't ask him why. "You'd better come in," she said. "Fisk's found something in the stove."

They briefed each other quickly, and went back into the house together. They found Fisk on his hands and knees shining a flashlight through the gaping door of the slow-combustion stove while Inspector Thorne bent beside him.

Inside the stove there was a thick bed of ash. But over to one side was a wavy pile of fine gray wafers. They would crumble at a breath, but you could see that they had once been a wad of lined notebook paper covered in handwriting.

"The fire was all but out when the paper went in," Fisk said.

"See those loops?" Steve craned his neck to see. "It's Klein's writing."

"We can't be sure of that, yet," snapped Fisk repressively. "Please stand back. This material is very fragile."

But even Thorne was finding it difficult to stand aside. He stooped, and twisted his neck to try to make out words on the flimsy scraps.

"Short lines. Looks like she's been making lists," he commented after a moment. "Dozens of lists." He straightened up, and frowned with disappointment. "School stuff, maybe."

"They could be poems," Tessa said quietly. "Astral said Klein wrote poetry."

. . . her poems were like her diary.

"You could very well be right," murmured Fisk. He took a breath and leaned even further into the stove. He remained motionless for a moment, then carefully withdrew his head, and breathed out. He closed the door of the stove and stood up.

"The material will have to be removed with extreme care," he announced unnecessarily. "But I think we can do it. If we are given some room."

"Why would she burn her poems?" asked Steve.

"An instinct for privacy?" Fisk suggested. "An ending?" His face was set, as though he understood.

Tessa stared at the stove. Was he right? Had Fiona Klein burned her most private work, then killed herself?

She seemed sad, when we said goodnight . . .

Thorne turned to Tessa and Steve. "You can't do any more here," he said heavily. "You know what you have to do. Get on with it."

They nodded and moved reluctantly away.

"And keep in touch," he called after them.

"He's frustrated," grinned Steve, as they left the house by the front door. "He wants this wrapped up fast and tidy."

"He also doesn't want this to be suicide," muttered Tessa.

Steve looked down at her. "I thought you agreed with me that she couldn't have killed herself."

"I'm not so sure, now."

"Come on! You really think Klein would have done that to the Brydies? She wouldn't. You know that. You met her."

"I didn't talk to her, Steve, you did."

"Can't you take my word for it?"

He was irritated.

You expect him to trust your judgment.

He doesn't know what I know.

They'd reached the paved area and Fiona Klein's car, where already two of Fisk's people were preparing for a forensic search.

"You really think they're going to find anything?" asked

Tessa, as she and Steve moved past the car and on down the driveway.

Steve shrugged. "Might be just a matter of elimination. But it's got to be done. There's a four-wheel drive mixed up in this somewhere. Klein's car is a four-wheel drive. Klein was back in the country earlier than she said. Klein went hot-footing over to Haven as soon as she heard that the body had been found . . ."

Is it possible . . . ?

Hold it. Take a step at a time.

"I think Klein might have had a thing about Astral," Tessa said slowly.

Steve stared. "What sort of 'thing'?" he demanded. "In love with her, you mean? What makes you think that?"

"It's just an idea," Tessa said defensively. "I might be completely wrong. But I think—I think maybe Klein broke up a long relationship and came back to Oakdale because of Astral."

"You reckon she decided after a few hours that it wasn't going to work, and jumped off a cliff on the strength of it? A woman like Klein?"

"I didn't mean that, exactly." Tessa rubbed her eyes. They were hot and prickling. The steep concrete driveway shimmered in front of her.

"What did you mean, then?" Steve was frowning as he walked.

"It's just—there are so many threads to this," Tessa said, keeping her voice as level as she could. "They all seem to tangle together. But none of them seem to lead anywhere."

"We've hardly started," Steve said stolidly. "It's a matter of taking one thing at a time. Working it through. We'll get there in the end."

"What if we don't?"

She hadn't meant to speak aloud. But she had.

He didn't answer. She could feel his distance, his withdrawal. He was staring straight ahead, pacing forward steadily.

Like he always does. While you rush off down side streets, tripping over your own feet . . .

"I think Klein could have helped us a lot," she said. It was a bid for attention, and they both knew it.

"Not much point in thinking about that now, is there?" he muttered, almost angrily. "Klein's dead."

The words hung in the air. They met each other's eyes. And suddenly it was as though a spark flashed between them.

Klein could have helped us a lot . . . Klein's dead.

Cause . . . effect. Problem . . . solution. For someone.

"And that's it, isn't it?" Tessa whispered.

Slowly, he nodded. "Yeah," he said. "I think you're right."

Twenty

Back in the car, it seemed obvious that the Ridge household should be their first port of call. Charles Ridge had been the agent in charge of letting Fiona Klein's house while she was away. He would, presumably, therefore be able to give them information on where she and her friend Nicki had been staying in Italy. Nicki would have to be contacted as a matter of urgency. Either she was Fiona's effective next of kin, or she could tell them who they should contact. And Heidi Ridge had to be spoken to about her sighting of Rachel Brydie—if indeed that had been a genuine sighting, not just an example of teenage melodramatics.

They phoned to say they were on their way. Charles, full of Sunday morning bonhomie that mixed rather uncomfortably with his expressions of shock and regret at Fiona Klein's death, of which he and his wife had been informed at first light by what he called "Freda's network," said he'd put the coffee on. Freda had just left for church with her mother, he said. She'd be very sorry to have missed them.

"I'll bet she will," said Steve, when he'd cut the connection. "The gossip at church'll be nothing to what she could have found out at home."

They stopped at the Oakdale cake shop to pick up breakfast—a chocolate croissant for Tessa, and two meat pies for Steve—and ate greedily as they drove to the Ridge residence, which they found without difficulty. The house was attractive with a large, well-tended garden and a view of the lake. Charles Ridge might make his living selling "mountain charmers" and "cute olde worlde cottages" to others, but his own bagged brick home, while built to a traditional design with corrugated iron roof and leadlight front door, was modern, convenient and low-maintenance in every respect. No drafts, sticking windows, squeaking floorboards or endless painting here.

They had coffee with Charles to the accompaniment of muffled cartoon sound effects and the laughter of children presumably watching early morning television in another part of the house. Charles, freshly shaved, in slacks, soft shirt and lightweight red wool jumper, his drying hair still showing the marks of the comb, seemed to assume that Fiona had met her death by tragic accident. Freda's network, he said indulgently, with a mild flicker of masculine superiority, was all het up about it—had all sorts of theories. But he himself wouldn't fancy living perched up on that cliff. Magnificent position. Very valuable property. But you'd want to have your wits about you.

"And between you and me, very windswept," he said, pursing his lips. He looked out with satisfaction at his own view—drama without danger, and well protected from the elements. He obligingly supplied both Fiona's contact number in Italy, recorded in his computerized diary, and the opinion that Nicki was in fact the person they should talk to.

"Don't know what the story is there," he said mysteriously, just falling short, Tessa felt, of tapping a finger on the side of his nose, "but the fact is, they were together for years. Quite an old married couple. Ha, ha!"

Making the most of Freda's absence, he helped himself to a second coconut cookie from the plate he'd felt justified in putting out in their honor. "Nothing wrong with it, these days, is there?" he said, eyes wide.

"You're talking about homosexuality, sir?" said Steve, just making sure.

"Well—yes." A trifle discomforted at this insistence on plain speaking, Charles glanced over his shoulder to make sure no children were present. Reassured on that point he leaned forward and lowered his voice. "It doesn't appeal to me personally, of course," he muttered. "But, I mean, as long as they're discreet, I don't see why anyone should take offense." He bit into the cookie. "Some people do, though," he added, with his mouth full. "Some owners won't have them in the house. Men or women. I had one vendor wouldn't even *sell* to them. Had a very good offer, too."

"Fiona Klein taught at the local high school, didn't she?" asked Tessa.

Charles nodded. "Certainly did," he said. "But there was never any trouble. As far as I know. Our daughter Heidi doesn't go to the high school, of course. She goes to St. Anne's. But she does have a few mates who—"

Suddenly he looked alert. It was as though Freda had materialized behind him and nudged him in the ribs. "*Was* there any trouble?" he hissed. "Is that why Fiona left the school? She resigned, you know. Didn't just take leave of absence. Freda thought that was funny, at the time. They would have hushed it all up, I suppose . . ."

"There was no trouble at all at the school to our knowledge, sir," Steve cut in firmly.

"Oh. Right." Charles looked slightly disappointed, cheated of the particularly juicy bone he'd thought he might have been able to lay at Freda's feet on her return from church.

"Is there anyone in Oakdale who knew Miss Klein well?" Tessa asked.

The plump man hesitated. "She saw quite a bit of Michael O'Malley, I think," he said, with some appearance of reluctance.

Michael O'Malley—the bookshop man. Again.

Michael O'Malley—who saw quite a bit of Fiona Klein— who disliked Rachel Brydie—who got a calendar from Michael O'Malley—who's loved by Lyn Weisenhoff—whose husband sold gin to Adam Quinn . . .

Small town.

Maybe.

"Michael's a member of the main street committee, but he wasn't at the meeting last night—touch of the flu," Charles was continuing, still with that awkward air. "He owns the bookshop two doors down from the wine shop. Nice chap."

"We'll have a word with him. Could you give us his address?" said Steve. "Or would he be in the shop today?"

Charles fidgeted. "Most likely at home. He's got other

people in the shop. Like I said, he's had a touch of the flu. Ah—his address. Ah—he's in Oakdale. 193 Furze Avenue."

Tessa glanced at Steve. Furze Avenue—the narrow road meandering across the ridge that ran almost parallel to Lily Lane. There was nothing but a creek and steeply climbing bushland between Furze Avenue and the backs of the houses on Lily Lane. Bushland through which anyone determined enough could climb, any time.

"We did a house-to-house along Furze Avenue yesterday," murmured Steve. "Asking about Rachel Brydie. Among other things."

"Oh, yes. Well, you would have," said Charles. He frowned at his coffee mug, turning it round and round. "So you might have seen Michael already, then."

"We didn't. But one of the others would have. If he was home. But they're local police, of course. They probably knew him already, if he runs a business in the village."

"Sure, sure!" said Charles heartily. "Oh, yes. They'd know him. Everyone knows Michael. Quiet chap. Nice fellow. So—will you still be having a word with him?"

"We'll have to do that, sir, yes," said Steve. "See what he can tell us about Miss Klein. We think she could have rung someone last night. Could have been him—if they were friends."

Still Charles twirled the coffee mug. Then he seemed to reach a decision. "It's a bit awkward," he said. "I don't want to make too much of it. But if you're going to see him—and someone's bound to tell you—the gossip round this place is—you can imagine—and you might think it was funny—" At this point, he seemed to dry up. He cleared his throat uncomfortably.

"Yes, Mr. Ridge?" said Tessa.

"Charles," the man said automatically. He looked up at her, his blue eyes round and startled as a baby's. "Michael did have a bit of a fling with Rachel Brydie years ago. Before Adam Quinn, of course. Years ago."

Michael O'Malley—who saw quite a bit of Fiona Klein— who disliked Rachel Brydie—who had a fling with Michael

*O'Malley—who's loved by Lyn Weisenhoff—whose husband
sold gin to Adam Quinn—who's dead.*

"You think he still cares about Mrs. Brydie. Is that it?"
asked Steve casually.

Don't make too much of it. Don't scare him.

"Oh, I wouldn't know about that," said Charles hurriedly.
Too hurriedly. "Freda always says he still holds a candle. Ha,
ha! You know how women are. But I just thought I should
mention—in case you thought it was funny that I didn't—
making too much of it—"

"Has Mr. O'Malley been away from work for long?" asked
Tessa impulsively.

Charles showed the whites of his eyes. "Oh—I don't know.
About a week, I think."

"What sort of car does he have, do you know?"

He gaped at her. "Nissan four-wheel drive," he said.
"Green. Like ours. Pretty much standard issue around here.
Roads aren't the best. But we've got the Merc. as well, of
course. Ha, Ha!"

Tessa and Steve exchanged looks. Steve stuck his notebook back into his jacket.

"Well, I think that's about it," he said. "Thanks, Charles.
Could we just have a quick word with Heidi, before we go?"

The man blinked at them. "Heidi? But I told you. She goes
to St. Anne's," he said, as though this expensive fact alone
should protect his daughter from such indignities as words
with the police.

"It's just a routine check," Tessa soothed. "About a car she
might have seen."

Only slightly mollified, Charles went to get his daughter,
who he said was still in bed. Heidi appeared a few minutes
later, heavy-eyed and wrapped in a pink dressing gown, a
well-developed, sultry young beauty with braces on her teeth
and an ultracool manner.

"She had a late night," said Charles. "You know how these
teenagers are. Ha, ha!"

"I wasn't asleep," said Heidi sulkily.

"We're running a bit short of time. Maybe Heidi could

walk out to the car with us," Steve suggested, standing up. "We can chat on the way."

Soul of tact.

He's got sisters.

"Fine, fine," said Charles, showing his teeth uneasily.

But Heidi had slumped down at the table. "I can't go out like this," she said. "Someone might see me."

"You look fine, Heidi. **Fine**," urged Charles. "Up you get."

"I can't, Dad." Heidi inspected her fingernails and frowned at a chip in the polish.

"Never mind." Steve smiled briefly, sat down again, and opened his notebook.

You only get one chance with him, kid.

Charles hovered uncertainly.

"We've had a report that you were at the lake last Sunday night, at about ten o'clock, Heidi," Steve began, getting straight to the point. "Could you please describe to us what you saw there?"

There was a short, deadly silence. Heidi's head was still bent over her fingernails, but she'd become unnaturally still.

Uh-oh.

"Ah—Heidi wasn't at the lake last Sunday night," said Charles Ridge, after a moment. "You've got your wires crossed there, I think, Steve. Ha, ha!"

"No, I don't think so," Steve said imperturbably. "Heidi?"

Heidi raised her head. She looked straight at Tessa. "I was home, last Sunday night. Baby-sitting," she muttered.

"Heidi, do you understand that we're investigating a suspected homicide?" asked Steve.

The girl nodded mutely. Her dark eyes swivelled in her father's direction, and instantly returned to stare at Tessa with wild appeal.

Get her out of this.

She asked for it. Let her face the music.

Tessa glanced at her watch and stood up. "You know, we really should go, Steve," she said. "Heidi, couldn't you just come with us as far as the gate? It'd save a lot of time."

"Oh, well. Okay." The girl scrambled with rather obvious relief to her feet and made for the front door.

Tessa turned to Charles Ridge. "Thanks for the help—and the coffee," she said casually. "We won't keep Heidi for long."

But by now Charles's face bore that baffled, irritated look of a parent who has realized that once again his offspring has been giving him the runaround. He was no fool, whatever his manner might imply.

Out on the driveway, Heidi seemed to have shed about five years. The drooping eyelids and supercilious half-sneer of the world-weary sophisticate had disappeared, and she had become a child in a panic.

"Dad'll kill me!" she moaned, biting at her lips. "I can't believe Melissa told you! It was Melissa, wasn't it? It must have been."

They didn't answer that, but instead drew her away from the house and the sight of her father peering from the front windows.

"Tell us about the car you saw, Heidi," Tessa said. "See if you can remember exactly what it looked like."

"It was nothing!" Heidi exclaimed, rolling her eyes. "I was there, just sort of walking around, waiting for—anyway, waiting around for this friend of mine—and suddenly I realized there was this car there, parked, in the mist."

"A four-wheel drive?"

"Yeah. See, that was the trouble. I got this real fright. Just for a second I thought it was ours." She grimaced. "I thought Dad might've followed me, or something. He said he was working, but that could've just been to trap me. I wouldn't put it past him to do something like that. I mean, Mum'd put him up to it, but she'd make *him* do it. She wouldn't miss her bridge night."

"The car must have looked a lot like yours, then," said Steve, flashing her a grin. He turned to look at the dark green vehicle parked behind them.

She shrugged. "They all look the same. I just thought it was ours for a second, because Mum had the Mercedes so Dad had taken the Nissan, and—" she wrinkled her nose "—and I s'pose I was feeling a bit—you know, guilty, or something, for sneaking out. Not that there was any *reason*," she added, her voice rising. "The kids were *fast* asleep, and *perfectly* all right."

"I'm sure they were. Okay, so you thought the car was yours . . ."

"Only for a second. But then I realized it couldn't be, because Crazy Rachel was in it. In the passenger seat."

"You're sure it was Mrs. Brydie?" Tessa asked. "Did you actually see her face?"

Heidi moved impatiently. "Not exactly her *face*. I mean, I couldn't see her *face*, could I? She was kissing this guy. Practically swallowing him." She shuddered. "Revolting," she added succinctly.

Steve rubbed his chin. "If you couldn't see this woman's face, and you were standing away from the car, behind a tree, and there was mist, I can't see why you're so sure it was Mrs. Brydie."

Heidi sighed. "I saw her hair. No one else's got hair like that. She always wears it hanging down. Middle-aged women shouldn't wear their hair down. It looks weird. Anyway, I know it was her. It was just like before. That's why I didn't want—"

"Before?" Tessa broke in, galvanized. "When, before?"

Heidi stared. "Ages ago. I mean—it's nothing. It was years ago. Before she got with Adam Quinn. When I was a kid. I was walking home from piano. I did piano then. Now I do flute. Mum makes me." She wrinkled her nose, sighed, and went on. "Anyway, I went down to the lake, on the way, to look at the ducks. Crazy Rachel was there in this car, with some guy—" she broke off, and looked, for a moment, surprised. "Actually, in the same sort of car, you know," she said. "A four-wheel drive. I hadn't remembered that, till just now. Isn't that amazing!"

She pondered for a moment on the vagaries of memory, then shrugged. "Wouldn't be the same guy, would it?" she asked rhetorically. "Not after five years or something. But anyway, she saw me looking, that time, and she actually got out of the car and screamed at me and started sort of chasing me. I just *ran*. I was *so* scared. All the kids said she was a witch. She's so weird. It was disgusting, too. She was half-undressed. You could see *everything*. Yuk!" She opened her eyes wide. "I actually had dreams about it afterwards, you know. It probably scarred me for life."

"You didn't see the man that time, did you, Heidi?" asked Tessa urgently. "When Mrs. Brydie got out of the car, for example? There would have been someone still sitting in the driver's seat, wouldn't there? Anything you can remember about him? Anything at all?"

The girl wrinkled her brow. "I was only a kid," she protested. "I mean, I hardly knew what they were *doing*, you know?" She squinted, as if making a heroic effort to recall the scene. "He had a white shirt, undone all down the front," she said finally. "And the bottom of his face was darker than the top. I think he had a beard."

"Adam Quinn had a beard," Steve said.

Heidi shook her head. "It wasn't him," she said positively. "He wasn't even here, then. And he didn't have a beard when he first came. He grew that, and his hair, after he went to Haven. Looked awful, I thought, whatever Melissa says. Made him look as much of a dropout as Rachel."

Tessa's phone rang. She answered, while Heidi, growing restless and glancing continually back towards the house, waited impatiently.

It was Russell Ingres. "We think we've found Rachel Brydie's hidey-hole," he said, his voice edgy with excitement. "In the bush, like we thought. Under a willow tree by the creek."

"Are you there now?" Tessa looked at Steve, signaling with her eyes that something was up, and moving casually away. He turned to Heidi and began asking her some final questions.

"Yeah," Russell said. His habitual reserve had disappeared. He was plainly, and exuberantly, imbued with the thrill of the chase. "You should see this place. It's a perfect spot to hide out—big as a small room, but you'd never know it was here unless you fell over it."

"What's she left behind?"

"Not a bloody thing," said Russell. "Cleared out. Bloody shame we didn't find it yesterday, but there you are. I don't reckon she's been camping here, exactly. I reckon she's been ducking down here whenever the police turned up. Well, that's all over now, isn't it?"

Tessa felt a wave of disappointment.

"So you're just inferring all this, then?" she asked. "In fact there's no actual sign that she was ever there?"

She wasn't interested in putting Russell down—just in getting at the truth—but his tone changed instantly.

"Oh well, we think she was, but it's just our opinion," he said stiffly. "The ground's trampled, and so on. You can make what you like of it. I was just told to call and let you know."

Mistake! Now he's miffed.

Miffed? Are we professionals, or aren't we?

"Look, we're on our way," said Tessa. "We'll be at Haven in ten minutes. How do we find this place?"

"No point in going to Haven," said Russell Ingres, still plainly offside. "This place is on the other side of the creek from there. Easier to get to it from Furze Avenue." He paused. "That's how we did it," he added finally—and resentfully.

We, who work while you big-note yourselves. We, who find out things while you swan around . . .

Furze Avenue.

"One-nine-three Furze Avenue, right?" snapped Tessa.

"Yeah," said Ingres, sounding at last surprised. "That's it. The back boundary of the property joins with the Haven boundary, at the creek, so we've been giving it a bit of pounding. Owner says he knows about the hidey-hole, but he doesn't know if Brydie's been using it, and he hasn't seen her. Sergeant McCaffrey says you'll want to have a go at him. Name of Michael O'Malley."

Twenty-one

Michael O'Malley's house was a small, modern construction of glass and dark-stained wood that had been fitted as unobtrusively as possible into its unfenced bushland block. A dusty dark-green four-wheel drive vehicle stood on a roughly cleared patch, screened from the house by a grove of gnarled old banksias.

"Could be the one," Steve murmured. "There's mud in the tire treads. If we can show it's been at Klein's place recently—or even at the lake—"

"The lake was a week ago," Tessa objected.

"If Brydie was in it, there'll be traces inside," he said, a little impatiently.

The front door was at the side of the house. They knocked, and waited a few minutes before the door was finally opened by a man in his early forties, probably, with an intelligent, serious face, a light-brown beard and gold-rimmed glasses. He was wearing pale blue jeans and a white shirt. He was Michael O'Malley, he agreed, when they asked him. He didn't seem at all surprised to see them. Presumably, he'd been expecting them.

He'd heard about Fiona Klein, first thing this morning. Floss, his assistant at the shop, had rung to tell him, he said. He expressed no grief, but his face was somber. He'd had the flu, so the story went, and he certainly didn't look well. There were deep shadows under his eyes, and he was thin and drawn-looking.

"We think Miss Klein might have made a phone call last night," Tessa said. "Did she ring you, Mr. O'Malley?"

"Yes," he said slowly. "Yes, she did. Just after nine."

He stood in the doorway, his hand on the doorknob. Plainly, he preferred to keep them outside, but when they suggested they might talk to him more easily inside the house, he didn't argue. He pulled the door wide and stood aside with a sweeping, ironic gesture.

They followed him through a light and airy living area, split-level, so as to fit neatly into the slope of the land. The trees that clustered around the house were visible from every one of the big windows, and all available wall space was lined with packed floor-to-ceiling bookshelves. Living here would be pleasant, Tessa thought. Michael took them through the living room and into the kitchen. He was making soup, he said. If they didn't mind, he'd go on with it while they talked.

The kitchen was small, without pretensions. The inevitable Harmony with Nature calendar hung on the wall next to a notepad and pencil. On the bench beside the stove was a chopping board on which lay carrots and garlic, and a knife.

Questioned, O'Malley was courteous, but withdrawn and guarded. Standing at the kitchen bench, meticulously scraping carrots and cutting them into chunks, he answered everything he was asked, but volunteered little.

"Fiona just rang to say hello, I think," he said. "She said that the Brydie girls were with her—and that they'd gone to bed. She asked if I'd heard any news of Rachel being found, and I said I hadn't. That was it, really. We didn't talk for long."

"Did she sound worried, or depressed?"

O'Malley seemed to consider this carefully. "No," he said, at last. "A bit flat, maybe. But she could have just been tired." He put down the knife and turned to face them. "You think it was suicide, do you?" he asked.

"It's a possibility," said Steve. "She'd burned a lot of her poems in the fire. We understand that she'd returned to Australia because her long-standing relationship had just broken up."

O'Malley's face remained impassive.

"Did you know about that, sir?"

"Yes."

But he's not going to talk to us about it.

"Her ex-partner's name is Nicole Phillips. Is that right?"

"They'd been together just over seven years," O'Malley said reluctantly. "Nicki can tell you anything you want to know about Fiona."

"We can't contact Miss Phillips. Her landlady, or whoever it was who answered the phone where she's staying, said she'd gone away."

"She's probably on her way home. I rang her this morning. As soon as I heard about Fiona. She said she was going to get the first plane."

Steve and Tessa glanced at one another. For some reason, this was the last thing either of them had expected.

But why? Of course someone would tell Nicole Phillips. Of course she'd come home.

For what?

Seven years . . . she loved Fiona. She wants to know why . . .

She wants to make sure we're doing our job.

She wants to say goodbye.

Tessa forced her voice into flat and unemotional tones. "Would you have expected Fiona Klein to have committed suicide, Mr. O'Malley? After your conversation last night?"

The man's sensitive mouth twitched. "If I had, I'd have done something about it, wouldn't I?" he said.

"You'd have gone over to see her?"

"Of course I bloody would!"

"And did you go over to see her?"

O'Malley frowned. "No, I didn't. I told you. We talked on the phone, that's all. Look, what are you—"

"A car like yours was seen outside her house last night."

"Well, I wasn't there. I was here. All night, if you're interested, though I suppose I've got no proof. It must have been someone else's car. God knows, there are enough four-wheel drives around here." Abruptly, he swung back to the work bench, picked up the knife and began scraping carrots again. "Is that all?"

"Not quite." Steve was frowning.

O'Malley irritates him.

Male. Competitive.

"Has Rachel Brydie contacted you in the last week, sir?" asked Steve.

"No, she hasn't. As I've told your colleagues, repeatedly. And as I've also told them repeatedly, I have no idea where she is."

"There's a place on your property—under a big willow tree, by the creek . . ."

The man's neck and shoulders tensed, but he said nothing.

Steve's voice strengthened. "A good hiding place," he said. "You know the place I mean, Mr. O'Malley?"

O'Malley recovered quickly. "Sure," he said evenly. "Of course I know it. I built this house. I know every tree and rock on the place. But I haven't been down as far as the creek for a while. I told the other police that."

"Do you recall telling Rachel Brydie about the willow tree, sir?"

"No. I don't recall that I did. But I might have. I can't swear to it either way."

"You didn't give her permission to spend time there in the last week?"

"No."

"You and Mrs. Brydie were close friends, at one time, weren't you?" asked Tessa, and watched O'Malley's profile. His mouth tweaked into a cynical smile.

"Close friends." How coy, Detective Vance.

What am I supposed to say? "I hear that you were at it like rabbits a few years ago"?

"Rachel and I were close friends at one time," he agreed.

"But you aren't any longer?"

"I think we're probably still friends," he said. "But not—close." The mouth tweaked again.

"When did you last see Mrs. Brydie, sir?" asked Steve formally.

Michael unhurriedly gathered up the finished pile of carrots from the chopping board and transferred it to a large cast-iron pan standing ready on the stove. "Oh, I wouldn't have seen Rachel for a good six months," he said. He poured stock from a jug into the pan, and clapped on the lid.

"According to information we've received, you were with

her in your vehicle at the lake last Sunday night," Steve said, losing patience and taking a chance.

Again the man swung around. "That's a lie," he barked. "That wasn't Rachel. What idiot—?"

He broke off, flinching.

Mistake. He got angry, and made a mistake.

"Who was it, then, Mr. O'Malley?" asked Tessa quickly.

"None of your business," the man snapped. "It's got nothing to do with this. Take my word for it."

"I'm afraid we can't do that, sir," said Steve.

Why not? He's obviously telling the truth. He was there, at the lake, but Rachel Brydie wasn't the one with him. And that means . . .

Not so fast. We have to make sure.

It's so tacky. A tacky sideline.

It's murder.

"Mr. O'Malley," Tessa heard herself say evenly, "this doesn't have to go any further than this room, if it's not relevant, but we have to know. Please tell us who was in your car with you at the lake last Sunday night."

O'Malley shook his head.

"Was it Rachel Brydie?"

"No!"

"It was a woman with long, dark hair. You were seen . . ."

"It wasn't Rachel." The man spoke through gritted teeth. "God, I can't believe this."

It was someone who wouldn't want it known. Someone he's protecting.

So—married. And a local. A married local woman with long, dark hair. A respectable woman who usually wears her hair up, so Heidi didn't think for a minute . . .

A sad-looking, gentle-faced woman, pushing at pins coming loose from her dark hair . . . Rochette, sardonic: "She shouldn't wear her hair long . . . some men've got a thing about long hair, but if you haven't got the wherewithal, there's no good crying for the moon."

"Was it Lyn Weisenhoff?" Tessa said aloud.

She watched Michael O'Malley's face change. Watched the sneer form.

"It was, wasn't it?" she persisted.

He shrugged, turning away, lighting the flame under the saucepan. "You seem to know all about it," he said. "Why ask me?"

Tessa glanced at Steve. Flicked her eyes towards the door.

Steve's frown deepened. Then he shrugged slightly, giving in.

"I'd like to see this spot under the willow tree," he said in a low voice, just loud enough for Michael O'Malley to hear. "I'll leave you to finish up here. Okay?"

"Sure," Tessa said.

"I gather there's a track down to the creek from the back here, sir," Steve said to the back of O'Malley's head.

"There's no track directly to the willow tree. Just follow the sound of baying," the other man muttered. His fists were clenched, pressed against the bench top.

Steve made no answer, and left.

Alone in the kitchen, Tessa and Michael O'Malley stood and listened to the gas burning under the pan, and the currawongs and magpies calling in the trees outside.

"Mr. O'Malley, we hear lots of things when a murder's being investigated," Tessa began quietly. "But we don't—"

"Stop it!" The man bent his head as if he was in pain. "Don't give me the standard treatment, for God's sake. Give me credit for having some vestige of intelligence."

"Mr. O'Malley—"

He turned and leaned back against the bench. A tic tweaked his lip, but his voice was steady. "Look, I understand," he said. "Someone saw poor Lyn and me making fools of ourselves at the lake last Sunday. Fine."

Poor Lyn.

"Someone assumed Lyn was Rachel," O'Malley went on. "It's a bizarre thought, but I can see how it could have happened. Lyn had let her hair down—" the tic became more pronounced, but he went on loudly "—to please me, I suppose. And Rachel and I used to go down to the lake sometimes. God, everyone knew that. It was the talk of the town, you might say. We weren't very discreet. Rachel didn't give a damn what people thought, and I—" His face darkened, and his head jerked in an impatient gesture of self-disgust. "I was too bloody besotted to care."

Too besotted to care.

"Why the lake?"

"I'd only been in town a few months. I was still building this place. Her daughters were at Haven. We liked the lake—it was convenient—God, what does it matter? Anywhere would have done. And did. Back of the bookshop. In the car. At the lake. In the bush. Nothing was ever planned. I never knew if it was on till it was on. It wasn't that serious—as far as she was concerned. It only lasted a few weeks."

"The affair ended when Rachel met Adam Quinn, is that right?" Tessa asked gently.

"That's right. Well over four years ago."

"Were you angry?"

"No. Not angry." His mouth twisted. "Devastated. In hell. Suicidal. Not angry. Rachel had the right to choose. Quinn was what she wanted. End of story."

"And Lyn Weisenhoff—?"

Again that jerk of the head. "Lyn's—a nice woman. Last Sunday night—it was a mistake. My mistake. A ludicrous, stupid exercise in self-indulgence. It had never happened before, and it won't happen again. Not that anything did happen. I couldn't—" He broke off, gritting his teeth.

Poor Lyn.

As if he'd read her mind, O'Malley glanced at Tessa angrily. "Look, you couldn't loathe me more than I loathe myself," he hissed. "It's made me sick."

"You've stayed away from the bookshop this week . . ."

"Because I couldn't face Lyn, knowing I tried to use her and couldn't even do that? Yes, you could put it that way."

"Are you still in love with Rachel Brydie, Michael?"

The man gave a snorting laugh. "I don't think love's the word for it."

"What is the word for it, then?"

"I don't know. Obsession, maybe. A form of mental illness." He laughed again. "Fueled by God knows what. I haven't touched Rachel for four and a half years. I've barely spoken to her. She cut herself right off. Every now and then she'd come into the shop—but she hasn't even done that for a good twelve months."

"One of those calendars is on her kitchen wall," said Tessa, pointing. "You give them out to regular customers, don't you?"

"Yes. I get them for practically nothing, because I carry the Harmony with Nature series of books. They're a bit tacky, but it's cheaper than sending Christmas cards."

"If you haven't seen Rachel Brydie for twelve months—"

He smiled bitterly. "This is detective work, is it? Rachel likes the calendars. They're useful to her, because they show the phases of the moon. I wanted her to have one. So I went round to Haven and put it in the letterbox just before Christmas. I didn't see anyone. I put the calendar in the box and stared at the gate for a while and then I went. That's all there was to it. Pathetic, isn't it?"

The lid of the pan rattled. The liquid inside was boiling. O'Malley glanced at it, and turned the flame down. His long, slender fingers were trembling.

"Does Mrs. Weisenhoff know—how you feel about Rachel?"

"Of course she does. She must. But we don't talk about it."

"And Fiona Klein? Did you talk about Rachel to her?"

"Sometimes. When I was feeling self-indulgent. She thought I was insane. She thought Rachel was poison. But she had an ax to grind. And as I told her, she was the last one to lecture me about obsessions."

"Because of Astral?"

He paused. "Yes," he said finally. He looked at her searchingly. "Did the girl—?"

"No one told me anything," said Tessa. "I inferred it." It seemed important, somehow, to tell this man the truth. She found she liked him.

He's neurotic.

He's a real person. Like Verna Larkin. Like Lyn Weisenhoff. Damaged, but real. Human . . .

"When Nicki got the scholarship, the chance to live in Italy for a while, I told Fiona to grab it," Michael said slowly. "Fiona loved Nicki. What she had with Nicki was real. This other thing—it—God, I told her—it was going to destroy her. Personally, professionally—" His brow wrinkled with strain.

"So she resigned and went to Italy."

He nodded. "I thought I'd done one useful thing, at least. I missed her—but I thought, it'll give her a chance. Give them a chance. But—it didn't work out. Fiona came back."

"Did she let you know?"

"Not beforehand. She rang me from some hotel in Sydney. She'd been there a couple of days. She was waiting for her tenants up here to get out. I didn't know what to say to her." He pulled off his glasses and rubbed at his eyes with the back of his hand. "What a bloody disaster! I told her she could come up and stay with me if she wanted. What else could I say? She was a friend. A good friend."

"And she came?"

"Oh, yes," he said tiredly.

"When?"

"On the Friday night. She had to wait, to pick up her new car—secondhand car, four-wheel drive, like the one she'd had before. Then she came."

"That was Friday a week ago?"

"Yes."

"So—was she actually here, in this house, on the Sunday night—the night Adam Quinn died?"

"I don't know. She left again, went back to town, sometime on Sunday night—while I was—with Lyn." O'Malley's voice was absentminded, dispirited. He didn't seem to think the timing was of any importance, except as a reference point for his own indiscretion.

"Michael, did Fiona see Astral, while she was staying here? She was so close to Haven—"

"She said she didn't want to see Astral till she was back in her own house. She said she knew she had to take it quietly. She had to calm down. She was in a state. She was—simmering with it." He glanced at the pan on the stove. "It was infectious," he added ruefully.

So you thought, "Why not?" You thought, why should I live like a monk? You couldn't have the woman you wanted, but Lyn was there . . . Poor Lyn.

Men are bastards. Even this one.

No one can be strong all the time.

"You won't have to talk to Lyn about last Sunday, will you?" O'Malley asked abruptly.

"We'll have to confirm," said Tessa, and watched the mouth twist again. "We'll be—"

"Discreet," he muttered. "Sure." He turned away, took the lid from the pan on the stove and started prodding at the carrots with a fork. "Maybe it'll be a relief," he said. "Lyn must have been going through hell, waiting for you to get to me. We knew you would, once you found out about Rachel and me. Who told you, by the way?"

The question sounded casual, but Tessa wasn't deceived.

"I don't think that's important, Mr. O'Malley," she murmured.

He shrugged, keeping his head down. "I was just curious. I thought it might have been Lyn's husband—Carl. He'd enjoy the idea of you giving me a hard time." He paused. "Not that he knows—about Lyn and me. But I irritate him, not being the macho, head-kicking type."

"Like he is, you mean?"

"Very much so. Which is why, if he finds out that Lyn's my alibi for last Sunday night . . ."

"He won't find out from us—unless it becomes absolutely necessary," Tessa said.

O'Malley turned and regarded her quizzically, the dripping fork still in his hand. He looked down at it, and turned back to the stove. "Are you finished with me, then?" he asked.

"For the moment. We'll probably need a formal statement. But that can wait a while. Will Nicki be staying here, with you, when she gets back?"

He laughed shortly. "No. She wouldn't stay here. She never wants to see my face again as long as she lives."

"Why?"

"She's decided to blame me."

"For Fiona's death?"

"For everything. The whole bloody, sordid, stupid, disastrous mess."

"That seems a bit unfair."

"You don't know what she knows. You'll have to talk to her and then decide for yourself if it's fair or not. She can blame me if she likes. It helps, if you can pin the responsibility on someone other than yourself when you're miserable. I just wish I could." He threw down the fork. "Look, if you want me again you'll have to come round. I'm going to unplug the phone. I don't want to hear any more about this. Will you let yourself out?"

Steve was already waiting in the car when Tessa left the house. He started the engine as soon as he saw her coming towards him through the trees.

"We're going round to Haven," he said, as she climbed into the passenger seat. "You can speak to Astral—you've got to do it sometime. I'll tackle Stoller. Ingres says he was washing his car this morning when the party turned up to go on with the search. At six A.M."

"What? Why didn't they tell us that before?"

"They say they didn't think it was important."

"Steve!"

"They didn't know about the car at Klein's house last night, did they? Anyhow, there might be nothing to it. Maybe Jonathon just likes a nice, clean car. We'll see." Steve let out the brake and eased the car onto the road.

Tessa controlled her impatience with difficulty. "Did you find the willow tree place?"

"Yep. It's a good spot to hide out, as they said, and it's obviously been used fairly recently. I had a quick look, but I didn't stay. Too many people have been tramping through it already. Fisk won't be happy."

Tessa lay back in her seat feeling limp. The conversation with Michael O'Malley had been exhausting, for some reason.

"Did you get anything more out of our friend?" Steve asked, after a moment's silence.

"Quite a lot, in a way. Not about the willow tree. He still says he hasn't seen or spoken to Rachel Brydie lately. But he admitted he was still in love with her."

Steve said nothing.

"I think he really was with Lyn Weisenhoff at the lake."

"For a quiet bloke he spreads himself around a bit," drawled Steve. "Just keeping in practice, was he?"

Tessa glanced at him. His mouth was set in a cynical line. She couldn't bring herself to tell him what Michael O'Malley had said about not being able to finish what he'd started with Lyn. It wasn't germane to the issue. And it would have been a betrayal.

"He said it was a mistake," she murmured. "One of those things."

"Mmm."

"Fiona Klein was staying with him for a few days before that."

Now she had his interest. "Tell me more."

She swayed in her seat as he swung the car around the corner, heading for Lily Lane. "She arrived Friday, and left Sunday. We were right. She broke up with Nicole Phillips and came home because of Astral. Michael disapproved."

I shouldn't have called him "Michael." It sounds too friendly. As though I'm on his side.

You are, aren't you?

"O'Malley takes a high moral tone, I gather," Steve's country drawl was even more pronounced.

"Not like that," snapped Tessa, exasperated. "He thought Fiona should keep away from Astral for her own good, that's all. He'd persuaded her to stick with Nicki and go away. When she turned up again he was worried about her. It threw him off balance. I think that's why he ended up with Lyn at the lake. Sort of."

Steve looked amused. "He told you that, did he?"

Don't say anything.

He thinks O'Malley snowed me.

Don't say anything.

Jamming his foot on the brake, Steve spun the wheel rather roughly to the right, and the car began to bump down Lily Lane.

Twenty-two

Jonathon Stoller was sitting on his back steps, hunched over a mug of black coffee. He was unshaven, and had dark rings under his eyes. He barely looked up when Steve joined him, barely returned Steve's greeting.

"Have they found anything?" he asked listlessly, staring out at the paddock.

"I think they've finished with your property now," said Steve, avoiding the question.

"That's good." The man lapsed into silence. Then he roused himself with an effort. "They said Fiona Klein killed herself."

"She fell from the cliff behind her house. We're not sure how, exactly."

"Will Astral—and the others—come back to Haven now?"

"They're there now, Mr. Stoller."

Stoller's head jerked up. "They're in there now?" His red-rimmed eyes were wide. "I didn't know that. Why didn't they tell me that?" He started scrambling to his feet.

"Detective Vance is with them at the moment," Steve said calmly. He watched as the man hesitated, wavered, then slumped down onto the step again. "I suppose you're anxious to see Astral."

"No. Yes! Well yes, of course I'm keen to see her. She's—she must be terrified. She didn't find the woman's body, did she?"

"No. It was found as a result of a police search."

"Thank God for that."

Steve decided to take a chance. "I understand you visited the Klein house last night, sir?"

Jonathon's jaw dropped. "I—how did you know that?" he spluttered. "No one saw me. No one saw me!"

"Your car was seen parked on the road at about nine-thirty. You washed your car early this morning, didn't you?"

"I—" Jonathon gaped at him, as though he couldn't understand the connection. "Yes. So what? I mean, I can wash my car if I want to, can't I?"

"Why did you wash it?"

"I just felt like it! Look, what is this?"

"I thought you might have wanted to wash mud off the tires, that's all, Mr. Stoller. Greys Lookout Drive has very muddy gutters. You might have wanted to remove any evidence that you'd been there."

"I just decided to wash the car. I wanted something to do, if you must know. I couldn't sleep. I haven't slept all night!" Jonathon clutched his coffee mug, wild-eyed and desperate. "Look, you don't think—I had anything to do with anything, do you? With Fiona Klein dying? I didn't even see her. I didn't see anyone. I just—went over there to see Astral. The phone had been left off the hook. Astral didn't know my mobile number. I wanted to make sure she was all right. That's all it was."

"And did you see Astral?"

"No! I told you. I didn't see anyone! I walked up to the house, and there were some lights on, and I sort of looked in the front windows, through the gap in the blinds . . ."

"You didn't knock at the door?"

"No! I—I'd started to feel funny about being there at all, and I was half-dead from climbing up that bloody drive. I looked in the front windows, into the sitting room, and there was no one there. The lights were on, but there was no one there. There was music playing. Some Celtic thing—chants and flutes and stuff. You know. It gave me the creeps, actually."

Steve said nothing. The CD they'd found in the player fitted Jonathon's description, and as far as they had been able to establish, there was no similar one in Fiona's collection. So it was playing just after 9:30. But according to Stoller it was playing to an empty room. If he was telling the truth.

Jonathon swallowed, and rubbed his mouth roughly with the back of his hand. "I stood there for a while, and then I realized that it was about twenty to ten, and Astral and the others were probably in bed and asleep," he muttered. "Astral says they always go to bed at nine o'clock, unless they're working in the garden. So that meant the only one up would be silver-hair—Fiona Klein. She was probably in the kitchen or something. But I didn't want to see her, did I? That was the last thing I wanted. I—didn't want to stay there. So I just left again, and came back here." He raised bleary eyes to Steve's. "That's all," he muttered. "That's God's truth. I swear!"

It was a reasonable story, given the man's personality, Steve thought. But was it true? If it was, and the living room was deserted when Jonathon came to the house, it could be that Fiona Klein was already outside with her killer by 9:40—or maybe already lying dead at the bottom of the cliff.

"Did you see or hear anything or anyone at all while you were there, Mr. Stoller?" he asked.

Stoller gave a strange half-shiver. "I didn't see anyone," he muttered. He moved restlessly. "But I had the feeling someone was there, watching me. From the bushes, maybe. I kept thinking about Quinn. What he looked like . . . And I thought—the mother hasn't turned up, yet. What if she's here. Hiding. Watching." Again he rubbed his hand over his mouth. "I crept back down the stairs and then I ran. I ran all the way back to the car, and when I got inside I locked all the doors. I drove home like the devil was after me." Suddenly he buried his face in his hands. "I don't know what's going on," he groaned. "Oh, God—I think I'm going mad!"

Steve stood up, sticking his hands in his pockets and gazing, as Jonathon had done, over the long, sloping paddock, into the shadowed pines. Was Jonathon Stoller what he seemed—a weak, shallow man who was way out of his depth? Or was he a weak, shallow man who was being very, very clever?

* * *

At Haven, the old house crouched under its vine-shrouded veranda. Hens pecked in the yard, crooning as they tore at the grass. In the shadows the spiders worked silently, increasing their territory, their webs spreading over the old wood, thick and white.

Standing in the middle of the yard, Tessa felt the atmosphere of the place close in around her like a lowering darkness. Brooding madness, spiked with malice.

This is an evil place. I don't want to be here.

Pull yourself together.

Something is here. Someone is watching me.

Moving quickly, she darted to the door of the shed in which Adam Quinn died and pulled it roughly open. Dimness. Rough old wood. Bare walls and roof. Littered floor. Nothing else. She spun around and ran to the toolshed, the outhouse, the potting shed, tearing them open one by one. The scuttling of beetles and spiders greeted her. Sticky web and vine tendrils caught at her clothes, face and hair. But no grinning face leered at her from the moldy darkness. No guilty hands reached out. She turned away, angry with herself, and strode to the house.

Pushing her way through the screen door, she hurried through the kitchen to the living room. But there was no one there. The house was dim and empty. Scrubbed, swept, bare. Over the fireplace the portrait of Adam Quinn flamed.

He watches us.

Tessa turned abruptly and went outside again, her heart thudding. She heard the screen door rattle shut behind her as she almost ran around the house to the back.

But there had been no reason to panic. Astral and her sisters were in the herb gardens. They were working, bending among the plants while Rochette Williams hunched uncomfortably on a wooden crate nearby like a disgruntled garden gnome. She cheered up immediately on seeing Tessa.

"G-day," she said brightly.

"I'd like to talk to Astral alone," Tessa said.

Rochette nodded. "They've found where Rachel Brydie's been hiding," she whispered. "In Michael O'Malley's place."

Tessa murmured something inconclusive.

"The boss was positive he was in on it," Rochette went on, glancing over her shoulder at the three white-clad figures bending amid the plants. "O'Malley. You know. He's a friend of Fiona Klein's. And he and Rachel Brydie were—"

"So I gather," Tessa said, rather coldly. "I've just been talking to him. It's a shame no one mentioned it to us before."

The animation disappeared from Rochette's face. She seemed to retreat into herself, drawing her chunky body into its uniform like a snail shrinking back into its shell.

Was that bit of spleen worth it to you? Now she's offside.
She's always been offside.
No. She's been trying to help. As much as she could.
Not good enough.

Feeling rather flat, Tessa left Rochette and walked across to the garden where the girls were working.

"Astral," she called. "Could you give me a minute?"

With that disconcertingly instant obedience that all the Brydie girls displayed on being given a direct order, Astral put down her weeding fork and stepped out of the bed. Tessa beckoned, and Astral walked towards her. Not fast, not slow. Her hands were grubby with the rich soil, Tessa noticed. The hem of her shift was rimmed with mud, and her bare feet were black to the ankles.

They walked together away from the herb garden, to the banks of lavender that led down to the orchard.

"Astral," said Tessa in a low voice. "I have to know if you saw or heard from Fiona Klein in the days before Adam died."

Astral shook her head, wondering.

"You're sure? We know now that she was here, in Oakdale, at that time."

So if you're lying, say so now. You'll be found out in the end.
She's not lying. You know she's not.

"I thought Miss Klein was in Italy," Astral said. "Until the moment you told us that she wanted us to stay with her, that is what I thought."

"Bliss and Skye as well?"

"Of course. It is what we all thought. They believed it, because I told them."

"Astral—there are things you don't tell Bliss and Skye. Isn't that right?" asked Tessa gently. "You didn't tell them, for example, about Jonathon Stoller, did you? You didn't tell them how close you and Jonathon were. How often you saw each other. You were—closer than anyone knew."

"Yes." Astral dropped her eyes to the lavender bush in front of her and began plucking at the fragrant gray leaves.

You always disobey . . .

"You and Fiona Klein were closer than anyone knew, too. Isn't that right, Astral?"

"Yes." Astral's slim fingers pulled at the lavender. The sweet, tangy smell rose warm from the bruised leaves.

"How did you manage to see her, once you'd left school?"

The girl turned her head to one side, as if to hide her face even further in her swinging hair. Her eyelashes brushed the curve of her cheek. She was astonishingly beautiful, thought Tessa. Like Bliss, she had her mother's looks—but in Astral, the striking features were fined-down and softened, giving her an air of tender fragility that tugged at the heart. It was hard to blame Stoller—or Klein, for that matter. For being attracted, at least. What they did about it was another matter.

"We met in the forest," Astral whispered. "She would come there on Wednesdays and Fridays, after she finished at the school. She would come down through the bush, from Furze Avenue, at the top of the ridge."

Tessa's heart thumped. "You mean she came down through Michael O'Malley's property?"

He didn't tell me that.

Why would he? No wonder Nicole's no friend of his.

"Yes. He said she could. He was her friend. He knew about us. And he did not believe that what we were doing was wrong." Astral's smooth forehead creased slightly. "It was not wrong," she repeated, as though arguing with herself. "It did not feel wrong."

She wasn't even sixteen when this started! And completely innocent. What was O'Malley thinking of!

Doing his old mate Klein a favor. Or maybe he got off on it. Maybe he watched. Crouching in the bushes, near enough to see . . .

No!

Tessa beat away the thoughts. "And you met Miss Klein twice a week for nearly a year and never told anyone?" she asked, keeping her voice level. "No one ever found out?"

"Bliss and Skye knew I went to the forest, but not about Miss Klein. I could not tell them. They would not have understood. They would have been afraid for me."

You do not learn . . . you always disobey.

"Only Michael O'Malley knew, and he would not tell. So we were safe. Sometimes Adam discovered that I had left my work, and then—" Astral's lips trembled slightly. She pressed them together, and continued. "And then he would correct me, for laziness." She lifted her chin. "But I always went again. It made Miss Klein sad, when I did not meet her."

Tessa bit her lip. What kind of woman had Fiona Klein been, emotionally blackmailing a young girl into something that she was beaten for? And why didn't Klein tell someone what Quinn was doing? Get Astral some help?

Because she was preying on Astral as much as Quinn was. She'd been the girl's schoolteacher.

She couldn't risk telling anyone.

Don't criticize Klein to Astral. She'll freeze up.

"It must have been hard for Miss Klein—knowing you were punished for coming to meet her. It would have made her unhappy, wouldn't it?"

Astral stared. "Oh, yes. Of course. But she did not know. I would not tell her such a thing."

But Klein must have known. She would have seen—

"If I had told her, she would have stopped coming to the forest," said Astral simply. "I did not want that. And how else would she have known?"

Tessa frowned. This was all wrong. Not at all as she'd imagined it.

"When you met—what happened? What did you do?" she asked abruptly.

Astral smiled, and even in profile it was wonderful to see her wistful face for a moment glowing and alive. "We had a special place," she said. "A secret place."

Tessa felt her stomach jolt. She knew what was coming next.

"It was on Michael O'Malley's side of the creek, where a willow tree hangs over a rock into the water," Astral went on. Suddenly she seemed eager to talk, to tell, to explain, to share.

"In the summer the tree made a cool, green room for us," she said. "The walls were soft green, the ceiling was green flecked with bright blue, and the sun made puddles of light on the floor. In the autumn, the room was golden. In the winter, the ceiling and walls were webs of bare branches where wrens and finches danced. We kept books there, in a box. We had biscuits, in a tin, and water to drink, with a cup for each of us. We read the books together, and talked about them. Sometimes we acted the plays—we took all the parts—half for me, half for her. It was—so good."

The smile faded. Her voice was tender with memory and regret. The clear, vivid picture her simple words had painted—the graceful willow boughs, the silver-haired woman and the slender young girl bent over a book together—effortlessly overwhelmed and replaced all Tessa's lurid fantasies.

"She was teaching you." Tessa felt her cheeks burning. She couldn't believe it. She'd been so wrong. So utterly wrong.

"She said—when I was older, I could leave Haven," murmured Astral. "She said that by then I would find the strength. The books would give me the strength. After I was eighteen, she said, no one could stop me. And no one could blame her, then, for helping me."

She swung round, her eyes now glassy with tears. "But then—one day, she was not under the tree, when I came. There was just a letter. She had left me a letter. She said she was sorry, but she had to go away. She said she had no choice. She said she and Nicki were going away to Italy, and they would be away for many years, perhaps forever. She said she could not bear to say goodbye, so she was leaving me the letter, and the books for me to keep. She said I must remember everything she had said, and leave Haven when I was old enough, as we had planned. She said it was better for us both that she leave. I could not understand!"

The last words were like a cry of pain. And there was no doubt about their truth. Astral had had no idea how Fiona

Klein felt about her or why the woman had decided she had to be ruthless, to tear herself away—as much for her own sake as for the girl's.

What an irony. Astral didn't tell Klein about Quinn, in case Klein stopped coming to see her. But if Klein had known, she would never have left. Did Astral dimly realize that, now? Was that part of the anguish?

"Do you still have the letter, Astral?" Tessa asked gently.

Why ask? You know she's telling the truth.

Check. Always check. Believe nothing. Believe no one.

This job has corrupted you.

"I left it in the box of books. I did not want to tear it up, or burn it. But I could not bring it here."

"Do you still go to the place? Read the books yourself?"

"No. I went once, after Miss Klein had gone. But it seemed—not good, to be there alone. I—I dug a hole and put the box under the ground, so no one would ever find it."

Dead and buried.

"Astral—did you ever tell your mother about your special place? Did you show it to her?" asked Tessa.

The girl drew a shuddering breath, and shook her head. "No one at Haven knew about it," she said. "No one at all. It is forbidden to cross the creek."

"I'd like to see the box of books," said Tessa gently. "Would you tell me where to find it?"

Astral turned back to the lavender. "If you wish it," she said listlessly. "It does not matter, any more."

Because Quinn is dead. And Fiona Klein is dead, too.

Tessa roused herself. "When you went to stay with Miss Klein last night, Astral, did you talk about—before she went away? Did you tell her the truth about Adam?"

"No. Bliss and Skye were always with us, and they were so afraid. But I had decided to tell her. I did not want her to go away again. I thought we would talk, later. I thought we had time. But . . . I did not guard my thoughts. And there was no time."

The hopelessness in her voice was terrible.

She's so young.

"There's still Jonathon," said Tessa.

Astral half-smiled. "Yes," she said. "Jonathon wants to help us, too. Perhaps he will try. But then——" Suddenly her eyes widened, and her lips parted. A look of dread crossed her face. She spun around to Tessa and gripped her arm. "Send him away!" she gasped.

They stood motionless together. Insects chirped in the long grass. The scent of the lavender hung in the air, mingled with the smell of chicken manure, earth and rotting wood.

"Astral—tell me where your mother is," begged Tessa. "Tell me!"

Rigid, the girl shook her head.

"Why not?" asked Tessa.

"We swore, Tessa," whispered Astral. "We swore on our souls."

Steve was still with Jonathon Stoller when Tessa called. "Have you finished there?" she asked.

"Almost. What's up?"

"A few things. I want you to come with me, to see something," she said. "That hiding place they found on Michael O'Malley's property—it's where Fiona Klein and Astral used to meet."

"Oh, yeah?" Steve's voice was laconic, but she flared up as though he'd made a salacious joke.

"Klein was teaching her. English literature. They read books together. That was all there was to it," she snapped. "The box of books should still be there. And a letter."

"They didn't find any books."

"Astral hid them. Buried them. And it was over five months ago. There wouldn't be any sign of it now. But Astral's told me where the place is. How long?"

"Two minutes," he said peaceably. "I'll meet you down by the dividing fence. There's a gap there, down near the bottom, where the hedge starts to break up."

"Right. And Steve?"

"Yeah?"

"Tell Stoller that Constable Russell Ingres is coming to keep an eye on him. He's on his way. Stoller should let him in, but no one else. Tell him to stay inside and lock his doors."

"Tessa—?"

But already, Tessa had cut the connection.

Steve glanced at Jonathon Stoller, slumped on the step, staring down at the tree line.

"I've got to go next door. Mind if I take a shortcut over your fence?" he asked.

"Help yourself," the man said sullenly. "What do I care? What do I care about any bloody thing?"

"In the meantime, you stay here. I'd like you to go inside, and lock your doors. A Constable Ingres is on his way here. He'll be driving a police four-wheel drive vehicle, and he'll have identification on him. Let him in, but no one else. No one at all. Okay?"

The man's nostrils flared. "What's going on?" he said loudly. "God, are you saying I'm in danger? Me? What have you found out?"

"We're just taking precautions, sir."

Jonathon stumbled out of his chair. He was pale and his forehead gleamed with sweat. "Why can't I go back to Sydney?" he demanded.

"You aren't in a fit condition to drive," said Steve. "Now look, you'll be fine. Just go inside and secure the house. Make yourself another cup of coffee. Constable Ingres will be with you as soon as possible."

He saw Stoller in, heard the key turn in the back door. Then the man's face appeared at the window, staring out, white and strained, through the smeary glass. He made no response as Steve lifted a hand in farewell.

Steve felt slightly uncomfortable about leaving him. The poor bloke was scared out of his mind, now. It might have been better just to leave without telling him to lock up. Ingres would be with him in a few minutes, and in fact there was no rational reason for believing that he was in any danger at all.

Tessa had a hunch—that was all there was to it, otherwise she'd have been more specific on the phone. And nine times out of ten Tessa's hunches were right off beam. The trouble was, every tenth time she was spot on. You were a fool to ignore her—especially with two people dead already.

Striding across the paddock, towards the fence, Steve

looked back once. Jonathon was still standing by the window staring after him. "You'll be all right, mate," he said aloud. Then he smiled wryly to himself. Jonathon Stoller was quite safe. With the doors and windows locked, he was secure.

But Fiona Klein's doors and windows had been locked, too. And that hadn't been enough to make her secure. She'd ended up twisted and broken at the bottom of a cliff.

Steve reached the fence and followed it down to where the hedge ended. Tessa was waiting there, a small brown shadow camouflaged by the cherry-laurel boughs. He wondered if she'd heard him talking to himself. It was a thing she did herself all the time. But she'd be surprised to hear him doing it.

He climbed over the fence and joined her. She looked pale and thoughtful. Her fair hair was soft and ruffled. There were dark smudges under her beautiful eyes.

"This is where Jonathon and Astral used to meet?" she said.

"That's right. The willow tree's right over the other side, almost at the other border."

"Right," she said. But she seemed in no hurry to go. Instead, her eyes were wandering over the long grass of the Haven paddock as it sloped down to the forest right in front of her.

"Stoller went to Klein's last night," Steve murmured, surprised that she hadn't asked. "It was his car Mrs. Rafael saw. He says he went up to the house, but he didn't go in."

"Do you believe him?"

"I don't know." He grinned as she raised her eyebrows. "Okay—now I'm the one saying it. But he's a funny character. He could be telling the truth, or lying his head off. And he did wash his car. Listen, what's all this about Ingres coming over to keep an eye on him? What exactly do you—?"

"Just a feeling I had." But Tessa was looking around vaguely. Suddenly, the urgency she'd exhibited on the phone had disappeared. "You can see where Astral walked through the grass," Tessa murmured. "Just the faintest tracks. But she's done it often."

Steve nodded. "Stoller says the forest down here's a refuge for her. The first time he saw her she was coming up from the forest." He grinned ruefully. "You read the notes. He thought he was having some sort of vision."

"She'd been crying," Tessa murmured, remembering.

"She had a lot to cry about, it turns out."

"Yes." She paused. "That was four and a bit months ago, about, wasn't it? In early January, a few weeks after Fiona Klein left?"

He couldn't follow her train of thought. "You mean Astral didn't waste any time finding someone else?" he hazarded.

"No." Tessa frowned. "I mean, no, that's not what I mean, exactly. I was just getting the timing straight. Just thinking . . ."

She started walking down through the golden grass, towards the pine trees.

"It'd be easier to cross the property here than to walk through the forest, you know," Steve called after her.

She took no notice. Irritated in spite of himself, he followed.

In a few minutes they'd reached the tree line, and were moving into the shade. Cockatoos shrieked above their heads. The creek gurgled and bubbled, unseen, at the bottom of the slope. The afternoon sun pooled here and there on the clumps of ferns and on the red and white toadstools that dotted the soft, brown forest floor.

Tessa stood looking around her. Her eyes were vague.

"Are you going to tell me what we're doing down here?" he said impatiently. "You do realize the whole place has been searched?"

"Maybe they weren't looking for the right thing," she said.

She wandered deeper into the forest, apparently aimlessly, looking at the ground, dwarfed by the great trees that rose dark around her. Then, suddenly, she bent and picked something up from the base of a cluster of fern. She held it out to Steve.

It was a small, dried-out bunch of rosemary—just a few sprigs, tied together with a grass stem. It was still fragrant.

"Rosemary for remembrance," she murmured. "This looks about a week old, wouldn't you say?" She looked up at him, and their eyes met. Steve felt a chill, as though the sun had gone in.

"Somewhere near here," she said.

Together they circled the fern clump, fanning out gradually till they found what they were looking for. The hump of earth was covered by a thick layer of pine needles, almost perfectly camouflaged as part of the uneven slope of the ground. You could have walked over it a hundred times, and not known it for what it was.

They called for assistance. And within half an hour another body was being uncovered at Haven. A skeletal body wrapped in a stained white sheet: an almost fleshless horror with long gray-streaked hair, a silver necklet bearing the shape of a crescent moon clasped around its neck, and the tatters of a long red dress clinging to its bones.

Twenty-three

"Been in the ground four to six months," said Tootsie, crouched low over the skeleton but showing, as usual, no sign of discomfort or distaste.

Thorne swore disgustedly. "Do you realize how much time we've wasted looking for this woman?" he spat. "Time and money?"

"It isn't yet confirmed that this is Rachel Brydie, Malcolm," observed Fisk, who was standing back watching Tootsie at work with his usual superior interest.

"Of course it's her," Thorne snapped. "Those girls have been spinning us a line all along. Tootsie? Cause of death?"

Tootsie looked up, rather haughtily. "It *looks*," she said, emphasizing the word, "as though she's been beaten to death. There are multiple fractures. Arms, ribs—" She pointed. "The skull is severely damaged in several places. I'm fairly certain it's a homicide, in other words. Even falling off the roof of the house would be unlikely to cause injuries as extensive as this. In my opinion."

Thorne nodded and turned away. He was furious. Not just because he'd been looking for a dead woman, Tessa thought. That had always been a possibility. The searchers had naturally looked for signs of recent ground disturbance in the forest, the nearby bush, and the gardens.

Thorne was angry because he'd been comprehensively fooled. He'd suspected everything the Brydie sisters said—except that their mother was alive last Sunday. That, he'd accepted.

They'd all accepted it. Yet they'd had no real reason to. Heidi's story of seeing Brydie by the lake had always been iffy. And everyone else they'd spoken to had said they hadn't actually seen Rachel Brydie for a very long time. But that had seemed quite natural. The woman, everyone said, hardly ever left Haven. Her daughters never left the property either. Adam Quinn was the only one who ever visited the village these days, they said. And Haven didn't welcome visitors. When you came to think about it, Rachel Brydie could have been dead for years, and no one would have known.

"Any idea of the weapon, Toots?" asked Steve mildly.

Tootsie shrugged. "I think it might have been a lump of wood," she said. "There are wood fragments in the bone, and caught in the shroud. But again, Steve—"

"All right," Thorne said grimly. "You can't confirm anything. But I know who can."

They took Bliss, Skye and Astral to the police station in Oakdale. The station, a small sandstone building with a veranda, gables and a steeply pitched iron roof, was conveniently but unobtrusively situated on the road that ran parallel with the railway line, at right angles to the main street.

In the days when the policeman in residence pottered in the front garden during his time off and his wife kept chickens in the backyard, in the days when a fire was kept up in the main office in the winter, and homemade lemon drink was served to people in distress in summer, the Oakdale station had no doubt been very charming. Now it was simply a cramped, inconvenient anachronism set in a glaring plain of concrete that had been marked out into parking spaces with white paint. The picket fence had long ago been replaced by rigid wire guarding a narrow border of severely disciplined evergreen shrubs growing through holes in black plastic that had been sprinkled with a niggardly mulch of pine-bark chips.

In the not-too-distant future, Tessa imagined, this police station would be closed. Sergeant McCaffrey, Russell Ingres and Rochette Williams, or their replacements, would be sent to join a team in a big, centralized establishment somewhere midway between Oakdale and the nearest other big village.

The new headquarters would have air-conditioning, sealed, tinted windows, ample parking and a hospital smell.

This old station would be sold. Possibly it would become a restaurant—yet another rival for Martin's. It would be made charming again. It would be refurbished inside and out. The concrete would be replaced by tasteful paving. The wire fence would be taken down and the picket fence restored. The back garden would sprout pergolas, courtyards, a fountain. And inside, sepia photographs of suitably ancient, and therefore unthreatening, groups of police would decorate the walls.

For now, however, the Oakdale station remained. Various attempts to make space, to bring it into line with modern requirements for power, heat and light, to accommodate new technology, had scarred and ravaged the interior, creating odd corners, awkward angles and an overwhelming air of clutter and make-do. But the interview room was a bare, white place without character or clutter. A space out of time.

There, confronted by the knowledge that their secret was out and their mother's body had been found, separated from each other and away from the spell of Haven, Bliss, Skye and Astral Brydie's control finally broke. As before, it was Astral who gave the best and most detailed account, but they all told the same story. A tale of Gothic horror.

It had begun just over four months before, on the fifth of January—the anniversary of the day Adam Quinn came to Haven, and the day he killed their mother.

Adam's anniversary, the only day ringed on the Haven calendar, was always a feast day, and this year was no exception. As always, Adam had killed a fowl. He did little work around the farm. He preferred to supervise. But he always killed the chickens. He would choose the one to die, then watch it for days as it pecked around, ignorant of its fate. When he killed it, cutting its head off with the ax, he insisted on an audience.

"He liked us to watch," as Bliss put it, softly, evenly. "It was for our own good. He knew it was good for us to understand, to remember how quickly death could come. And that the weak must bow to the strong."

That night, Rachel Brydie was cooking the dinner. The

special dinner, for Adam's birthday. There was the chicken, stuffed with onion and herbs, and many vegetables from the gardens, cooked together in a baking dish. It was very hot in the kitchen—far hotter than it was outside. Rachel was nervous, because Adam was in the kitchen, watching her. He was impatient. He had been drinking. More than usual. Rachel had worked slowly, worried by the heat, and the dinner was very late. It was growing dark, and the moon was rising, when at last everything was cooked.

"Mother lifted the baking dish from the oven, and carried it to the kitchen table, where the big platter was," said Skye, her voice flat and lifeless, her hands, for once, still in her lap. "She began to lift the chicken onto the platter. Then, somehow, her hand shook. The chicken slipped from the fork. It fell onto the floor, and the platter fell down after it, breaking into pieces . . ."

"Adam was angry because the feast was spoiled," said Bliss, her beautiful voice trembling at last. "He shouted at Mother. He called her a clumsy fool. He hit her across the side of her head with his hand, and she fell, pulling the baking dish down with her. The vegetables scattered on the floor. Mother screamed, because she had fallen, and the hot fat had splashed her legs and arms . . ."

"Mother was crawling on the floor. She was trying to gather up the food," whispered Astral. "She kept saying, 'I'm sorry, I'm sorry.' I tried to help her, but Adam screamed at me to get back, to leave her alone. She was crawling—crying, slipping on the fat, crushing the food, spoiling it more and more. It was in her hair, on her clothes . . ." Her face contorted. "Adam kicked her in the back. Then he caught up a piece of firewood from the basket by the stove and hit Mother with that. She screamed and tried to crawl away from him, but he kept on and on. I tried to pull him back, to hold his arm so he could not hit her any more. Bliss did, too . . ."

"Bliss and Astral tried to stop him, but I did not," said Skye. "I wanted to help Mother, but I knew it would do no good. And it would make Adam angry. So angry." Her voice faltered, and she closed her eyes. Her lids were so thick and pale, her eyelashes and eyebrows so light, that for a moment it looked, in the yellow light of the interview room, as though she had no eyes at all.

"We were at fault, to interfere," Bliss said. "We made Adam far angrier than before. Angrier than he had ever been. He threw us aside. He kicked and struck at Mother over and over again, shouting. Finally she lay still. Blood was coming from her nose and from her mouth and ears. Adam felt her wrist. He said she was dead, and that we had killed her because we had raised our hands to him. He said that Skye was as much at fault as Astral and I were, because she had stood by and let us attack him . . ."

"He made us wrap Mother's body in a sheet, and carry it down to the forest," Astral said, her eyes dark with the memory. "Her body was very heavy. We could feel it still warm, through the sheet, and the blood soaked through to our hands. I wondered if she could be still alive, but she did not move. I thought, Miss Klein has gone. Now Mother has gone.

"We went down through the long grass. We went very slowly. It felt like a dream. It looked like a dream. Adam walked in front of us, carrying the spades. He was wearing his purple robe. He was very tall. The moon was full. It lit our way, making the night like day, though with no color. I did not know Jonathon then, but I had watched him. I thought, if he was home, he might see us. But he was not there. His house was dark." Her voice sank to a whisper. "There was no one to see . . ."

"Adam chose a place under the trees," said Skye. "He marked out the space, and told us to dig. When the hole was deep enough, he rolled Mother's body in. Then we put the earth on top of her, and he stamped it down . . ."

"We covered the place with pine needles, so it would be hidden," said Bliss. "Then Adam made us swear never, never to tell, while we lived. He made us swear, on our souls. He told us that we were bound to him in blood forever now, in this life and beyond the grave, and he would know if we should ever betray the trust. The place where Mother lay must never be marked by any sign. We must never tell anyone that she was dead." She raised anguished eyes to stare at the door of the plain, white room. "We have betrayed the trust," she said. Her strong mouth quivered.

"It's all right, Bliss," Tessa said helplessly. "Bliss, believe me, Adam won't be back. You're free of him, now."

But Bliss stared at the door, as if waiting for it to open and Tessa felt a chill, as though the girl's fear was seeping into her own soul.

The story of Rachel Brydie's death and burial was terrible. But for Tessa the story of what came after was in its way even more horrifying.

When they came back from the forest, Bliss, Skye and Astral cleaned the kitchen. Adam watched them do it. Then he took Bliss into his bedroom and shut the door. Skye and Astral clung together, listening to her screams.

And that was only the beginning of their new life, alone with Adam Quinn. As the weeks and months passed, he seemed to grow stronger and stronger. He became enraged more and more often. He watched their every move. He went to the village most afternoons, for supplies, and to drink at the hotel, and then they had an hour of freedom. But he told them that he knew what they were thinking. He knew everything they did. Every now and then, after dinner, he took one of them into his bed. He said it was necessary, since they had caused their mother to die. They never knew which one it would be, or when it would happen. They dreaded it—waiting, not knowing.

"Did you wish Adam would die?" they were asked, one by one.

And one by one they answered: "He said he could not die."

But Adam Quinn had died.

"They're flimflamming us," said Thorne. "As McCaffrey puts it, I can feel it in my liver."

Tessa made no comment on that. She stood in the cluttered office, in front of the desk Thorne had appropriated, staring over his shoulder and through the window at the railway line across the road, feeling like a schoolgirl.

You've even got your hands behind your back.

A silver train passed, running smoothly on its tracks. Going down, to the city.

"Can they go back to Haven tonight?" she asked. "They want to."

Thorne looked grim. "I haven't even thought about that," he said. "I'm not finished with them yet."

That desk's too small for him.

Too small for his ego.

"Where's Steve?" he asked restlessly.

He's uncomfortable, dealing with me.

Do you blame him? You're acting as if he's the enemy.

He's always like that.

"Steve went out for a walk. To get some air."

To stretch his legs. To look in Ridge Real Estate's window. To relax. To pace himself. I should have gone with him.

It wouldn't have done any good.

"You still think they killed him, Malcolm?" She'd had to force herself to call Thorne by his name. But she didn't want to call him "sir." Not in the present situation. She felt bullied enough already.

Thorne gave a thin smile and swung around in his chair to face the window. "I have no opinion," he said. "All I know is, they've lied to us from the start."

"They had to. They felt they had to. They were scared."

"Scared of being charged with murder, maybe?" Thorne swung around and faced her again. "You realize they inherit all Quinn's money, don't you? He went up to that solicitor two doors down from this place and made a will in their mother's favor just after he moved in with her. Everyone round here knows about it. He talked about it. It was no secret. Now those girls get the lot. Millions."

Tessa couldn't speak. She stared at him in disbelief.

He held up his hands. "I'm not saying that's germane, Tessa. I'm not saying they knocked the man off for his money. I'm just saying it could have been a sweetener."

"What do you *mean*?"

Thorne's face hardened. "I mean, we don't have to look for a financial motive for the Brydies. We've got motives coming out our ears. Quinn beat their mother to death in front of them. He kept them virtual prisoners for months. He brutalized them, and he terrified them. They had the motive. They had the means. They had the opportunity. They cleaned the gun, disturbed the body and swept out the shed around the body. There's no suicide note. There's no classic murder-suicide pattern."

"There's no sign Quinn was restrained or forced to lie down in the shed, either."

He shrugged. "He still could have been drugged or poisoned."

"Tootsie doesn't think so."

He raised his eyebrows. "The toxicology results aren't in, to my knowledge."

"So are you suggesting they killed Fiona Klein as well?" asked Tessa coldly.

He gave her a sideways glance. "I wouldn't charge them with that. The experts have only just started on the papers we found in the stove at Klein's house, but it's clear they are poems, and from what they've made out so far a lot of them are about love. I think Klein could have jumped."

"No. I don't think so."

"You spoke to O'Malley. You know the story." Thorne was being unnaturally patient.

He knows you're tired. Overinvolved. Watch it, or he'll take you off this case.

"Fisk found the box of books and magazines, buried at that willow tree cubby-house place," Thorne went on. "They were right where you said."

"Where Astral said."

"Yes." Thorne adjusted his glasses, glancing at a note in front of him. "Not in a bad state, considering. The tree offered good protection from the weather. In the box there was also a round tin containing eight chocolate-chip cookies—very stale, obviously—a plastic bottle of water, two plastic cups. Klein's farewell note was there too. Substance the same as your report."

He leaned forward. "Think about it, Tessa. Klein gets herself away because she thinks she's getting too fond of the girl—Astral—and it's dangerous. She goes off to Italy with her girlfriend, but she can't hack it. She breaks up that relationship, comes home, finds the girl she's obsessed with has killed someone, thinks it's her fault, and decides it's all too hard. She burns her poems, goes outside, walks out towards the clifftop and just doesn't stop."

Makes sense.

No!

"Astral says she didn't tell Klein anything last night," said Tessa.

"Well, she would say that, wouldn't she?" At last, Thorne was showing signs of impatience. It was almost a relief. "For God's sake, Tessa—didn't Klein say Astral had a flair for drama, or whatever? That's teacher's code for being a good liar, isn't it?"

"Rachel Brydie was an actor," Tessa said.

"Right. My point exactly."

"I mean, it would be natural for Astral—all of them—to have inherited the talent. It doesn't mean they're using it. Does it?"

Thorne pushed away a cup of half-cold coffee and stood up. He looked straight at her. "You're the one who's dealt with Astral Brydie the most, Tessa. I want you to go back in there and take her back through the night Quinn died. Steve can sit in. When's he due back?"

Tessa looked at her watch. "About now."

"Good. He sits in. But you do the talking."

"I've already—"

"We haven't had it all, Tessa. Not by a long shot," he interrupted. "And I want it all. I want the whole story again, in full. I want every detail checked. Quinn thrashed the girl last Sunday, didn't he? When? Where? Why? How did she feel about it? How did her sisters feel?"

"He'd beaten her before," Tessa murmured. "You can see the scars . . ."

You always disobey . . .

"You've heard of the straw that broke the camel's back, I presume?" Thorne pushed his hands into his pockets. "You want me to take this on myself, Tessa? I'm happy to do that. You can keep right out of it, if you don't think—"

"No—no, it's fine," Tessa broke in hurriedly. The last thing she wanted was to abandon Astral to Thorne. Or even to Steve. She didn't want to abandon Astral at all.

He knows that. He's using that. He knows you'll get more out of her than anyone.

There's nothing more to get out of her.

Then why are you afraid of questioning her?

I don't want her badgered.

Not true. You're scared she'll slip up.

She didn't do it.

You aren't sure. You still aren't sure . . .

"Tessa?" Thorne was watching her. The low afternoon light streamed through the window, glinting on his glasses.

"Just thinking," she said. She firmed her lips. "I want to take in the bunch of rosemary I found in the forest. It'll help."

Without comment he left the room. He came back seconds later with the tiny bouquet, which looked somehow even more pathetic encased in its plastic evidence bag.

Tessa looked at it. She felt she already knew its story. She'd known it from the first moment she saw it lying abandoned on the forest floor.

Now she was going to find out for sure. Astral was going to tell her.

Twenty-four

When Tessa put the packet of rosemary on the interview room table, Astral shrank back.

"You took this to your mother last Sunday, didn't you, Astral?" Tessa asked.

"Yes," the girl answered through stiff lips. "I took it to her grave. I was at fault."

"How were you at fault?"

"I betrayed the trust," Astral went on, so softly that it was hard to hear her.

"Speak up, please. How did you betray the trust? Whose trust?"

"Adam's trust. We had sworn we would not mark the place. But I disobeyed. I had visited the place where mother lay. Many times. Then, on Sunday, I took the rosemary to her. I guarded my mind, but he knew."

"Who are you talking about?"

"Adam," said Astral, her voice barely more than a sigh. "I betrayed the trust. I took flowers to the grave. I spoke to the stranger. I let the stranger—touch me."

"Who do you mean by 'the stranger'?"

The girl looked at her. Her soft eyes were bewildered. "Jonathon," she whispered. "I told you."

This is awful!

You've got to do it by the book.

"When did you leave this rosemary at the grave, Astral? When exactly?"

"It was last Sunday, in the middle of the afternoon. I thought Adam had gone to the village. I thought it was safe."

"And was it safe?"

The girl was staring straight ahead. Even from across the table, Tessa could feel her fear.

"It was not safe," she said. "Adam knew I was false. He pretended to go out to the village while we worked in the gardens, but he did not. He went down to the forest, and hid himself, and waited for me. And he saw. He saw everything—" She broke off, her eyes blank with remembered terror.

"What did he see, Astral?" said Tessa relentlessly. She was very aware of Steve, sitting by the door. Aware of the tape recorder, silently recording every word.

"He saw me go down to the forest, and put the rosemary on the grave. He saw me go back to the long grass, and meet Jonathon by the fence. He saw us speak. He saw me return to the forest and go through the fence, to Jonathon . . ."

"You went to Jonathon's side of the fence?"

"Yes." Astral's head drooped. "Jonathon asked me to do it. We had met in the forest before, because Jonathon said we would be hidden there. But the fence was always between us. Last Sunday—was different."

"Speak up a bit, please, Astral. It's hard to hear you."

"I am sorry." The voice was dead. But obediently, Astral had raised it.

Don't say you're sorry. Don't do what I say! Don't feel so defeated, so hopeless. Everything's going to be all right. I'll help you.

Go on!

"What did you do, with Jonathon?"

Astral's head was still down. "He kissed me. We had kissed, before, over the fence. But this was different. His mouth was hot. He—touched me. His hands were soft. Not like Adam's hands. He did not hurt me. He took off his shirt, and put it on the ground. We lay down. He was breathing, so much, so hard. He said my name. His voice sounded— strange. Then he rolled on top of me. He was warm. I closed my eyes. I felt him push up my dress. Then I felt him inside me." She winced, and tears rolled down her cheeks.

Tessa writhed.

Bastard! Men are bastards!

Did she ask him to stop?

"Did you ask him to stop?"

"No." This possibility had obviously never occurred to Astral—at the time, or afterwards. "It was what he wanted."

"So—"

"It was like Adam. But not like Adam. Jonathon was gentle. I did not have to—do anything. He asked me for nothing. He did not hurt me."

That's twice she's said it. "He did not hurt me."

Big deal!

It was, to her.

"And it was over—so quickly," Astral was going on. "Like with the sparrows, or the wrens."

Poor Jonathon. Just too eager. Four months of aching balls . . .

Cynical bitch!

"And when he had finished, he cried." Astral looked up, and now her eyes were almost surprised. "He cried. I thought—he was hurt. But he said, no. He said he loved me. He said he was sorry. I did not understand."

So many things you don't understand.

"What happened then?"

"We lay still for a while. Then I told him I should go. But he said no. He began to kiss me again. He started to pull my shift up, higher and higher. Past my stomach, and up to my chest. I saw that he wanted to take my shift off." Astral's smooth girl's forehead puckered, and her voice rose. "I tried to stop him, so he would not see—"

"What, Astral?"

The voice dropped again. "It is not permitted to undress in front of strangers."

In case they see the scars. Tell the cops. Put Adam Quinn away, where he belongs . . .

Adam Quinn's dead.

I'm glad. So glad. May he rot in hell.

"But Jonathon did see," Astral said. "He felt the marks on my back, and then he looked. He—he was very angry. I tried to explain. I said that I disobeyed, very often. That—it was necessary that I be corrected. But Jonathon would not listen.

He said he was going back to the house with me. He said he was going to talk to Adam."

Tessa forced herself to stare straight ahead, though more than anything she wanted to turn, to look at Steve.

Astral clenched her fists on the table. "I was so afraid. I told him, no. I begged him to leave me, to go back to the city."

"Astral, didn't you want him to help you?" asked Tessa.

"Jonathon could not help me," the girl said simply. "He could not fight Adam. He is too soft, too gentle. He did not understand—what Adam was. He did not know about—Mother. He thought Mother was with us. He did not understand that we were tied to Adam, in blood, and could never . . ." She drew a shuddering breath.

"At last he agreed to go. It was late. He said—next week. We would talk again, next week. He fastened his clothes. And he went, back up to his house, and then away."

Tessa leaned forward. "Did you actually see him go, Astral? Think carefully. Tell me exactly what you saw."

Astral's forehead creased again. Plainly, she didn't understand the point of the question. But she answered obediently. "I watched from the trees as he went up to his house. He went inside and closed the door. A little later, not long, he came out to his car, with a bag. He put the bag in the car, and started the car, and drove away, around to the front of the house and up the driveway, to the gate. Then he opened the gate, and drove through."

"But you couldn't see all that, from the forest, could you?"

"I could not *see*, once the car was at the front of the house," said Astral patiently. "But I could hear, and I know the sound." She looked up, meeting Tessa's eyes. "I have heard it, many times," she said.

I have heard it many times. As he drove away, back to his world, leaving me in mine.

"What did you do then?" asked Tessa.

The girl was silent. She clasped her hands, pressing them against the table. The knuckles were white.

"Astral?"

"I went back to the Haven side of the fence," Astral said, in a low voice. "I turned to go out of the forest. And then, Adam was there."

Again, it was as though the words had caught in her throat. She swallowed.

"What did he say to you, Astral?" Tessa prompted.

"He said nothing. But I knew, from his face, that he had been there, hidden, all the time. He had heard, and seen . . ."

That dark face, those shadowed eyes. A mask of rage.

"He took me by the arm. Here." Astral touched her upper arm.

Yellow-brown marks on soft flesh, a grip of iron.

"He took me to the grave. The rosemary was there. He picked it up, and threw it away. Then he took me back to the house. Still, he did not speak."

Out of the forest, through the long grass, through the orchard. The man, tall, powerful and filled with rage; the girl, terrified, stumbling beside him on bare brown feet. Her sisters, startled, white-faced, looking up from their work in the gardens . . .

"In the house, Adam spoke. Not to me. To Bliss and Skye." Astral's voice wavered. She was trembling. "He told them that I had broken the trust. He said that I was evil, and full of filth and lies, and had defiled Haven and betrayed him. Then he corrected me. It was . . . bad. Worse than every other time. Skye cried and screamed. I remember her screaming. Bliss did not scream."

"Didn't they try to help you?" Tessa asked evenly.

Astral shook her head. "They knew—what he would do. They remembered what had happened to Mother. They did not want me to die."

Another warm, broken body to wrap in a sheet, to carry to the forest, under the moon.

Then there would be only two . . .

"But afterwards—when Adam had gone to his room— Bliss came to me and lifted me up. She took me to my bed. She gave me water to drink. She washed me, and put the salve on me. She calmed Skye, and made her still."

Bliss, the oldest. The grave, watchful one with the beautiful voice. Doing what she could, but seeing no hope of remedy, intent only on surviving, enduring. Skye, weak, terrified, be-rating her sister, who put them all in danger, who always dis-obeyed . . .

"Tell me the rest, Astral," Tessa said. The plain little room was utterly silent. She knew Steve was very near, but she couldn't hear his breathing.

"The rest is the same," said Astral. "There is nothing more that I have not told you." She gave an odd little shake of her shoulders. "Perhaps, if I had told you everything, at first, you would have understood," she said. "But I could not tell."

"Astral . . ."

The girl was staring straight ahead, her eyes unfocused. "Adam had corrected me, but it was not enough," she said. "So he gave us the drink. He set the fire. He had to purify Haven. Purify himself. He knew he would live again. He meant for us to die. But we did not die. We lived on, in wickedness." She drew a shuddering breath. "And Adam knows. He watches us."

Tessa reached across the table and took the small, work-roughened hand in her own. "Astral, surely you don't really believe that?" she urged. "You've read. You've learned about the world—from Miss Klein, and Jonathon. Can you still be-lieve that?"

Tears slipped slowly from Astral's eyes.

"I had begun to doubt. But now I know that I was wrong," she whispered.

"Because of Miss Klein? Is that it? Is it because Miss Klein tried to help you, and now she's dead?"

"Yes. Adam came for her. Adam is waiting his time. Soon he will come for us. Then we will pay."

"She didn't actually see Stoller leave. Maybe he didn't," Tessa whispered, as she and Steve left the interview room to-gether. "Maybe he parked his car halfway up the drive or something, waited till late, when he thought the women would be in bed, then went in and killed Quinn. He's besotted with Astral. He'd just seen all the old scars on her back. He didn't tell you a thing about that little interlude in the forest, did he?"

"No," Steve said grimly. "He left that interesting piece of information right out."

"And why? Unless he knew we'd see it as a motive." Tessa felt a surge of excitement. She stopped and pulled Steve's arm to make him stop. She didn't want to have this discussion in front of Thorne and Sergeant McCaffrey.

"He could have tricked Quinn out to the shed," she said. "Held the gun on him. Forced him to lie down on the floor . . ."

Steve's brow wrinkled. "It's tempting, but I can't see it, Tess. It's full of holes."

"Why?"

"Stoller wouldn't scare someone like Quinn. Stoller's all talk and angst, no do. He-man stuff, no way. But if I'm wrong about that, if it was Stoller, he wouldn't have been able to set up the thing to look like a murder-suicide. Not on his own. Someone would have had to give him Quinn's gun, or show him where it was. And there's the fire. Stoller didn't want Astral and the others to die, did he? So if he lit the fire in their bedroom, he did it with their cooperation."

"Well, then—" Tessa hesitated.

"You're going to say, maybe he did? Well, frankly, I don't see that either."

"I thought you'd jump at the idea."

He grinned, but the smile didn't reach his eyes. "Mr. Predictable, am I?"

"I didn't mean that!"

Steve leaned his back against the wall and looked at her. "I don't think they did it together because I'm certain—as certain as I can ever be—that Stoller had no idea he was going to find a corpse in an advanced state of decay in that shed yesterday morning. He was still shocked to the back teeth when I first saw him. Chucking wine down his neck as fast as he could go, babbling, sick, shaking like a leaf. If he'd done the murder, with the Brydie girls as accomplices, it just wouldn't have happened like that, would it?"

Tessa was downcast. She could see that he was right.

Aren't you supposed to be the hotshot?

I'm tired.

Isn't he tired? But he hasn't stopped thinking.

"Plus," Steve went on, ruthlessly hammering the last nail into the coffin, "if Stoller had done the thing with their cooperation, he would have had to know that Rachel Brydie was dead."

"Why?" asked Tessa weakly.

"It's just about inconceivable that he'd leave her out of the equation," Steve said. "Her daughters were obviously very close to her. If she was alive, if she really had just been out for a while, they would probably have told her exactly what happened when she came back. Stoller couldn't know how she'd take that. She could have gone straight to the cops. He wouldn't have taken that risk. Not Stoller."

"So maybe he did know."

He shook his head. "I don't think he had the faintest idea."

"Why are you so sure?"

"Because this afternoon, when I told him I was leaving, and to lock his doors, he was bloody terrified. He wasn't acting either. He went dead white, and broke out in a cold, visible sweat. He thought just what I think you did, when you rang me. He thought Rachel Brydie was around somewhere. He thought Rachel had killed Fiona Klein—and that he was next. How could he have thought that, if he knew she was buried under the pine trees?"

He shrugged. "So Stoller couldn't have done it with the Brydies, but he couldn't have done it without them, either. So he didn't do it at all."

"But still," said Tessa, rallying, "he didn't tell you the truth—all the truth, did he?"

"No. And I'll follow that up. But I don't think—I really don't—that there's going to be any joy for us in it. We're still in the dark."

Something stirred in the corner of Tessa's mind. She struggled to see it clearly, but it scuttled out of sight.

"What is it?" Steve was looking at her quizzically.

She shook her head. "Something . . . I feel there's something I've forgotten. I just can't . . ."

"Stop trying to force it," he said. "I know you. It'll come."

*   *   *

In the end, Thorne had to let the Brydies go. There was no valid reason to hold them any longer. Even Sergeant McCaffrey couldn't urge that there was. McCaffrey did point out, however, that they might not be safe at home. Local feeling, he said, was running very high. A lot of the blokes in town had drunk with Adam Quinn at Swans. They liked him. The kids all loved him. The women liked him too. He was always very polite to the ladies.

"Except the ones he lived with," Steve said dryly.

McCaffrey sniffed, and glanced at Tessa.

It's on the tip of his tongue to say they probably asked for it.

But if that's what McCaffrey had nearly said, he thought better of it. "Hard to believe," he contented himself with saying.

Russell Ingres was not so discreet.

"Those women'd drive anyone crazy," he said. "Up themselves, the lot of them. Weirdos. They were happy enough to have Adam, when he first moved in, from what I hear. Happy to have his money. Happy to live on him."

Pig!

He didn't see Astral's back. He didn't hear the stories. He doesn't know . . .

That's no excuse. There's no possible excuse for . . .

"Are you sure you're in the right job, Constable?" Thorne said.

"Pardon?" Ingres's red face seemed to swell.

"According to the testimony we've received, Quinn was a killer, a rapist and a sadist," said Thorne, ice dripping from every word. "I suggest you give that a bit of thought."

How about that?

Tessa looked at Steve. He was staring out the window.

He doesn't like seeing people put down. Even people like Ingres.

McCaffrey stirred uncomfortably. "Russell, you go out to Haven, will you?" he said. "Just keep an eye on things. Get yourself something to eat first. Then get on. We don't want any louts getting in there tonight, mucking things around, frightening the women."

Ingres mumbled, grabbed his cap and made for the door, looking at no one.

"I'll get Rochette to take over from you later tonight, Russ," McCaffrey added. "She'd better get some sleep first. She was up almost all bloody night. Okay?"

"Sure," Ingres was out the door. He didn't look back.

"Think I'll have another go at Stoller before he leaves for town," Steve said.

Thorne adjusted his glasses. "He's staying on," he said. "Taking a few days off work, to keep an eye on things up here, he says."

"Keep an eye on us, does he mean? Keep an eye on developments? Stay close to the Brydies?"

"I'm not sure what he means. And I take your point, Steve. He needs to be watched. And he needs to be questioned again. But if he's involved in this he's played it pretty cool so far. He's not going to blow it by running out at this stage, is he? Leave him for tonight. You and Tessa go back to that guest house place and get some sleep. Have a chat with him in the morning. He'll be there. He's organizing a solicitor for the Brydies, by the way."

"They don't want a solicitor," Tessa said. "I've asked them quite a few—"

"Stoller's getting them one anyway," Thorne cut in. "He seems to think he can talk Astral into it, if he gets her alone."

With an air of relief, he then left them to it. He was going back to Sydney. They could report to him there, he said. By tomorrow lunchtime the Brydies would have seen their solicitor and had their psychiatric assessment. He'd decide then how to proceed.

"Don't find any more bodies till at least eight tomorrow morning, if you don't mind," he said to Tessa as he got into his car. She smiled obediently at the joke, but her lips felt numb and there was a sour taste in her mouth.

Callous bastard.

He's a professional. A survivor. One day, if you stick with this job, you'll probably be like him.

I'll never be like him. I'd rather be dead.

Knock on wood. Don't tempt fate. You've got another night here. Another long night.

Nothing's going to happen.

Knock on wood.

⌐ Twenty-five ⌐

Tessa and Steve drove back to Bide-A-While.

"All pretty inconclusive, isn't it?" Steve said. He was restless now the need for activity had passed. He was driving slightly faster than usual.

"What do you think will happen at the inquests?" asked Tessa. She lay back in her seat, and closed her prickling eyes. She tried to work out how many hours she'd been awake, but couldn't.

Steve frowned over the wheel. "Murder in the case of Rachel Brydie, suicide or an open verdict on Adam Quinn and Fiona Klein. The Brydies'll have to attend, you know."

"Yes." Tessa sighed. It was hard to imagine Bliss, Skye and Astral at a coroner's inquiry. Or anywhere else but here.

"We'll have to get them some proper clothes," she said.

"The solicitor will do that." Steve glanced at her quickly. "You're too involved with them, Tess."

"No, I'm not."

He pulled up the car outside Bide-A-While. "Thorne's right," he said. "They had the best possible motive for killing Quinn. A whole raft of motives, in fact."

Her body was very heavy. We could feel it still warm, through the sheet, and the blood soaked through to our hands . . .

. . . he corrected me. It was . . . bad. Worse than every other time. Skye cried and screamed. I remember her screaming. Bliss did not scream . . .

"If a motive was all we needed, our job'd be pretty easy," Tessa snapped. "Lots of people have motives for murder. It doesn't mean they go and do it."

"As I said, when you were talking about Stoller." He yawned, and got out of the car. She got out, too, slamming the door behind her with unnecessary force.

Petulant.

"What happened last Sunday—it points just as much to suicide as to murder," she said, as they walked to the gate. "I can't understand why you're all happy to put Fiona Klein's death down to suicide, but not Quinn's. I would have thought Quinn was a much more likely candidate. He was unbalanced, for a start. His twisted little empire was falling apart, and he was in danger of being exposed. He saw Astral put flowers on her mother's grave. He saw Astral with Jonathon. He saw Jonathon find the scars on her back, and threaten to confront him. He must have known that Jonathon wouldn't be put off for long. He must have suspected that Astral had told Jonathon about her mother, or that she would as soon as Jonathon came storming into Haven with a bunch of social workers or police . . ."

"I agree," Steve said reasonably. "But if murder-suicide was what Quinn had in mind, why didn't he dispatch the girls properly? It was always on the cards that the gunshot'd wake one of them up—as it did."

Dispatch?

"Why no note?" he went on. He held the gate open for her, followed her into the dark garden. "And why kill himself in a filthy, stinking shed? Why lie down in rubbish and pull the trigger when you've got a nice comfy bed inside the house? Suicides usually make themselves comfortable."

"Okay—so he's not a classic case," Tessa snapped. "So what? If he'd killed himself in bed you and Thorne would have been positive the girls had done it. Now you're saying that they killed him *because* he died in the shed. You can't have it both ways."

She looked up at him. The corner of his mouth had tightened.

He thinks I'm being overemotional.

You are. Calm down.

They paced the gravel path, towards the house. "He said he'd been defiled," Steve said dubiously. "He could have decided the shed was symbolic or something."

It was a peace offering, of sorts. And it was another way of looking at it. A fresh way, that made sense.

He's thinking rationally. You're not. You're feeling, not thinking. You're haunted by nightmares. You can't forget . . .

"Maybe after he'd beaten Astral, he suddenly realized what he'd become," Tessa murmured. "Maybe dressing himself up in that robe and lying down in filth *was* his suicide note."

Steve made no answer to that. Plainly, that seemed to him an unlikely flight of fancy. They climbed the steps to the veranda wearily. The front door was locked. They rang the bell, and after a few moments Melissa opened the door. She didn't return their greeting—just stood back sulkily to let them in.

"Heidi's been grounded again," she muttered, as they passed her. "Her father wouldn't even let me *speak* to her."

"Sorry about that, Melissa," said Steve. "But we had to find out, didn't we?"

"Well, it turns out Mrs. Brydie was dead all the time. So it was all for nothing!" The girl's eyes filled with angry tears. "And people are saying Adam did it. As if!" She kicked the door closed, and the leadlight rattled dangerously.

The two bedroom doors opposite the living room were open, now, with signs of cleaning in progress. Verna Larkin's head popped out of the second door, the one marked "Wattle."

"Oh, you're back," she said. She smiled, but her eyes remained cool. She, too, had obviously heard the news, and didn't like it. "These rooms will be ready soon, if you'd like to change. You're on your own here, now."

"Oh, thanks. But the rooms we've got will be fine," said Tessa. She realized she'd spoken for Steve as well, and glanced at him apologetically.

"Yeah," he said. "Thanks for the offer, Verna, but we're okay. We'll probably be leaving here tomorrow. We're just going to catch up on some sleep now. Don't worry about us."

Verna came out into the hallway. She was wearing bright blue rubber gloves and carrying a cleaning rag. She put one hand on her hip.

"They say Fiona Klein jumped off the cliff beside her house last night," she said, and watched them narrowly.

"We're still not sure exactly what happened," Steve said. "There'll have to be an inquest."

Melissa, still lurking sullenly by the front door, sniffed loudly.

"Melissa, get in and finish that bed, will you?" said Verna. Melissa slouched across the hall to the door of "Waratah" and lingered there.

"All sorts of stories going round," Verna continued, turning back to Tessa and Steve. "They say you're claiming Adam was some sort of monster. They say those Brydie girls are going to get off the whole thing."

"Verna, we really can't tell you anything," Steve said. "Not at this stage."

Her strong mouth quivered. "It's easy enough to slander a man after he's dead," she hissed. She swung around and went back into the bedroom.

Tessa and Steve went on down the hall, aware of Melissa's reproachful eyes burning into their necks.

The house, silent and empty, had become unfriendly.

"They don't like it," Tessa murmured, as they turned into their own corridor.

Steve didn't answer. They reached his door. "Sleep," he said. He stretched, and looked at his watch. "It's eight o'clock. When did we last eat, Tess?"

"I don't know."

I've never felt less like food in my life.

"I might grab a sandwich in the kitchen, later," Steve said. "Verna said we could help ourselves."

"That was when she was feeling friendly."

He grinned tiredly. "She'll come good," he said. "They're like that in the country. Loyal to the people they like. They don't change their minds about people as easily as townies do."

"This isn't really the country."

"Feels like it."

Tessa walked to her own door and opened it. Mauve shimmered inside, wall to wall. She leaned on the doorjamb and looked around at him. "They only care about Quinn, you know," she said bitterly. "Have you noticed that? None of

them care about Fiona Klein. Or Rachel Brydie. Fiona and
Rachel didn't fit into their narrow little idea of what women
should be like, so they can die, and no one cares. But they
loved Quinn. Because he shouted drinks at the pub. Because
he was a good bloke. Because he was a star, but he actually
talked to them."

"Your mate Michael O'Malley claims he cared about
Fiona. Rachel Brydie, too," Steve said.

"Michael O'Malley's—different. He's not a real local."

He nodded slowly, as if taking that comment in. That, and
the attitude that lay behind it. "Well," he said. "I'll see you
later."

He went into his room, and quietly closed the door behind him.

Afterwards, Tessa could barely remember stripping off her
clothes and getting into bed. Sleep engulfed her the moment
she lay down. But it wasn't pleasant. It was as though a door
had slammed, imprisoning her in a pitch-black room full of
things that crawled around the walls, things she suspected,
but couldn't see. She woke, suddenly, hours later, knowing
she'd been dreaming but unable to remember what about, her
heart beating violently, with the feeling that she was late for
something, that she'd forgotten something she had to do.

She looked at her watch. It was one minute to midnight.

The witching hour.

*Coincidence. You went to sleep at eight. You always sleep
four hours, then wake, when you're worried. You know you
do. Everything's normal. Normal.*

She sat up, running her fingers through her tangled hair.
She turned on her bedside light. There was a bottle of spring
water and a glass on the bedside table. Another thoughtful
Bide-A-While touch. Suddenly she was overwhelmingly
thirsty. She broke the seal on the bottle and gulped half the
water down without stopping.

She put the bottle down and sat, panting slightly. The
feeling of panic slowly drained away, leaving her heavy and
listless. She became aware of a dull headache hanging over
her eyes. Her handbag was lying on the floor beside her bed,

underneath the tumbled pile of her discarded clothes. She bent and reached for it, fumbling for headache pills.

She swallowed the pills with more gulps of water.

Midnight.

Astral, Bliss and Skye would be asleep now, at Haven, in that small, bare room with three beds in which, despite everything, they felt secure. Would they dream? Would the mist, crawling at the window, menace them?

Adam is waiting his time. Soon he will come for us. Then we will pay.

Out in the yard the hens would be asleep, too. They would be roosting, in their warm, smelly shed, their heads tucked under their wings, their blank eyes covered by wrinkled eyelids, the wire netting of their prison protecting them from the prowling cats, dogs and foxes that otherwise would scent them out, and kill them.

Did spiders sleep? Or did they crouch motionless in their webs all night, waiting for the tremor that would tell them a night insect had come blundering into the sticky net. Waiting to rush out, to sting and wrap and sting and wrap . . .

He made us wrap Mother's body in a sheet, and carry it down to the forest. Her body was very heavy. We could feel it still warm, through the sheet, and the blood soaked through to our hands . . .

Tessa stood up quickly. Too quickly. Her head pounded. She closed her eyes and rubbed at her forehead.

You haven't eaten. Get something to eat.

Not hungry.

Sandwich, and tea. Help you sleep. Get rid of the headache.

She picked up her clothes and dumped them on the bed, but the idea of clambering back into the stiff, brown cloth was repellent. She went to the cupboard and rummaged in her bag. She found her old cream polo-necked jersey, some baggy moss-green slacks and a pair of thick green angora socks. They were barely respectable garments, long past their use-by date, but they were comfortable and smelled of home. That's why they were in the bag. They'd rescued her from discomfort in strange places many times over the past few years.

She pulled the clothes on, relishing their warm softness and familiarity, but her hands were clumsy, and her whole body felt heavy and awkward. She stood in front of the mirror and ran a comb through her tangled hair. A pale, haunted face with huge eyes stared at her from the glass.

Her body was very heavy. We could feel it still warm, through the sheet, and the blood soaked through to our hands . . . It felt like a dream . . . Adam walked in front of us. He was wearing his purple robe. He was very tall. The moon was full. It made the night like day, but with no color . . .

Quickly Tessa left the room, closing the door on the stifling mauve with relief. She walked down the hallway, past the bathroom and Steve's door, towards the breakfast room and the kitchen beyond. Her socks made no sound on the rug, but the old floorboards beneath creaked under her weight.

The breakfast room was dark, one table for two set and waiting for the morning, but a dim light showed under the door that led into the kitchen. Did Verna usually leave a light on? A hostessly habit, to accommodate guests who felt peckish in the night? Or was someone there?

Tessa pushed the door. It swung open and she saw Steve standing at the kitchen bench holding a half-eaten sandwich in one hand, and pouring boiling water into the teapot with the other. He looked around and smiled at her. His hair was ruffled, and dark stubble roughened his face. He was wearing battered corduroy trousers and a blue sweater. He looked wonderful.

"I thought you might turn up," he said. "Tea?"

"Yes, please."

Unhurriedly, he clapped the lid on the teapot, covered it with the knitted tea cozy and put it on a tray already set with two mugs, milk and sugar.

"Verna left it all ready for us," he said. "Food as well." He indicated a large plate of sandwiches beside the tray. The plastic wrap that had covered the plate was half pulled away. Steve stuffed the rest of the sandwich he'd been eating into his mouth, picked up the tray and carried it to the table.

Tessa grabbed the sandwich plate, and followed.

"I thought I wasn't hungry," she said, sitting down. But the sight and smell of the food was making her mouth water. She took a sandwich and bit into it. Fresh bread. Smoked salmon. Black pepper. Cream cheese.

"Good," she mumbled, with her mouth full.

He laughed.

They sat eating in silence for a moment. The clock ticked. The blinds were drawn, hiding the night. Tessa was glad of that. She took another sandwich. Chicken, lettuce and mayonnaise. Steve poured the tea and handed her a steaming mug. Tessa sipped, and sighed with pleasure.

"That's better," she said, and closed her eyes. "Oh, I'm so tired."

"Did you sleep?"

"Like the dead. But I dreamed . . ."

It felt like a dream . . . Adam walked in front of us, carrying the spades. He was wearing his purple robe. He was very tall . . .

Her eyes opened. She put down her mug, and ran her fingers through her hair. Steve was watching her.

"You've got to learn to switch off, Tess," he said softly. "Give yourself a break."

"I can't—" she began, and stopped.

He waited.

"I can't seem to stop thinking about things." She wrapped her hands around the mug of tea, letting the heat soak through to her bones. "I hate this case."

That sounds so childish.

"I mean, we've seen horrible things before, of course we have," she stumbled on. "But this—there's something so claustrophobic about this. It's all wrong. It's like—an evil thing with no beginning and no end. All the threads—all the details—they're winding round and round on themselves and on us and through everything, and they stick and cling, like spiderwebs. So we struggle, and get more and more tangled up—and all the time something wicked is watching, from a dark corner. Very near . . ."

"God, Tessa!" Steve grimaced. "Look, just forget all that stuff. You have to make yourself stand back. Get your perspective straight. Think through it."

"I can't *stop* thinking about it all. It's all there. But there's something I'm not seeing. I know there is. There's something I've seen, or heard, or noticed that doesn't fit. And I can't think what it is. It's driving me crazy."

"You have to put up with loose ends sometimes. They go with the job."

"What if we never find out the truth? What if there's an open verdict on Quinn, and the files are never closed? Astral, Bliss and Skye will have to live with that forever. Ordinary people don't know them, don't know the details. They just read the papers. They'll just see motive, means and opportunity. And they all know about the girls inheriting Quinn's money."

"Double motive," Steve agreed, and took another sandwich.

"The only motive, as far as Oakdale's concerned," said Tessa bitterly. "Oakdale won't hear a word against Quinn." She drew a deep breath. "It wouldn't be so bad if the girls would go away somewhere. But they won't. They'll never leave Haven now. They'll live on here, with everyone, everyone in the whole town, believing they killed Adam Quinn."

"It's still possible they did."

"Quinn wasn't drugged, Steve. Tootsie and Fisk haven't found a thing, And even—"

Don't say it!

"Tess—"

Tessa bit her lip.

Her body was very heavy. We could feel it still warm, through the sheet, and the blood soaked through to our hands . . .

"And even if they did," she muttered defiantly. "Even if they did kill him—why should they suffer for it? Why should *we* or anyone else make them suffer for it? Quinn was evil, mad—a monster. He deserved to die."

"It's not our job to decide who deserves to live or die, Tess," said Steve quietly.

"Don't lecture me!" she hissed. Again she ran her fingers through her hair. Words and pictures scudded across her mind like clouds across the night sky.

*The moon was full. It lit our way, making the night like day,
though with no color . . . Adam marked out the space, and
told us to dig . . .*

The silence lengthened.

*. . . when the hole was deep enough, he rolled Mother's
body in. Then we put the earth on top of her, and he stamped
it down.*

Stop it!

Tessa dropped her hands to the tabletop and looked up to
meet Steve's steady eyes. "I'm sorry," she said. "I know
you're right. I'm being self-indulgent. Stupid." Her fists were
clenched.

Steve leaned across the table. Their hands were almost
touching. "We could talk it through," he said. "Would that
help?"

"I don't know." Suddenly, Tessa shivered.

"Finish your tea," he ordered. "Warm yourself up."

Obediently Tessa drank. The hot liquid was comforting.

"Steve, you're a man—"

"Last time I looked."

"No—seriously." Tessa frowned. "What makes a man do
what Adam Quinn did? What sort of mind did he have, that
he'd enjoy making those women so terrified of him? Brutalizing them?"

Steve shrugged, pouring himself more tea. "Like Stoller
said, megalomaniacs make up their own reasons for things.
The really interesting thing to me is why the women let him
do it."

"What?!"

"Why did they let him do it? Rachel Brydie had brought
up those girls alone all those years. She'd insisted on the
family living her way. She'd resisted officials who wanted to
interfere—all that. And Bliss and Astral, at least, seem pretty
strong characters, however neurotic they are. Why did they
let this guy take over, and grind them down?"

Tessa felt her face flushing with anger. "I can't believe
you're blaming them because they—"

"I'm not blaming them," Steve said calmly. "I'm just
asking the question. I'm a man, so you ask me why Quinn did

what he did. Okay. You're a woman so I ask you why Rachel Brydie and her daughters let it happen."

"I'm not going to start defending them to you. It's—"

Steve shook his head. "I wish you'd stop seeing this as an attack, Tess. I'm not attacking anyone. I really want to know. Look at Quinn's history. He might have had talent. He might have been charismatic. But he had no center. He was a drinker, and a druggie. He had a breakdown when the fans didn't love him any more. As far as I'm concerned that means he was weak. Weak as piss."

"Weak in one sense, maybe, Steve. But he was big. He was powerful. Tootsie said he had muscles like iron."

And he was a man.

Don't say that.

"And he needed to dominate. He had a male need to dominate."

"Not all men need to dominate," said Steve, as she'd known he would.

"I'm not saying they all—"

"You're being simple-minded, Tess."

"You're trying to dominate me right now, Steve!"

"Fat chance."

He doesn't know how threatened I feel.

How do you know he doesn't feel threatened as well?

"I don't threaten you, do I?" Tessa demanded aloud.

"Not in the slightest." He relaxed, and grinned at her teasingly. "I'm not the type. If you feel like flexing your threat muscles, and Michael O'Malley didn't satisfy you, have a go at Jonathon Stoller."

Jonathon could not help me. He could not fight Adam. He is too soft, too gentle. He did not understand—what Adam was.

"You really despise Stoller, don't you?"

Steve frowned. "He's pathetic. He gets involved with a half-crazy seventeen-year-old and hasn't got the guts to either keep away from her, or bail her out of a horrific situation. He keeps her like a pet, for the weekends. He lies his head off to protect himself. He drinks to stop himself having to face what he is."

"At least he's still here. He could have gone back to the city."

"He's not here to look after Astral. Under all the dithering, he's looking after himself. Like he has from day one."

Tessa sighed.

"Why do you think Astral talked to him when she did, that first day?" asked Steve suddenly. "He'd already owned the place next door for eight months or something. She'd never done it before."

Miss Klein had gone. Now Mother had gone too.

"Before, she had Fiona Klein," Tessa said. "But Klein left her. Her mother had just been killed. She'd been visiting the grave, she was lonely, miserable, vulnerable, and Jonathon was standing there, by the fence, watching her . . ."

Steve reached for her cup and started pouring more tea for them both. Tessa stood up and restlessly paced over to the window. She drew the blind aside and looked out. Across the courtyard, towards the end of the new wing, a light was burning. The room next door to Melissa's, Tessa calculated.

"Verna's still awake over there," she said.

Steve added sugar to his cup and stirred. "Your tea's here."

Tessa turned back to face the room. From here the big kitchen, no doubt so full of life, color and movement during the day, so much the hub of the house, looked like a stage set when all the actors, and the audience, had gone home. Steve looked somehow incongruous, sitting at the long table all alone, with the tea tray set primly in front of him.

All the houses in Oakdale look like this now. Dim. Quiet. Everyone sleeping.

But Verna's not asleep.

Tessa paced. She stopped to look at the Harmony with Nature calendar on the wall near the phone.

Compliments of O'Malley's Bookshop.

She'd seen three of these so far. And of course there must be many more. All over Oakdale.

Charles and Freda Ridge probably had one in their kitchen, marked with soccer dates, bridge nights, ballet concerts. Lyn Weisenhoff, too. Poor Lyn, thinking of Michael O'Malley whenever she marked off a day.

Jonathon Stoller wasn't a bookshop customer. But he

wouldn't have used the calendar anyway. He probably had a neat little diary—black and slim, to match his mobile phone. Fiona Klein wouldn't have used it either. She would have told Michael O'Malley to keep it. Its self-conscious environmentally friendly tone would probably have irritated her.

They're cheaper than Christmas cards.

Tessa's eyes wandered over Verna's calendar, marked and ringed and scribbled all over with appointments and reminders. Evidence of a busy, active life, full of birthdays, anniversaries, films to see, places to go, appointments to keep. Whatever her past sadnesses and trials might have been, Verna Larkin hadn't let them get her down.

At Haven, the calendar notes were all about work. Only one date ringed. Evidence of a bleak treadmill of a life, with a nightmare at its heart.

Michael O'Malley's calendar was unmarked. What was that evidence of?

Suddenly the dates and scribbles blurred in front of Tessa's eyes. She blinked, transfixed.

"Tessa?"

She registered that Steve was speaking to her, but she couldn't respond. She stared at the calendar, every muscle rigid. Everything was tilting—shifting—

Something wicked is watching. Very near . . .

"Tess!"

She moistened her lips, and moved away from the calendar, towards the courtyard door. "Don't go," she managed to say. "I'll be back."

She let herself out into the misty night. She skirted tables and chairs, moved under the vine-draped awning on the far side of the courtyard, and knocked at Verna Larkin's door.

In a few moments the door swung open. Verna stood there, surprised and anxious, her auburn hair tumbling over her voluptuous shoulders and breasts, a turquoise dressing gown thrown hastily over her black satin nightdress.

"Is something wrong?" she whispered. Her voice was husky and slightly slurred. She smelled of gin, perfume and cigarettes.

"Verna, I need to talk to you," Tessa murmured. "You've got something to tell me, haven't you?"

And without another word Verna stood aside, to let her in.

Twenty-six

Steve sat in the kitchen, waiting. Ten minutes passed. Fifteen. Twenty. Several times he thought of getting up and going back to bed. A couple of times he thought of going over to Verna Larkin's room, to see what was happening there. But in the end, he hadn't moved. He'd just waited.

It occurred to him that he wouldn't do it for anyone else. He wouldn't just wait, without knowing what he was waiting for, with no explanation. He wouldn't have done it for Tessa Vance, when he first started working with her. Why was he doing it for her now?

She'd got to him, that's why.

Tessa was hung up on this case—there was no doubt about that. Unprofessional, Thorne had called her yesterday. If Thorne had seen her as she looked tonight—pale, haunted, wide-eyed—like a frightened street kid half her age—he'd have ordered her back to Sydney.

But Thorne would have been wrong. It wasn't a matter of how anyone might feel about Tessa Vance, Steve told himself. It wasn't a matter of feeling protective. Plainly, she didn't want to be protected. It was a matter of logic. The fact was, Tessa got things wrong, but she got things right, as well. And it was the right things that counted. If it hadn't been for Tessa they'd still be looking for Rachel Brydie, for example. And whatever she was doing in Verna Larkin's room, she was doing it for a reason.

The courtyard door opened, and Tessa slipped into the room. She was tense, almost shuddering with nerves. Steve said nothing. He didn't stand. He didn't ask her what she'd been doing.

279

She walked quickly over to him. "I want to go back to Haven," she said. "Now, Steve."

"It's the middle of the night," he said mildly. "And what's the point? They've searched the whole place. They didn't find anything."

"They weren't looking in the right place, Steve," she said fiercely. "They weren't looking for the right thing." He realized she was simmering with anger.

"What is it, Tess?" he asked gently.

She swung around, to tell him.

The car bumped down Lily Lane, headlights flaring in the mist. At the turning circle Tessa got out. The purr of the car engine, the twigs and gumnuts crackling under her feet, were the only sounds as she moved through the damp, clinging whiteness to open the gate. There was a light below, glowing faintly through the trees that surrounded the left-hand driveway. Jonathon Stoller, as she had suspected, was still awake.

Steve eased the car through the leafy tunnel that led down to Haven. The mist pressed against their windows, blinding them. He swore softly.

"Sorry," said Tessa, as though the darkness, the mist, the twists and turns were her fault. Suddenly she yawned.

Tension.

Steve hunched over the wheel, peering through the windscreen. "Yeah. You could have chosen a better night for it," he said. She was suddenly flooded with gratitude for his calm, his confidence, his experience, and his strength.

The sprawling bulk of the house loomed up to the right of them, and the headlights picked up the gleam of Rochette's parked car. Steve pulled up beside it and cut the engine.

"She'll be inside," he murmured. "I'd better go and tell her we're here."

"Not yet. Not till we're sure."

"No choice, Tess. She's on her own, and she's on guard. If she hears intruders, she'll be out with her gun drawn. Do you fancy getting shot?"

"She wouldn't shoot."

"She might."

But as they climbed from the car they heard the screen door creak and rattle shut, and saw the gleam of a flashlight through the mist. Then Constable Williams was calling in a low, gruff voice: "Police, here. Who is it?"

"Steve Hayden, Rochette. Tessa's with me," Steve called back.

There was the sound of footsteps on the boards of the veranda, and then the flashlight was bobbing towards them. There were a few complaining clucks from the chicken house.

Rochette's surprised, pale face swam out of the mist. "What're you doing here?" she demanded, in a piercing whisper.

"We just want to look around a bit," Tessa whispered back. "You just go in. Don't worry about us."

Rochette gaped at her.

"Go back inside, Rochette," said Steve. "We'll call you if we need you."

Rochette's brow wrinkled. Her eyes were alive with curiosity. But, recognizing the voice of authority, she ducked her head and turned back to the house.

They watched her go. The mist closed around her stocky figure almost immediately, but the glow of the torch marked her progress. Once, it flared more brightly as she swung around to stare back at them, but she could see them no more easily than they could see her, and within moments they heard her feet on the veranda boards, and the screen door softly rattling shut as she returned to the house.

"Okay," said Steve easily. "Let's see what's up."

Together they walked to the shed where Adam Quinn had died and pulled open the door. The sweet, foul smell of death still hung faintly in the stuffy air. Perhaps it always would. Perhaps it had permeated the old wood, soaking in, becoming part of the place. They shone their flashlights around.

The packed-earth floor had been swept clean where the body had lain. Only a white outline marked the spot where Adam Quinn had died. Fisk's team had fossicked in the debris of straw, dead leaves, chicken manure and grubby feathers that lay in shallow, stinking drifts around the walls, inspected the bales of lucerne hay at the back, and disturbed the bags of chicken feed that were stacked near the door.

But Tessa wasn't interested in the floor. From the doorway, she shone her flashlight up, at the rafters. The old wood lowered above them, rough, brown and bare. A single spider beginning a web in a corner froze as the light hit it.

"See?" she whispered.

"There could be some reason," Steve said doubtfully.

But Tessa's heart was thudding. Her stomach churned with sickness. She knew she was right.

They went into the shed. Mist crept in after them, but neither of them wanted to shut the door. The space was small, and what they wanted to do wouldn't take too long. They separated in silence, moving to opposite walls. Darkness lay between them. Their flashlight beams were focused on the old wood as they searched it, centimeter by centimeter.

"Here!" exclaimed Steve suddenly.

Tessa spun around, and crossed the shed to join him. He was standing about halfway along his wall. His flashlight beam made a yellow circle on the wood, at a point just above his shoulder. There, a small tack protruded from the wall. A tiny fragment of colored paper clung to its head.

Tessa stared at the tiny thing, hardly breathing. "So there you are," she said finally.

"It's not much."

"We don't need much. And we've got the other."

"It'll be a hell of a job to prove it in court."

There was a sound from the doorway. Both of them spun around. Rochette Williams was standing there. Steve's flashlight shone directly into her face. Her pupils were dilated with nervousness and a trace of fear. Behind her stood Bliss, Skye and Astral in their white nightgowns, gray woollen shawls wrapped around their shoulders.

"They heard you, and got up," Rochette muttered. "I told them not to come out. But I couldn't stop them. I mean . . ."

"It's okay, Rochette," said Steve.

She licked her lips. "What are you doing?" she asked. "I mean, what were you looking at, on the wall?" She started, and glanced over to her left. "Hey!" she shouted roughly. "Who is that! Hey, you!"

Steve stepped forward swiftly, and moved out of the shed, brushing past Rochette. Tessa followed. A dark figure stood stock-still beside the parked cars, just visible through the mist.

"Jonathon!" called Astral suddenly. Her face broke into a smile of welcome and relief.

Stoller came towards them, blinking in Steve's torchlight. His eyes were bleary, his hair was ruffled, and his shirt hung partly out of his trousers at the front. Astral ran to him, and he put his arm around her slim shoulders. "I saw them come in," he mumbled to her. "Thought I'd better—" He rubbed a hand over his mouth and turned to Tessa and Steve. "What're you doing here in the middle of the night, waking people up and dragging them out here into the cold?" he demanded. "Some kind of fascist thing, is it? You can't talk to them in the middle of the night. You've got no right to come—"

"We have a perfect right, sir. We're checking the crime scene," Steve broke in calmly. "Astral, Skye and Bliss came out of the house of their own accord, despite Constable Williams's advice that it wasn't necessary, and her request that they stay where they were."

Stoller boggled. "That right, sweetheart?" he slurred in Astral's direction.

She nodded, her eyes wide and frightened.

She's never seen him like this.

The man shrugged, and wiped his mouth again. "All the same, it's pretty sus, if you ask me," he muttered. Again he turned to Tessa and Steve. "I don't know what you think you can do about anything in this," he said belligerently, waving his free hand at the darkness and the mist. "You can't see a bloody thing."

Tessa came to a decision. "We've seen what we came to see," she murmured, carefully not looking at Steve. "Come over here, Mr. Stoller. I'll show you."

"Tessa—" Steve warned, but she took no notice.

"Come over here," she repeated, beckoning.

Jonathon stumbled towards her, still gripping Astral with one arm.

Tessa stood at the shed doorway, and again she shone her torch onto the rafters and down the walls. Rough, brown, bare wood gleamed in yellow light. She turned to her audience and raised her eyebrows.

"There's nothing there, is there?" Rochette Williams blurted out.

"Well, I can't see anything," Stoller growled.

"There is something, actually," said Tessa. "But what I want you to notice is what isn't there."

Deliberately, she looked at the Brydies, one by one. Bliss. Skye. Astral.

"You know, you nearly got away with it," she said, conversationally.

There was a stunned silence.

"You could do everything else," Tessa went on, as though she was talking about the weather. "After you killed Adam Quinn in his sleep, you had nearly a week to make the change. You could move all his possessions out of here, and into your mother's bedroom. You could rip all his posters and clippings off the walls, and pull rotten boards away. You could dump leaves and chicken mess all over the floor. You could haul in feed bags and bales of lucerne and old tools and make this place look like no one had ever lived in here, ever. But you couldn't make the vines climb through the gaps. And you couldn't make the spiders come in and spin the webs that should have been hanging on every rafter and filling every crack, like they are in every other shed in the yard. I suppose even witches can't do that."

Bliss, Astral and Skye stood frozen in the doorway, expressionless and silent.

"What are you talking about?" spluttered Jonathon Stoller. "What are you saying? Are you saying—?"

"You've been under a spell, Mr. Stoller," Tessa murmured. "Just like us. But it was nothing to do with witchcraft, really. Just good acting. And good gardening."

She smiled. "It was a matter of planting the seed of a lie, in you—the independent witness they needed. It was watering the lie, and feeding it, just a bit, every weekend, and watching it grow and ripen, month by month. And then harvesting it. All at the proper time."

"What's she talking about? Astral?" Jonathon asked, bewildered. Astral clung to him. "I don't know," she whispered. "I don't understand."

"Astral, it's all over. You blew it, frankly," Tessa said, looking her straight in the eye. "Remember how you told me about burying your mother, after Adam Quinn had killed her?"

Her body was very heavy. We could feel it still warm, through the sheet, and the blood soaked through to our hands . . .

"You told me how you carried her body down to the forest, through the long grass, under the full moon. The picture stayed with me. Like all your pictures."

Adam walked in front of us. He was wearing his purple robe. He was very tall. The moon was full. It made the night like day, but with no color . . .

"I couldn't forget it. You did it so well. But your mother was killed on the fifth of January, Astral. You all insisted on that. The anniversary of the day Adam Quinn came to Haven, you said, though I think it was probably your mother's birthday, wasn't it? We'll have to check."

Astral stared straight ahead. Her face was blank.

"But the fifth of January was a new moon night. The calendar in your own kitchen says so. The Harmony with Nature calendars all over Oakdale say so, but I hadn't noticed till tonight." Tessa's voice hardened. "You're very talented, Astral. I never doubted you for a moment. But that one little lie broke the spell. Suddenly, I realized that if that picture wasn't real, maybe none of them were. I realized that we'd been seeing this whole thing through a lens you held up for us. And if that lens was distorting . . ."

Skye whirled around to her sister. "This is all your fault, Astral!" she screeched. "You always have to show off, and go too far. Didn't Mother always tell you . . . ?"

"Shut up!" hissed Astral. She was still standing rigidly still, but suddenly her beautiful face was twisted with rage.

"Everything we told you happened," said Bliss. Her

beautiful voice trembled, but only slightly. "We told you the truth."

Tessa nodded. "You were clever," she said. "You knew that lies work best when most of the details are accurate. That was the plan. You told us what happened. But you switched the main characters around so the whole picture was distorted. And I believed it. Totally believed in Adam Quinn, the sadistic, dominating monster; your mother, the helpless, pathetic victim. But I only had your word for it that that was how it was. Your word, and Jonathon's."

Astral seemed hardly to notice that Jonathon had shrunk back from her, and was pulling his arm away. "I was confused about the moon," she said coldly. "I just made a mistake."

"No," said Tessa. "I think you were just carried away, creating the most dramatic picture you could think of. Like Skye says, you always go too far, Astral. Especially when you know you've got your audience in the palm of your hand."

She sighed. "I should have realized. There were so many things—you pretended you didn't understand phones, for example. But you'd seen Jonathon use his. You acted as though you knew absolutely nothing about modern life, but I saw some of the books and magazines you'd read with Fiona Klein. No one could read those and stay as ignorant as you pretended to be."

Rochette Williams's small, bright eyes were almost starting out of her head. "You're saying they've been lying all the time, Tessa? About Quinn being a bastard? About him beating them, and Rachel? But the scars—"

"It was Adam Quinn who was the victim," Tessa said quietly. "He was the weak, unstable one—the one looking for humiliation and punishment. He was the one who was bullied and degraded, who worked like a dog on this place every day, and was given his ration of alcohol every night so he could drink himself into oblivion out here, where they made him live."

"Not us!" shouted Skye. She was shuddering all over. "It was Mother. Mother! She was the one."

Bliss's hand darted out and gripped her arm so tightly that she shrieked.

"Maybe she was, when she was alive," said Tessa. "But after she was dead and buried, you took over. You treated Adam Quinn just like she had. And after a week or two, you decided to kill him."

"Why would we do that?" asked Astral, rigid, half-smiling.

"Because he'd seen you beat your mother to death, in the kitchen, on the night of her birthday. Who was it who really dropped the dinner on the floor that night, Astral?"

The hot fat splashed her arm, and she screamed. She scrabbled on the floor, trying to gather up the food, ruining it more and more . . .

"That part of the story was true. It was something you'd really seen. But it wasn't your mother on the floor, was it? Was it Bliss, or was it Skye? Bliss, I think. She's the oldest. She would have been in charge of the dinner."

Astral's lips opened. "I told you the truth," she said tonelessly.

She won't give in. She'll never give in.

Skye's the weak link.

"You told me a story that was part truth, and part a lie," said Tessa. "It wasn't Adam who flew into a rage because the feast was spoiled. It was your mother, kicking and screaming at Bliss lying on the floor in that mess of vegetables and fat and broken china. You tried to intervene, to help her, just as you said. Skye didn't. Skye was too afraid."

Tessa turned her gaze to Skye. The girl's mouth was hanging open, her lower lip loose and moist. Her eyes bulged.

The weak link. Soon . . .

Tessa looked back at Astral.

"Adam stood back, too. He was too drunk, probably, to do much anyway. But you tried to help Bliss, and when your mother pushed you away, you didn't give up. You'd had enough, hadn't you? Fiona Klein had gone. She'd left you, just as you were starting to realize that your mother wasn't the be-all and end-all. That your mother was wrong. That you didn't have to put up with the treatment she meted out. The work. The restrictions. The beatings—"

Skye whimpered, her arm pinched white under Bliss's grip. Astral's face didn't change.

"So you grabbed the piece of wood from the basket, and you hit your mother over the side of the head with all your strength. And she fell to her knees on the slippery floor, and then you went on and on and on . . ."

There was dead silence.

Deliberately, Tessa lowered her voice. "You told Quinn he was implicated. You convinced him to help you bury your mother in the forest, and made him swear not to tell. You knew Rachel wouldn't be missed in the village for a long time. She hardly ever left Haven. She had Adam to run her errands for her, and pay for the things she needed."

Again, she looked at Skye. "You know, if you'd gone to the police then, even after your mother was buried, things might not have been so bad," she said softly. "There was severe provocation. You all had scars to show how badly you'd been treated . . . but you never even thought of that, did you? Because after the shock of what had happened had passed, maybe the very next day, you'd thought of something else.

"You were free. You'd be free to stay at Haven in peace, or leave, free to do whatever you liked—if it wasn't for Adam Quinn. Adam, who you all despised, who knew your secret, and who had all that money. If you got rid of Adam, and blamed him for your mother's death, you'd be safe, and rich, and all your troubles would be over. So you made your plan. And the next week, Astral engineered a meeting with Jonathon Stoller, the next-door neighbor who could be your accomplice, without knowing it."

She heard Jonathon moan softly.

"You can't prove any of this," said Bliss, her face as calm and still as untroubled water.

"Yes, we can," said Steve, from the shadows. "Now we know what we're looking for, we can prove Adam Quinn slept in the shed, not in the house. We can prove he worked the garden, didn't just supervise. We can prove that it was your mother's portrait that hung in the living room for years, not Adam Quinn's. There'll be forensic evidence you couldn't get rid of or disguise, even in a week. Take it from me. You went for the big lie, and the lie's going to be shown up. And that's what's going to bring you undone."

"My God! My God, I can't believe this!" Jonathon Stoller's face was ashen. "She was using me. She even let me . . ."

Astral glanced at him, and an unmistakable expression of distaste flickered across her face.

He cringed away from her. "You were acting, all the time. I believed you. I thought you were suffering . . ."

"Hah!" snorted Rochette Williams.

"We did suffer!" shrieked Skye. She tore away from Bliss's grip on her arm, and whirled round to stare, wild-eyed, at Rochette. "You know!" she cried. "You saw us, at the school. You know how it was. We never had proper clothes, or friends, or nice things. We couldn't cut our hair. We had to work all the time. Mother never let us have books, or a television set, or even a radio. She corrected us for the smallest thing—"

"Skye! Be still!" ordered Bliss, her handsome face still rigidly calm.

But Skye was beyond caring what Bliss or anyone else said. Tears were running down her cheeks. She scrabbled at Rochette's sleeve. "She said it was because she loved us, and had to protect us. But whatever you did, however hard you tried, it was never good enough. She made you feel like you were nothing. Bad, and stupid and nothing."

She drew a shuddering breath. "At first, when Adam came, things were better. A bit better. But then it got bad again, and then it was worse than ever. And Adam just let her do it. She'd scream at him, and slap him on the face, and he'd just cry. He'd wear what she told him, and drink when she told him, and sleep where she told him. He liked it. And he never helped us. Never!" Her voice rose in a screeching wail of pain. "I'm glad she's dead. I'm glad he's dead. I'm glad we killed them. Glad!"

Twenty-seven

After the Brydies had been taken away, Steve took Jonathon Stoller home. The man seemed numb with shock. He looked around at his little sitting room as though he'd never seen it before.

"She won't be coming back, will she?" he mumbled.

"Astral? No," Steve assured him.

"I can't take it in," Stoller said, still staring around the room. "She was just using me. She was lying to me, all the time." He slumped down at the table.

"You can think yourself lucky she did lie to you, mate," said Steve. "She hadn't lied to Fiona Klein. That's what signed the poor woman's death warrant."

"Astral killed her?" said Jonathon dully. "Fiona Klein? Astral killed her?"

"We think so, though she hasn't admitted it, and I don't like our chances of proving it in court."

Jonathon stared at him blankly. "I don't understand," he muttered. "Why would Astral risk it?" He shuddered. "Is she just mad?"

"Not in the way you mean. Astral had no choice, in her view. She had to do it because Fiona knew the truth. Rachel Brydie was still alive when Fiona went away. The plan to kill Adam Quinn hadn't been made. Astral had no reason to lie to Fiona about him. We think that Fiona knew perfectly well, through Astral, that Adam Quinn was under Rachel's thumb, not the other way around—that Rachel made the rules at Haven, and ran the place with an iron fist in a gardening glove."

He smiled grimly. "Astral thought Fiona was safely far

away, in Italy for years, so it didn't matter. But then Fiona turned up, at Haven, just at the critical moment. It must have been a terrible shock for Astral. Fiona could have destroyed the whole elaborate charade at a stroke, if she'd known what the girls were saying to us. But she didn't know. And she was killed before she could find out."

"But—didn't you talk to her? That first day?"

Steve grimaced. "Not for long. Not about the main issue. There were a few things she said that should have warned me, but—" He broke off. There was a dull thud in the pit of his stomach whenever he thought about Fiona Klein sitting talking in the car with him. A few more minutes' conversation—a couple more questions—and she might be still alive.

He straightened his shoulders. "If you're right, I'll leave you, now," he said to the slumped man at the table. "We'll be in touch."

"I'm going back to town in the morning," Jonathon Stoller muttered.

"That's okay. We've got your mobile number."

Stoller looked up, watery-eyed. "I'm going to sell this place. I'm never going to come here again."

Steve murmured something appropriate, and left him.

Again, Tessa and Steve didn't get back to Bide-A-While in time for breakfast. They returned to it mid-morning to field Verna's avid questions, sleep for a few hours, pack, and sign the bill. Then they left again to join Rochette for a late lunch at Martin's before going home.

She was waiting for them at the same table they'd had on Saturday night. Her little eyes were sparkling.

"I heard Skye's spilling her guts. Putting them all in," she said with relish, as they sat down.

"She says Bliss and Astral thought up the whole scheme and she just followed along, because she was too scared to do anything else," said Steve.

"Probably true. I feel a bit sorry for her, really." Rochette screwed up her nose childishly. "But I still don't like her," she added. "And if you ask me, she wanted Adam's money as much as any of them."

They scanned the menu, and all decided on soup. Leo Martin, Rochette said, was famous for his soups.

"Fiona Klein's friend Nicole was at the station when I left, you know," she added. "Just back from Italy. She reckons Fiona told her that Rachel Brydie treated the whole family like her servants, and that Astral despised Adam Quinn because he was so weak. Like all men, Astral said, apparently."

Juliette came to take their order, slim and smiling as before.

Everything's like it was before. And nothing is.

"You know, you guys really know how to operate," Rochette went on, when they were alone again. She leaned towards them, over the table. "I didn't realize. Started to think you didn't know what you were doing, as a matter of fact. But you knew exactly what you were doing, didn't you? All the time. Talk about playing your cards close to your chest!" She shook her head in frank admiration.

"It wasn't quite like that," Tessa said faintly.

She glanced at Steve, feeling guilty, but he just grinned and changed the subject.

"They'd thought of every little detail, to make the story work, hadn't they?" he said. "Right down to taking it in turns to seduce Quinn, so that later they could claim he'd forced them into sex. Astral did the same thing with poor old Jonathon Stoller, to make the story of Quinn going crazy with rage on the night he died more believable. Bliss even beat Astral with the cane, the same night, so there'd be fresh cuts over the old scars, for us to see at the proper time."

"Gross!" mumbled Rochette, looking sick.

"Yes. Horrible." But Tessa wasn't talking about the beating. "Bliss and Astral just loved it, in a way, didn't they?" she said. "Working out this sick, obsessive plan. Then putting it through. What you said, Steve—'at the proper time'— that's the operative phrase, isn't it? They made sure everything happened in its season. They orchestrated every move, revealing things to Jonathon, then to us, gradually, so it would all seem natural." She looked down at the tablecloth. "I swallowed it whole."

"We all did," said Rochette. "The bit about Quinn ruling

the roost at Haven, anyhow. Why wouldn't we? It's what you expect, isn't it? Men beating up women, bullying them. You never think of it being the other way round. It happens, though." She considered this, with her head on one side. "Skye said he liked it," she said, after a moment. "Remember that?"

"Not really," Tessa lied. Again, she glanced at Steve. She'd told him what Verna Larkin had admitted last night, in that warm bedroom that smelled of perfume, gin and cigarettes. But they'd agreed they weren't going to tell anyone else, unless it was absolutely necessary.

Verna had ended the affair with Adam Quinn because, as she put it, S and M wasn't her thing. Especially the S bit. She'd tried to please, she'd told Tessa. She didn't mind playing games, and she'd try anything once, or twice, or even a few times. But she didn't like it. And Adam's pathetic need for punishment and degradation hadn't stopped at a few slaps in the face.

"So I knew what must have been going on with Rachel Brydie, behind the bedroom door," Verna had told Tessa, arms folded tightly across her breast, color burning high in her cheeks. "It made me feel sick, honestly it did. But I never said a word to anyone. I mean, I didn't want to—tell Adam's secrets, did I? And I've got Melissa to think of. And my friend—Duncan. Neither of them knew that Adam and I—"

"But when we started talking about Adam being violent, and terrorizing Rachel, you couldn't believe it," Tessa interrupted gently. "Is that right?"

"Of course it is. It was just—ridiculous. I thought of saying. But I just—couldn't bring myself to it." Verna pressed her lips together, and shook back her tumbled hair. "Anyway," she said, with a show of careless bravado. "You guessed it for yourself. I'm not surprised, given the way I ran off at the mouth. So that's that. Will you have to tell anyone?"

"We'll try not to," Tessa had promised.

And as it had turned out, they hadn't even had to try. Skye had broken down, and Nicole Phillips had turned up to repeat everything Fiona Klein ever told her about Astral and Rachel Brydie, and the household at Haven. Fisk, what's more, was having a field day amid the litter gleaned from the shed, hap-pily proving beyond doubt that it had been moved from else-where and dumped where it lay. There was no need to add any more fuel to the flames that were consuming the painstaking edifice that Astral and Bliss had constructed.

"That woman must have been a doozy," said Steve. "Rachel Brydie, I mean."

He's been thinking about it, too. He feels threatened.

Tessa found herself smiling.

"She was," said Rochette, with her mouth full. "I told you. Scary. Crazy Rachel. All the kids knew."

She told me. The whole town told me. Why didn't I listen?

You were too busy listening to Astral. Lovely, gifted, spe-cial Astral. Who killed out of rage, fear and greed, just like anyone else.

"That first husband who killed himself. Wonder what he went through? And the guys who fathered the kids. She just used them," Steve went on.

"Yeah," Rochette said placidly. She glanced at Tessa's somber face. "And if anyone's having the heebies about putting those women in, because of what their mother did to them," she added loudly, "they shouldn't bother. Plenty of kids have had lousy childhoods and beaten it. I've met a few. And anyhow, that's not our business. It's not our job to decide who gets punished and who doesn't, is it?"

Tessa avoided Steve's eyes.

Their soup arrived, and they began to eat. It was pumpkin, sprinkled with nutmeg. It was hot, rich, delicious. Tessa found that she was ravenous.

"I don't feel sorry," she said. "Because of Fiona Klein. She wanted nothing but good for Astral, she loved Astral, and As-tral lured her out onto the clifftop behind her house, and pushed her over. Skye said she did, anyway, and I believe her. The very sight of Fiona Klein sent Skye into hysterics on Sat-urday. She knew why they were going to stay with Fiona. She knew what Astral had decided to do."

"And if Rachel Brydie was a devil, Adam Quinn wasn't. He had as much right to live as anyone," Steve said. "Poor, pathetic bastard. And they killed him, while he slept, in cold blood. To get his cash, and save themselves. So they were as bad as their mother was, really. It's all just a matter of how you look at it."

"You still thinking of buying a place up here, Steve?" Rochette asked hopefully.

"I might. Charles Ridge has a couple of places that might be good. I'll see. I wouldn't mind getting out of the city more. When I can. When I'm not on call I could drive up, for weekends."

"Like Jonathon Stoller."

"*Not* like Jonathon Stoller."

Rochette buried her nose in her soup. "You better bring Tessa with you, I reckon," she said slyly, looking up at them over her spoon. "Get some color into her cheeks, eh? Get rid of the tension."

She never stops.

What are you scared of?

"That'd be nice," said Tessa recklessly. She felt Steve's eyes on her and looked up. His eyes were warm, challenging. She felt herself beginning to blush.

"Hey, it's working already," gurgled Rochette.

Steve glanced at his watch. "We better get going, Tess," he said casually.

Tessa murmured agreement, and pushed away her plate. Her heart was thudding in her chest. She couldn't have eaten another mouthful of soup if she'd tried.

"Already?" Rochette protested. "You haven't finished your soup. And what about coffee?"

But Steve was already calling for the bill. "Sorry, Rochette. No time. We've got a long ride home." He glanced at Tessa. "Right?"

"Right," she echoed.

"And you've got some private talking to do as well." Rochette was gleeful now. "That's it, isn't it?"

Steve smiled, and stood up. "Constable Williams," he said softly, "you'll never know."

If you enjoyed
SOMETHING WICKED,
then go back to the beginning . . .

SUSPECT
by
Jennifer Rowe

The First Tessa Vance Novel

Published by The Ballantine Publishing Group.
Available at your local bookstore.

The mysteries of

JENNIFER ROWE

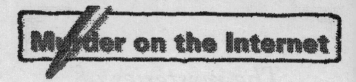